REQUIEM, MASS.

REQUIEM, MASS.

a novel

JOHN DUFRESNE

W. W. NORTON & COMPANY

New York London

For information about permission to reproduce
selections from this book, write to Permissions,
W. W. Norton & Company, Inc., 500 Fifth Avenue,
New York, NY 10110

For information about special discounts for bulk purchases,
please contact W. W. Norton Special Sales at
specialsales@wwnorton.com or 800-233-4830

Manufacturing by RR Donnelley, Harrisonburg, VA
Book design by JAM Design
Production manager: Anna Oler

Library of Congress Cataloging-in-Publication Data

Dufresne, John.
Requiem, Mass. : a novel / John Dufresne. — 1st ed.
p. cm.
ISBN 978-0-393-05790-4 (hardcover)
1. Problem families—Fiction. 2. Massachusetts—Fiction.
3. Domestic fiction. I. Title.
PS3554.U325R47 2008
813'.54—dc22   2008001343

W. W. Norton & Company, Inc.
500 Fifth Avenue, New York, N.Y. 10110
www.wwnorton.com

W. W. Norton & Company Ltd.
Castle House, 75/76 Wells Street, London W1T 3QT

1 2 3 4 5 6 7 8 9 0

For My Friends,
Especially Those Whose Lives I've Borrowed

Acknowledgments

Portions of this book appeared in different form in *Bat City Review*, *The Pinch*, and *The Pedestal*.

I want to thank my friends and family for helping me on the journey, and in particular Doris Bartlett, David Beaty, Jill Bialosky, Keith Blate, John Bond, Mary Bonina, Kim Bradley, Don Bullens, Anjelica Carroll, Alan Dayton, Tom DeMarchi, Kevin Harvey, John LeBow, Richard McDonough, Debra Monroe, Marie Monroe, Leonard Nash, Don Papy, Fran Quinn, Eve Richardson, Tom Swick, Elizabeth Weber, Dan Whatley, Evan Wondolowski, and Nina Zaragoza. And, of course, Cindy and Tristan.

The past is what you remember, imagine you
remember, convince yourself you remember,
or pretend to remember.

—HAROLD PINTER

REQUIEM, MASS.

What Is This Thing Called, Love?

AT FIRST I pretended that all of what follows here—all three hundred or so pages—that all of it happened to someone else and not to me, to someone I made up, a boy named Bix Melville. Bix at twelve was a lot like me at twelve, but not exactly like me. For example, he was decidedly more self-assured when talking with Dr. Courtney Rinehart than I ever was talking to my mother's shrink. Bix was also more wistful and quick-witted than I. He was the me I wish I had been. Bix once told his little sister Chloe (in the role of my sister Audrey) about how certain songs, when you hear them again on the radio, will cause your skin to shiver and bump, and that's because you love the song even if you hadn't realized it till just that moment. Bix told Chloe that the skin doesn't lie.

Bix was just as shy with his Betty as I was with my Veronica. But he was more imaginative in his pursuit—if that's not too strong a word—of her. Bix built a remote-controlled blimp which he fitted with a camera. He flew the blimp over Betty's house and snapped photos of her backyard, and occasionally of

Betty and her mother, Clara, sunbathing. Myself, I've always been mechanically disinclined. Best I could do was walk past Veronica's house twenty times a day, whistling like I didn't have a care in the world, imagining my startled demeanor when she would lean out her window and call my name, which she never did. Bix saw faces, not always human, everywhere he looked—in electrical outlets, in grains of wood, in plumbing fixtures, on the abdomens of spiders. And he took comfort in their gazes.

So I wrote about Bix Melville, and I wrote about him in third person, thereby distancing myself even further from the unwonted and baneful events of my own childhood. In this way, I figured, among other things, that I would not embarrass family and friends, would not hurt or otherwise upset and anger the people I care about and who might still care about me. Plus if anyone ever said, "You shot your father!," I could deny it. I was calling the novel *Almost Touching, Almost True*. Here's how it began:

Bix Melville's story begins many years ago when he sat in the parlor of his second-floor apartment and tried to explain to his mother, not for the first time, that he and his sister Chloe were her children, and not, as Mom contended, shrewdly crafted replacements. They were not from another planet; they did not work for the government; they were not here spying on her. Mom blocked her ears and hummed "To Sir, With Love." Chloe slumped on the sofa, her cat asleep on her head, her cowgirl boots up on the coffee table where they did not belong. Chloe had her mother's psychology book opened to a page of photographs of a monkey making faces to express fear, anger, joy, alarm, confusion, and sadness. Chloe made a face like an electrical outlet and said, "Bix, look at me. I'm startled!"

I showed the manuscript to my sweetheart Annick. Annick's a freelance theatrical set designer, a part-time real estate stager, and a generous reader, who enjoys counseling my so-called literary career, such as it is. We were out on the deck at dusk, folded into our Adirondack chairs, sipping our postprandial cocktails. We heard *hunk hunk* and the flutter and whistle of an ibis's wings and looked up to see him rise above the mangroves, a tree snail in his decurved red bill. Annick draped her leg over my knee. I browsed through the new Archie McPhee catalogue while Annick vetted my draft, a pencil—a #2 Sanford Earth Write—in her hand. The pencil had an orange, wedge-shaped eraser slipped over the ferrule. I can't write with pencils myself. The scratch of graphite on paper hurts my teeth. The pain was worse when we had to use that miserable, thready, yellow arithmetic paper back in grammar school. The only way I was ever able to do my long division was to make these analgesic but irritating-to-everyone-else susurrant noises to cover the hiss of the pencil. We all have our curious aversions, I suppose. Audrey could never stand the feel of suede against her skin. Annick gags at the smell of pears. Blackie Morrissey was, maybe still is, afraid of milk.

Annick took notes. Occasionally, she tsked. I ordered a Shakespeare action figure and some Evil Clown Nesting Dolls. Spot was over by the steps, gnawing through a log-cabin birdhouse that until that morning had hung in a tamarind tree in the Llinases' backyard.

"HANDMADE, AMIGO," Raul Llinas told me. He shook his head, lifted his eyebrows. "Very expensive." He took a receipt out of his guayabera pocket and quite ceremoniously unfolded it.

I said, "Dogs don't climb trees, Raul."

He pointed with his chin at Spot. "What that is in the doggie's mouth?"

"Yes, he has it now, but—"

"Gnatcatcher."

Was he calling me a name?

"Charming gnatcatcher family lived in that birdhouse."

"What do I owe you?"

ANNICK HUMPHED. At what? I wondered. At a redundant adjective? a flimsy verb? some motiveless behavior? an inexplicable phrase? a self-regarding passage, perhaps? So much can go wrong. I turned up the stereo, closed my eyes, and lost myself in Charles Trenet's "La Mer."

She said, "Did you even hear a word I said?" and I was back on the deck.

Annick lifted her leg off my knee. She slipped the pencil behind her ear, eraser end up, held the manuscript in both hands, lifted it twice like she was weighing it, leaned toward me, and said, "Why the masquerade?"

And then we heard a splash. Sometimes a monkey will dive from a mangrove after a crab. If he catches it, he'll crack it open on the retaining wall by the fence. We listened. Other times a monkey will toss a squirrel into the canal. It seems to be a sport with them. We heard a rustle in the trees and a scream. I switched on the yard lights. A yellow-crowned night heron squawked, leaped to the fence, turned her hunched back to us.

I said, "It's fiction."

She said, "It doesn't breathe."

Annick suggested that I tell the story simply. Artlessly. Genuinely. Transparently. For once in my life. "Just do it like this: 'Once upon a time in Requiem, Massachusetts . . . blah, blah, blah . . . and they all lived happily ever after. Amen.'"

"My mind doesn't work that way."

"A to Z, Johnny. Zig to zag. Beginning, middle, end."

"In that order?"

Spot sniffed at the $85 nest he'd unhoused. He stood, backed up, woofed at it, lay down, rolled over. He looked at the nest upside down, and he whined.

Annick said, "It's your childhood. Call it memoir."

"I would have to change some things."

"That's what memoirists do."

"Just seems easier to make it fiction."

"What's easy have to do with it?"

"I'm used to lying."

"If you call it memoir, no one will believe it. If you say it's a novel, people will assume you're writing about yourself."

I made two dry martinis, up, with twists. I put Israel Kamakawiwo'ole on the stereo. Hawaiian music is not Annick's cup of tea. I hate it when you spend fourteen months on a 322-page manuscript, and your honey tells you that you haven't started yet. I came back with the drinks. I said, "All right, how about this, then?"

My new and hastily constructed narrative strategy went like this: The central character is a reporter for the *Requiem Standard-American*. He stumbles across a story about a woman he once knew, went to high school with or something, and this woman believes that her two children have been abducted by aliens and replaced by very clever androids. (And, in fact, some folks living in Requiem all these years later may recall that *my* own dear mother was once the subject of a story in the *Manhattan Tattler*, the headline of which read "Martians stole my baby." The tabloid ran my sixth-grade class photo with the story, only they airbrushed antennae to my forehead.) The *Standard-American* reporter, Jimmy Tivnan, knows the story can't be true, but he smells an even better story between the lines. So he calls his old classmate, Carla Todd Melville, arranges a luncheon meeting at Arturo's, and so begins his investigation. "I'll call it *Let's Get Lost*."

Annick said, "Write it like it happened. A little invention here and there might be inevitable."

The fact is I have often written about my family, but always my family in disguise. Like my sister might be a brother or a younger cousin. My father might be blind or going blind or he's suffering visual hallucinations, eye problems being my favored metaphor for parental disinterest. My own mother, as the mother in the story, might be a country singer who has run off with the charming and devilish pedal-steel player. Often my mothers are so normal and predictable that they fade into the background and often vanish from the final drafts. One father was a lineman for the electric company who abandons his family and moves to Tahiti, of all places, with another woman, leaving his wife to take up with a series of eager, ruddy-faced, and unreliable suitors. In one story the narrator's dad dies when he drives his drunken self through the guardrail, onto the ice, and into the waters of Lake Purgatory. In another, a terminally ill father has a fortunate and heartwarming reunion with his estranged son just before the father dies. Once I made my father the narrator's uncle, and as the uncle he was most like my father—a compulsive and flamboyant liar, a man unable to tell or recognize the truth and completely indifferent to it. He'd lie like an unfelt smile, lie without blushing in the presence of people who knew the truth.

In my dad Rainy's defense I have to say this. He could charm the knickers off a nun. People loved Rainy. Wherever he was, he was the center of attention. His lies were never malicious. Here's an example of what I mean. This was Rainy's kind of lie. He once took me to the wrestling matches at Mechanics Hall. He told me he knew all of the wrestlers personally. He put two fingers together, said, "Me and Rocca, we're like this." He told me about their home lives. "The Beast has a boy with polio. Sad."

When I asked him why don't your wrestling friends ever stop by to visit, he said, "We'll have Rocca over for dinner. How about that? Soon. Wait'll you see him eat. Eats like a, like a friggin' wolverine." When the matches ended, Dad took me back to the dressing rooms. He just nodded at the guard and kept walking. He said hi to the wrestlers, all in various stages of undress, and they nodded. We watched Argentina Rocca shower while Dad congratulated him on the magnificent dropkick that sent Joey Maestro to the mat. I had never seen a naked man. I looked at my Keds.

Lies could also be excuses. One night at supper when we were all giving him the silent treatment for coming home two days later than he said he would, Dad said, "So you want to know why I'm late? Is that what you want to know? Is that it? I was busy saving the lives of twenty-four people. That's right. That's how come. While you were sitting here eating your bonbons and watching TV." He put down his knife and fork. "I was delivering a shipment of medical supplies to Mexican Hat, Utah. Highway 316 was washed out in the flash flooding, so I had to drive the Mokey Dugway, a treacherous road for a sedan, never mind for a big rig. I'm just easing out of a hairpin turn on a stretch of gravel road when I see ahead of me a church bus with its right front wheel off the road, in the air, and the bus itself tilting over the edge, fifteen hundred feet above the Valley of the Gods." And here he set a wax bean at the edge of his dish to illustrate. "On the side of the bus it says THE SANCTIFYING JUBILATORS. I hoped to hell they were saying their prayers. I heard moaning from inside and crying and wailing. Someone sang 'Swing Low, Sweet Chariot.' I told them, 'Don't one of you move an inch. Don't even move your eyes. I'll have you out of here pronto.' Long story short, I got the chain wrapped around the bus's frame and pulled them back to the surface. I figure I had maybe two inches of leeway before I went over the side myself, backing up the way I was.

Anyway, the story was in all the papers, and I am in all their prayers."

The thing is, I believed him at the time and admired his courage and humility. Of course, I also believed he'd been a cowboy named the Cheyenne Kid and had also pitched for the Boston Braves after returning from Korea. In one game against the Dodgers, when his arm grew weary in extra innings, he borrowed Warren Spahn's glove and pitched the twelfth inning left-handed and won the game. I wonder if my gullibility encouraged his lies. Or was it the other way around? He would tell people we met these gratuitous and fruitless lies, like he'd say that he and I had won the father/son fishing derby at Lake Purgatory on opening day—kid caught a seventeen-inch rainbow—when we hadn't even gone fishing. He'd say it in front of me. I suppose he counted on my being too embarrassed or puzzled to ever correct him. And I never did.

He told us all one time that he was occasionally asked by the government to transport certain top-secret items from Point A to Point B. "I shouldn't even be telling you this," he said. "I don't ask questions. I do my duty to my country." Then he asked me if I'd ever read "A Message to Garcia." I said I had. It was mandatory reading at St. Simeon's. "It's not very good. More like a sermon." And then Dad quoted from it about the man who does his work when the boss is away and how that man is the cornerstone of civilization. And I said, "What the author didn't write would make a good story."

What Annick was asking me to do was to strip away the pretense and let Rainy and Frances be Rainy and Frances. Let Audrey be Audrey. Me be me. (Me be I?) But how do you write your own truth without casting doubt on the truths of others? You don't, Annick said.

So we drank to the launch of the memoir. I said I'd call it *My*

Future Just Passed. Annick tapped my knee, said I'd probably think of something better, not to worry. She kissed me. Spot woofed. He wanted his kiss, too. Annick called him over and kissed him, meaning she let him lick her face. And then he kissed me. And then his tail knocked over Annick's martini. He jumped back. Annick told him it was okay, he was a good boy, yes, he was. She swept up the glass.

Annick said, "My mother used to say there are two kinds of people in the world. Folks who look at their reflection in a pond and folks who dive right in."

I told Annick what my mother always said. "The mask is more real than the face." And in the morning I began to write my life.

If the Phone Doesn't Ring, It's Dad

THE TROUBLE I want to tell you about began in 1968 when I was twelve, when my mother, who had already suffered two "breakdowns," whatever that means, was getting crazy again, when my father decided to absent himself from our lives, when my sister Audrey and I were threatened with foster care and separation, when we were saved by the kindness of neighbors, some of whom did not exist.

On the last Saturday of September, in our kitchen at her thirty-fifth birthday party, my mother, Frances, still recognized Audrey and me, but she didn't seem to like us all that much, didn't find us clever or endearing, despite our effervescent efforts. Audrey folded the "Happy Birthday" napkins into little sleeping bags— Mom thought they looked like coffins—and snuggled the plastic utensils inside. I scrambled eggs in one frying pan, fried bologna in another, grilled bread in a third. Mom sat at her place, smoking a Pall Mall, flicking her ashes onto the linoleum floor. She complained about the elastic chin strap on her party hat. It chafed her skin. The pointy hat matched her heliotrope robe. I turned the bologna, stepped away from the splattering grease. Audrey switched the radio to the country station that she liked. Bob Wills and His Texas Playboys. Audrey asked Mom to dance the Cowboy Twist with her. Mom slurped her coffee, looked at the telephone, and said, "Where did you come from?" Audrey danced alone.

I said, "Mom, he'll call. Don't worry. They're in a different time zone out there in Colorado."

"Is that right, Einstein?"

Audrey said, "Mom, you need to be sweet on your birthday." She clicked her boot heels together.

Mom said, "I named you after Audrey Hepburn, and you are nothing like her, young lady."

Audrey spun once so that her blue gabardine Annie Oakley skirt opened, lifted, and wrapped itself around her legs. "Who's Audrey Hepburn?"

"By the time little Audrey Hepburn was your age, she had already sung 'White Cliffs of Dover' for the British royal family. That's who Audrey Hepburn is."

"I'll sing for the royal family."

"I doubt they'll want to hear 'Take Me Back to Tulsa.'"

"We bought you a present."

Mom picked a speck of tobacco from the tip of her tongue. "A present? I'd rather have a future." She waved smoke away from her eyes.

"What are you talking about?"

"Ask Chef Einstein over there."

Dad had been on the road for five weeks. He had left town in a driving rainstorm, hauling a truckload of scallops to Kansas. From Kansas he'd drive his next load west. After he left, Mom, as usual, lost what little interest she'd had in cooking, cleaning, in getting dressed for the day. Audrey and I kept Dad's postcards on the fridge: Rupert, Idaho, Christmas City, USA; Welcome to the Oak Tree Inn, Vaughn, New Mexico; University Student Center, Eugene, Oregon; Pony Express House, Austin, Nevada; St. George, Utah, Gateway to Zion. Audrey thought it was a hoot that all the towns had first and last names, but how did George become a saint? Dad's messages were brief. He'd tell us how many miles he'd logged since the last card, and he'd tell us how he missed us, hated to be away, couldn't wait to be home.

Dad was an independent long-haul trucker, and in those days it seemed he spent two months on the road for every week he spent with us. That's normal, he told us. Someone's got to pay the bills, he said. Someone's got to bring home the bacon, keep the wolf from the door, pay the piper. Dad had the habit of repeating the same thing in several different ways. This can get on your nerves. Maybe you know people like that. Anyway, for all that Dad worked, we never seemed to have much money.

Audrey freshened Mom's coffee, poured glasses of cherry ZaRex for her and me and a bowl of milk for Deluxe, our malleable cat. Deluxe sat in Audrey's old high chair, a tin Little Red Riding Hood teacup of Friskies in the tray in front of him. He looked at the milk and then at Audrey. He blinked and meowed.

"You're welcome," she said.

Mom thought cats were evil, were emissaries from the dark side, but had learned to tolerate Deluxe because he didn't act much like a cat when she was around. Deluxe ate his Friskies one nugget at a time. He'd pick up a chunk in his left paw, bring the paw to his mouth, and crunch. He'd pose in any position you arranged him in. He loved playing marbles and a rather pandemoniac game of checkers, played possum, fetched spitballs, and swam in the bathtub. Audrey took him for walks in a baby stroller up and down O'Connell Street. Sometimes when she did, she'd dress Deluxe in a silver cape (and then he was Super

Deluxe) and he'd deluxuriate in his sedan chair, cradling his fluffy
catnip mouse.

ONE DAY when Audrey was seven, I was in the apartment—
Mom was getting her hair done at Bev's Unisex—when I heard
the back doorbell ring. Audrey stood there on the porch with
an emaciated brindled coon cat puddled in her arms. He was
purring so ecstatically, he couldn't move. His mouth was opened
and his eyes half closed. Audrey told me that the cat had told her
he'd been walking all over Requiem searching for a gray house
with a blue tricycle in the yard.

"Can we keep him, Johnny Boy?"

"He might belong to someone."

The cat looked up at Audrey. She said, "He told me he's alone
in the world."

"Maybe he's lying."

"How can you say that? Look at his face. Look at his little pink
sandpaper tongue."

The cat looked at me stalwartly, blinked twice, widened his
mouth in a mute meow.

I said, "What do we tell Mom?"

"That he's been here all along."

WHEN I served the food, Mom rolled her eyes. "This crap again?"

I said, "If you want birthday cake, you have to eat every bite of
your supper."

Mom squirted mustard on her eggs, poured ketchup on her
bologna, and spread peanut butter on her grilled bread. Audrey
made a bologna and egg sandwich, cut it into triangles.

I said, "So who did you name me after, Mom?"

"Your father's father."

"What did he do?"

"Grabbed my ass every chance he got."

"What did he do for work?"

"He drank."

Audrey told us that Nestor Fulta grabbed her ass in the school-yard. Mom said if he does it again, kick him in the cojones. Audrey said she didn't mind it, actually. I told her she should mind it.

Mom rolled her bologna into a tube and ate it like a cannoli, the ketchup dripping down her chin, oozing out the other end, plopping onto her robe. Deluxe crunched a Friskies nugget. We heard Caeli Beauchemin upstairs walking across her kitchen. Deluxe put his front paws on the tray and stood. He looked at Audrey. He looked at Mom. He looked at the crucifix over the pantry door. He looked at me. Audrey said, "Number Nine: Embrace the silence."

Audrey was a huge fan of Dr. Valentine Bondurant. Dr. Bondurant operated the School for Champions in Dallas, Texas, and he was the star of a Sunday morning infomercial where he promoted his thirty-three Secrets for Success. Audrey ordered his book and memorized the secrets, his bondurants, determined as she was to win friends, influence people, and make something stunning of herself.

Mom said, "Did you notice today?"

I said, "Notice what?"

"The petulant clerk at Sterling's. The hobo in the window at Charlie's. The bus driver. All the same person."

"What are you talking about?"

"Bad disguises—it's like he wanted me to know."

"Why would anyone go through all that trouble?"

"It's not obvious?"

"Did you take your medicine today, Mom?"

She blew smoke in my face. "You're starting to look like your father."

Audrey lit the candle, put out the light, and carried the chocolate cake to the table. We sang "Happy Birthday." Mom held her
hands over her ears and smiled. Then she blew out the candle,
picked it out of the cake, and licked the frosting from the stem.
She broke off a piece of the candle and chewed it. Audrey held
up her glass of ZaRex. "To Frances, long may she wave." We
toasted. Mom cut the cake, and Audrey served.

Mom said, "Did you bake the cake, Johnny?"

"Bought it."

"At Iandoli's Market," Audrey said.

We were raised to believe that any food bought at a store or a
restaurant was superior to anything you could possibly make at
home. Those people were professionals, after all. Poor people
cook food. Rich people order it. Poor people bake their own
pastries—who else but the idle poor would have that much time
on their hands?

I couldn't afford the cakes at Iandoli's, but I had no alternative.
A Twinkie with a candle would have been pathetic. I went near
closing and asked Mrs. DePasquale if I might have a discount on
a birthday cake for my mother.

"Your mother's White Owl, right?"

"Yes." People called Mom White Owl because she looked like
the woman in the cigar commercials who wore a white feathered
headdress.

"And you want to buy her a cake?"

"I only have a dollar." I didn't, of course, tell her I'd taken that
dollar a dime at a time from my mother's pocketbook. Getting
the money was easy; keeping it was difficult.

"I haven't seen White Owl in a dog's age."

I explained that the cakes on display were about to become
day-old cakes and couldn't be sold as fresh tomorrow, so instead
of tossing them into the Dumpster, why not make a little profit?

Mrs. D. said whatever they didn't sell went to the nuns at St. Simeon's. I was in the eighth grade at St. Simeon Stylites School, and now I knew that the dear sisters weren't sharing their goodies with the boys and girls. I said, "Don't you think Sister Sylvanus and Sister Mary Clare have had enough cake already? They'll be diabetics if you keep feeding them."

I was in luck. Mrs. D. showed me a cake she'd decorated earlier. *Happy Birthday, Eleanor.* No one had picked it up. Mrs. D. smoothed away the *Eleanor* with a frosting knife. We wondered what could have happened to Eleanor's erstwhile benefactor. Mrs. D. figured Eleanor's no-account husband had ordered it, wanted to surprise her, do something considerate for once in his trifling life. He was probably in the doghouse now or would be soon because he didn't buy that gold necklace she wanted at Sharfman's. So this morning he of little brain got the bright idea of making it up to Eleanor with a birthday cake. Moron. Then he felt so proud of himself he stopped off at the Cat Dragged Inn for a quick one—to celebrate his beneficence.

I said, "You've been giving this some thought."

She looked at her watch. "By now he's on his sixth highball. By now he knows it's too late to even bother going home."

I got the cake for free.

Mom opened her gift, a bottle of Jean Naté après le bain. She dabbed a little behind her ears, behind Audrey's and Deluxe's ears. Deluxe shook his head and sneezed. The kitchen chimed with citrus and pepper. We all had a second piece of cake. Mom asked how the Sandiland twins were doing. I told her they were fine, last I saw them.

"Will the Sandilands be around this weekend?"

"I'll ask."

"I'm thinking of having a little party now that I have the proper eau de toilette. An adult party. I was thinking that maybe you two could sleep over at the Sandilands'."

Audrey said, "Little Cher is so cute."

"I thought the twins were George and Gracie," Mom said.

Audrey shook her head. "Sonny and Cher."

I told Mom that I'd check with the Captain, even though I wasn't sure that leaving Mom alone at a party was such a good idea.

Audrey said, "Sonny told us a poem he made up. Want to hear it?"

"Shoot."

"'My Two Birds' by Sonny Sandiland. *The mother bird ate two worms and died. The father bird did not die. He hit the pole, but he did not die. He flew away.* The end."

"It doesn't rhyme."

I said, "Sonny is stretching his poetic wings."

Deluxe sniffed his cake, nudged it with his paw toward the side of the tray. Audrey put her head on Mom's shoulder. Deluxe nudged the cake a little farther, looked at me watching him, meowed. The phone didn't ring. I didn't know it just then, but this was the last good night the three of us would ever have in our home.

There were no Sandilands, by the way. No flesh-and-blood Sandilands. I made them up. They were going to be the Marches, August and Jan and their four charming daughters, April, May, June, and Julie, but Audrey didn't want all those girls around and did want a less military name. At first there were just Earl and Ivy Sandiland and their basset hound, Alfalfa, whom Audrey and I would care for when the Sandilands were supposedly out of town, which always coincided with Mom's more erratic episodes. But then Audrey wanted children, so the Sandilands had twins. It was an unplanned pregnancy, but they were thrilled. So now we babysat instead of dogsat. Not long after the children were born, Alfalfa was struck and killed by a garbage truck on Harvey Street. I blamed myself for the death, but Mrs. Sandiland, bless her heart, told me she'd never been able to break the dog of the habit of chasing garbage trucks.

When Audrey and I needed to be out of the house, like when Mom would shake Audrey and scream in her face, the phone would ring, and I'd answer it, tell Mom the Sandilands needed us pronto—they'd decided on the spur of the moment to go dancing at the Club Trocodero. They'd be out late and we'd need to sleep over. Sometimes in summer, the Sandilands took us with them on vacation to Nantucket. Earl Sandiland was a captain of industry. He owned Sandiland Manufacturing, the world's largest maker of quality dental equipment. Everyone who knew him called him Captain, including his wife, and he called her his First Mate.

Going to the Sandilands' usually meant sneaking upstairs to Caeli's apartment. Her full name was actually Regina Caeli, but she went by Caeli, pronounced *Chay-lee*. She was a legal secretary for a big-shot downtown attorney named Nunziato Ferraro, whose photo she kept on the dresser in her bedroom. In the photo, Attorney Ferraro stands on the sidewalk outside the Black Orchid, his cashmere overcoat draped over his shoulders. Caeli kept a key for us under the slatted doormat in her back hall. In the old days before Caeli moved in, we'd go to the cellar, which was cool in the summer and warm in the winter if we laid our sleeping bags by the furnace. That way we could sneak upstairs if Mom went out and use the toilet, play with Deluxe, raid the fridge. If Caeli was entertaining a gentleman caller, we stayed downstairs with the Morrisseys, Red, Violet, and Blackie. Red was a retired meter reader for the city water department. He had a goiter on his neck the size of a cantaloupe and liked to sit out on the front steps listening to the Red Sox broadcast. In winter, he spent his days ice fishing. Violet sat in her armchair and read six romance novels a day. Every day. They worshiped their boy Blackie, an independent filmmaker. We slept in what had been their daughter Garnet's room. When Mom asked where all the

babysitting money went, we said right into our college fund
accounts that the Captain had set up for us at the Requiem Five
Cent Savings Bank.

Mom said, "College?" and then she laughed. "My, my." She
tapped me on the nose with her finger, cocked her head, made
her Shirley Temple face, and said, "My wittle dawings have qweat
big pwetensions." Deluxe pushed the cake over the rim of the
tray, pulled his ears back, and stared at me.

I SLIPPED the burning cigarette out of Mom's fingers, took a
puff, and coughed. I dropped the butt into Mom's bowl of
melted chocolate royal ice cream. I pulled the afghan up to her
neck and turned off the TV. She groaned and opened her eyes. "I
was watching Johnny Carson." And then she closed them. Dad
never did call to wish her a happy birthday, to let her know when
he'd be home, to say how much he missed her, missed all of us.
I closed my eyes and saw him at the movies, sitting up front with
a box of popcorn in his lap. He's laughing like mad at the movie.
I can't see what he sees, just the light from the screen reflecting
off his face. He's laughing so hard there are tears in his eyes. I
wondered if Dad thought about me and what I might be doing
while he was on the road. Like he's driving his rig across the
desert and he sees a forest of saguaro cacti, and he thinks, Johnny
would love to see this. I need to take him with me on my next
trip. Johnny and Audrey. Hell, the whole family. Make it a vacation. And he looks across the seat and pictures me sitting there
studying the road atlas, estimating our time of arrival.

I checked on Audrey before I went to bed. She was wide
awake. "Audrey, you have to sleep sometime."

"Where do you think Dad is tonight?"

"At the movies."

"He never takes us to the movies."

Deluxe stuck his head out of the pillowcase, meowed. Audrey dangled her rosary beads at him. He swatted the crucifix.

"What if they put her in the hospital again?"

"Dad'll come get us."

"How will he know?"

Deluxe grabbed the beads in his paws, rolled over, and fell off the bed. He shook his head, let out a throaty meow.

"Parents have a sixth sense."

"Don't jerk my chain, Johnny Boy."

The Nuns Didn't Teach You
to Write Like This

S ISTER CASILDA SAT at her desk, turned her chair to face the windows, rested her cheek on her fist, and stared out at Requiem. We students were supposed to be writing the answers to the "Let Us Pray" questions at the end of Chapter 30 in the *Baltimore Catechism*, the chapter on contrition: *Elizabeth says: "Anyone who commits even one mortal sin does more harm than hundreds and hundreds of earthquakes ever could do." Elizabeth is* **right**. *Which are the* **four** *reasons we should have contrition for mortal sins?* My job, my duty, was to turn back a page and copy out the answer to catechism question #176: *We should have contrition for mortal sin because it is the greatest of all evils, gravely offends God, keeps us out of heaven, and condemns us forever to hell.* Why would someone, some Father Michael A. McGuire in this case, want children to believe that their willfully missing Mass one Sunday is more devastating than the destruction of cities, the deaths of hundreds of thousands, is equivalent to the rise of fascism, is more vile than Harry Frazee's selling Babe Ruth to the Yankees for thirty pieces of silver?

Whom I wanted to write about here was the merciful and gracious God of great kindness that Father Dolan had talked about in his Sunday sermon, a God who would have laughed at Father McGuire's absurd declaration, the long-suffering One, abundant in goodness, plenteous in mercy, slow to anger, an unrivaled God, too secure in his perfection and majesty to forsake and damn his bewildered children, a God worth attending to, in other words, like the cryptic trickster, the moving finger who wrote on Belshazzar's wall, *Mene, mene, tekel, upharsin,* "It has been counted and counted, weighed and divided." But I knew this would result in another conference with Monsignor Reilly, who creeped me out big time. Monsignor's lips glistened when he spoke, and he tended to spit when pronouncing his plosive consonants. When he talked about sin, his blue eyes rolled back in his meaty head. The last time we'd chatted in the living room of the rectory, he asked me in a strained whisper if I'd ever touched myself down there, and I said indeed I had—isn't it cool? He began to tremble and turn red. He called me a cur, a viper, a scoundrel, the scum of the earth, and he took me by the shoulders and shook me, told me to kneel and beg the Lord for forgiveness. Better I should sever my offending hand than suffer the fires of hell.

When I think about those school days now, I'm amazed I survived with my faculties somewhat intact. One afternoon in fifth grade, I was blindsided by Sister Sylvanus while kneeling on my chair reciting the Apostles' Creed with the class. She caught me on the side of the head and knocked me to the floor, where she proceeded to kick me in the back and pound on my arms, which covered my head. She lifted me off the floor and shoved me in my seat. My crime was that I'd decided not to spend my lunch hour in the church hall watching a movie about Father Damien and the lepers. I played basketball alone in the schoolyard. I reminded Sister that she'd told us we had a choice. She told me I'd made the wrong choice and slammed my head into my desk. When I got home that afternoon, Blackie Morrissey was sitting on the front steps reading *Rolling Stone*. He asked me who tore my shirt and bruised my cheek. I told him the story. He said he'd have Sister killed if I wanted. Make it look like an accident. "I'll just call Dave Brin—he's itching to whack a nun." I told him that was crazy. She's like a hundred anyway. How long can she last? He said he'd cover the cost. He said, "This is a church with a lot of explaining to do."

I looked up from my catechism and followed Sister Casilda's gaze out the window. I saw Spastic Jack Kazmierczak going through his facial contortions outside Tony's Spa, saw Bev's Unisex Salon, the paved schoolyard, and beyond the schoolyard, the Cat Dragged Inn and the triple-deckers of O'Connell Street. Sister toyed with the crucifix below her guimpe. She was, I knew, looking beyond what I could see, looking at what might have been or might still be. I wondered what she saw. Whatever it was, it was far from Requiem. Without turning her head, Sister said, "I don't want to hear any whispering, Mr. Ludy." Billy Ludy made a goofy face and flipped Sister the bird. I thought Candace Kane was going to cry. She closed her eyes and moved her lips in prayer. During lunch, which we ate at our desks, Smooch Penney didn't touch his salami and cheese sandwich. He seemed lost in sadness. He just stared out the window. He shook his head. I said, Smooch, are you okay? He said, Sometimes I just want to stick my dick out the window and fuck the world.

After lunch, I volunteered to sweep up the classroom while the others took recess in the schoolyard. Sister was cleaning her desk, dusting the statue of the Virgin, polishing the reception bell she tapped to summon our wandering attentions or to still our commotion. I asked her what her real name was. Before she was a nun. She smiled. I asked her where she grew up. She didn't talk like she was from Requiem. She told me that her life before taking her vows was insignificant. I asked about life in the convent. Do you get to watch TV? Do you guys sleep in your pajamas? Eat Oreos in bed? Do you and the sisters play games? She told me that was all none of my business, told me I'd missed a pile of dirt under Thomas Simone's desk. I asked her what color her hair was under the veil, the wimple, and the linen headband. She told me my question was impertinent.

We were studying the Battle of Tours in history class when I got distracted by the name Charles "The Hammer" Martel, so I missed the discussion of how the Frankish warrior stopped the invading Moslem horde dead in their heathen tracks. Instead I was imagining a three-fall North American heavyweight title match at Mechanics Hall between Gorgeous George and Charles "The Hammer" Martel. There I was, ringside with my dad, peanuts and Moxie in my hands, cheering on The Hammer, when I somehow heard Candace Kane declare that God knew all along, of course, that Martel would crush the Islamic army of aggression. God knows everything, doesn't he, Sister?

Sister said, "He certainly does, Candace. He has what's called 'infallible prescience,'" and she spelled it out and had us write it in our notebooks. I wrote it on my hand and then raised that hand and suggested that if God knew the future, then there could be no such thing as free will, which you yourself, Sister, said last week that we did have, said that Judas chose to betray his Savior. If God knows what I'll choose, it's not a choice. I don't get it. How can you have both free will and—I read my hand—infallible prescience? Sister said I wasn't supposed to get it. It was a sublime mystery, she said. The judgments of God are inscrutable.

I said, "If God created me knowing I would sin, then isn't he responsible for my sins?"

Sister hooked her thumbs into her cincture. "What did you just say?" That's when Sister Superior chimed in on the intercom and told Sister to send me to fourth grade immediately. Audrey was in fourth grade. This wouldn't be good.

"May I, Sister?"

She pointed to the door. "Don't speak to me."

I stopped by the stairwell beneath the rows of class pictures. There she was, my mom, Frances Packard, class of 1951, in a white angora sweater, a pearl necklace, and short upswept blond hairdo. Her eyes were clear and dark. She was smiling. I wished I'd known her then, before she came unhinged. I thought what I should have said back in class was if I have free will, then I choose not to believe in God, and all this doctrinal prattle means nothing to me. *Prattle* was the Word-a-Day in the paper that morning. Use it ten times in a sentence and it's yours. *What's this mindless prattle on the radio? It's all just children's prattle.* Seven more.

When I got to the fourth-grade class, Sister Mary Geronimo was pounding on the closet door, demanding that Audrey open it and come out. I told Sister that wouldn't work. "Audrey can't be forced, Sister." The last time I'd been in this classroom I had had a wad of Juicy Fruit gum on my nose and an I'M STUPID sign pinned to my shirt. Punishment for chewing gum in school.

Sister said, "She keeps saying she isn't here."

"Maybe she wishes she weren't."

"I called your mother."

Audrey said, "Is that you, Johnny Boy?"

"The woman who answered didn't know who you two were." Sister heard laughter and turned. She clenched her fists and stepped toward the class. She pointed to a boy in the back row wearing a red flannel shirt and a thin blue necktie. One of the O'Briens. She said, "If I have to go back there, I'll gouge your eyes out, boy." She told the class to fold their arms on their desks,

lay their empty heads in their arms, and close their eyes. If she
heard a peep from anyone, she'd beat them all to within an inch
of their odious lives. She agreed, reluctantly, to stand at the back
of the room while Audrey let me into the closet.

I said, "Man, it's dark in here."

"If you're in the dark long enough, you can see," Audrey said.
We sat on the floor. "How does that work?

"Your eyes adjust."

"How?"

"Audrey, why are you in the closet?"

"Sister left the key on her desk."

The fact was that Audrey liked being in small, dark spaces. She
usually did her homework under her bed. As a toddler, she sat
behind the curtains. All you'd see were her legs extending into
the room. She'd turned her bedroom closet into a clubhouse. She
had a lamp in there, pillows, books, a transistor radio. Mostly she
sat in there and talked to herself.

She said, "Where's thence?"

"What?"

"Jesus will come from thence to judge us."

"He'll come from the future."

Audrey thought about that. "If we went back to last week,
we'd be coming from the future."

"I think so."

Audrey stood, dusted off her maroon uniform skirt, wiped the
toes of her cowgirl boots on the backs of her legs. "Are we going
to sit here all day, Johnny Boy?"

"Let's go."

"Bondurant Number Twenty-five: Overcome your fears."

YOU CAN get three hundred days off your sentence in purgatory
just for saying, "My Jesus mercy." The reduction is called a par-

tial indulgence. So in one minute, you can reduce your suffering and torment by six years. You get five hundred days' partial indulgence for this prayer: "Most Sacred Heart of Jesus, have mercy on us." What this all adds up to isn't clear, eternity being such a slippery concept and all. Eternity minus three hundred days is an awful lot like eternity. Three hundred days fewer than always. But let's say you are particularly devout, that you're Joan Noonan and you go to seven o'clock Mass seven days a week, and so you only get a hundred years' punishment for your meager venial sins (you once uttered an oath under your breath when you slammed your finger in the car door, and you lied to your mother about liking her unnerving beehive hairdo); well, then you can erase that century of flames right there in your living room while you eat lunch and watch Arnold Stang devour a Chunky bar, and you can be in heaven before the commercial's over. If you happen to die just then.

Sister Casilda hadn't spoken to me for a week, not since the free-will episode. Hadn't called on me, not even when I was the only one with my hand raised, the only one who knew that the largest lake in Europe is Lake Ladoga. Hadn't made eye contact. So to get back into her good graces, I figured I'd tell her why the boys smirked and giggled every time she told us to recite one of those brief, pious utterances. In that way I would eliminate her confusion, settle her agitation, and protect her from further humiliation. So I stayed after class, walked to her desk, and told her not to call the prayer an ejaculation. *Ejaculation* has another meaning, Sister. She looked at me and blushed, fumed, seemed to rise in her seat, and then she hit me on the side of the face with her Little Town of Bethlehem snow globe. I couldn't hear out of my left ear for days.

Once Upon a Time

WHEN I WAS nine years old and Mom was at Four Crowned Martyrs Hospital having trouble having Arthur, the baby she lost, and Audrey was staying with my aunt Pepper in Taunton, and Dad was either with Mom or he was down at the Cat Dragged Inn "decompressing," as he put it, I had a fourteen-year-old babysitter who ate my food, stole Mom's costume jewelry, snooped through Dad's dresser hoping to find a smutty novel, and locked me in my room while she smooched and smoked pot on the couch with her boyfriend, Thing 1. I kept Fig Newtons in my sock drawer, so I didn't go hungry, but I was nonetheless disappointed because I had hoped for something more intimate in our relationship. Her name was Garnet Morrissey, and she lived downstairs. (She would not be around for our troubles, but she was the person who opened the door for me and let the future rush in. And this book is for her.) I suppose I had a crush on her. Garnet had long, wavy black hair and dense brown eyes. She wore wire-rimmed glasses and black leotards. She had two smiles. One reflected amusement with just a slight lift of the right side of her mouth, which engaged a dimple. The other, more luminous smile involved her eyes and eyebrows, nostrils and cheeks, and could express either hilarity or rage. I dreamed of her singing me to sleep, massaging my brow with her delicate and soothing fingers. I was certain that if I whimpered, if I bravely confessed to how frightened I was, how terribly lonely I was, Garnet would climb into bed with me, and we'd snuggle, and I'd watch her while she slept.

When Thing 1 wasn't around, Garnet would tell me all about his ass and his lips and his rock band Gloria's Sunset (which actually had a racy regional underground hit at the time called "A Glans in Your Direction"). She told me she was mad to live, couldn't wait to grow up, but dreaded growing old. I didn't know what she was talking about. I understood children and adults to be different species. One could not become the other. Garnet said she couldn't imagine living beyond thirty. What would be the point? "Leave a beautiful corpse," she said. And she laughed. "Do you think I'm beautiful?" she said. In fact, Garnet lived to be fifty-two.

After Sister Syncletica slammed Garnet's head against the chalkboard for alleged insubordination, Garnet borrowed a switchblade from Chopper DeProspero in the ungraded class, and she held the knife at Sister's doughy throat, cut through the linen coif, in fact, while Sister wept and apologized to Garnet in front of the tenth-grade class. Garnet got expelled, of course, and she was surely headed for hell, but first she headed to Bob Cousy High School, which she attended sporadically. When she was sixteen and she could, Garnet quit school altogether and moved in with Thing 1, and they had a baby girl, Sophie Anne. But then Garnet started bringing men home for sleepovers, and that put a strain on the relationship. After a while, the long-suffering Thing 1 got tired of sleeping in his daughter's room,

tired of cooking breakfast for unwanted guests, and tired of writing songs about betrayal and about coke-snorting, late-sleeping
reprobates and poseurs, and he moved out with Sophie Anne.

When she was thirty, Garnet got her first real job as an LPN
and visiting nurse, which was how she met Karl, a Vietnam vet
with post-traumatic stress disorder. While Karl was still under
house arrest, Garnet arrived each afternoon with his serotonin
reuptake inhibitors, his trazodone and clonidine. Karl had done
some nasty things while he was afflicted, like pimping his girlfriend, punching her unconscious, putting a passed-out drunk's
open mouth on the edge of a curb and stomping the back of his
head, but now Karl was turning his life around with the help of
pharmaceuticals and herbs, which mellowed him out. These days
he wrote letters to the editor of the *Requiem Standard-American*,
attended city council meetings religiously in order to badger the
pro-development city manager and to advance his own libertar-
ian agenda, and he planned to run for public office so that he
could help this great nation return to its roots. Who doesn't want
a second chance? Who doesn't love a story of redemption? Garnet couldn't resist. Karl had memorized the Bill of Rights. He
swept Garnet off her feet.

When she was forty, Garnet began losing her balance, tripping
over her feet. She felt a tingling in her fingers and seemed clum-
sier than usual. She and Karl were doing a lot of heroin in those
days, and she chalked the symptoms up to euphoria. Around this
time my own marriage collapsed, and I briefly dated Sophie
Anne. She told me her father Brad, no longer known as Thing 1,
had moved to Austin, Texas. She didn't see much of her mom
anymore. She told me about her minister, Billy Bartlett, and
about her job at the Department of Public Works. She liked
them both. She let me kiss her on the cheek.

At forty-five, Garnet had to quit her job when she was diag-
nosed with multiple sclerosis. The disease advanced rapidly, and

soon she was in a wheelchair. She became a burden to Karl, who told her, Baby, I didn't sign on for this detail. He didn't leave for good, but he did leave every night after supper and went down the block to the Olde Towne Tavern. Garnet didn't see why he couldn't take her along. He laughed at that idea. He could give her ten reasons why. She didn't think she should have to beg for sex. She was trapped in their second-floor apartment. Unless Karl carried her down the stairs, she was imprisoned. She wanted to move to a wheelchair-accessible house. She wanted to move to Florida to where Sophie Anne had moved. In Florida she could be independent. Then when Karl went out for a drink or wherever, she could call Sophie Anne. They could chat, go shopping. She told all this to her brother Blackie, who told her that when she was ready to leave that asshole Karl, he'd be by in a cab to pick her up, bring her home. She said, This *is* my home.

On Christmas Eve, Garnet asked Karl to please stay in for once. She had bought him a gift, a hash pipe and an ounce of Nepalese black hash. They smoked a bit, watched *It's a Wonderful Life*, ordered pizza. Eventually, Karl said he needed some air. Garnet said, Open the window. When he put on his toque, she cried. That's right, he said, I'm going to the bar. Bingo! Garnet followed him to the back hall and grabbed his jacket. He slapped her hand away, and took the stairs two at a time. She screamed. He told her to shut the fuck up. She tried to stand and lost her balance, tumbled down the stairs, the wheelchair bouncing off her back. Karl called her a cunt, told her she could just lie like that until he got home. And he went to the bar.

I couldn't know the part I just told you about, of course, but from what I've learned about Karl, I'd be willing to bet that I'm right in essence if not in detail. When she woke up in the hospital, Garnet didn't remember a thing. Karl told her that he found her on the landing when he got home, and he called the ambulance immediately. If only the landlady had been home, he said, and lowered his head. Garnet suffered spinal damage and lost the use of her arms.

Bad got worse. Garnet couldn't eat or take meds without help. She couldn't get high if Karl didn't want her to. Her only connection to the world was a headset and voice-activated telephone which dialed the numbers she recited. Karl meanwhile met a woman named Diane at the tavern. Diane had some miles on her, but Karl was wise enough to realize that he was going to seed himself. Diane also had a husband back at their flat upstairs over a Jewish bakery. He was a rummy and mostly oblivious, but she and Karl couldn't very well fuck with the husband in the bed with them, now, could they? Karl's bright idea was to move Diane into his and Garnet's apartment under the pretense that Diane could help out with Garnet's care. Diane's bright idea was that they should steal Garnet's Cylert and Wellbutrin and sell them on the street. Garnet lay in bed at night listening to them carrying on, laughing, whooping, falling down.

Garnet finally got hold of Sophie Anne, who by then had a husband and a baby of her own. Garnet told Sophie Anne that she feared for her life, that Karl and his whore were stealing her meds. And then she asked Sophie Anne what the baby's name was. Prudy. How old? Six months. The husband's name? Alex? What's he do? In the Army in Iraq. Sophie Anne asked her mother if she'd called the police. Garnet told her the cops wouldn't come there anymore. Sophie Anne said, Tell the asshole to leave. I did; he won't. Sophie Anne said, Mom, we can't take you in. We have no room. You need to be in an assisted living facility with people who are trained to care for you. Garnet hung up. She called Brad and left a message on his machine. Between sobs, she begged him to come and get her, said he was the only person in the world who could save her. She pleaded. Karl is trying to kill me.

Brad listened to the message with his wife, Robinella, who

told him he had to do something. What can I do? he said. Robinella hugged his waist, laid her head on his chest. You could go to her. Let her know she's not alone in the world. Brad called his daughter, and they agreed to meet in Mass. in three days. What will we do? We'll figure something out. He had to find someone to sit in for him with the band for the week or ten days he'd be away. When he got off the plane in Providence, he checked his cell phone for messages. One: a male voice told him that Garnet was dead, that her body was in Four Crowned Martyrs. That's it. No explanation. No condolences. No introduction.

Garnet died just two weeks ago, about the time that Annick and I were out on the deck discussing my manuscript. A memorial service was held at St. Simeon Stylites. Friends and family gathered to say a few words about Garnet, about tribulation and storm clouds, about the furnace of affliction and the bread of tears. Brad held his granddaughter in his arms, stared into her dense brown eyes. Sophie Anne summoned tears that would not come. The body was being held for burial at a later date. The Requiem police are calling the death "suspicious." Garnet died from an overdose of Avonex which sent her into a fatal seizure. Here I go again: Karl, I'm sure, or Karl and Diane, shot Garnet up while she slept. She would not have felt the stabs in her thigh.

Diane went back to her husband to wait out the medical examiner's investigation. Karl's staying with a buddy from the surveying crew. Karl and Diane have been asked not to leave town. When Karl was asked if he could explain how Garnet could have injected herself, he said no, sir, he couldn't, but she was a remarkable woman, indeed. A third of all murders in this country go unsolved. I remember Garnet and I sitting at my kitchen table, way past my bedtime. She was eating my Wheaties, and she asked me if I wanted a sister or a brother, and I said, Do I get to choose? I watched her left eyebrow lift and her right dimple appear.

I Know You Are, But What Am I?

DELUXE SAT ON the bathtub drain and batted a marble, a blue and yellow swirly, around the tub. In her bedroom, Audrey packed her pink and black vinyl GOING TO GRANDMA'S overnight bag for our babysitting sleepover at the Sandilands'. Mom was in the kitchen baking her tomato soup cake and whipping up her signature Honolulu dip for the party. Cocktail franks in barbecue sauce simmered in what Audrey called the clutch oven. Mom had been talking nonstop to Arthur since we'd gotten home from school, telling him mostly about the lives of people on *The Guiding Light* and *Search for Tomorrow*. Someone named Jo has a daughter, Patti, who's having an affair with a married man. When I reminded her that Arthur was dead, she took the cigarette out of her mouth and smiled. She licked the wooden spoon and said, "Is that right, Mr. Memento? Well, let me tell you that my relationship with your brother Arthur is the only honest and dependable relationship I have. So put that in your pipe and smoke it."

"You could try talking to your flesh-and-blood children once in a while."

"Arthur knows how to listen."

"You could talk about—"

"Without interrupting."

I watched Audrey fold her clothes and allowed myself to think that this time Dad might not be coming home, that he had already vanished into the heartland. I was, of course, being melodramatic, which was my way in those days. But I also knew how easily such a disappearance could happen. Dad could drive his rig off some foggy mountain road, and no one would ever find him. Or if they found him, then his body and his wallet would be burned to ashes, and no one would know how to contact his next of kin. Or he might knock his head on the corner of a motel medicine cabinet and get amnesia. I'd seen just this sort of thing happen on TV plenty of times. You get conked on the head, and you lose your memory. Only another conk on the head will get it back, but once you're conked, you don't know that any more than you know your name or the names of your children, if you have any children. You don't even know what memory is. Or Dad could get waylaid by bandits. Bad guys rob trucks these days the way they used to rob stagecoaches back in the Lone Ranger's days. Dad told me that's why he kept a pistol stashed under his driver's seat.

Audrey held a maroon and white Stormy Petrels T-shirt to her shoulders and checked herself in the vanity mirror. (We were the St. Simeon Stylites' Stormy Petrels.) She said, "Both our grandmothers are dead. So what do you think Mom was trying to say when she bought me this overnight bag?"

Just so you know, Audrey possessed a whimsical fashion sense. She wore her oversized cowgirl boots with every outfit, including her maroon plaid school uniform. The uppers were red with white shooting stars; the vamps were white with pointy blue toe boxes. We'd found them one Saturday morning at the St. Vincent de Paul Thrift Store. Audrey liked wearing corduroy slacks under her skirt and tucking the pants legs into the boots. Her hair was jet-black like Dad's, and shoulder-length in those days. She was fair and freckled and had a gap in her front teeth. She could whistle with her mouth closed. I told her to pack her pajamas, and I ran downstairs to get the mail. From the porch I saw Veronica Carrigan, whom I had a crush on, carrying a grocery bag and getting on the eastbound #5 bus. Probably going to stay with her father and his girlfriend for the weekend. They lived in Wheelock, just outside of Requiem. They didn't have lawns in Wheelock; they had mud yards. That's what Veronica told me. Mud yards, broken fences, and cars up on blocks. And all the dogs in Wheelock were mangy and mangled. They either had one eye or three legs or their tails were hacked off or their ears were chewed up.

I came back upstairs and read Dad's reassuring postcard from Jerome, Arizona, Ghost Town City, to Audrey. He wrote that he was off to Flagstaff to pick up a load of—and I couldn't read what he'd written—to deliver to St. Louis. When I showed Mom the postcard, she laughed. I said, What? She said, isn't it funny that the invisible man is in a ghost town? I'm tired of his shit.

I showed the card to Audrey. "So he's on his way home," I said.

"How do you know?"

"He's driving east. Pick up and deliver."

Audrey sucked at the strand of hair in her mouth.

I said, "You do know what deliver means, don't you?"

She pulled the hair from the corner of her mouth. "To take the liver out of."

"I'm going downstairs to talk to Blackie."

Audrey cocked her head. "Are you?"

WHAT SENT me to Blackie was the letter from St. Simeon's addressed to my parents. I'd opened it on the stairs. Sister Superior and Monsignor wrote that they were concerned, were, in fact, alarmed at Audrey's peculiar and disruptive behavior, and they were sending the school nurse, Miss Delilah Berthiaume, and the guidance counselor, Sister Mary Eustochium, to our home for a consultation on Saturday at noon. Tomorrow. I was hoping Blackie would know what to do.

Blackie was my parents' age, but looked older with his thin graying hair and his paunch. Out of the house he wore a kind of uniform—black T-shirt, black chinos, black loafers, and white socks. That afternoon he wore a wine-colored robe over his lime-green pajamas—he'd just gotten up—fluffy blue house slippers, and a hairnet. His face glistened with some kind of gel. He wore a gold and ebony ring on his left pinky. The ring was a welcome-home (from prison) gift from Miss Teaspoon, Blackie's good friend and constant companion.

Miss Teaspoon was taller than Blackie by several inches. She was thin to the point of frailty and stood with a slight stoop. Miss Teaspoon certainly had a first name, but I never heard anyone use it. Blackie insisted that they were not romantically involved, but they were devoted to each other. I don't recall any public displays of affection, but I did notice that when they spoke with each other, they spoke quietly, leaned in, looked into each other's eyes, and finished each other's sentences. Miss Teaspoon's eyes, by the way, were an alarmingly pale blue, so hueless as to seem defenseless against the light. Blackie's eyes were gray.

Miss Teaspoon and Blackie were partners in Copperhead Films, and Blackie, the creative half of the team, was then at work on what they hoped would become the company's first movie, *The Devious Dr. Diabolus*, about an evil civil engineer who commands a squadron of robotic assassins and aims to over-throw the Canadian government. The movie's heroes are a Mountie named Shep Warner and his fiancée, the scientist Tinkerbelle Houghton. Blackie had promised me a not-insignificant role in the movie, and I thought it might be nice to be someone else for a while.

Blackie had served four years in the county jail, but he wouldn't tell me why. "The past is past," he said. "Kaput. Finito, Benito. We have to live for the future, Johnny." I'd once overheard his mother, Violet, on the phone telling someone that Blackie had been betrayed by the Judas who led the cops to the naked man stuffed in the trunk of a stolen car. "I was young, and I was foolish," Blackie said. "Young, foolish, drunk, and immortal."

We sat at the kitchen table. Blackie put on his reading glasses, sipped his coffee, and read the letter from school. Violet brought out two china saucers with white paper doilies on them. She put three Oreos on each doily and set the saucers before us. She served us apple juice in red-striped glasses. She stood behind Blackie, her hands on his shoulders, and smiled at me. She said, "It's so sad about Timmo." Her nephew Timmo Donovan had died just the week before. He was waterskiing on Metacomet Pond, trying to execute a 360 when a mallard flew into his face. Timmo died of a blunt facial trauma. Donny O'Leary, who'd been driving the boat, said he turned around and Timmo was gone. Patsy Flynn, who was supposed to be watching Timmo, had passed out drunk in the back of the boat. Donny found Timmo and hauled him onto the boat. He found the mallard's remains and turned them over to the detective in charge of the investigation. Violet said, "God have mercy on his soul."

Blackie said, "Someone should have yelled, 'Duck!'"

Violet slapped his head. "You're wicked, you! Show some respect to the dearly departed." And she laughed, blushed, and excused herself.

Blackie took a Phillies panatella from one robe pocket and a can of air freshener from the other. He lit the cigar with a series of quick puffs. He told me there hadn't been a straight face at Timmo's wake. He exhaled the smoke, sprayed the air with Glade, and fanned the smoke with his hand. I coughed. He held up the letter. "Well, this powwow should be a hoot."

I said, "I don't want it to be a hoot. She has to act normal."

"That's your answer right there."

"What is?"

"Acting," he said. He blew a smoke ring, watched it rise and expand. He puffed and sprayed.

"What are you talking about?"

"I'll tell Frances the meeting is a screen test. She's to play the very sane mother of two adorable, well-behaved children. The nurse and the counselor are actors, we'll tell her. We'll improvise."

"That won't work."

"She's a trouper, your mother."

CAELI SAT at her dining room table applying her makeup. Audrey sat beside Caeli, her hair held away from her face with a turquoise sweatband. I sat at the front window, watching down on O'Connell Street to see who might be arriving for Mom's party. I saw Tom Bergie in his wheelchair, flipping the bird at a passing motorist. Tom sold newspapers downtown, but his dream was to become a nightclub comic. He idolized Lenny Bruce. Tom's dream was our nightmare. He wasn't funny. He was toxic. Blackie and I saw him perform on open mic night at the Y-Not Coffee House. Tom had a snare drum in his lap with which he played his own rim shots. He opened with this line: "I don't do stand-up." Ba-doom BA! He ranted against the recent Democratic convention. He called the delegates the spawn of Satan. He scowled at our silence, made eye contact with all eleven of us. He described lady Democrats as "corn-fed, no-makeup, natural-fiber, no-bra-needing, sandal-wearing, hirsute, somewhat fragrant hippie chick pie wagons," which not only didn't make sense, but wasn't, as I said, funny. Tom dismissed us as unhip and naive and told us to fuck ourselves. Blackie stood and applauded as Tom rolled off the stage. I asked him why. He told me this was conceptual art and very witty in a grim and insolent kind of way.

The last time I'd seen Tom, I was at the counter at Charlie's Soda Shoppe drinking a chocolate frappe. Tom tried what he called a joke out on me. He said, "What's worse than having termites in your piano?" I didn't know. He said, "Having crabs on your organ." I didn't laugh, he slapped me on the back of the head. I called him an asshole. He said, "I know you are, but what am I?" Jeez! Tom could hit you, but you couldn't hit him back. He was a hemophiliac. He could die from a paper cut. I figured he was coming to the party and was waiting for someone to carry him up the stairs.

Caeli blotted her lips on a Kleenex, wiped her front teeth with her finger. She told us that Nunziato would not be coming to the party. Friday night was his night with the family, with Carmela and the kids, Junior and Rosalie. Family night was sacred to Nunziato. Nothing interfered with it. "He's sweet like that," she said. "Takes them out for supper at the Black Orchid, then for a few strings at Rock and Bowl."

Audrey said, "If Nunziato is married to Carmela . . ."

"What am I doing with him?" Caeli held Audrey's chin in her hand, brushed some blush on her cheeks. She worked the blush with her finger. "Life is more complicated than you know, sweetie. Now close your eyes, please and thank you."

"He's your boss," I said.

"Reason number one. A lawyer's work is never done."

"Number two?" Audrey said.

"Nunzie is a man with—how do I say this? He's more man than one woman can handle."

Audrey said, "Bondurant Number Ten: Reject all thoughts that weaken you."

Caeli said, "How do I look?"

Butchie Franklin walked up O'Connell Street playing his flute and balancing a case of beer on his head, flattening his enormous Afro. Butchie claimed to be descended from Masai warriors, which may have been true. He was a tall drink of water. Six-four, six-five. Sometimes he stood in front of Charlie's and jumped straight up and down for fifteen or twenty minutes. Audrey called him Pogo. Sometimes he put his face right into yours and shouted what sounded like babble, but was, Butchie claimed, Purko, and may have been. When Butchie was five, his father Bunny lifted Butchie over his head and tossed him off the Cadillac Street overpass onto the expressway. Butchie landed in the bed of a pickup, but only for a moment. He bounced, struck the pavement, and rolled into the weedy right-of-way. His bones healed, but his brain did not. Butchie would sometimes space out and not respond to anything or anyone around him for several minutes. You could shake him, scream in his ear. Nothing. Other times he let out piercing shrieks for no apparent reason, and then he'd laugh so hard the laugh turned to a coughing fit, and he'd hold his sides and double over. Bunny was found to be insane, by the way, and lived out his years at Bridgewater State Hospital wearing a football helmet and leather mittens.

Butchie walked up to Tom, put the flute in his pocket, laid the case of beer on the sidewalk, took out two bottles, and opened them with the church key hung from a chain around his neck. He sat on the case and they drank. Biscuit Sweeney arrived, and they all slapped hands. Tom pointed to our second-floor apartment. Butchie disappeared with the case. These three characters were headed to Mom's party. That was not a good sign. Biscuit's job, if that's what you'd call it, was running errands for some of the local merchants. Buying a coffee, walking to the mailbox, hosing down the sidewalk, and like that. Whatever he made, he spent on beer. He lived with his mother, Pearl, a Realtor, who wore large flowery hats. Biscuit had a wicked underbite, a thick and glossy lower lip, and a face as flat as a dinner plate. He didn't exactly resemble a biscuit the way people said, but there was in that face, I thought, the insinuation that when Biscuit was in the oven, all of his features bubbled to the surface and then cooled at delivery and settled back toward the skull. Tom hopped on Butchie's back. Biscuit folded the wheelchair and hauled it up the stairs. I told Caeli she ought to get down there pronto before any trouble started.

Audrey and I played Monopoly following her improvised rules, which were always capricious, but, curiously, did not always work in her favor. The police department might be on strike, so there would be no reason to go to jail. Instead, you could take your ill-gotten gains and go directly to Boardwalk. New York Avenue might be closed for construction, and you'd be left cooling your heels or spinning your wheels on Tennessee Avenue for several turns. Oh, no! A Rottweiler has been slammed by a car on Oriental Avenue or has been—oh, the humanity!— flattened by a freight train on the B&O line. Audrey was always the race car. I was always the old shoe.

We went to sleep close to midnight, and the music downstairs was still pumping, "La-La (Means I Love You)" by the Delfonics. God, they were slow-dancing down there. I didn't want to think about it. I put the bolster over my head and fell asleep. I was awakened from uneasy dreams by someone yelling, "Audrey!" Once I got my bearings, I switched on the light and followed the voice to the spare room. I found Audrey, wide awake, on her back, shouting her name to the ceiling.

I said, "What are you doing?"

"I like the noise of my name."

His Haws

I SHOOK AUDREY awake at eight. She swatted my hand away and buried her head beneath her pillow. I tiptoed to Caeli's bedroom and eased her door shut. I washed up, got dressed, and woke Audrey again at eight-fifteen. She kicked at the blankets and growled. I fixed myself a bowl of Wheaties as quietly as I could. While I ate, I read a compatibility test in Caeli's ladies' magazine. Question number one: *Are you jealous to the core?* Well, I did sometimes wish that I had a three-speed English racer like Eddie Dumphy, a maroon Raleigh, but I never begrudged Eddie his bike, so I supposed I was emulous but not jealous. Not to the core. Number two: *Are you smart or shy?* Are they mutually exclusive? I wondered. Was there some meaning to *smart* that I didn't know about? There's brain-wave smart, of course. (And I was not that.) There's smart like, *That's a smart-looking bow tie, Junior.* But certainly you can be both fashionable and shy. There's smart like, *I've had just about enough of your smart talk, young man.* Hmm. Maybe *shy* was the problem. I knew about *shy* as in *bashful*, about *shy* as in *lacking: I believe the guy's three bricks shy of a load.* I knew about *shy* as in *fear*. But I still didn't get it. The test wasn't so easy as I thought it would be. Eight-thirty.

I drew Audrey a bath and woke her up again. Audrey knew that if she didn't get up on the third rousing, I'd have to resort to dripping cold water on her face, and she hated that. She walked to the bathroom with her eyes closed and her arms out in front of her. A sleepwalker. A zombie. She cracked me up. I had to steer her around the chairs and table and past the fridge.

I went downstairs through the front hallway and into our apartment. I picked up the record album covers off the floor. Rusty Warren, Doug Clark, Redd Foxx. I slipped the covers into the hi-fi cabinet between Mario Lanza and Jack Teagarden. The Ouija board was opened on the coffee table, but the planchette was missing. Wouldn't this have been nice for Sister and the nurse to walk in on—racy records and fortune-telling equipment? *Tell me, Ouija, will Johnny and Audrey be attending St. Simeon's school come Monday?* Big fat no. Not to mention the opened bottles of beer on the floor. I opened the windows. Someone had draped a brunette wig over the globe of the table lamp. Did this mean someone went home hairless? I folded the blanket on the couch.

Deluxe was dead asleep in his Easter basket on top of the TV. He was limp, a melted cat. I lifted a paw, let it drop. His eviscerated catnip mouse was draped over the side of the basket, its cotton husk still damp with saliva. I whispered in Deluxe's ear. It twitched. He managed to open his eyes when I said, "Tuna." His haws were raised to half-mast, which meant he was either sick or unreasonably tranquil, inordinately snug. I scratched him under the chin, and he cooed. Then he purred like an idling diesel. He'd live, I figured. I heard a drawer open in the kitchen. I went in to see Mom.

A man in a glen plaid suit was opening and shutting the cupboard doors. I said, "Where's Frances?"

He turned. He had on this black-and-white op-art necktie, all concentric circles, and when he moved, the circles seemed to spin. He said, "You must be Johnny."

"And who are you?"

He smiled, leaned over the table, and shook my hand. "Keefe Smith."

Keefe was balding up front, but had thick, wiry, wild black hair on the sides and back, and a matching brushy mustache. He wore oversized aviator glasses with red frames that kept slipping down his nose, so that he had to lean back to see through the lenses. "Do you have any coffee, Johnny?"

"Instant."

"Cream?"

"Powdered milk."

"Black, then."

I put the kettle on.

"Sugar, I hope."

"Fine, superfine, confectioner's, light brown, dark brown."

"White."

"Cubed? Crystals?"

"Cubed."

I fetched the sugar bowl. "And *what* are you?"

"Friend of your mom's. We went to St. Simeon's together a million years ago. I'm a reporter for the *Standard-American*."

I got him a Teamsters mug, a plastic spoon, and the jar of Folgers. I said, "Those are smart-looking shoes, Mr. Smith."

"Keefe."

They were black tasseled loafers.

"Thanks. Flagg Brothers. Twenty bucks."

I watched the kettle until it whistled.

He said, "The Sandilands?"

I poured the water in his mug. He stirred the coffee, smelled it, winced, dropped in three sugar cubes. They wouldn't melt. He took a tube of Ben-Gay out of his jacket pocket, squeezed a healthy bit into his palm, and then worked the Ben-Gay into his scalp.

I said, "What are you doing?"

"I'm going bald, if you hadn't noticed."

"I noticed."

"And I'm having a hard time accepting it."

"The Ben-Gay?"

"Is supposed to regrow the hair. Something about the camphor and menthol opening the follicles. Pepper's supposed to do the same thing."

"You could try Tabasco."

"I have. And safflower oil, and onions, and Dr. Crinite's Do-Gro, and evening primrose oil, and hot lavender and balsamic compresses, and sulfur balm and Dead Sea mud. I've tried them all."

"Try a hat."

"I understand I'm playing the fool, trifling with these trash remedies, but I can't help it. I like my hair too much."

I said, "Why are you here?"

"Drank too much last night."

"You don't want to be late for work."

He checked his watch. "Where do they live? The Sandilands."

"The west side."

"He's such a big shot I'm surprised I don't know him."

"The Captain hates publicity."

"You got anything to eat? A muffin, maybe? Bagel?"

"Devil Dogs."

"Perfect."

He got icing on his mustache. I handed him a paper towel.

"Your mother, she's a doozy."

"She likes to put on a show, pretend she's unconventional. My father, however, is a certified madman."

"White Owl told me Rainy was dead."

"She likes to tell stories."

"Cancer, she told me. Testicular."

"He drives a truck."

"That's an odd thing for her to say."

"She gets to appear to be strong that way and yet vulnerable at the same time. Wounded yet . . ."

"Plucky?"

"Invincible."

"I assure you there was no funny business between White Owl and me."

Keefe took a deep breath, and I could see that he was about to launch into a long explanation about how these peculiar circumstances—a strange balding man in the kitchen, the lie about Mom's marital status—might lead one to suspect some hanky-panky, but that's when Mom shuffled into the kitchen in her Kotex slippers. Her hair was up in blue Spoolies and she was smoking. She tugged the belt of her robe and looked at me. She said, "Coffee, presto." She sat at the table and coughed.

Keefe said, "Talk about smart-looking footwear."

The slippers were Mom's invention. She was going to patent them. She laid one pad down flat—that's the one she walked on. The second pad she looped and glued into a strap that she slipped her little foot into. Some people should not be allowed to have a glue gun.

I reminded her that she had a screen test in a couple of hours. "You should get ready. I'll clean up."

"And I'll be going." Keefe pushed his glasses up his nose. He thanked me for the breakfast. I didn't see him again for another thirty-some years.

Spilled Milk

TODAY IS MOTHER'S day, and this morning Spot surprised Annick by leaping on the bed and waking her up with a kiss. The two of them are down at the beach playing surf Frisbee, and I'm here at my desk interrupting the flow, if not the course, of our story because of something I just remembered about Mom. This happened when I was ten. It was a Saturday morning, and Dad was at work, pumping gas at Desrouges' Flying A. Audrey sat in her closet reading *Five Little Peppers and How They Grew*. Mom and I were on the couch listening to Harry Belafonte records and eating Sky Bars. Mom put her arm around my shoulders and kissed the top of my head. Harry had to leave a little girl in Kingston town. Mom told me that when she first learned that she was pregnant, she tried to abort me by holding her mother's hand and jumping off the kitchen table twenty-five times a day for twenty-five days. She sounded wistful, said she and her mother had never felt so close. She was twenty-two then, Catholic and unmarried. "So you can see what kind of awkward position your coming put me into."

"Mom, that's a sin."

"When that didn't work, your grandmother, bless her heart, made me some pennyroyal tea. It's what they used in Canada."

"She had eighteen brothers and sisters."

"She would have had twenty-seven. We tried Queen Anne's lace seeds, vitamin C, falling down a flight of stairs."

"Why would you want to kill me?"

"Let's not be melodramatic, Johnny. You weren't a person then, were you? You were a problem."

"So what changed your mind?"

"Sometimes I wonder what my life would have been like, you know. Maybe I wouldn't have married your father. I could have gone to college, maybe, to secretarial school, gotten my derriere out of this hellhole."

"Sorry."

"What's done is done." She broke off a square of Sky Bar, handed it to me. Vanilla nougat, my least favorite. "Maybe I could have been someone. That's all I'm saying."

I wondered about my father's role in this noxious business. When Mom told him her secret, making it their secret, did he hesitate in marrying her? Was that pained look on his face what drove her to the kitchen table? As a kid I thought a lot about my close call with nonexistence. What would it have been like not to have been? What or who would have taken my place in this world? What would have been right here in this space where I sit at my desk with my fountain pen in my hand in Dania Beach, Florida? Air? Emptiness? Space? Ether? There would be no desk, of course, and Annick Pascal would be in love with another man, and Spot . . . poor Spot!

(By the way, I'm talking about my beloved grandmother Grace, mind you, the woman who loved me more extravagantly and resolutely than anyone ever has. Grace's husband, Mr. Burt

Packard, shop foreman at New England High Carbon, vanished from Requiem when Grace was pregnant with my mother and has not been heard from since. Grace always said, Good riddance to bad garbage, whenever Burt's name was mentioned, the only ugly comment I ever heard her make about anyone. She practically raised me until I was six and a half, and she died of a not-unexpected heart attack, died on her kitchen floor with a lit Herbert Tareyton cigarette in her fingers.

Grace had gnarled, arthritic hands, swollen knuckles, twisted fingers. She had been a seamstress all her life, but when I knew her she was having a hard time doing the fine handwork. Whenever she sewed clothing on the Singer machine in her bedroom, I'd sit on the linoleum floor by the treadle and play games of construction and demolition with the darning eggs and bobbins. I can remember the intermittent drill of the machine, the sizzle of rain on the roof and window, and Grace humming one of her songs from the forties.

I don't think of myself as a superstitious person [although I do think that if I'm watching the Marlins and they're ahead, then I can't change the channel or they'll blow the lead], but I never break an egg in a dark, shadowed place. I never leave a sliced onion on the counter. Why let discord in the door? And if I drop a spoon, Annick has to pick it up. I know that if I'm interrupted in the making of a bed, I'll have a sleepless night. I keep to these habits because Grace taught them to me. When I look at the blue flame of a candle I remember how Grace told me the blue meant a spirit was in the room with us, and I remember when she told me that—at the kitchen table, on a summer morning, the two of us eating cantaloupe à la mode, the ice cream dripping down my chin. She had been telling me about her brother Romeo whose birthday it was, and who died of influenza when he was nine.)

I asked Mom how she felt when I was born.

"I was in a great deal of pain."

"You weren't happy to see me?"

"I threw up every morning for seven months."

"So then you must have been relieved, at least."

She took off the Belafonte and put on the Mario Lanza, *The Student Prince*. "You had a pointy little head. Your father called you Dinny Dimwit."

"Who's Dinny Dimwit?"

"A friend of Willie Winkle's."

"Who?"

"You were not a pretty baby."

I keep my parents' formal black-and-white wedding portrait here on my bookcase between my Jack Kerouac bobble-head doll and my View-Master stereoscope. Rainy and Frances. Mister and missus. Rainy's in a white shirt, white tuxedo jacket, black slacks, and black shoes. His black bow tie is crooked. He's wearing a light pink, I would guess, boutonniere. His black hair is combed back in a neat little pompadour. His hands are folded at his waist, left over right. He's wearing a gold watch, the one he still wears, a Lord Elgin with a second hand where the "6" should be, stares soberly into the camera lens. I once asked Frances why Dad didn't smile for the photo. She said, His teeth.

Frances's short hair is crowned with a rhinestone tiara. A starched lace veil is pulled off her face and falls over her shoulders to her waist. Her gown is satin and lace with a beaded insert at the neck. The sleeves are long. The full skirt is not so unlike a three-tiered wedding cake. She holds a tussie-mussie of tea roses in her hands and a string of rosary beads. Her head is held back; her smile is nervous, reserved, and shows mostly in her wide eyes and her raised brow.

I stare at the photo and try to look through the eyes to the thoughts and feelings simmering behind them. I see that Dad understands he now has his chance to become a new man, a mature and enterprising breadwinner, and he knows he is up to the challenge. He sees this new life spread before him like a holiday dinner, and he's as hungry as a wolf. Mom is still a little queasy. She couldn't eat a thing, thank you. She doesn't even want to look at food, not even at the lacy wedding cake from Gannon's Bakery. She's weary with being the center of attention. She'd like to sneak away, toe her shoes off, sit, put her feet up, and smoke a cigarette. And I know I'm there, too, curled on my back, trying out my parts, stretching my fingers, opening and closing my new mouth.

Annick's mom, Nettie, called this morning after Annick and Spot had left for the beach. She thanked us for the flowers. What do you call them? I said, Peruvian lilies. Nettie's husband Frank Nissen—her third husband, not Annick's dad—died in his bed last summer, and now she's finding her romance on the Internet and hoping that some greater-Phoenix-area senior citizen will sweep her off her feet the way Big Frank did. She said, You don't know what it's like to be dating against the clock, Johnny. No, I don't, I said. Big Frank was a brassy, banjo-bellied old goat who slapped waitresses on their asses, picked his teeth with a matchbook, and referred to his genitals as Little Frankie and the Twins. You could be at breakfast with Big Frank and Nettie, and he'd wipe the yolk off his mustache and lips, slap his chubby hand on the table, look over at Nettie, and say, What do you say we pay Little Frankie and the Twins a surprise visit? And Nettie would blush and smile, and the two of them would excuse themselves and pad off down the hallway to their bedroom. Big Frank, I thought, was an acquired taste, like deep-fried Twinkies, but Nettie loved that geezer to death—quite literally, as it turned out.

Nettie told me about her last-night blind date, how the first thing the guy asked was did she have a car. Yes, I have a car, she told him, a mocha Lincoln Town Car with a sunroof. Is that all you're interested in? "I let the fool take me to dinner at Lo-Lo's Chicken and Waffles. And then he got steamed when I wouldn't let him drive. Said it didn't look right, the woman at the wheel. He asked me if I could chauffeur him to the VA on Monday morning. Imagine."

I was still trying to imagine the dish of chicken and waffles.

She said, "Before that it was this little Sicilian, came up to my shoulders. Just off the spaghetti boat, this one. Right out of the gate he wants to know how I feel about sex. Where's the romance anymore, Johnny?"

"Times have changed," I told her.

"After we ate I told him, 'Have a sweet life, Massimo.'"

WHEN KEEFE left, Mom said she'd take her bath. I cleared the dishes and wiped down the table. I put an onion in a cereal bowl and put the bowl on the coffee table to cut the stench of smoke. Audrey came in the front door, and Deluxe hopped down from the TV, meowed, chirped, performed his figure-eight dance between Audrey's legs, and then collapsed in a pile at her feet so that she could stroke his back, rub his belly, scratch his head, and tickle his chin. I opened the windows, turned off the stereo. Audrey pointed at the limp and purring Deluxe and whispered, "Catatonic." Why didn't I hear the water running? I said, "She went back to bed." I asked Audrey to go tell Mom to shake a leg.

The last time Mom had checked into the hospital, Dad took Audrey and me along to see her. "Your mother's been driving in the breakdown lane again," he told us. Audrey had a get-well gift for Mom. She had drawn and colored a picture of a hooded merganser—Audrey's favorite bird. But the nurses at the front desk wouldn't let us up to see Mom. Too young. So Dad gave us money and told us to wait for him in the cafeteria. He shrugged. He took the hooded merganser. "She'll love this, Audrey."

Audrey ordered a black cow. I got a strawberry frappe. Audrey said, "Loons aren't crazy."

The man at the corner table was talking to himself in sign language. He seemed upset. His T-shirt said, PAIN IS WEAKNESS LEAVING THE BODY.

"That's what the ambulance driver said Mom was crazy as."

"He was joking," I said.

The man at the corner table brought his cigarette closer and closer to his eye. It was the width of a nickel away from his pupil. It hurt my teeth just to look. I shut my eyes. When I dared to open them again, the man was taking a puff and Audrey was over talking to the doughnuts. The man looked at me, smiled, and pumped his eyebrows like Groucho Marx. And then Audrey was gone. I found her finally in the chapel standing in front of a statue of the Blessed Mother. If you're Catholic, you know the statue I'm talking about—Mary's barefoot, and she's standing on the spine of a snake. This is one gal you don't mess with. Audrey was in front of the statue, but she was staring at the blank wall beside the statue. She said did I see anything on the wall. No, I didn't. She said if you stare at the statue long enough and then move your eyes to the white wall, you'll see the Blessed Virgin who isn't really there, but is appearing to you as she did to the kids at Fatima. And you can talk to her, and she'll listen until she fades away. "It's a miracle, Johnny Boy."

So, of course, I knew what Audrey was doing in Mom's bedroom now, staring at the wall above Mom's bed. I said, "Did you try to wake her up?"

"She told me she was feeling crispy."

"I'll get the sponge."

I shook Mom and reminded her about the screen test. I told her the actors would be here in like thirty-five minutes. Audrey held the sopping sponge about a foot over Mom's face. "I'll count to three, Mom. And then Audrey squeezes."

BLACKIE SAID, "Frances, you look simply famishing, my dear."
Mom wore a simple black sleeveless dress, black espadrilles, a
white silk scarf tied around her head, and amber rosary beads
around her neck. She looked, I thought, like a slim and elegant
nun from the future. Blackie kissed her cheek, took her by the
hand, and led her to the sofa. He picked up the bowl with its
onion and put it in the Easter basket. "We'll have the children sit
with you." He surveyed the living room, slid the rocker closer to
the coffee table, and shook his head. "We can't have a nun sitting
in a lawn chair, now, can we?"

Mom said, "What is it I'm supposed to be doing again?"

"Acting."

"And who am I?"

"The concerned mother."

"And these are my kids, I take it."

"Your beloved children."

"Just so you know, they aren't."

"They are."

"If they were my kids, I'd love them, wouldn't I?"

And that's when I realized this could go very wrong should
Mom decide to go public with her delusions or lies or whatever
they were. And if she went public, then maybe this wasn't just a
game she was playing.

She walked to the hutch and stared at a family photo we'd had
taken in a studio three years earlier. Mom loved the whole Olan
Mills experience. We sat for a portrait whenever she had a
coupon. There are the four of us in white shirts, black slacks,
and bare feet. Dad's standing to the left with his arms crossed,
and he's grinning at the camera. Mom's leaning into him, and
she has her left hand on my head, tousling my hair. I'm looking
up at my hair. My feet are crossed. Audrey's on her tiptoes, hug-
ging me, with her eyes closed like she's making a wish. We're all

draped in Christmas bulbs. Mom said, "These are my authentic children here."

Blackie took Mom by the shoulders. "I don't know what's going on with you, Frances, but for the next hour or so these two adorable children standing here are your kids, and you love them to death." He put the photo on the coffee table. "If you need the picture to help you remember, then stare at it."

"I might love them, but I'm not *in love* with them."

"We'll go with that for now."

Mom closed her eyes, took a deep, slow breath, exhaled with a drone, and nodded. "What do I want?"

"To keep the family together."

"What's pulling us apart?"

"Your recent erratic behavior for which you are now being treated and which you deeply regret."

"What's my motivation?"

Blackie looked at me, back at Mom. "It's what mothers do."

"I'm kind of over motherhood."

"This isn't about you, Frances." Blackie put his hands on his knees and leaned toward Mom, put his face inches from hers, and whispered, "It's about the children."

"The replacements."

Blackie asked me, "Is your mother on any kind of pills?"

"Lots."

"Why don't we give her a few?"

Mom said, "I'm having a bit of a hard time holding on, you know. To all this. But like I told the husband, I'm just going through a phase. I'll be fine. I've gone through phases before: sweet little rock 'n' roller, pre-Raphaelite aesthete, Betty Crocker, ball-buster. I survived them all. And this too shall pass. I'll be fine. I don't know why it happens." She shook her hands and then her arms and then her shoulders. She stretched all the muscles in her face. "I can do this," she said.

Blackie sent me to the kitchen for a chair. "We'll sit Sister in the rocker and the nurse here." He regarded his set. He said, "Do you have a Bible we could put on the coffee table?" I got the Douay-Rheims from the junk drawer in the kitchen. "Perfect," he said.

Mom looked at me and smiled. "My jewelry."

"What about it?"

She snickered. "You stole my seahorse brooch."

"Why would I steal it?"

"That's what I'd like you to tell me."

"You probably misplaced it like you misplace everything else."

"I have an elaborate jewelry storage and inventory system which you know nothing about."

Blackie said, "That'll be our visitors."

Mom said, "I know what you're trying to do, Johnny."

Blackie said, "Is anyone going to get the door?"

Audrey headed downstairs.

Mom opened her compact and looked at herself in the little mirror. She said, "The smaller the mirror, the more it's me." She tapped a cigarette from her pack and leaned back into the sofa. She said, "Sometimes when I sit I become part of the sofa, and then it's hard to move or talk or anything."

Blackie told her to lean forward; maybe that would keep her separate.

She said, "Does that ever happen to you?"

When Sister Mary Eustochium and Nurse Berthiaume arrived, I took Sister's black knit shawl and Nurse's Irish fisherman's sweater and brought them to Audrey's room and dropped them on the bed. When the ladies took their seats, Blackie clapped his hands and said, "Action!"

Sister said, "Pardon me?"

Mom said, "Have we had this conversation before?"

Sister looked at Nurse Berthiaume.

Blackie introduced himself as our favorite uncle, said he'd stay out of our hair. He stood behind our guests. "Pretend I'm not even here."

Deluxe rubbed his body along Nurse Berthiaume's legs. Then he leaped onto Sister's ample lap, purred, curled, settled, tucked his tail under his chin, and shut his eyes.

"He's a good judge of character," Mom said.

She said, "What's his name?"

"Saul of Tarsus," I said, fingers crossed to void the lie.

Audrey walked in wearing her First Communion veil and carrying a tray of snacks—yellow and white cubes of cheese speared with red plastic toothpicks, Ritz crackers spread with deviled ham, and a blue anodized aluminum tumbler of Slim Jims. She curtsied, offered each of us a napkin and snack in turn. Sister declined politely. Nurse Berthiaume had one of each. Deluxe lifted his head and sniffed. He kneaded Sister's thigh and returned to sleep. When Audrey excused herself, Mom remarked at what a thoughtful child Audrey was, always had been. A blessing.

Nurse Berthiaume took a small green and copper beanbag ashtray out of her capacious black pocketbook and set it on the coffee table. She lit up a Chesterfield.

Sister said, "Actually, we're here to talk about your Audrey."

Mom said, "My Audrey?" She shook her head, smiled. "Audrey belongs to the world."

Sister said, "We're concerned about her behavior."

"Her health and well-being," Nurse Berthiaume said.

"As you should be," Mom said.

There followed a catalogue of Audrey's alleged aberrant behaviors. The closet incident, of course, the face painting, the squid on the desk, the confetti storm, the hamster release, the bubble-blowing, the ventriloquism—

"The what?" Mom said.

Sister said, "She can throw her voice."

"Talk with her mouth closed," Nurse Berthiaume said.

"And this has caused some innocent young ladies to be unfairly punished," Sister said.

Mom looked at me or whom she took to be my replacement, I still wasn't sure. "We should get her on *Amateur Auditions*." She put her cigarette to her lips. I lit it for her with my new Sacred Heart Zippo, a rash gesture, since I'd stolen the lighter from Smokey's News and Tobacco. I liked the burning heart with the crown of thorns around it. I liked the smell of butane. I knew stealing was a sin, and I wasn't proud of it, and I knew I'd have to confess eventually, but I also knew that Father "One Hail Mary" Donega would make it all better in thirty seconds. No matter how or how often you had sinned, your penance was one Hail Mary. Bludgeon your grandparents to death with a tire iron, one Hail Mary. Miss Mass on Sunday, one Hail Mary. Steal a lighter (me), assault your teacher (Dave Brin), all the same. And so on Saturdays all the teenagers and young marrieds lined up outside Father Donega's confessional while across the church Monsignor screamed at some old woman who had slipped a dollar out of her husband's slacks to buy milk for the family.

Nurse Berthiaume said, "There are times Audrey doesn't seem to be there. You talk to her, and she stares at you in silence."

Blackie said that Einstein didn't talk until he was like ten or something. He caught himself butting in, apologized, said, I'm not here, and zipped his lips.

Nurse Berthiaume blew three impressive smoke rings that swirled, jiggled, and widened as they rose toward the ceiling. Audrey put her finger through the third, looked at Nurse Berthiaume, and said, "Now we're married."

Nurse Berthiaume cleared her throat and said, "We're worried that she might be having petit mal seizures."

Audrey sang, "Star of tomorrow, who will it be . . ."

Nurse Berthiaume asked Mom if she had ever had Audrey evaluated by a neurologist.

"I've seen no reason to."

Audrey pointed at Sister and sang, "With your vote it could be me . . ."

"She has conversations with people who aren't there," Sister said.

"It's called prayer," Mom said.

"It's up to you . . ." Audrey sang and cake-walked out of the room.

Sister and the nurse exchanged glances. Deluxe sat up on Sister's lap and stared at her while she spoke. "She seems to be impervious to discipline."

Nurse Berthiaume said, "Incapable of controlling her impulses."

As if on cue, Audrey walked back into the room for her reprise with a black lace mantilla in place of the white veil. She folded her hands and sang "Ave Maria" in Latin, only she didn't know all the words, so she stopped after what sounded like "Domino's take-home."

Mom crushed her lit cigarette with her thumb and index finger. She said, "I see what's going on here, ladies." She slid the clinched butt behind her ear. The flame wasn't quite out. A strand of her hair blazed and went out, like a spark from a Tesla coil.

Sister said, "What did you just do?"

Mom said, "You may say what you want me to hear, but I hear what you don't want to say."

Sister said, "I don't know what you're talking about."

"Loud and clear."

This wasn't going well. We needed a distraction. I tried lighting my tie on fire. Mom held out her hand for the lighter. I gave it to her. She hit me on the head with it. I whimpered, She said, "You really want something to cry about?"

I said, "It hurt."

She addressed our guests. "Sister Basilla taught me all about this in British lit. She told us the real text is the subtext." Mom raised her eyebrows and smiled. "You say something, Sister, and I'll translate for the peanut gallery."

"This is insane, Frances," Sister said.

Mom turned to us. "Frances knows the truth about her children."

Nurse Berthiaume said, "Frances. Look at my eyes and listen to my words. What do you think that we think that you supposedly know about your children?"

Mom translated. "'We have your children, and they are in grave danger.'"

Sister looked to Blackie for help. Mom said she wanted her kids back. She wouldn't go to the cops, promise. No one had to know.

Sister said, "Where's your husband, Frances?"

Mom said, "You can dispense with the charade, my dear."

I said Dad was away on business.

"We had hoped he'd be here."

I said, "He'd rather be here than anywhere. Trust me, Sister."

Audrey held out her arms and Deluxe leaped into them. Sister brushed cat hair off her habit. Deluxe swatted Audrey's mantilla.

Nurse Berthiaume said, "Because we need to discuss getting Audrey the help that she so obviously needs."

Mom said, "My Audrey?"

"And that you seem unable to provide."

Sister said, "She needs a thorough psychological examination, a neurological workup—"

"And perhaps a round of therapy," Nurse Berthiaume said.

Mom said, "There are some mothers who would tell you two Nosey Parkers to fuck yourselves."

Oh, shit. Blackie brought his hands to his head. Audrey hid a smile behind her hand. Sister sat up. Nurse Berthiaume leaned forward. I put my arm on Mom's shoulder wishing her back into character, holding her still.

Someone from the kitchen, it sounded like, said, "Attagirl, Frances!" I looked at Audrey. She grinned and stared straight ahead.

Mom said, "But I'm not that kind of gal, girls. I'm a mother with the best interests of her children at heart. Isn't that right, Blackie?"

Sister said, "Perhaps our meeting here is over."

The voice from the kitchen said, "Bondurant Number Twenty: Always have a Plan B." And with that Blackie stepped backward across the parlor, eased the door open, and slipped out of the apartment.

I said, "Maybe Audrey could see Mom's psychologist."

Sister said, "Mom's psychologist?"

"Dr. Christian Reininger," I said.

"German," Mom said. "Need I say more?"

The phone rang. I answered. Blackie said, "I'm your dad. Put the penguin on."

"Dad?"

Mom said, "I'm not here," and then, "Who am I supposed to be again?"

I gave the handset to Sister and held the phone on my hip. "What a coincidence," she said. She turned and looked around the room. "Yes, I see." She sat back in her chair. "I think we're finished playing games here." She lifted her left eyebrow and looked at Nurse Berthiaume. "I think you know exactly what games, Uncle Blackie, if that's who you are."

I tried to lift just one eyebrow. That way I would look both duped and incredulous. Couldn't do it.

And then Sister asked Mom just what on earth was going on here, and Mom said, "Isn't it obvious, dear?"

Nurse Berthiaume picked at her teeth with a Requiem Savings and Loan matchbook and sucked at the loosened bits of Slim

Jim. I saw that the tops of her feet had swelled over the tops of her black shoes.

Sister told Mom, "You'll be hearing from us."

Blackie came up the back stairs as our visitors left by the front. He said, "Well, we can expect unpleasant repercussions, I'm afraid."

Mom said, "I fucked up, didn't I?"

"You did what you could." Blackie looked at me. "How long has she been like this?"

"Has she been like what?" Mom said.

"You're addlepated, Frances."

I said, "On and off for a while."

Blackie said, "Let me see your hand."

Mom seemed surprised at the blister on her thumb. Audrey went for the Neosporin. Mom blew on her blister. "I don't know why they have it in for me."

"The nuns?" Blackie said.

"The impresarios."

"Who?"

"You think they tell you who they are?"

I said, "Dad's going to have to straighten out this mess."

Mom waved me over. She held my arm and sniffed my neck. She leaned back, looked me over, turned me around. She shook her head. She said, "You could call it a blessing, I suppose. Or a curse?"

"What's that, dear?" Blackie said.

"How I can see into people."

"Like the Visible Man?" Audrey said.

"In*to*, not in*side*."

"How do you do it?" Audrey said.

"By dipping my toast into the blue yolks of your sunnyside eyes."

"What if I close them?"

Blackie said, "And what do you see, Frances?"

"All the levels of deceit. All the cunning nuance and the blistering intentions."

"Must be scary."

"I can't be lied to, in other words."

"How long have you been able to do this?"

"Always, but I only lately realized I could."

Over the years I'd come to realize how uncommonly susceptible Mom was to suggestions regarding her physical condition. I said, "You look like you've got one of your migraines coming on."

She closed her eyes and massaged her temples. "I should probably lie down," she said.

Dad, in fact, did call that night from a motel near the Wilbur Cross Parkway in Wallingford, Connecticut. He told me he'd be home in the morning—what did I think of that?—and asked to speak to Mom.

"I'm fine, thanks," I said.

He said, "How are you, Johnny?"

"Audrey's good, too."

"Can't wait to see you," he said. "I miss you guys. A whole bunch, a bushel and a peck."

They were still talking when I went to bed. I could hear Mom's voice, but not what she was saying. And I was soothed. It was like listening to the radio from the kitchen on a snow day and hearing Dick Larson's serene and creamy voice on the WREQ Breakfast Club, catching every few of his words as he tells me how aromatic and scrumptious his coffee is this cold morning and how he wants to thank the people at Holiday Doughnuts for schlepping it in. No school in Requiem, he'd say. No school in Spindleville. No school in Boxboro-Foxboro.

A Show of Affection

I WOKE UP at four A.M. when I heard a clatter of dishes in the kitchen. Mom was already up and dressed in a yellow sleeveless blouse, red clam diggers, and rhinestone sunglasses. She was sipping coffee, stirring a pot of butterscotch pudding on the stove, and jabbering away a mile a minute about what she and Dad were going to do when he got home: breakfast at the Broadway, shopping at Bradlees, seeing the new Steve McQueen movie at the Loew's Poli, pizza at the Wonder Bar, blah blah blah. I didn't mean to, but I startled Mom with my question.

"Jesus H. Christ, Johnny, don't ever sneak up on me like that. I could have had a heart attack. My God. And no, I am not talking to Arthur again. Arthur's in heaven."

I peeked in the pantry and saw that she had already made a Swans Down chocolate cake with double fudge frosting and a chocolate cream pie. I said, "Are you going to clean up this mess or am I?"

"That's completely up to you," she said.

And then it was noon, and Audrey and I sat at the kitchen table with our bowls of pudding. Deluxe, still dusted with flour, watched us from the top of the fridge. Audrey split the pudding skin with a spoon and poured a cruet of cream into the crack. She ate the creamy pudding first and saved the skin for last.

Dad had gotten home at nine-fifteen. At 9:21 he and Mom slipped into their bedroom, locked the door, stuffed the keyhole with tissue, and had been there ever since. Audrey said, "What do you think they're doing in there, Johnny Boy?"

"Probably sleeping. Mom was up all night."

"Mom squeals in her sleep now?"

"Probably dreaming."

"I think they're intercoursing."

"What?"

"Mom and Dad."

"They are not."

"It's what moms and dads do."

"How do you know?"

"Everybody knows."

And I knew that Audrey was right. Intercourse was indeed what our parents were gleefully up to in there. They were "doing it," I realized, even if what *it* was was not completely clear to me. I mean, I understood, or thought I did, the nimble mechanics of intercourse, but not what surely had to be its graceless choreography. I understood what was done—if not exactly how—but not why someone would choose to do it. Sex had always been (for *always* read eight months) an exhilarating, if somewhat shameful and private activity, a filthy practice referred to in the confessional as "the sin of self-abuse," a barbarous passion best kept secret, a foolhardy enterprise that would lead inevitably to blindness and madness if Father Carrigan, Veronica's uncle Robert, were to be believed. So inviting another person to share in your depravity did not seem all that noble or considerate. And I cer-

tainly did not care to think about it, didn't want to picture my
mother and father engaged in their naked and preposterous cal-
isthenics. And I may also have been jealous, of course. They had
each other to play with. They didn't seem to need Audrey and
me around. I said, "How about a piece of pie?"

"Alamo," Audrey said, meaning with ice cream.

Six months or so earlier, I'd been playing Wiffle Ball in the Iandoli's parking lot with Paulie Langevin when it started to pour.
We ran to the gazebo in the Genatassios' backyard, and for some
reason, while we sat there waiting out the rain, Paulie, who was
in high school already, decided to lecture me on sex. He said,
"You know your dick?"

"Of course I do."

"It's called a penis. And a girl's unit is called a vagina." He told
me I could look up the words in the dictionary and read all about
them, which I doubted because I couldn't even find *shit* or *jizz* in
my *Ivy League Pocket Dictionary*. And then Paulie explained copu-
lation, and when I asked him who was the guy who figured this
out, he said there was nothing to figure. It just feels so good, you
can't stop yourself.

"Can't feel good for a girl."

"Ever touch yourself?"

"Of course."

"Then you know what I'm talking about. It's like touching
yourself squared."

I asked him how he knew all of this, and he told me they
teach it to you in high school, and that was maybe the hardest
thing to believe that he had told me. "They have to," he said.
"It's like the law."

Until that stormy afternoon, I'd never heard of intercourse,
and then suddenly the topic seemed to be on everyone's lips.
Even in the schoolyard. Had this been going on all the while, and

I simply didn't have the language to admit it to my little world? One night Timmy O'Toole, Vincent Mulhearn, and I were pitching pennies against the school steps. Mulhearn was an A student, a teacher's pet, a brown nose, not a brainiac, but one of those kids who volunteered to clap the erasers after class and whose homework was always punctual and presentable. College material, the nuns liked to say. And he was the best dancer at St. Simeon's, star of the Girls' Club dances, better even than the girls. He wore a sports jacket and bolo tie to the dances and slipped quarters into his white-buck penny loafers. Mulhearn liked to hang out with the knucklewalkers like Caesar Cormier, so he could rile them up and then watch the ensuing carnage. He told Caesar one day that Diz Nadeau called him a lard-ass. Caesar duct-taped Diz four feet up a telephone pole and punched him in the stomach until he puked.

O'Toole was the funniest kid I knew. He had bright red hair, blue eyes, and a deep, resonant voice. He could sing like an angel, and Mr. Gallipeau was always trying to get him in the church choir, but when Mr. Gallipeau himself spoke or sang, he had these threads of saliva running from his upper lip to the lower lip, and it grossed O'Toole out. O'Toole memorized lines from movies he saw on *Boston Movietime* and would fall into character at the drop of a hat. You could be sitting in Tony's Spa drinking a Blennd, and O'Toole would say, "A boy's best friend is his mother," or "That's quite a dress you almost have on." And he knew things like that the major export of the Katanga Province of the Belgian Congo was copper, and he might bring that up in the middle of a conversation about the Red Sox. Or he'd say hi and then, "Don't even talk to me if you don't know that the trailing arbutus is the state flower of Massachusetts." He'd pretend not to be looking when we walked down the sidewalk, and he'd slam into a light pole, collapse to the ground, bounce back up with an embarrassed smile, make a show of brushing himself off, and say he was okay, no problem at all, thanks. I laughed every time he did it. He carried a starter's gun in a shoulder holster.

Mulhearn stood up straight, tugged at his creased dungarees, told us he had a wicked boner. O'Toole said, "His rod and his staff shall leadeth him. But mostly his rod." I wondered what had brought the boner on, but not enough to ask.

Mulhearn said, "Got a hankie I could borrow?"

"Use your socks, needledick."

"I'll get blisters."

"On the little mister?"

"On my feet."

"Then you're pulling the wrong appendage."

O'Toole told Mulhearn to think about his mother, and that image seemed to settle him down. I took Mulhearn's last five cents, and we sat on the steps. O'Toole lit up a Camel and told us he'd fucked his little sister Kathleen, and it was fabulous. I laughed. He didn't. I could see O'Toole staring into his past about a foot in front of his face. I don't think he ever looked any farther than that again.

"She wouldn't say so," he told us, "but I could tell she loved every moment of it." He bit his knuckle. "Every night from now on . . ." He pumped his fist like a piston.

Mulhearn piped up with the news that all African women have pussies with teeth. Said he'd read it in *National Pornographic*.

The last time I saw O'Toole he was just back from Vietnam. He'd joined, he said, so he could be there when we lost, could enjoy the humiliation firsthand. He was waiting for the bus in front of City Hall. Told me he was living alone in a room over a tavern on Park Ave. I told him I was at Requiem State studying English. He told me I'd grow up someday. He showed me a business card with his name, number, and a skull and crossbones logo, told me he made a living, a pretty good living he said, breaking people's legs, arms, necks, you name it. Have club, will travel, he said. I asked him about Kathleen. Skank, he said. All of them. Kathleen, Mona, Nora, Brianna. Skanks.

A month later I read his obituary in the paper. Timothy X. O'Toole had driven his motorcycle into the side wall of St. Simeon's Church. No skid marks. Apparently he started at the top of O'Connell, gunned the engine, and aimed for the church. He was doing over a hundred, they figured, when the bike blasted through the picket fence. *He leaves his loving parents, Eamon and Bridie O'Toole, and four adoring sisters . . .*

Vincent Mulhearn became an independent insurance agent. Still is. He sponsors Little League and softball teams. He's a deacon at St. Simeon's. You're in good hands with Vincent Mulhearn.

I went to the library that afternoon right from talking with Paulie Langevin. I went to the enormous unabridged dictionary on the table by the bust of FDR. Only I'd misheard *vagina* as *regina*, and what I found at the entry was a small map of Saskatchewan with a star at its capital. Since then I've thought of Saskatchewan as a female province, a province of mystery, and a place I'd like to visit someday. Maybe go to Flin Flon, which straddles the border with the masculine province of Manitoba. I got out an atlas and saw that they had Saskatchewan as yellow, which is completely wrong. They had Alberta—despite the name, a masculine province—correct as green. States, provinces, and countries come in colors just like flavors come in shapes. Massachusetts is lavender. Montana is pink. Wisconsin, red; Minnesota, a slate blue; South Carolina is orange; Missouri is brown. Anyway, mishearing can lead to knowledge, and ever since that day I've felt a kinship with the prairie province and have tried to learn as much about it as I can.

By two o'clock Audrey had had enough. She pushed her cow-girl hat back on her head, grabbed her crayons and a paper bag, and wrote a note: *Trapped in kitchen! Help!* She slid it beneath the bedroom door. She found a kabob skewer in the junk drawer and poked the tissue out of the keyhole. She knocked. She wouldn't stop, wouldn't go away. I joined her. We yelled.

AUDREY CLAMPED on to Dad's leg like a starfish on a clam, so he had to walk around the apartment with her attached. Audrey, he said, sweetheart, you're getting too big for this. The only way he could coax her off the leg was to give her the gift he'd brought back from the trip—an Old Glory lariat, which had a small string you held on to while you swung the red crepe paper streamer which was the lariat proper. When you twirled it in a loop or a figure eight, the lariat hummed. Audrey loved it, and so did Deluxe, who lay on his back and flicked his paw at the streamer every time it swept by his face.

Dad wore a clean white T-shirt, blue chinos, and tan moc-casins. His hair was slicked back with Dr. Gray's Wave-Set. He had a small triangle of tissue pasted to his chin where he'd nicked himself shaving. He smelled mossy like English Leather. He sipped his coffee and told us how good it was to be home, how much he missed us all. So I said why not take us on your next trip. He said the insurance company wouldn't go for that. And any-way, you can't be missing school. School's too important. I told him that actually it wasn't so important. All that our nuns seemed to care about was religion and silence. The other day, I said, Sister Casilda didn't know the capital of North Dakota and didn't even seem curious to find out. Mom put out her cigarette and said that she was going to make us salmon croquettes for supper. How does that sound? Dad had a better idea, thank God. Let's celebrate, he said. Let's go out to eat. Mom went to slip on a dress and grab a sweater. Dad gave me my gift, a Swiss Army knife with a spork, a knife, a nail file, and a pair of scissors attached. Told me he'd gotten a deal on it at Chief Yellowhorse's Trading Post in New Mexico. Traded an adjustable wrench for the knife and a box of Little Debbie snack cakes.

We owned a rusted-out tan and white 1959 Ford Custom 300 Business Sedan that Dad had bought from Franco Desrouges for seventy-five bucks. Franco sweetened the deal with a pair of snow tires and a steering wheel knob with a photo of a pinup girl holding a sombrero in front of her naked body. We drove to Speedy's Drive-In, which was where we almost always ate. We loved eating in the car for some reason. Dad flashed his head-lights, and the carhop skated over to us. Audrey ordered her usual boiled hot dogs on grilled rolls with ketchup and relish. I ordered a pint of fried clams. Mom and Dad had lobster rolls. I ate the clams with my Swiss Army spork. When she finished half her roll, Mom opened the car window and lit up a cigarette. This would be one of the last days of Indian summer. Speedy's would be closing soon for winter.

Mom told the story—like she always did—of how she and Dad met for the first time one night at Speedy's. Love at first sight, she said. She pointed. Right over there. Dad was with Rose-mary Faford. They'd been down the lake watching the subma-rine races. Mom had been at White City riding the Whip with Jackie Gillette. "Your father saw me in Jackie's Chevrolet, and he couldn't take his eyes off me."

Audrey said, "Jackie had a Buick."

"She's right," Dad said. "Buick Roadmaster Riviera with a sun visor."

Mom said, "Jackie and I were going steady, but your old man was just too handsome for his own good." Mom stared through the window of Speedy's. "Jackie's a plumber now. And you know what plumbers make an hour."

"What do cowgirls make?" Audrey said.

"Big trouble for cowboys," Dad said.

Mom said, "And Rosemary became a nun after your father broke her heart."

Dad smiled and shrugged. "What a waste," he said.

"And so when Rosemary went to the girls' room, I sent Jackie in for cigarettes. I jumped in your father's jalopy, and we drove off into the sunset."

"And they all lived happily ever after," Dad said.

Mom said, "When you're in love, you're above the law."

Then Audrey told us how she likes to plan out her conversations before she has them so that she knows what she'll say, what the other person will or can say, and in that way, she said, she gets to live the same conversation more than once, so her life is longer than anyone else's.

I LOST most of my mementos a couple of years ago when Hurricane Fritzy missed us but a tornado it spawned leveled the neighborhood. I don't even remember most of what I lost, but every once in a while I'll recall some keepsake I don't have anymore, like the photo of Garnet and me on our front steps. I was squinting into the sun, I remember that, and my right elbow was on Garnet's bare left knee. Her left arm was around my shoulder. Thing I took the snapshot, and his long shadow ascended the staircase like a Cubist silhouette. Some things I lost I'm probably better off without—like the giddy photographs of my happy wedding. I still have my Swiss Army knife. In fact, it came in handy after the storm when Annick, Spot, and I camped out in West Lake Park for two weeks before we could move into a FEMA single-wide. And I still have Audrey's cowgirl boots, a shoe box full of St. Simeon Stylites report cards, and a wicker hamper stuffed with Super 8 home movies. I took the movies out of the closet this morning, got the projector from the

garage, aimed it at the fridge, and watched the movie taken at
Speedy's.

Mom and I are in the car, and Audrey's pretending to be taking our order. She's got her cowgirl hat strung over her back, and
she's writing down our order on one of those plastic lift-and-
erase drawing slates. She bows to us and walks away smiling into
Dad's camera, not even looking where she's going, and so I keep
my eyes on her because I think she might walk into the path of a
car, and so I don't see Mom waving into the camera, throwing a
kiss like she's saying goodbye, going away, don't see it until this
morning, thirty-seven years later. And I see myself staring out
the windshield, my hand on the door latch, ready to scoot, if I
have to, after Audrey.

IT WAS Dad's idea that we all drive out to Brookfield Orchards
on the first Sunday in October if it didn't rain. We'd buy a bushel
of Macouns and a couple of Halloween pumpkins, and maybe
stop at Hot Dog Annie's on the way back. So on Sunday morning after nine o'clock Mass, we piled into the car, stopped at
Desrouges's for two bucks' worth of regular, and drove down the
block to the Cat Dragged Inn, where Mom and Dad proposed to
launch our festive day with Bloody Marys. They purchased our
consent with the promise of State Line potato chips and Polar
cola. Mom and Dad sat at the bar, chatting with Rags Rafferty,
the bartender. Rags only ever talked about two things: the Red
Sox and people who should be shot, an ever-expanding group
that included, first and foremost, corrupt politicians, profligate
priests, and Communists, as well as people who toss their gum
on the sidewalk, people who park in the space that you've cleared
of snow, hippies, homos, the Beatles, people who drive slowly in
the passing lane, Communist sympathizers, peaceniks, Yankees
fans, thieves, people who only go to Mass on Christmas and

Easter, lawyers, ex-wives, ungrateful children who don't call their parents, men who swear in front of women, Puerto Ricans, Madalyn Murray, salesmen, people who don't order their own french fries but then go ahead and eat some of yours, bankers, bad tippers, doctors, welfare cheats, cops on the take, the sons of bitches from the IRS, plumbers, the sanctimonious buttinskis from the Bishop's Fund, people who drive Japanese cars—"It's like they never heard of the Bataan Death March"—drug addicts, and women's libbers. Rags always had something to talk about.

Mom had been a tad manic since Dad got home, but was otherwise cogent. Dad didn't want to hear a catalogue of Mom's antics. Let's just live in the present, why don't we. Nothing we can do about what's been done, is there? She has her good days and her bad days. We all do. Remember the day I shot the television?

Audrey and I sat at a Formica table with our exotic breakfasts and watched wrestling on TV. George the Animal Steele was chewing the stuffing out of a rope buckle. Everest Sweeney was pounding on George's noggin with a metal chair. Audrey loved George for the fur on his back, and she was worried that Everest would flatten him with a Big Avalanche. I didn't tell Audrey this, but a couple of months earlier when Everest was in town for the matches at Mechanics Hall, Jay Laprade's older brother Dave ran into Everest at the Waldorf Cafeteria and they started chatting. Everest asked Dave if he'd like to give him a hand job, and when Dave said not really, Everest said he was sorry and cried. He didn't mean anything, he said. He was just lonely.

Audrey also loved the fast-talking Saladmaster guy who did the commercials. "Shush, Johnny Boy. Chris Saladmaster is on." Chris held up a battered pan and asked us if we had a bathtub this pitted, black, and discolored, would we take a bath in it? Audrey said, "We do, Chris, we do." Chris said, "Shucks, no. So why cook with utensils like this?" The Saladmaster seven-ply surgical stainless steel cookware cleaned like a water glass, featured pistol grips and inverted lids for easy storage, and on each lid, a little policeman whistled when the water boiled—guaranteed for as long as you lived. And then what Audrey really liked: Chris said, "Look at this for abuse," and then battered the pitted aluminum Brand X pan with his own stainless steel beauty until the side of the Brand X pan caved in. All of this in two minutes.

I walked to the bar and asked Dad if he was ready. He told Rags to get us more chips and tonic. "The apples'll wait," he said. One Bloody Mary led to another. A half dozen old Lithuanian men stopped in for their after-Mass shots and beers. Bruno Sammartino pinned the Masked Marvel after a devastating belly-to-back Suplex. Chris came back with his Saladmaster all-purpose kitchen appliance and proceeded to slice, dice, cut, peel, shred, puree, grate, chop, sliver, string, waffle, trim, snip, and ridge any number of fruits and veg-e-tables, as he pronounced it.

By the time the football game started, the bar had filled with Teamsters all wanting to buy Rainy a drink and talking about their French-Canadian girlfriends and reliving their summer vacations in Camp Ellis, Maine. Mom was laughing, and that was nice to hear, but I simply couldn't watch TV anymore. I could feel my brain cells crinkling, drying up, and flaking off the wetware. Maybe if they turned on the cartoons, the Stooges, anything but the drone and misery of sports. Audrey asked me for my "Swiss shiny knife" so she could carve *Audrey loves George the Animal* into the bench. I told her Rags would pitch a conniption fit. I said, "We could go home if you want. Slip out the door. Wouldn't anyone miss us."

One time when I was ten, Dad took me ice fishing out to Three Mile Pond in Old Furnace. At least that was the plan. We bought our shiners at Pete & Shorty's Bait and made it as far as the St.

Charles Hotel. I played bumper pool while Dad talked to a guy named Rub whom he hadn't seen since high school. He lied to Rub about his three seasons in Triple-A ball with the Rochester Red Wings and his cup of coffee in the Bigs with the Braves. Eventually, Rub helped Dad out to the car and into the passenger seat up front. He told me to keep the windows cracked. The cold air would sober Dad up in no time. He's a good man, don't you forget that, buster. Dad explained to me how to shift. It makes an H, he said. First, second, third, reverse. My feet didn't reach the pedals, so I had to stand and lean against the seat. I drove the Hudson home at ten miles an hour because I couldn't get the car out of first. Dad said, What's so hard about an H, Johnny? A three-dimensional H, I said. I'm not used to depth in my letters. When we finally got home, the shiners were frozen in their cylinder of ice in the bucket. They were trapped there in mid-swim, it looked like, bowed like parentheses and canted to their sides. Looked like time had stopped for them.

Audrey fell asleep at the table. Dad, I said. He looked at his watch and slapped his forehead. Where does the time go? He and Mom had a doch-an-dorris, and then we walked up the hill to home. Audrey said, "Look at this for abuse." She told me that last night she had dreamed that we all went out to the orchard, only all our apples had worms in them, and when you tried to pick up a pumpkin, the top came off in your hand and the whole orange deal collapsed like a flannel balloon. I heard Mom giggle and Dad do his Pepe Le Peu imitation. Zee cabbage does not run away from zee corn beef. Audrey asked me if I knew what was worse than finding a worm in my apple. I didn't. Half a worm, she said, and broke out laughing. I heard Dad say, Don't start with me, Frances.

DAD TOOK me along to the Mass 10 Truck Stop in Shuttleville where he was getting his '66 Freightliner serviced. I asked him if this meant he'd be leaving again soon. He said he couldn't very well earn a living sitting on his can all day, now, could he? We passed the Jesuit college up on the hill, and Dad asked me if I ever wondered what went on up there. I told him he should get a job where he could stay at home like normal fathers. Something fishy about all those priests, he said. You never see them walking our streets. You could be a janitor, I said.

"I'm a trucker, Johnny. That's what I am."

"Be a milkman. Drive a little truck."

"I got 10/40 oil coursing through my veins."

I told him how badly the meeting with Sister and the nurse had gone, how the school wanted to send Audrey to therapy, how if Mom kept acting nutty and if he stayed gone, there was a good chance that Audrey and I would end up in foster homes.

"This ain't Russia. They can't do that."

"If you were home, you—"

"I can't be in two places at the same time."

"I'm only asking you to be in one."

"How about on the way home we stop at school and talk to the nuns?"

"You will?"

"Straighten them out."

"They think Mom's bananas, you know. And I think they're right."

"She's running on a tough stretch of road right now. Dangerous curves. Frost heaves."

"And they're not sure you even exist."

I sat in the cab while Dad walked to the service bay. I flipped the sun visor and saw a family photo tucked into a pocket, a picture we'd taken at Olan Mills in happier days. In this one Audrey's a smiling baby in a pink smock on Mom's knee. Mom's wearing a crooked but engaging smile and a pearl necklace.

Dad's standing behind all of us, and he's kind of leaning in over Mom's shoulder. I'm standing beside Mom, Audrey's squeezing my finger. My hair's so blond it's white. And I'm winking. When I was that age, like four or five, I loved winking for some reason.

I looked under the driver's seat and pulled out the purple cloth Crown Royal sack. I knew the bottle had been replaced with the pistol. I checked to see that Dad was not on his way back already, and I opened the sack. The gun was black, almost blue, and looked like it had been greased with Vaseline or something. I was afraid to touch it. I closed the sack and slid the gun under the seat.

DAD AND I went to the café while the truck was being worked on. Dad asked me what I wanted to be when I grew up.

"An adult."

"You might regret it."

"I know—these are the best years of my life."

"Get yourself a trade. Electrician, drywaller."

"I thought I might be a teacher."

"That's good, too. Nothing wrong with teaching. Nothing at all. No, sir. Keeping the barbarians at the gates. Noble profession. Not just for women anymore."

Our young waitress wore a black sleeveless jersey and a black skirt. She was quite heavy, and her name tag was askew. Dad cocked his head to read it. "That's funny," he said to her. "Your name's Dot, and you work at a truck stop."

She said, "How's that funny?"

"D-O-T. Department of Transportation."

"It's short for Dorothy."

Dot was sweating, and there were toast crumbs on her breasts and belly, and I was sorry she had to work in a restaurant and be tempted by food all day long. She took our order without writing it down even though she had a stubby pencil jabbed into her hair and an order pad in her apron pocket. I was sure she'd get it wrong. My poached eggs would be hard and my toast white.

Dad blew on his coffee, looked out the window at Route 12, and took a sip. He spoke to the passing traffic. "I should never have been a father. I wasn't cut out for it."

"Excuse me?"

"Like you said, I'm a miserable dad—"

"I never said—"

"I'm missing in action."

"Why are you telling me this?"

"You know there's people who've traded their babies for travel trailers and television sets. Other folks abandon their children in all manner of squalid places." He slurped his coffee. "Sick sons of bitches."

Dad told Dot he didn't order the home fries. She said, I think you did. He said he'd eat them anyway. Not a problem, Dot. She asked me did I want a refill of—what was I drinking? Orangeade, and yes, I would. My eggs were sunnyside. Dad always said you can judge a person's worth by how he treats a waitress. That's when your true character shows through. I'd remember that a few years later when I saw *Five Easy Pieces* and Jack Nicholson humiliated the waitress, and everyone in the theater thought it was so funny, and I thought he was an arrogant bastard, and the movie was ruined for me. I just didn't care about him anymore. I wanted to see what the waitress's apartment looked like, what letters she'd gotten in the mail, what books she was reading. Did she have a pet for company, a parakeet, maybe. I said, "So why aren't you cut out to be a father, do you think?"

He shrugged.

"And by the way, it's too late to decide that now."

"I'm doing the best I can."

Maybe I rolled my eyes.

He said, "Well, excuse me for earning a living, for putting food in your mouth, clothes on your backs. You're ungrateful sometimes, I swear. Just like your mother."

"Were you cut out to be a husband?"

"She doesn't make it easy."

And then he stared out the window. He said, "Every woman thinks she can change the man she marries. Every man eventually says, You knew what I was like when you married me. Women like projects. Men like the illusion that they are free."

"Aren't we?"

"I'm stretched thin, Johnny. You don't know how thin." He pushed his plate aside, lit up a Lucky Strike.

"If you were here, you could make her get help."

"I can't make her do anything."

"What if something happens while you're away?"

He took out his wallet, fished out a business card, and handed it to me.

I said, "Who's Roscoe Deschenes?" Roscoe lived in Monroe, Louisiana.

"He's a good friend. You call this number. A woman will answer. She'll know how to reach me."

"Roscoe's wife?"

"She is."

"Where's Roscoe?"

"On the road."

"How's she going to know where you are?"

"She'll find me. Track me down. CB radio." Dad took a ten-dollar bill from his wallet and left it on the table. "So who do we have to talk to at school?"

"Sister Superior."

"Is she with the Justice League of America?"

"The who?"

"Sounds like a superhero. Wonder Woman and Sister Superior."

"Misbehaving students don't stand a chance."

"What are her superpowers?"

"Sarcasm and derision."

"Big words, little boy."

"I've been reading the dictionary. Did you know there's a word for the annual outing of the employees of a printing firm?"

"You're making this up."

"Wayzgoose. I'm not."

"You're a funny kid."

SISTER SUPERIOR, despite her erstwhile heroic station, was squabby of stature, built like a teapot. She greeted us at her office door and waddled behind her desk and sat. Her rosary beads clacked against her chair. Dad sat across from her, his back straight, his feet on the floor. I was to stand. I folded my hands behind my back and rocked up on my toes and back on my heels. I hated the smell in there—lilac air freshener. He complimented Sister on the healthy glow to her skin and mentioned that every single item in the room had been transported by truck. Sister said she didn't recall seeing Dad at Mass recently. Or ever. On the road, Sister, he explained. Sister said she had taken the liberty of checking into the family's weekly donation envelope, but couldn't find the record of one. She hadn't noticed any of us at October Devotions.

"To be frank, Sister, I've lapsed a bit. Pray for me."

"I'll make a novena." Sister fingered the crucifix below her guimpe. "I have to tell you that the school has notified the Welfare people with regards to our concerns over the well-being of the children."

"You had no right."

I stared at the Infant of Prague up there in his corner pedestal, a porcelain doll with a gold embroidered robe and a red crepe de chine cape. And he stared at me.

Dad said, "The children are fine, I promise you."

The Infant winked. He tossed up the globe he held in his left hand and caught it. I shut my eyes and shook the image from my head. The Infant rolled his eyes, whistled like nothing miraculous had just happened. With his right hand he made a pistol with his thumb and index finger. Pointed it at Sister.

Sister said, "Then there should be no problem, should there?"

"Audrey's a bit high-strung; I'll admit that."

Sister said, "Your wife Frances was a student of mine. Eleventh-grade history."

The Infant waved me over, but I was glued to my spot.

Sister said, "I understand that Frances has had a history of nervous breakdowns."

I looked at the Infant and shrugged, tried to lift a foot. Sister asked me if I needed to go to the basement, which was the school's euphemism for toilet. I said I didn't.

"Don't?"

"Don't, *Sister*."

"Then quit your little dance routine."

The Infant stared straight ahead. Butter wouldn't melt in his mouth. Sister put her left hand on a tortoiseshell box that I knew contained the knucklebone of St. Stephen, the first martyr, a bone which leaked blood every year on the anniversary of his execution—stoned to death by a Jewish mob.

No, Sister told Dad, your son is not a good student, in fact. He's a daydreamer, a Mr. Fidget, who refuses to work up to his potential. I was harmless enough, she said, but doomed to a life of mediocrity and aimlessness. Our Lord, she said, hates the malingerer.

Dad stood, said he hoped it wouldn't be necessary to take

action, legal or otherwise, against the school. And by *otherwise* I mean *incendiary*. Sister said something about the only law being God's law. Dad stormed out. I apologized to Sister for my father's anger and for his inflammatory metaphor—I backed out of the room and closed the door.

I caught up with Dad on the front steps. I said, "Well, that went swimmingly."

"Bitch! The family, Johnny, that's the bedrock of America."

AT SUPPER Dad announced he was leaving Monday morning. Had a load of office equipment to deliver to Dallas. In Dallas he'd pick up a shipment of Dixie Cups and haul them to Seattle, and from Seattle, who knew. Figured he'd be back in two, two and a half weeks. Three, max.

I said, "We need you here to keep us on the straight and narrow. You heard what Sister said. I'm a malingerer."

"He's a thief," Mom said.

"I am," I said. "I steal and I don't know why."

"Well, stop stealing," Dad said.

"I lie. I cheat. I covet. I bear false witness. I worship false gods. I'll go to hell and it'll be your fault."

"No, it'll be your fault," he said.

Mom extinguished her Pall Mall in the mashed potatoes. Audrey slid off her chair like she had melted into a pile on the floor. Deluxe climbed on her belly, licked her face, kneaded her chest, and purred. Mom said, "Who are you people?"

Dad said, "We don't need to listen to your loopy shit right now, Frances."

Mom picked up her dish and heaved it at Dad, covering him in potatoes, gravy, and string beans. Dad looked at me. "And you expect me to stay in this fucking nuthouse."

Geography

L AST NIGHT LONG after Annick and Spot had retired to their beds, Annick with her Joyce Carol Oates novel and Spot with his sock monkey, Hamlet, I sat up in the living room watching sitcoms on TV with the sound muted, listening to Brahms sonatas on the stereo. I had been experiencing intermittent shivers in the heel of my right foot for hours, like the heel was a cell phone set on vibrate and I kept getting calls. I was sure this was an early sign of MS or something and my body had been putting through a 911 to my brain. Once again hypochondria had murdered sleep.

I had the Rand McNally road atlas opened on my lap, and I was staring at North Dakota, a river shy of rectangular perfection, trying to lose myself, distract myself, trying to imagine what the main street in Livia looked like, and then having imagined a row of empty storefronts, a Rexall drug, a Lutheran church, a line of diagonally parked pickup trucks, a feed store, a boarded-up Rialto movie theater, a gas station/bait shop, and several poplar-lined blocks of Craftsman bungalows, I watched the house catty-corner to Dell's Diner, the blue house with white shutters and a light on in the kitchen, waiting to see if someone would step out onto the front porch and walk to the steps, stare up into the starry spring sky, and inhale the cool air rushing down from Saskatchewan. And when she did, when a barefoot woman in jeans and a sleeveless white blouse sat on the steps and buried her face in her hands, I wondered what on earth she could have been thinking about that hurt so much. And then I heard the whistle of an approaching train. She raised her head, wiped her eyes. A squeal of tires from down the street. The howling of her neighbor's bird dog. It occurred to me that I could now write this Livia woman's story, the story of a mother whose boy has fragile X, whose husband is a memory and a monthly child-support payment. I could do what I like to do—make things up—and I could leave my memories and my mother where they belong.

I looked across the room at the TV, at the ironically named Will and Grace, and thought what if they lived in Livia and knew my barefoot young mother? In Livia they could own twenty times the house they had in Manhattan, of course, but then they would not be Will and Grace, would they? Place is character in a way that time, maybe, is not. In thirty years, Will and Grace will still be Will and Grace. Would the actors ever consider doing a reunion show in thirty years, so they could know how their other selves were doing? They're sixty-something and still look better than most of us. Sleek and comely. Let's say Grace has just lost her husband. And maybe the death was humorous, like he'd had a conversion experience, was slain in the spirit, and he was being baptized by a rock 'n' roll preacher in a pool at a Baptist church in Waco, Texas, and the preacher reached for the microphone while they were both up to their armpits in water, and they were electrocuted. The Lord works in mysterious ways, and who are we to question his wisdom? Will has survived—although that may be too optimistic a word—he has endured, lived through a protracted battle with colon cancer. They meet for dinner and cocktails at Will's place in Riverdale. They reminisce, which gives the producers a chance to air footage from vintage shows. They haven't seen each other in, what has it been, Grace, five years? How did we let that happen?

I sat there and every few minutes felt myself on the verge of tears, felt uncomfortably frangible and brittle. The music stopped, and I heard ringing in my ear. When I picked up my pen, my index finger and my thumb trembled. This had never happened before. A new surprise every day. I put down the pen, looked at the palsied hand. My heel buzzed. Anything I wrote now would be mawkish. I knew it. I've been here before.

Of course, I could have gone to bed and cuddled with Annick, but I wouldn't be able to sleep, and Annick sleeps the sleep of the dead or the innocent, and soon I'd be kicking the sheets, punching the pillow, the flimsy goddamn pillow—it's like sleeping with my head on a washcloth—soon I'd be back there with Mom, going over and over some wretched scene or other in my head, hoping that if I remember it differently this time, then maybe the future just passed will change, maybe all our family's lives will be bountiful if only I can see now what I missed then, going over the day Mom carved my father's name into her forearm with a blue double-edged razor blade, and I had to paint iodine on her arm with a pastry brush and wrap it in a clean dish towel, and then call Dr. Christian Reininger, who asked me what I'd done to upset her, and when I reminded him that she'd slashed RAINY not JOHNNY, he clucked his tongue and told me to put her on the phone. Do you realize what time it is? he said. Better to sit up then and write. Sometimes you have to start with the drivel. You have to plant your seeds in shit if you want your flowers to bloom.

But I was still writing shit in the morning, even after I'd changed pens, drunk a pot of coffee, switched ink from black to peacock blue, walked around the block, seen the sunrise, put away the Office Depot tablet and used the Evidence-brand tablet. So I stopped writing and read an essay on Atlantic salmon by Edward Behr. The author was visiting salmon farms along the Bay of Fundy in New Brunswick. I came to the clause, "we drove a few minutes along the unspoiled shore," and I suddenly saw very clearly from his road an unmentioned whitewashed house at the top of a treeless hill overlooking a rocky, wave-tossed cove, and I realized that I had been there, and I knew what Behr did not, that the house, long abandoned by its family, had been converted to a restaurant, and I remembered the dark and rusted interior, the cozy bar, the linen tablecloths on the pine tables in the two small dining rooms, one a step higher than the other, the print of Théodore Rousseau's *Market in Normandy* over the mantel, a crackling fire in the fireplace, the fragrance of cedar logs. I felt like I'd been there with someone else, but I could not remember whom. The kitchen has a back door that opens to a view of the expansive bay. The two-lane blacktop, down the hill where Behr drives, leads, I know, to a forested highway where one might expect to find fir, pine, and spruce, but I see aspen, maybe from another memory, a drive through Colorado, perhaps. And then I wasn't so sure that this memory was accurate. I've been to New Brunswick, but never to the coast. Could I be remembering County Clare instead? Mendocino? Mount Desert Island? Maybe the images were not from memory but from a dream or a book or a song or a movie. (You see the trouble with memoir.) There's no sign to name the restaurant, and I don't recall a name. I do remember that it closed several years ago, but I don't know how I know. Out of business due to an economic downturn and an exodus of young people to Montreal, to Toronto, to Vancouver.

There's a path behind the restaurant that runs along a cliff, and I know if I follow it (perhaps I have) I'll come to a two-story farm-house. And on my way I'll see a man in a tweed greatcoat, cap, and wool scarf, standing there, staring out over the water. He'll look like Samuel Beckett. I'll say hello and smile because I'm American and I can't help it. He'll ignore me. He'll take a paper from his greatcoat pocket, unfold it, read it, refold it, repocket it.

ON THE Wednesday after Dad left for Dallas, while Mom was off lying to Dr. Christian Reininger and Audrey was, I hoped, safely slumped at her desk in her fourth-grade classroom, I skipped school—Caeli called in my excuse (the grippe, Sister, wicked bad)—and went along with Blackie and Miss Teaspoon to the St. Anthony Nursing Home on Casimir Street to film an interview with the oldest person in Requiem, maybe the oldest person in the world, for all we knew. Blackie wanted to keep Nora McCabe alive after she died. And, who knows, maybe we could use some of the footage in *The Devious Dr. Diabolus*. She could be the Queen of the Laurentian Shield or something. We loaded the camera, film, and sound and lighting equipment into Miss Tea-spoon's Rambler. Nora Maureen McCabe was born in County Kerry, Ireland, on the day that Abraham Lincoln was assassinated by the actor John Wilkes Booth.

I *loved* movies. Blackie *believed* in them. Movies made me cry. I'd go into the theater in the bright sunshine of the afternoon, and I'd come out into the darkness, and that's why I thought I felt sad. Darkness meant impending bedtime, and I resented sleep as life stolen from me. Blackie told me that we cry at movies because the screen goes black and the lights come up, and we look around and find ourselves back in the same disappointing world we were in two hours ago. For a while, he said, we got to live a richer life, and then in a flash here we were back in

Bleaksville. But Bleaksville, Blackie said, was an illusion. What's on the screen, that, my friend, is real. Film is forever. Film does not change, is not subject to whim and circumstance. That's why you can trust it. Film builds its own truth. It preserves what we did not see and hear as well as what we did see and hear. It's honest and reliable in a way that memory and dream can never be.

The nursing home had adopted a greyhound as a community pet. His racing name had been Fleetafoot, but everyone there called him Baby. Baby's presence and timid behavior were meant to calm the patients and elicit their tender impulses. Baby had grown up chasing rabbits in the Oklahoma Panhandle, and Baby could not climb stairs, so he turned out to be more of an inconvenience than they'd bargained for. He spent most of his day curled under the receptionist's desk, snoring, farting, and twitching in his sleep. Baby followed us to Nora's room, his nails clicking on the tile floor, his head low, his tail tucked and curved to a hook.

Nora slept while we set up the equipment. The attendant Brad told us she slept eighteen hours a day. The heat in the room was jacked up to ninety degrees. Nora wore a sweater over her hospital gown and a green wool hat with a shamrock on the front. Blackie took off his cardigan. When Nora woke, Brad fed her a few spoonfuls of raspberry gelatin. She drank a sip of her cold tea. Blackie introduced himself.

"Emmet your da?" she said.

"My granda," he said.

"I knew Emmet."

"From Kerry?"

"From the AOH."

Nora told us that the secret to her longevity was that she never married. "A married woman could not last." She closed her eyes. "My sister Bondi married an O'Dwyer and had seventeen kids.

Can you believe it? My sister Ellie had thirteen by Frank O'Mara. Neither of the girls could keep their knees together. Both of them dead now forty or fifty years. I hardly remember what they looked like." Nora told us her ma took in laundry, died of consumption, never made it to America.

Blackie said, "Tell us about your da."

"He died by the side of the road."

Blackie showed her a photo of President Kennedy.

Nora took a magnifying glass from the bedside table and studied the photo. She nodded. "I know him. Who is he?"

"JFK. He was president."

"Looks like a boy I knew in Kerry. Something O'Donovan. A layabout with lovely eyes and frisky hands. Always going on about knickers and knockers. I miss him."

Blackie said, "What do you think happens when we die, Nora?"

"I don't. Think about it."

"Maybe you'll live another twenty years."

"The boredom will kill me soon if the cancer don't."

"You have cancer?"

"In my dreams."

"Anything you'd like to do before you pass?"

"I'd like to go back to Kerry. But who would take me? And who would I know when I got there?" She told us she'd outlived her family in Ireland and in Requiem except for the shiftless nieces and nephews who never visit. "We'll all be forgotten, won't we?"

Nora dozed off several times in midsentence, and when she did, Miss Teaspoon sat in the comfy chair by the window, and Baby sat beside her with his brown head in her lap. Miss Teaspoon scratched his tapered muzzle and sang "All the Pretty Little Horses." When we eventually left the room, Baby followed us down the hall to the foyer. You could see that he was trying to casually insinuate himself into our little entourage, that he wanted us to take him home or at least away. Outside, he stood on the front porch beside Brad and whimpered, barked, wagged his ropy tail, and whined. Miss Teaspoon threw him a kiss and promised to visit. She sang, "Go to sleep-y, little Baby," and waved goodbye.

We'd parked the car down the block in front of a brown and mocha triple-decker at #47. I didn't know it then, of course, but in twelve years I'd be living in the third-floor apartment in this tenement. As we packed the equipment into the Rambler, three girls in pigtails, obviously sisters, walked toward us in matching camel-hair coats and turquoise scarves. A blonde, a brunette, and a redhead. When they saw us, they whispered to each other, giggled, ran up the steps, and disappeared through the front door into the house. I met the red-haired sister again six years later in the registration line at Requiem State College. She told me her name was Anne. I asked her why it said MARTHA on her student ID. She was given *Martha*, she said, but chose not to use it. In fact, her real first name turned out to be *Mary*. She legally changed it to *Emma*, shortened it to *Em*. I called her *Alice*. She called me *Jack*. At any rate I was smitten. I asked her if I could look at her class schedule and then signed up for all of her classes. I majored in Alice. I began to walk by her house several times a day, hoping she would be looking out her window, sitting on her piazza, working in her garden, and she would see me and call out my name, and I would appear incredulous and would say, "You live here!" and she would invite me inside to meet her sisters, to eat gingerbread, to browse through her books. I never told her about seeing her that day years ago, never told her how her laughter had disconcerted me. We dated through college. We married. She pursued a teaching career. I read books, wrote stories, floated from job to job: taxi driver, extruding machine operator, janitor, shipping clerk, short-order cook. When it became clear that I had no fiscal ambitions and insufficient ardor and that she could not live with who we were and who she was, our marriage ended. Here's how we lost our hold.

In those early days when Alice was playing at being Ruby Tuesday, her allure involved a slightly mannered, ironic innocence and a studied whimsy. "I'm sorry," she might say when we awoke in her bed, "but I don't believe we've been properly introduced. I'm Siam, like the country. And you are . . . ?" She told me that all of her previous beaus had been uncomplicated athletes named Jimmy, if you can believe that, all seven of them, all genial Catholic-school boys, fiercely devoted to her but intellectually circumscribed, the sort of earnest and eager young fellows who would drop to the floor in a heartbeat and give you twenty snappy push-ups if you so much as intimated that maybe they couldn't do ten. She told me that courtship with a Jimmy was not unlike training a seal to balance a ball on his nose. She said, You probably couldn't write me a sonnet, I'll bet.

After we married, Alice settled in to her new role as the missus. "This is all I've ever wanted," she told me, "a home of my own." She smiled and rested her head on my shoulder. "Let's buy a cat and a wood stove." She cleaned, she cooked, she shopped, she entertained, she kept up appearances. But when the domestic role ultimately proved unfulfilling or unsettling or both, when the novelty wore off and it became clear that I was not about to strike it rich in the manual labor business, and we would not be moving into the house in Truro that she'd fallen in love with, and not long after she'd read *The French Lieutenant's Woman*, Alice began to reinvent her homespun self as a tragic heroine. Those sweet and amusing boyfriends suddenly became dope-snorting, girlfriend-abusing delinquents who had alternately punched and screwed her into submission.

Her unbearable yet inexorable attraction to bad boys became the customary subject of her after-dinner conversation with friends and acquaintances. One Jimmy, we heard over coffee and date-nut bread, forced a loaded pistol into her mouth (it's how she got the chipped tooth), spun the barrel, and squeezed the trigger. Another Jimmy, the Gregg Allman look-alike to whom she would be engaged tossed her out of his speeding pickup on the expressway (it's how she got the ugly scar on her elbow). I chose not to challenge her stories so as not to embarrass her in front of guests. And what did I know, really? Maybe the jovial Jimmys were the lie. And maybe I didn't want to know the truth. And what was the harm in a few fantasies? Who doesn't want to seem outrageous and louche? When I asked her one night in bed if she wanted me to get rough during sex, she laughed.

I said, "What's so funny?"

She said, "Just act like you're interested."

"I don't understand you, Alice."

"I know."

I sat up. "You seem to prefer your made-up life to our real life."

"You think it's made up?"

"Stop this!"

"It's all one life."

"I know you, Alice."

"You don't even know yourself."

"Your life isn't tragic."

"Why would I need tragic when I already have ordinary?" And then she touched my shoulder. "Sometimes you treat me like a doll or a statue or something. I'm flesh and blood. I don't want to be on a pedestal. I want to be on the floor."

"Don't degrade yourself."

"Jesus, what did they do to you?"

She accused me of lacking passion, said if she'd wanted

chivalry, she'd have married some elderly industrialist. I told her that for marriage you need compassion as well as passion, and respect and kindness. She shook her head, put on her sleeping mask, and turned away from me.

Alice would make things up about me and announce them to our friends. One night she said that I thought *The Feminine Mystique* was irrelevant and histrionic, which forced me to deny it resoundingly, at which point she held up her hands defensively, maybe even flinched, said she was sorry she even brought it up, and cast a sidelong glance at our friends, like, *Whoa, what's up with His Majesty!* She cleared away the dishes while our guests looked for their coats and hats. When I confronted her later, she said she was having some fun, trying to get a rise out of our politically correct friends, and it worked like a dream.

"At my expense, Alice."

"You can afford it."

If she heard an intriguing nugget of gossip or, more often, if she read a slice of a novel that tickled her, she would claim the rumored or literary life as her own. She read about an artist's model, and that same night she told us about her experiences as a nude model for a handsome and dissolute Italian painter and about how she became addicted to exhibitionism. She'd been the other woman in several affairs and wasn't concerned about her betrayal. She was also addicted, we found out on another evening, to gambling, and her losses forced her to take a job as an exotic dancer in a windowless club on Route 12, and that led to three-ways with generous regulars and to a brief affair with another dancer—you know how it goes. "Only a woman knows what a woman needs," she told me and the Robertsons. Char choked on her triple-berry crisp, and Brew looked at me, like, *You poor bastard.*

Way back when, one snowy Sunday morning when Alice and

I were first living together, we were curled at either end of the couch with coffees and afghans and sections of the *Boston Globe*. Alice said, "Oh, my God!" and put down her paper.

"What is it?"

"This guy I used to know died."

The guy, Aras Kopka, was an acclaimed cellist who had studied with Pablo Casals in Vermont. Alice and Aras met when their families rented adjacent cabins one July on a lake in Fitzwilliam, New Hampshire. Aras had been onstage at a music festival in Interlochen, Michigan, when he was struck by lightning. Maybe you remember when that happened. He was twenty-eight.

The cellist stayed dead for several years, and then I found a letter (that maybe I was intended to find) on the kitchen counter, a letter that Alice was writing to some woman she knew from yoga class, a mother of a four-year-old, apparently, who had recently lost her husband to leukemia. In the letter Alice explained that she had also lost the love of her life, Aras, her betrothed, and when he died, a part of her did, too. She had to learn to breathe again.

After supper that night, while Alice and I were doing the dishes, I told her that I'd read her disturbing letter, and frankly, I said, I was worried about her. "Maybe you should see someone, a professional."

She rinsed a dinner plate and handed it to me. We had this heavy Franciscan Ware china, tan flowers on brown, that always made me think of torch-lit medieval dining halls. She said, "I know a hawk from a handsaw, buddy. I don't need to see anyone. I know what's what."

"You're writing this insane letter to a person you hardly know. I don't get it."

"I know you don't."

Alice wouldn't see a counselor, so I did. The night before my first and, as it turned out, my only session, I wrote out and memorized what I was going to say. I told Dr. Madonna how Alice's bizarre lying or fantasizing or whatever it was, was driving me crazy. I read him the Aras letter and explained that Alice had only known him casually.

He said, "She does seem to be in mourning, but not for the cellist."

"It's a total fabrication."

"But the emotion isn't."

"Mourning for whom, then?"

He shrugged. "Any theories?"

"Maybe for the person she never was." I felt terribly insightful.

"Tell me why you're here today."

"I'm trying to understand what's going on with her."

"What's going on with you?"

"I don't know what to do. I was hoping you'd tell me."

"What would you like to happen?"

"I want Alice to get back to her lighthearted self."

"Why?"

"Well, she wouldn't be in pain."

"And?"

"She'd be happy again."

"And?"

"And I wouldn't have to put up with her self-absorbed bullshit."

He smiled. "We seem to be getting somewhere."

I sat back in my seat and apologized.

"Sometimes we say the most when we don't say anything."

What hadn't I said?

"You haven't mentioned the future of the marriage. Does it have one?"

"I don't know."

"Why don't you know?"

"Maybe I'm not in love with her."

"And that would make you a bastard. How could you live with yourself, walking out on a woman so emotionally in need?"

"She is needy right now."

"She's certainly not manipulative and selfish."

"Listen, I'm no day at the beach. She's put up with a lot."

"What did she do to you?"

"She's not to blame."

"You're angry, and you're not just angry with Alice."

So that's my story. Alice opened the door with her lies, or whatever they were, and I walked way. I couldn't take it anymore. She'd become unreachable. Turns out that she wasn't crazy. Last report I got, she was married, teaching, and a mom. She could not have been telling the truth or at least not the whole truth or at least not nothing but the truth.

Her take on the marriage would be different, of course, something like, she was in pain, and I did not comfort her; she was out of control, and I let her drift away; she needed me, and I ignored her. She liked making up stories, that's who she was, and what did it matter, no one was hurt, but I couldn't deal with it. I walked my lazy ass out of her life at the first sign of trouble. Guilty as charged. I didn't try very hard, did I? In my silence I may have encouraged the lies, made them necessary, even. When I think of her now I don't see her trying to shock the guests at dinner, I see her sitting in bed, eating an orange, and reading Charlotte Brontë.

There's a third way to think about the marriage: This was a story of two people who mistook charm for love, who believed that they were in love and inviolable, but who found out that they were not in love and were, in fact, forsaken by love and by each other. At any rate, the marriage was over, and so began the lost years, about which the less said the better.

Living with Herself

WE MOVED UP to O'Connell Street on Harp Hill a
month before Arthur was not born. We'd been liv-
ing in the Jonas Rice Housing Project out by Purgatory Lake, and
I had to ride the school bus across town to St. Simeon's. I was in
the first grade, and everyone else on the bus was more interesting than I was. Donald Hoey could whistle with his fingers in his
mouth, a whistle so shrill and piercing it could break glass. Jere-
miah Fitzgerald swore he saw Donald crack the windshield on
his uncle Obie's Studebaker. When Donald whistled in Doody
Mero's ear, Doody's ear started bleeding. Robert Roy could, and
on most days did, recite the entire texts of Marvel comics, and
while I found the stories themselves witless and dreary, I admired
Robert's unbounded enthusiasm and wished I'd had some
equally zealous and quixotic obsession. Robert wore black chinos
with a cloth belt sewn in the back with a silver buckle. I loved
that useless belt. Huey Moran had enormous hands and feet, tiny
blue eyes, and never spoke to anyone on the bus, didn't read,
didn't look out the window, stared at the back of the seat in front

of him, his face as blank as an egg. His nickname was "Vacancy,"
but no one said it while Huey was around. Years later—I was in
college—Huey was shot in that great empty face as he walked
along an Oregon highway minding his own business. A man in a
pickup truck pulled alongside Huey and leveled a rifle out the
window. Huey's brother Moonie told me at the wake that "Huey
was somewhere he didn't belong. Stay with your own, Johnny.
They're the only ones who give two shits. Capisce?"

One morning, I had been watching two girls in the seat across
the aisle braiding gum-wrapper belts when I heard Rosalee
Acciardi tell someone who wasn't there to fuck himself, and I
looked over to see her hold her hand in the flame of a lit match
without flinching. Rosalee was a high school girl, and every
morning she bummed a Lucky Strike off our morning driver, Mr.
Wells, who was either sweet on Rosalee or afraid of her or both.
Mr. Wells got sick that year and wasted away before our eyes. He
grew so gaunt in his last weeks that he frightened some of the little kindergartners, who slumped in their seats and cried. Mr.
Wells was all teeth and eyes and angles at the end. And then one
day he was gone. Our new driver, a burly man named Mr. Short-
sleeve, intimated that we kids had killed Mr. Wells. Mr. Short-
sleeve said he knew all about project trash like us and said he
didn't want any guff from any of us, wouldn't stand for any non-
sense. Got it? He walked down the aisle and back, eying each of
us and nodding slowly. Okay, then, he said. We understand each
other. He clapped his hands and took his seat. He fired the
engine and ground the gears.

This particular bitter and blustery day in January was so cold
that even the cool kids wore balaclavas and ski pants or else
wrapped scarves around their faces and stuffed newspapers in
their galoshes. But I had no mittens because I had lost them like
I lost everything else, and Mom was sick of my irresponsibility

and was going to see that I learned my lesson. My fingers hurt so much that I cried. In the bus, I sat on my hands, but when the hands got warmer, the fingers throbbed even more. I was frightened by the stabbing pain. On the line from the bus stop to the school, Rosalee Acciardi took my school bag from me, draped it over her shoulder, and took off one of her woolen mittens and slipped it over both of my hands. She took me to the girls' lavatory and ran cold water over my hands at the sink. She told me sometimes you need the opposite of what you think you need. Then she brought me to my classroom and told Sister Polyxena that she'd "like to muckleize the kid's old lady." Sister rubbed my hands in hers and told me to offer my suffering up to the Sacred Heart. I couldn't stop crying. I couldn't move my fingers. My hands were on fire. I wanted to sleep. Sister put my hands under her arms and sang "Salve Regina" over and over. Sister Superior showed up with a pair of unmatched gloves, a suede right and a knit left, and gave them to me. She told Sister Polyxena (Pretty Polly-O, we called her) that she'd certainly speak with my mother.

When I got home that afternoon, the back door was locked. The extra key under the mat was missing. I buzzed the bell and Mom came to the door. "Can I help you?" she said.

"It's me."

"Me?"

"Johnny."

"You do look an awful lot like my Johnny, but he's not a baby like you are." And she stepped back and closed the door.

I banged on it. "This isn't funny!" I heard Audrey calling my name.

This pretense of nonacquaintance soon became Mom's favorite little game, one she would spring on me in department stores, on crowded elevators, at bus stops. And when I would eventually and inevitably cry, then Mom would say, Oh, yes, you *are* my little crybaby; I recognize the whine. And she'd hold me, pat my shoulder, and kiss my head, say, There, there! She tried this game on Audrey, too, but Audrey was all too happy to be someone else. She'd say, Actually, madam, you don't look at all like my beautiful mother, and if you touch me, I'll scream. And with that she'd walk off, and I'd fetch her back.

I also cried whenever Mom sang "Hush, Little Baby." The song made me sad and still does. I think the message that depressed me was that nothing was ever going to turn out happily. Whatever I had, it wouldn't sing or shine or pull or bark. It would turn to brass, break apart, or fall to pieces. So Mom would sing it to me at bedtime. She loved the song, I think, loved the idea of Mom replacing all that fails, and she wanted me to overcome my morose and silly aversion to its sentiments. And then I couldn't sleep. I'd lie in bed and listen to the voices from Caeli's apartment above me. She and Nunzie talking and then not talking. I couldn't hear their words, just the music of their voices, but I didn't need to. I could tell from the pitch and tone of their speech what they were saying. That's how cats and dogs know what you mean. Those nights I felt like a dog.

My belabored point is that I had grown used to Mom's games and had long since stopped crying over them, so when she told me, after Dad had left for Dallas, "As soon as I get my real kids back, you two are right out the door," I didn't pay much attention. Funny as a crutch, Mom. But then her joke grew more elaborate. She told me during Carson's monologue that she couldn't take much more of this, of playing along with our treacherous dumb show, and she hoped that I would carry that message to my puppet masters. She slumped back in the easy chair, said she was growing weary with it all—the constant stress and everything. She swished her feet around in the plastic basin—she was soaking them in Epsom salts. She gave us credit for doing our homework—we clearly understood the intensity of a mother's love. I told her to just stop it, okay? What she wanted to know, she said, was why. I told her I was going to bed. What have you done with my children? she said.

So I could either believe she was being cruel or I could believe, what? That she was coming unglued? I spoke very calmly. "Mom, I wish you would stop telling Audrey that you're not her mother."

"I *am* Audrey's mother."

"And Audrey's asleep in her room right now?"

"As far as I know."

"So who did you call an imposter at the supper table?"

"Your assistant, partner, whatever she is."

"And where's Johnny?"

"You tell me."

"They're going to take us away from you."

"Your overseers?"

"The Welfare."

She leaned her head back, closed her eyes, and massaged her temples. "Maybe then I'll get some peace and quiet."

"And then what'll happen to us?"

She opened her eyes and spoke to the ceiling. "They'll recycle your parts." She lifted a foot from the basin and dried it with a dish towel. Then the other.

"Do you know how this makes me feel?"

"Feel?" She lifted her sarcastic left eyebrow.

"Sad."

"Should I play my little violin?" She leaned forward in her chair. "Look, I know you're only doing your job, but this has gone on too long. I miss my babies."

I FOUND out accidentally that Mom's delusions did not extend to the telephone, that they were somehow triggered by our physical presence. I called her from Caeli's to tell her that Audrey and I would be staying over at the Sandilands' to watch Steve and Eydie while the Captain accepted a lifetime achievement award at a regional dental convention.

She told me about my inscrutable replacement, how he had disturbed her footbath the night before. When I asked her how she knew I wasn't the replacement, she said she'd know me anywhere. I said, "Is he there now?"

"If he is, he's being very quiet."

I told her I'd be home shortly to pick up our overnight bags—always packed and under my bed.

"Be careful, honey. You're being monitored."

"No, I'm not."

"That's what they want you to think."

THERE ARE times I can look at a smooth wall and see a textured pattern, shut my eyes, look again, and the crosshatching has become herringbone, so I know the eyes play tricks. Just last week I was in Austin for a writers' conference and ran into Sharon, an old friend, in the vestibule of the convention center. Her previously blond hair was now a light raspberry shade of red, and I wondered why she'd tinted it. She told me she was getting married again, and I figured, new house, new name, new dreams, new hair, new person. I went to her panel the next morning, "The Eyes Don't Have It: Blind Authors from Homer to Borges." (Sometimes you just have to accept coincidence, as lame and unconvincing as it may seem.) And her hair was blond. So had she been wearing a wig when I first saw her or had she re-dyed her hair back to its natural color, or had I made the whole color change up?

That's what I thought then—well, not really what I thought, I suppose, what I hoped then—that Mom's eyes were not always, but were sometimes, unreliable. Maybe all she needed was a trip to a good eye doctor to find out what was garbling the visual message. When I went downstairs to fetch the overnight bags, Mom was poised and alert. She was dry-mopping the floor and told me she was going to use her free night to catch up on her sewing. I didn't say, What on earth are you talking about? You've never sewn in your life. I smiled. She told me not to forget our toothbrushes.

I said, "I'm not an imposter, you know."

She said, "That's a funny thing to say."

"Sometimes you think I am. Someone else, I mean."

She leaned the mop against the stove, opened the fridge, and took out a bowl of broken glass, this dessert she liked with cubes of Jell-O, crumbled graham crackers, and whipped cream. She got herself a spoon and sat at the table.

I said, "Is there something I could do to see it doesn't happen again?"

"What would be nice," she said, "what would be nice is if you would listen to me the way my therapist does."

"Dr. Reininger is odd, don't you think?"

"Is he?"

"He's always washing his hands."

"Germs are spread by way of filthy hands."

"There's a sink in his office."

"It wouldn't make much sense for him to walk out during a session, now, would it? The man's a professional."

"There are no replacements, Mom. Just me. Just Audrey."

She held out her arms. I leaned in for a hug. "You really splashed on the Jean Naté this morning."

She held me at arm's length. "You're shimmering."

All right, maybe not an eye doctor. I had another theory. When we were not in Mom's presence, when she had to imagine us, she imagined us perfectly. And the real Audrey and I could not live up to the ideal.

PRECIOUS MEMORIES was a game Caeli invented where you pretend to know some famous person, and you recount the time that you and this celebrity, Marlon Brando, let's say, went cross-country skiing in the French Alps, and you came upon an injured and unconscious skier, and you saved his life, and that skier turned out to be Prince Albert, and later at the lodge, over hot toddies by the crackling fire, long after Marlon has gone off to bed or to wherever it is he goes, the prince confides in you that all is not peaches and cream between him and Princess Grace, and you can see that maybe he has eyes for you, but your heart belongs to Nunzie, and you let the prince know that, and he is grateful for your forthrightness, and the two of you become fast friends, and you still exchange holiday greetings and the occasional breezy chronicle. Or maybe you were on safari in Kenya with the Mutual of Omaha guy on the trail of the elusive white rhino when you came to a clearing, and you looked up, and there were Elvis Presley and Tuesday Weld clinched in a smoldering yet snowy embrace—you've stumbled onto the set of *Bwana Wanna Rock*, and the two of them very much want you in their movie. You'd be perfect as Tuesday's younger, lovelier sister.

You can be older than you are in your memory. You can remember the future—you and Tommy Sands at your oldest daughter's Vegas wedding—because when you take your last breath, you realize—and this realization is all the heaven you get—you realize, Caeli said, that everything that ever happened, happened in an instant—she snapped her fingers—and not just what happened in your own little life, but the entire beginning, middle, and end of existence, of the universe, the whole megillah. Time, she said, we made it up. Like we made up God. We needed

God because we have to have someone to talk to when we're alone and desperate.

So Audrey, Caeli, and I sat on the floor in Caeli's parlor with mugs of hot chocolate and a bowl of Toll House cookies, telling stories. Caeli said she spent every summer of her youth with Brenda Lee riding their horses Ermine and Blast through the majestic purple mountains of Mississippi. At night, after a chuck-wagon supper and showers, they'd sit out on the porch of the ranch house, which was owned by Brenda's record company. They'd drink lemonade, watch the fireflies, and admire the pretty cowboys smoking cigarettes outside the bunkhouse. On one of those nights, Brenda sang "My Daddy Is Only a Picture" for Caeli as the sun went down in the west. "I guess I didn't have to say 'in the west.' As the sun set. As the blood-red sun set."

Audrey said, "What did Brenda wear to bed?"

"Flannel pajamas with cowgirls on them. I still cry every time I remember that night." Caeli sang about the angels taking Daddy to heaven and blotted her eye with a tissue.

Audrey recalled the evening she spent with St. Gerard Majella in 1753. St. Gerard could be in two places at the same time, so while he was on his knees in supplication in the monastery chapel, he was also in the vineyard teaching Audrey to fly. Audrey told us that Gerard was very light and hollow-boned, and when he lifted off the ground, he sounded like someone shaking out a pillowcase. I heard sirens coming up O'Connell Street. Audrey said how you fly is you empty yourself. Emptiness is purity. It's not easy to do, of course. You have to release your thoughts through your pores and let the light shine in. When you're pure enough, you will rise off the ground. And then all you do is look to where you want to go. The body follows the eyes.

Before I could launch into my story about watching the northern lights in the Yukon with Muhammad Ali, the pair of us like giants in this village of diminutive and gracious Eskimos, the sirens from the street went quiet, and we realized we had stopped hearing them, and now their absence was unsettling. Flashing red lights stunned the parlor windows. Caeli touched her throat. "Violet's heart."

We heard a ruckus on the front porch and then the clomping of feet on the stairs. Red Morrissey yelled, "Fire!" We ran to the kitchen. Caeli felt the door, sniffed the air. We hurried down the back stairs to the sidewalk. Out front, we saw the medics loading someone into the ambulance. Red told us, "False alarm" and sipped his beer. Blackie said, "She's going to be all right."

I said, "Your mother?"

"Your mother." He held my arm, told me to stay here and watch Audrey. He'd go to the hospital.

"I'll come with," Caeli said.

I said, "What happened?"

Blackie said, "Where's your sister?"

I found her on the back porch, Deluxe cuddled in her lap. She said, "You were just going to let him fry."

"I forgot."

Audrey kissed Deluxe on his head. He yawned, laid his chin on Audrey's arm, blinked at me, and shut his eyes.

I TOLD Violet I should call my dad.

"Does he have a telephone in his truck?"

"I've got an emergency number."

"Let's wait till Blackie gets home with the news."

Audrey and I were in our pajamas and up way past our already liberal bedtimes, but we all knew we wouldn't be going to school in the morning, and I found it a bit exhilarating. We'd be sleeping in Garnet's room, me on the bed and Audrey and Deluxe under it. Right then, Audrey was in the parlor with Red, playing

Crazy Eights and watching the Bruins on TV. Audrey loved hockey. Her favorite expression those days was, "Jesus saves! Esposito rebounds!" Violet and I were at the kitchen table, both of us peeking occasionally at the Kit-Cat clock and listening to the phone for that faint click that came just before the ring. I was drinking Welchade and nibbling on nonpareils. Violet drank her Salada tea. I read her the saying on the tea bag's paper tag: *A man who says his wife can't take a joke forgets that she took him.*

Violet asked me about Veronica. "She's your girl, isn't she?"

I shrugged. "I like her."

"Her brother was killed."

"In Vietnam."

"That's ten boys from Requiem." She shook her head.

When Veronica's brother Pinky came home from boot camp, before they shipped him to Asia, he took a ride on the back of Duke Duquette's Electra Glide. The two of them rode out to the reservoir, smoked some dope, and talked about the chopper shop they'd open after Pinky's tour. On the drive back Duke took a turn off Bell Ave. a little too sharply, hit a patch of sand, and laid the bike down. It didn't seem so bad. Pinky got right up. Some angry-looking scrapes on his left arm, a sore elbow, but otherwise okay. He was thinking how a broken leg might not have been entirely unwelcomed—keep his ass out of 'Nam—and he joked to Duke how they'd have to try that one more time. But Duke didn't laugh. His forehead had been split open like a melon, juices leaking to the pavement. Veronica's mom told everyone who would listen that her son's survival was a miracle. God wasn't finished with Pinky Carrigan, not just yet. God had plans for Pinky, megaplans. A week after Duke's funeral, Pinky caught a Trailways bus back to Fort Dix.

For a while after Pinky died (friendly fire) I was afraid to talk to Veronica. Finally she cornered me in Charlie's. I told her I was sorry. She said she couldn't get over the loss. "It's not that he can't be with me. He always will be. It's that I can't be with him."

I changed the subject and asked Violet how come she liked to read all those romance novels.

"They take me away." She told me she'd probably read a hundred thousand or so romance novels, and her all-time favorite was called *Her Persian Lover.* I told her she should write one herself, and then Blackie could film it.

She shook her head. "A movie's a lazy way to tell a story."

"Did you and Red have a romance?"

"We weren't thrown together like in the books. We grew up together. Next-door neighbors. Twelve years in the same classrooms. From when we were toddlers everyone knew we'd get married. So did we. We had no black moments, nothing that prevented us from being together. No mystery and no mayhem. No outside agitator, no stumbling block, no monkey wrench."

"You got the happy ending."

"We did." Violet stared into her cup. She folded her napkin in a triangle. "I don't expect romance in my life. I'm just glad it's out there in the world. It makes me happy to know that."

I HAD been sitting up with Red in the parlor when I nodded off on the couch and dreamed I was in an empty room that had no doors or windows. I didn't know if it was day or night, winter or summer. I did know that somewhere inside was a source of light because I could see, but I could see no shadow. I also knew that I was dreaming, and I tried my best to insinuate an exit into that room, the way you can do when you know it's a dream. They knew what they were doing, the people who invented the jail cell. And then I thought, I'll get out the same way I got in, only how did I get in? A trapdoor. Of course. I felt around the floor for the telltale groove, and then the lights went out, not in the dream, in the parlor, and the sudden darkness woke me up. I heard the whisper of vinyl as Red settled back into his easy chair. He said, "Everybody knows that I drink, but nobody understands my thirst."

And then we heard Blackie saying goodnight to Caeli on the porch. He came in and sat on the couch. Red slid his whiskey glass and the bottle across the coffee table to Blackie. Blackie said, "She's had her stomach pumped. She'll be fine in the morning. She took some pills, then changed her mind and called for help."

I said, "What time is it in Louisiana?"

ROSCOE DESCHENES'S WIFE asked me who was calling, please. I told her I was Rainy's son. "I've heard all about you," she said. She told me her name was Stevie, asked me to hold on a sec, and told someone to get his face out of the dog's dish. "How many times do I have to say it?" She apologized for the interruption. She said, "Lord, it's like some people were raised on pig farms."

"Could you give my father a message?"

"Be happy to."

"Tell him to call me. It's an emergency, tell him."

"Hold on, sugar." She put the phone down. I heard a child barking.

"Johnny."

"Dad? What are you doing . . . What's going on?"

"Visiting. I dropped in on a friend. Passing through town, thought I'd be sociable. In the neighborhood and all."

"Well, you have to come home," I said, and I told him why.

"You two okay?"

"We're with the Morrisseys."

"All right. I've got a load to dump in Jackson, and then I'll bobtail it home."

"Who's that growling?"

Dad cupped the phone, said, "Stevie, don't you think the boy ought to be in bed by now?" And then he asked me for Mom's room number at the hospital, told me to go to bed, he'd call Mom and me in the morning.

We said goodnight. Before he hung up I heard him say, "He bit me in the leg, Stevie. I think he broke the skin."

I borrowed a flashlight from Blackie and took it to bed. I read from a volume of Garnet's diaries. This one's title was *Perpetual Diary and Daily Reminder* and was one of four. The diaries weren't hidden away. Garnet had often read to me from them. Audrey snored beneath the bed. On October 4, 1967, Garnet wrote, *Everyone thinks when I pull one of my stunts, as Mom calls them, it's because I want the world to look at me. I do want them to look at what I do, so that they don't see who I am. Today I imagined that my parents and brother died in a terrible accident, and I had to identify the bodies. I did not feel sad. I felt tall. The Red Sox lost today. Thing 1 is despondent.*

Concessions

I WAS KEEPING MY mother's appointment with Dr. Christian Reininger since she wasn't up to it. Her teeth throbbed, she told me; her eyes burned, and all of her internal organs were pressing up against her skin. Miss Teaspoon came along with me so I wouldn't feel like a juvenile delinquent, not being in school and all. People would be staring at me if I were alone, I knew, wondering what no good I was up to, and one of those gapers just might be the truant officer, an avenging angel in a wool suit and fedora, a character I'd read about in stories and seen in the movies, and figured was likely patrolling the mean streets of Requiem, hunting down wayward children, exiling them to reform school. Only fresh kids, Violet told me, chippies and hoodlums, roamed the streets on school days. And I knew she was right.

I had, in fact, a year earlier, skipped school with Chas Wrixon. I had no good reason to skip, just that Chas asked me nicely, said he didn't want to be alone. Chas, on the other hand, had good reason to hate school. The nuns were forever sprinkling him with holy water to drive out the devils and asking the rest of us to pray for the salvation of his soul. We played pool at the Strand with two brothers named Brothers, Tee and Dee, who beat us like yard dogs and laughed at our incompetence. We ran into a guy that Chas knew named Bobby Sham, short for Shamgochian. Bobby Sham was this compact guy in his fifties, maybe. Hard to say. Trim, tidy, and snug. He was shorter than we were, but fully grown. He was someone you'd think of if you needed a portable man for any reason. His brown hair was cut in a boy's regular, short sides and a half-assed quiff up front set with Brylcreem or Wildroot Cream Oil or something. His skin was flaky and raw. He limped enough to need a cane, and he carried a walnut one with a pink rubber cup at its tip. His green plaid shirt was buttoned at the collar. The index and middle fingers of his left hand were stained with nicotine. He lived in the Hotel Royal on Front Street in a room over a corset shop. Which was where we ended up. Chas seemed right at home. He opened the top drawer of Bobby Sham's dresser and took out a deck of playing cards with pictures of naked women where the pips should be.

The room was dim and smelled of yeast, like maybe something was fermenting in a closet, only there was no closet, only a metal armoire with a busted door. The only chair in the room was attached to a telephone table on which sat a ticking alarm clock and an old Brownie camera. A black plastic transistor radio sat on the windowsill and a shadeless wall lamp hung above the iron rails of the bed. The springs of the bed squeaked when Chas and I sat. Bobby Sham never unzipped his poplin jacket, never stopped smoking, never moved from the center of the room, never smiled, not even when he laughed. When he laughed, he coughed. Chas never took his eyes off those cards. Bobby Sham asked Chas about his job. Every Sunday Chas worked for his uncle Ray at the Proutyville Rod & Gun Club, loading charcoal skeet onto a trap in a bunker. Eight hours of that in the freezing cold. Chas said it was okay. Bobby Sham aimed his cane like it was a shotgun and followed the flight of an imaginary pheasant across the room to Chas's face and fired. Bang! Chas fell back on the bed. I noticed a dull and dented Brand X saucepan on a hot plate on the dresser. I wondered why Bobby Sham had allowed this despair to take over his life. I felt the sun through the window on the side of my face. Bobby Sham was saying something, but all I heard was a humming. He hung the cane over his elbow and closed his eyes. I told Chas we should leave. He told me to wait for him downstairs.

We ended up later at the lunch counter in the Trailways bus terminal drinking chocolate frappes. Chas told me he had enough money to get a bus to Bismarck. Where the hell is Bismarck? It's colder there than here, I told him. North Dakota. He said he had a good mind to hop on the bus and leave anyway. I told him he was having too much fun right here in Requiem. He said, I am? And then he said, You're kidding, right? We watched Slim Diggins load luggage onto the departing buses. Slim was six-foot-four and thin as a crane. He had no chin to speak of, was all nose and larynx, and his nose was running. He wore his Trailways parka unbuttoned and an aviator cap with fur earflaps, but he didn't snap the button on the chin strap, so the flaps swept out from his head like wings. Somehow his cigarette clung to his glossy lower lip even as he talked to himself a mile a minute.

Everyone in Requiem had a theory about Slim: he was a millionaire; he'd been an orphan; he'd been raised by nuns in a convent; he was the illegitimate son of the actor who played Joe Palooka; he owned a dozen triple-deckers on Harp Hill; he'd been a child prodigy, a mathematical genius, summa cum laude at Req Tech, who either: (a) took a one-way trip on Owsley acid, or (b) was exposed to ungodly amounts of radiation in the Bikini Atoll H-bomb tests.

Slim took a break and sat at the counter beside us. Chas offered to buy Slim a coffee. Slim ignored him three times. Chas said, You don't have to be an asshole. I said we should probably leave. Before we did, Chas whispered something—Fuck you, I suppose—into Slim's left ear. Slim didn't flinch.

I would meet Slim again eighteen years later at James Dean's grave in Fairmount, Indiana. This is kind of hard to believe, I know, but it happened. I was driving back to Requiem from Arkansas, where I was going to grad school. (This was after the dissolution of the marriage.) I figured to drive ten hours the first day, which would take me to Indiana. I thought, What would I want to see in Indiana? So I drove to Fairmount and checked into the Hoosier Motor Court. In the morning I got directions to Park Cemetery. Once there, I crept along the loop road, hoping to find a sign that would direct me to the grave. I parked the car in front of Clystia Ballinger's final resting place, got out, and surveyed the landscape. I thought if I were an undertaker, where would I bury a movie star? Hmm. I know, I know—in the ground. I didn't have all day, but I figured I'd wander through the headstones for twenty, thirty minutes and maybe get lucky. Just when I was thinking why don't they bury them in alphabetical order, I noticed a tall gentleman in a tweed overcoat standing on a low rise a hundred yards away. I didn't want to interrupt what might be his grieving with my insignificant question. But then I noticed that he wasn't praying. He was smoking and looking around. As I headed his way, I could see he looked a lot like Slim Diggins, but what were the odds? And then I saw it was Slim Diggins. How could this be? His hair had thinned and gone gray at the temples. I said hi, and he told me he was standing watch over Jimmy's grave, and he nodded to the plot beside us.

I said, "James Dean's?"

"Someone's stolen the headstone."

"You're Slim Diggins."

He seemed pleased that I knew him, but didn't ask me how I did. He said, "I flew in as soon as I heard the news." He told me he was a family friend; in fact, the family considered him one of their own. Mark—whoever Mark was—had driven him out to the cemetery this morning. Slim was staying in Jimmy's old room. A patrol car drove through the gate, and Slim waved to the policeman, who waved back. They'd been roommates, he and Jimmy, back in New York in the fifties. He said, "Juvenile delinquents."

"What?"

"Took it. Took the headstone."

I never saw him again. I don't know if he's dead or alive. I Googled him just now—what the hell. *Did not match any documents.*

MISS TEASPOON and I stopped for lunch at J. J. Newberry's. She slid her purse onto the shelf beneath the counter. We ordered grilled-cheese sandwiches and Frostie root beers. Miss Teaspoon said she was happy to be living in this day and age when two pals could relax and have someone cook their meals while they chatted and watched people.

I said I thought it was a bad idea to have the cosmetic department so close to the lunch counter. All I could smell was lilac. "Makes my head ache. Makes me think of my gran's bedroom. It's like I'm back there again tugging on the white tufts of her chenille bedspread. I can see the white coat button at the end of the pull string for the light, the wall socket without a faceplate. The snow globe on her bureau."

"And it smells all lilac-y?"

"They used to make me nap in there in a crib when I was little. Me, a bottle of warm milk, and a stuffed green clown."

Hank Michaels sat across the U from us. I knew his name

because it was embroidered on his jacket: *Hank Michaels, the Signing Balladeer*, only I think it meant *Singing*. He sat there drinking coffee, drumming his fingers, and mumbling to himself. He tipped back his felt cowboy hat, pushed the glasses up his nose, chewed on the stub of a cigar, and stared at the ceiling.

Miss Teaspoon looked at the menu photo of a BLT. Two triangular sandwich halves, three stacked pickle chips, a small pile of french fries. She said they really could have used a snake in the picture. "One of those thick, sleek green ones."

"An eastern smooth," I said.

"Newberry's ought to have someone like Hieronymus Bosch doing their menus. *Still Life with Corned Beef and Cobra. Banana Cream Pie and Jackal.*"

Hank pardoned himself, apologized for the interruption, and asked us what rhymed with "so heroic."

Miss Teaspoon said, "Paregoric."

Hank squinted.

She said, "It does if you sing it right."

When I told Miss Teaspoon that I was nervous about talking to Dr. Reininger, she said then I was in the right place at the right time—who better to talk to about my anxieties than a psychiatrist?

"So do I tell him I don't think he's a normal person?"

"He might take offense." Miss Teaspoon wondered if Mom was not crazy at all. Maybe she had just opened some other doors of perception that we were too dim-witted to understand. "All that we can think is not all that we can know."

I looked at her.

"Just a theory, mind you."

We stopped by the pet department to say hello to Mynah White, this talking bird they had in an enormous cage. He said, "Awesome, dude," and "Excellent," and then he rang like a telephone. And that got me thinking about why they do that—why some birds will repeat the song or the speech that they hear. Are they lonely? You make a noise, you get attention. Are they desperate for any kind of company? Does the chatter help them survive somehow? Miss Teaspoon thought they do it because they can't not. And that made me think about Dr. Reininger and his hand-washing.

THE DOOR to Dr. Reininger's office opened and a heavyset young woman with a bit too much lipstick on stepped out looking dazed or drugged or sleepy. She looked at me and at Miss Teaspoon, turned to Dr. Reininger, and said, "Is this your bitch?"

Dr. Reininger said, "This is inappropriate behavior, Betty." He opened the waiting room door, showed her the hallway.

Betty said, "Because if it is . . ."

"I'll see you next week, Betty."

"And the week after that," she said.

Dr. Reininger nodded to me, told Miss Teaspoon we'd be fifty minutes, turned on a white-noise machine on the floor by the office door, and closed the door after us with a hankie over the knob. He went to the sink and washed his hands. He had told me once that he washed his hands in warm, not hot, water for fifteen seconds, the time it took to recite the Lord's Prayer, because to wash for fewer seconds would not kill the bacteria. I'd been to the office before with Audrey and my mother and noticed then what I noticed now—that you could look around the office and not learn a thing about the man who worked here. No family photos, no diplomas, awards, or commendations, no tchotchkes, no magazines, no artwork, no knickknacks, no drawings by kids thanking him for visiting their class at Maureen Powers Elementary School. I wondered what he was hiding or what he was hiding from. Did the anonymity of the furnishings comfort him?

The fringe on the oriental rug beneath the coffee table was perfectly straight, like it had been combed.

Dr. Reininger wiped his hands with a paper towel and said, "Let's get going, shall we?" I sat on the cozy black leather chair. He shook his head. "You sit there." In the smaller but still comfy upholstered chair. I told him the joke about the morbidly depressed obsessive-compulsive who wanted to kill himself but couldn't get the gun clean enough. He asked me if I thought illness is funny. I said it can be.

He sat with his clipboard on his lap, closed his eyes, and said, "What goes on between your mother and I in our sessions is confidential."

"Me."

"What?" The eyes opened.

"Your mother and *me*."

"My mother?"

"Your grammar."

"My grandma?"

"You need the objective case. 'Between your mother and me.'"

"You're not one of those obnoxious pedants who gets their kicks by correcting other people's grammar, are you?"

"*His* kicks. And no, I'm not."

He clicked his ballpoint pen four times and then four more times. He said, "Do you always slouch in your chair like that?"

"So is this like confession?"

"Excuse me?"

"The session."

"Like concession?"

And I was thinking, yes, like con sessions where lies are sold, but I wouldn't have been attending to the surface of the conversation if he hadn't made a big deal about my grammatical corrections. "I'm here about my mother, but if you can't—"

"I can tell you this. Your mother is in a lot of pain."

"She says I'm not her son."

"I know she does. She may have a rare condition we call Capgras's syndrome. But the tests aren't conclusive. But here is my considered, my professional, opinion. Frances does know you're her son, but because of this . . . this disease, let's call it . . . in her head, she feels no emotion for you."

"She does so."

"And that is a cause of great distress to her. So she denies that you are who you say you are. She couldn't live with herself otherwise."

"What am I supposed to do about that?"

"What would you like to do?"

"Audrey needs her mother."

"Does Johnny?"

"What's wrong with your foot?"

He uncrossed his legs.

"The big shoe," I said.

"I have a clubfoot," he said. "So did Byron."

"Byron who?"

"Lord Byron."

"The wrestler?"

"Poet. 'She walks in beauty, like the night or cloudless climes and starry skies.' Byron swam the Hellespont."

"How bad is she?"

"*Bad.* That's an interesting word choice."

"I've got a mother and a father who don't want to be my parents."

"It's not always about you, Johnny."

"If the Welfare gets involved, then they'll separate Audrey and me."

"And how does that make you feel?"

"I can't let that happen."

"That's not what I asked you."

I drew a tissue from the pop-up box, blew my nose until it honked, dropped the tissue on the coffee table. I sniffled, wiped my nose on the heel of my hand, and wiped the hand on the thigh of my dungarees.

Dr. Reininger stiffened, bent forward, stared at the tissue like if he averted his eyes, it might leap at his throat. "The basket," he said.

"What?"

He pointed his chin at the side of my chair. "The tissue," he said.

I flipped the tissue in the metal wastebasket.

Dr. Reininger told me that sometimes what we call mental illness, insanity, is actually a creative response to an incomprehensible and frightening world. It's self-preservation. "She's a woman of enormous courage."

"How can you make her better if you think she's healthy?"

"Perhaps she only seems confused to you and me because we don't understand her personal symbolism, her peculiar syntax. She is speaking metaphorically, and our job, our duty, is to try to understand her metaphors."

"I don't know what you're talking about."

YEARS LATER—I may have mentioned my lost years already—I was in therapy myself, thanks to Blue Cross, with Dr. Nandadulal Ghosh, Ph.D., MSW, who had some difficulty with the pronunciation of English. All of his *f*'s were *p*'s. What are your pears, Johnny? Why do you all the time peel pustrated? (I conjured an unpleasant image there of *pustrated* that has stayed with me. In it I see my seething self pounding my fists against my knees until a fetid, sulfur-colored liquid bleeds from the scabs on my hands, the oozy debris from my necrotic emotional tissue.) Are you, in pact, apraid to pail?

When I felt anxious in a session, I might inappropriately lash out at Nandadulal. ("Call me Dr. Ghosh. We are not priends.") "Doctor," I'd say, "I frequently feel fearful, fretful, full of frenzied, unfocused fantasies."

"This is punny to you?"

"Sorry."

"Pace the pacts, Mr.—"

"Call me Johnny."

"You are an emotional slattern."

Worse than his pronunciation, however, was his inability to understand me, the Requiem accent, I suppose. So I'd often have to repeat to him what I found loathsome to say in the first place, what I found humiliating and shameful. "You what your pather?"

"When I was a kid, I shot him."

"You tried to kill your pather. My gosh." He sat forward in his seat.

"I didn't want to kill him."

"Just wound?" He scribbled in his notebook. "Splendid!"

Which naturally led to a discussion of my manhood.

"How do you peel about your penis?"

"My fenis?"

"Your cuckoo bird. Your plonker. What do you call it here? Your organ?"

"We call it a Hammond."

"Do you admire your Hammond?"

"It's useful."

"Super. Do you ever play with it?"

"If you're asking am I Ham-fisted . . . "

His smile told me he was.

Or if I said, "I want to be good, and I want to be seen as good, and that's not good. I'm weak. I'm afraid that people will see that and leave me."

"Why do you think they will?"

"Because they have."

"What have you done to them to make them leave?"

"Not given them enough."

"Hmm . . ."

"I've grown tired of them."

"Excuse me, what?"

"They can sense it, I think."

"They can sense . . ."

"That I don't need them."

"And they leave you."

"Yes."

"You haven't left them."

"Correct."

"Convenient."

"What?"

"You heard me, Johnny. Loud and clear."

"I'm afraid to be alone."

"And yet you've managed to do just that."

"Why am I so afraid of not being liked that even when creeps turn away from me, I'm upset, angry, and obsessed with wanting to know why?"

"Yes, why is that?"

"I'd like to beat them."

"Would you like to explore that anger?"

"Even you, Nandadulal, you don't act like a human being with me."

"Would you like to beat me?"

"Do you care about me?"

"Do you think I do?"

"Puck you, Nandadulal."

"Now we're getting somewhere."

Beauty

M OM HAD TAPED her eyes shut with Audrey's zebra-striped Band-Aids and then tied a silk kerchief over them. She stuffed her ears with cotton balls, swallowed a Benadryl with a glass of warm milk, leaned back in bed, and pulled up the covers. I sat on the stoop with Blackie, waiting for my father to show up and make everything all right again. Deluxe stretched himself out under the hedges by the front walk and watched Audrey play hopscotch with her invisible friend AbracaDebra.

Blackie asked me if I'd noticed how you never see a nun alone in public. They're always in a pack. A *waddle*, he called it, as in, *A waddle of nuns clogged the canned vegetable aisle at Iandoli's*. "They are women of mystery, Johnny."

Audrey said, "Your peever's on the line, Little Debbie, but you get a do-over."

Deluxe twitched his tail, chattered, and clicked. He'd spotted the white-eared squirrel beneath the mountain ash.

Blackie said, "She's a cute one, that Sister Godzilla."

"Casilda."

"I'm willing to bet she has a bitchin' little body under that habit."

"You shouldn't be talking like this."

"Most of them are dykes, you know."

Deluxe waggled his fanny, crouched, and slunk across the brown patch of lawn. That's when the mockingbird swooped in and pecked him on the noggin. The squirrel climbed the tree and barked at Deluxe, who pretended the recent insult had not occurred.

Blackie said, "I'm going to ask her out."

"No, you're not."

"To the movies, maybe. And then, who knows?"

"You'll go to hell."

"I plan to take her to heaven."

"What about Miss Teaspoon?"

"I've told you we're not . . . not romantically enmeshed. We're not embrangled in an amorous way."

"Does she know that?"

"I wonder what Casilda would look like in an angora sweater."

Deluxe walked over to the hopscotch court, plopped himself down in heaven, and licked his paws. I looked up O'Connell Street, hoping to see my father's truck cresting the hill. Sargie Galvin stumbled out of Charlie's and leaned against the plate-glass window. He seemed to be reasoning with himself. He couldn't get his cigarette lit.

I said, "I'll pray for you, Blackie."

Sargie zipped his baseball jacket—HARP HILL POST 323, ZONE 4 CHAMPS, 1954. He slipped his hands into his pants pockets and summoned the resolve to walk his drunken self home up O'Connell. Three o'clock and his day was done. Sargie lived on Emerald Street with his mother, slept in the only bedroom he'd ever slept in. His father, Ace, had died of liver cancer, and his sister Helen was a Carmelite nun in Danvers. Mrs. Galvin worked part-time as a receptionist for the bus company and sang in the St. Simeon's choir. Blackie waved to Sargie as he passed our house. "Monsignor Galvin!" he said. Sargie stopped and blessed us, making a sweeping sign of the cross. "Bless your asses," he said. His right eye was bruised, a front tooth was missing, had been for as long as I'd known him. He'd pissed his pants. His face was ruddy; his blond hair was just fading to gray at the temples. You could see beneath the swollen features that he had once been a handsome guy. Blackie told me that Sargie had played center field like an angel—he didn't run, he glided; every spectacular catch was effortless, every throw to the plate, on the money. He could have made the Bigs—even got a phone call from Tom Yawkey—but then he fell into the bottle.

"Maybe he'll crawl out," I said.

"He made a choice. Some choices you don't get to do over."

"I didn't say it would be easy."

Sargie stopped in front of Charbonneau's Shoes, leaned against a station wagon, and puked into the gutter. Steam rose from the vomit in the cold air.

"I was with him when he had his first drink," Blackie said. "It was my idea. He was a star; I was a fuckup. We tapped a Harry outside Mulcahy's Package Store and got two fifths of Gilbey's gin. I drank mine that night and slept in the schoolyard. I saw Sargie the next day at the doughnut shop, and he was still drunk. And he had a half a bottle left. He told me the secret was, you drink a glass of water every hour, and it keeps you drunk. And he's been drunk ever since."

I couldn't have known it then, of course—on the stoop there watching Audrey hop on her booted foot—but there would come a time in my life—a rattling, but not toppling, bump in the

road is how I prefer to think of it now that I'm behind the wheel
again—when I behaved as wretchedly as Sargie Galvin ever did.
This was after Alice (we're calling her) and I had separated. This
was also after I'd lost my counseling job (I was finally using my
head) at the Crisis Center, Inc. Because why? Because I'd told our
glib and swinish director at a staff meeting that I did not approve
of the bureaucratic direction our agency was taking, and he told
me the obvious, that I had trouble with authority, and I told him
to fuck himself, and he asked me did I want to take it outside.

I lost my way after that. No wife, no cozy lodgings, no money,
no ambition, no dreams—just what I'd wanted. I took a studio
apartment in a bleak little rooming house. I waited, as Kafka
advised, for the world to offer itself unmasked, to roll in ecstasy
at my feet. I rolled my own cigarettes, stole toilet paper from
public restrooms. I applied for food stamps. When the unem-
ployment checks ran out, I took day-labor jobs on landscaping
and house-painting crews, spent my pay on cocaine, which was
fun but expensive, so eventually I gave up the studio, bought a
used sleeping bag at the Salvation Army Thrift Store, and slept in
parks, in the weeds by the railroad tracks, on the floor at friends'
apartments, in movie theaters, and at the library. And it was at
the library that I ran into an old friend on even harder times.
Katie Cullen and I had acted together in college—in a production
of Ionesco's *Exit the King*. Katie played Queen Marguerite—she
was beautiful, elegant, and appropriately high-strung, perfect for
the part. I played the Guard, the army of one, with bearskin hat
and halberd. "Recollections of recollections . . . we invoke you."

After graduation, Katie moved to New York to try her hand at
professional acting, but was unable to land any significant roles.
Mostly she ushered at small off-off-Broadway venues. And then
her parents died within weeks of each other, and Katie returned
to Requiem. We left the library and walked to Moynihan's Bar.

She swallowed a Tuinal with her peppermint schnapps. She told me she'd had a breakdown and had lost her parents' house, *her* house, to the bank. She had been staying at the battered women's shelter until today when they found out she hadn't been battered at all and had, in fact, been stealing from the other women. She fell asleep in the booth. We began to keep company.

The worst thing about living in public is, of course, that you have no privacy. Let's say you're having a tiff on the Common with your manic-depressive and melodramatic girlfriend (because, let's say, she snorted all the toot you were saving for after a hard day's work). Everyone walking by your bench now knows your abject business. What might, in the privacy of your living room, pass for normal if somewhat belligerent behavior can seem outrageous, dangerous, even psychotic on the street. Especially if your sweetie enjoys an audience. Especially if she yells out lines like, "What is it with you and my asshole, you sick fuck?" Or if she conjures a role from memory and screams, "There was a second back there, yeah, there was a second, just a second, when I could have gotten through to you, when maybe we could have cut through all this, this CRAP. But it's past, and I'm not gonna try," but nobody catches the Albee allusion, and you squeeze her shoulders to try to calm her down, but she blubbers and asks you not to beat her again. All of this can erode a relationship rather quickly. That and the abrupt, uncomfortable, and furtive sex beneath the rhododendrons at Tommy Heinsohn Park or in the dank and fetid bathroom at the public inebriate shelter. What might have passed for thrilling at sixteen was, in fact, clumsy, dopey, and unpleasant, not to say embarrassing and sordid.

If I hadn't had the pen in my hand and the pocket notebook on the table, I'd've been staring at, but not paying attention to, whatever game was on the TV over the bar. It had come to that—

I could only concentrate lately when the pen scratched the paper, could only escape the odious here and now by scribbling. And the here and now there and then—sitting in a booth at Moynihan's, nursing a Schaefer draft, and waiting for Katie—was the last place on earth I wanted to be. (I wanted to be in Paris or Amsterdam or Idaho.) Without the visual evidence of authentic, if not exactly nimble, thought, my mind lost confidence in itself and sought the soothing narcotic of distraction and amusement. Katie was off shoplifting in the lingerie department at Filene's, and part of me, a large uncharitable part of me, wanted her to get caught. Not because arrest would teach her a lesson—I was not so naïve—but because then she would be out of my hair—out of my hair and taken care of. I was making a list in my pocket notebook. *1. Call Larry—work. 2. Call José— 1/2 gram. 3. Frommer's Europe on $10 a Day. 4. Laundry Thursday. 5. Toothpaste and floss.*

A gaunt and somewhat round-shouldered guy walked in and took a seat at the end of the bar. I couldn't take my eyes off him. Maybe a dozen other guys had walked into the bar since I'd been sitting there, and not one had attracted more than my momentary attention. There were fifteen guys at the bar, but the new guy was the only intriguing one. He nodded to Eddie and held up two fingers. It wasn't his thinning hair or the mossy teeth. It's odd how that happens, and it happens all the time. Something about a person suddenly reaches out to you and draws you in, and when it does, you find yourself imagining that person's story. I was already thinking that he had a trunkload of secrets he could barely keep closed. If the shame in there were ever to leak out, he'd be devastated. And then I realized what had drawn me to him were his eyelids. They drooped just a tad, not like he was tired exactly, but like he was wary maybe and just a little bit overwhelmed by what he saw. When he turned to watch the game, I went back to my list a new man. I guess I decided to imagine my own life. I wrote, *What are you doing, Johnny? What do you want?*

I wanted not to live outside. I wanted to be unscented and clean-shaven. I wanted a home with a sink, a shower, and a toilet, a tranquil little flat with cushioned furniture and table lamps. I wanted a console radio with a dial that glowed in the dark, an enamel-topped kitchen table, a toaster, a bread box, and a cast-iron skillet. I wanted clean sheets and photographs on the walls. Venetian blinds, hardwood floors, and a mudroom. I wanted a cheery sanctuary, not unlike, I realized, the Morrisseys'. Evidently I was clinging to the past, moving on but not growing up. I wanted to read books and not paint houses. But who would pay me for that? How badly did I want it? Not badly enough to actually do anything about it.

I was becoming isolated from the few friends I had. I couldn't drop in on them with Katie in tow. I'd tried that already. She'd stolen a mounted digger wasp from Humphrey Dunt's insect collection. I brought it back, but Hump said, No more. She insulted Bailey Harold's wife Tiffany by telling her she was extremely graceful for a cow. Katie could be perfectly sane for twenty minutes—all you really have to do, after all, is keep yourself still and see that one sentence connects with the next. *Sanity* is just another word for *appropriate*. But then she'd uncork herself and say something like, "Satan has left the sign of the beast on your forehead." Later on, while we were bedding down behind the Stoddard mausoleum at Hope Cemetery, she'd tell me it was a joke. They would have let us sleep on the couch, I said. I knew that I was fast approaching the Sargie Galvin line and knew that once I had, there would be no do-over, no redemption.

I was writing all of this down, feeling like I was taking the first step on the road to finding myself, when Katie walked in wearing a floppy blue corduroy hat. Evidently she'd passed through the Filene's millinery department. She walked to the bar, put her arm around the new guy, and kissed his cheek. Interesting. He handed her a highball glass, and the two of them joined me in the booth. They sat across from me, flank to flank. Katie introduced me to Tombo Pflug. Pleased to meet you. Tombo took a small bottle out of his shirt pocket and tapped several clear drops into each eye. He blinked and shut his eyes. He told me he'd been born without tear ducts.

"Isn't that cool?" Katie said.

"So you can't cry?" I said.

"Never have."

"What do you do when you feel like crying?"

"I never do."

"You're a lucky man."

"When I was a kid, I would scream and whimper, but you can't keep doing that."

Katie pulled her purloined chemise and panties out of her purse, finished the last of her brandy, excused herself, and went to the ladies' room to change and freshen.

Tombo said, "She's an actress, you know."

I nodded. "So what do you do, Tombo?"

"I try to be in the moment."

"Does that pay well?"

"She's got quite a voice. And I've got a band looking for a lead singer."

"So why aren't you auditioning her right now?"

"Pawned my Fender. Get it back with the next disability check."

"What's the name of your band?"

"You know Katie, then?"

"We go way back."

"You've dated?"

"We have."

"Good in the sack?"

"I am."

"SewerSide."

"What?"

"The band." And he spelled it for me. "We used to play a lot at the Blue Plate. Maybe you've heard of us."

I hadn't.

"Before that we were Deathwish Dumpster."

"Doesn't ring a bell."

"Offhand Butterfly."

"Nope."

"Music's a hard way to earn an easy living," he said. "So I've got a day job." Tombo leaned to his left and slid his wallet out of his back pocket. He took out a laminated piece of paper and handed it to me. A personal ad he'd taken out in a magazine called *Swing Shift*, offering his stud service to guys who wanted to watch Tombo boink their wives or girlfriends. Tombo promised discretion and enthusiasm.

"How's business?"

"Picks up in the winter."

Someone dropped coins into the jukebox and put on J. Geils, a local band that had made good: "Freeze-Frame."

"It's like anything else," Tombo said. "You're always dealing with cum-twangs who want a discount, who want to pay you with checks or credit cards. They bust your balls."

I said, "You know what? I don't belong here."

Tombo said, "Hey, I didn't mean you had to pay to watch. Jesus, what kind of guy—"

"Tell Katie I had to run." I slid out of the booth. I hurried down Main Street to Central like someone might be after me. I checked in to the Holiday Inn by the expressway. I tossed my change of clothes and backpack into the coin washer, went back to the room, and took a long, luxurious, and steamy shower. Then I called Larry. He said he could put me to work for at least six months. We'd be painting the American Antiquarian Society. I'll be there at eight, I said. I set the alarm for seven. I asked for a wake-up call. I ran out and bought myself a fifth of Hennessy and a Sky Bar. I retrieved my dried laundry. I found an episode of *Newhart* on the TV. I loved that show. Alice and I used to watch it. Larry, Darryl, and Darryl were running the Minuteman Café while Kirk was in the hospital. I felt happy, alone in that room in the dark. I loved how the people on the show cared about each other. I closed my eyes and listened to the hum of the traffic. I walked to the window and looked down on the glowing sign for the Hawaiian Buffet next door.

I sat at the little desk and wrote in my notebook about how I knew I'd escaped, but I didn't know how. Something significant had happened in the bar—a dope slap from Tombo. I felt a part of the world again. I remembered Audrey saying, "Abandon your history, Johnny Boy." One of Valentine Bondurant's keys to success. That's how you move on—by letting go. Well, I was never going to graduate from Dr. Bondurant's School for Champions. Maybe I wouldn't even move on. But I knew I couldn't give up what had just helped to save me. I saw myself on the stoop with Blackie, and I wanted to be that boy again, the kid who would do whatever he could to save his sister Audrey. The last time I saw Sargie, he was wearing a black silk baseball jacket and was stumbling up Plantation Street toward home. I told him I was sorry about his mom. She'd died a week earlier. He sucked in his breath, took the measure of me. He wanted to say something. He raised his left arm and his eyebrows, bit his lower lip, shrugged, belched out his breath.

I saw Katie another half dozen or so times, always from a discreet distance. I watched her age twenty years in a couple. Her lipstick and mascara became more emphatic. Her hair thinned. She had this habit of turning her head sharply like she had just heard someone calling her name. After I had left Requiem, I heard from Dooley Raymond that Katie had somehow gotten behind the wheel of a station wagon and killed a pedestrian, a ninety-something-year-old decorated war veteran and his beagle. Hit-and-run, Dooley said. I suppose she went to jail. I don't know if she's dead or alive.

Dooley, who used to keep tabs on old friends for me, told his wife after thirteen years of marriage that he thought he would be happier as a lady. His wife Peg called me and asked me to talk some sense to him. I'm not sure if Dooley and Peg ever divorced, but he went ahead and had the operations, moved out to Rutland or Barre or somewhere like that, changed his name to I-forget-what, and took a job as a librarian. I hope she's happy. I hope she reads this and drops me a letter.

WHEN DAD pulled up out front I noticed he'd had an inscription stenciled in blue Gothic letters over the back window of his white cab. I'M IN LOVE WITH YOUR BEAUTY. As soon as he jumped down from his seat, Audrey was all over him. She climbed up his back, wrapped her legs around his chest and her arms around his neck. Dad galloped up the walk, did a couple of hops on the hop-scotch court, and said, "Johnny, how's your mother?" He didn't wait for an answer. He hurried past me and through the front door. He didn't even scratch my head. Blackie did. And he clapped my shoulder. He said, "Fathers—you can't live with 'em; you can't live without 'em." He lit a cigar. I'M IN LOVE WITH YOUR BEAUTY. What was that about? Welcome home, Dad.

You think about your life at all and you begin to see patterns. I find myself expecting to be ignored. I'm always surprised when anyone pays attention to me, even if the attention turns out to be pretense or simple good manners. I teach college to support this writing habit. I got a call a while ago from a colleague at a university who asked me to apply for a job. I was so flattered that I did. I went to the interview. This was just a few years ago. Annick didn't want me to apply. Why would she want to leave Florida? she said. Wait, I don't want to start there. Let me move forward a bit and then back up.

Knife in the Head

Quantum entities that have interacted with each other remain
mutually entangled, however far they may eventually separate
spatially. It seems that nature fights back against a relentless
reductionism.

—JOHN POLKINGHORNE

I'M IN AND out of sleep at the Quality Inn when I dream that
I'm offered a teaching position at Whitman College, not the
Whitman College in Walla Walla, Wash., where Diane DiPietro
teaches, but the Whitman College that is simultaneously in
South Florida where I live and in Requiem, Mass., where both
Diane and I grew up. This apparent synchronicity is an illustra-
tion of what's going on at Planck length: 10^{-43} seconds—the
shortest anything can get, the boundary where the roil of scrambled, granular space, the quantum foam, is so furious that there
is no left or right, no before or after, no here or there, no *there*
there. The dream Whitman New England campus is a single
wood-frame building across from L'Hospice de St. Francois, the
nursing home for French-Canadians, where I worked as a dutiful,
if sullen fourteen-year-old, washing dishes, peeling potatoes, and
frying French toast.

I accept the Whitman job offer, and I immediately regret my decision. Teach *what* and to *whom*? I can't find the dean or anyone else who can help me. The professors, all of them men with pasty complexions and stooped shoulders, wear plaid flannel shirts and salt-stained hiking boots. Each holds student essays in his hands. I'm depressed already about my pension. I want to tell someone that I'm pretty sure this campus is my uncle Honore's old triple-decker. If I look off the back porch, I should be able to see his fifteen-foot Elgin V-bottom and his boat trailer in the driveway. I wake up when the door to the next room slams—salesman, I figure, headed off to the airport, has to be in Cleveland for a nine A.M. PowerPoint presentation—"Mistaking Articulation for Accomplishment"—and I realize it's Ash Wednesday, and I'm visiting a Methodist university in the heart of the heart of the country. Requiem, Mass., is the *Heart of the Commonwealth*. Walla Walla, Wash., is *The Land of Many Waters*.

Walla Walla's founding Whitman was the missionary, Dr. Marcus Whitman, who, along with his wife Narcissa and staff, was massacred by the Cayuse when the Indians found his medical care wanting during a measles epidemic. The dream university's eponymous Whitman sang of himself, or he made candy, or he yodeled—I don't have the handbook yet. Walla Walla is fifty-seven hundred miles northeast of Pago Pago (pronounced *Pango-Pango*) and fourteen hundred miles southwest of Flin Flon, a city straddling the Manitoba-Saskatchewan border and named for Professor Josiah Flintabbatey Flonatin, a character in J. E. Preston Muddock's science fiction novel, *The Sunless City* (which Flin Flonians insist their city is not—it is built *on*, not beneath, a rock).

MY FRIEND and host Hillary and I have breakfast at the Bob Evans (home of the sausage pinwheel) across the highway from the Quality Inn before I speak to her class. We've known each

other since our academic exile in Binghamton, New York, City of
the Square Deal and the poisoned river, where pink beach balls
dance in the foam of the spillway. I tell Hillary how I'd gone back
to Bingo recently to see old friends and went to a party for a visiting writer at a student's flat on the south side. The poets had
arrived first and sat in a circle of chairs in the small parlor; all the
poets were balding and blond, and each held a slim book in his
gracile fingers. The poets had brought along their groupies.
They began to sing Tom Paxton songs. I went to the kitchen for
spiedies and rum.

   The sky is sheet-metal gray here in the heartland. The air is
damp and raw, feels like snow. Hillary shares a nickname with an
old girlfriend of mine and a medical condition with me. The
name is Button, the condition, tinnitus. My left ear rings and
clicks constantly, chimes on occasion. Both of Hillary's ears ring
with several distinct notes, like an irritating song, a brain worm
you can't get out of your head. Silence increases the volume,
which may be why we keep on talking. We'll never know quiet
again, nor the source of the phantom noise. I show Hillary photos of Spot and Annick. Hillary wants to know where I got the
phrase "knife in the head" that I used in a story that she assigned
her students to read. I tell her from a Bruno Ganz movie of that
name, and she says that she used the same phrase in a poem, and
got it from the movie *Montenegro*, which I loved. Yes, the man
with the quite literal knife his head, unlike Bruno's metaphorical
Messer im Kopf. And then I remember that before I fell asleep in
the room last night, I had watched a newsmagazine report of a
man with a seven-inch serrated kitchen knife buried to the hilt in
his brain. We saw the X-ray of the blade angled through the
spongy gray matter, rather like a pie server through pudding.
The man survived with only a little nerve damage to his left hand
and a slight stutter.

I tell Hillary I visited her alma mater a few months back for a job interview. I tell her I didn't get the job that I was asked to apply for. We order Egg Beaters and Sausage Lite. She leans toward me. I tell her the whole story.

THE TRIGGERING town where I had my actual interview, where Hillary went to school, is 214 miles east-northeast of Walla Walla, 2,340 miles northwest of my home, 5,477 miles northeast of Pago Pago, 824 miles south-southwest of Flin Flon, and 1,478 miles west-northwest of the Bob Evans Restaurant. My plane was delayed four hours in Minneapolis. I called my friend James in Dinkytown to come sit with me at the airport, but James was not at home. The last time we'd sat and talked about books was at George's Majestic Lounge in Fayetteville, Arkansas. We drank PBRs and sat by the fireplace. It was Eudora Welty's eighty-somethingth birthday. James remembers the birthday of everyone he has ever met.

Hillary reminds me that she once lived in Minneapolis and knew my friend James when they both served on the board of a literary center. She found him intense and quite brilliant, but acerbic. I found a bar modeled after a bar in a TV show, modeled after a bar on Beacon Street in Boston, only here at the terminal Cheers one of the walls was missing, and nobody knew your name. I drank beer and imagined this town I was going to: raised wooden sidewalks on the main street; snug taverns serving red-eye, mulled cider, and sarsaparilla; looming mountains shawled in snow; rusted Ford pickups idling in front of the pharmacy; log cabins, their cracks chinked up with moss; children skating on a pond, bundled against the wind. Yes, I could live there.

I arrived at the Garden City's airport sometime after midnight, after a stop in Great Falls, to where a former Requiem County man, David Brown, had moved a year earlier, changed his name

to Nathaniel Bar-Jonah, butchered a ten-year-old boy, and fed
him to the neighbors. A few months later when I read of Bar-
Jonah's arrest, I recall that night I stared out the airplane window
at Great Falls, thinking this is where the Corps of Discovery
faced eighteen miles of mosquitoes, gnats, and rattlesnakes on
their portage over cactus-covered land and where Captain Lewis
was attacked by a grizzly, a cat "of the tiger kind," and a "buf-
faloe." Lewis wrote in his journal, "It now seemed to me that all
the beasts of the neighbourhood had made a league to distroy
me . . ." Bar-Jonah wrote in his journal, *Lunch is served on the patio
with roasted child.*

I waited for the hotel shuttle and talked with a fellow traveler
on his way to Polson. He told me we were standing in the banana
belt of Montana. When I touched the door of the shuttle, I got a
shock of static electricity. I checked in at the Edgewater Motel on
the Clark Fork River, on the site, I was told, of what had been a
famous poet's house.

THE DEAN of the College of Arts and Sciences tells me that his
wife is from Requiem, the Kevin Bacon of cities, but he can't tell
me much of anything about salary (it's negotiable), health insurance (a couple of your big firms), or tenure and promotion (it's
up to the department), which makes me wonder why I'm even
talking to him. He tells me I'll get a handbook that explains
everything. He tells me his wife's maiden name, but it's not one
I recognize from Requiem. I try to imagine his wife, and I see a
university logo sweatshirt with a white lace collar sewn onto the
neck. I see swollen knees and white sneakers. I see a floral print
skort. The dean seems neither carefree nor careful. He seems
pacific. He tugs at his knit tie. He runs his fingers along the edges
of my file. He leans over the file and breathes as if the file is a pot
of steeping tea and he's trying to inhale the steam of its mean-

ing. When I summon his diminished attention and ask about the
benefits package, his eyes glair over like he's developed nictitat-
ing membranes, and, in fact, he does look a little froggy. Squat,
slick, smooth, and plushy. He looks sedated by the light slanting
through the window. All in the handbook, he says.

He smiles like he might have enjoyed being more helpful this
morning, but I don't have to tell you what that can lead to—more
and more questions and answers, a chuckle or two, and then a
cordial lunch at Front Street Pasta and Wraps, an eventual,
inevitable friendship, invitations to dinner, an exchange of holiday cards, family trips to Glacier. Life gets terribly roiled and
scrambled very quickly. The dean shifts in his chair, leans back,
folds his arms, glances at his watch, gazes at his telephone, asks
if I have any further questions. I say, How do you like Montana?
He twists his class ring, says, It's not for everyone.

HILLARY AND I order more Bob Evans coffee. I tell her how I
thought the reading and the fiction workshop with the students
at her alma mater went quite well. After the workshop I walked
the Hellgate Canyon Trail and then went to the UC for a bagel
and a Diet Dr Pepper at Soups and Such. I bought lip balm, eye
drops, saline nasal spray, throat lozenges, and hand lotion at the
bookstore and then walked to the English Department. The man
at the next Bob Evans table tells whomever it is he's talking to on
his cell that he's on his way to the La-Z-Boy Gallery right now.
Almost there. Need to hang up before I wreck.

The English chair can barely speak. I lean forward, turn my
good ear to his voice. Mostly he nods at everything I say. Apparently, yes, there *is* an adjunct slot for Annick in the theater department and, yes, the local public schools *are* exemplary, and, yes,
the salary *is* competitive and *is* commensurate with experience
and publication. Apparently, anything is possible in Grizzlyville.

The English chair is more forthcoming than the dean, but he is not a bundle of information, and he is without enthusiasm. He's pleasant enough, if not effusive. But he seems dazed, like a bear who's stirred too early from hibernation. I wonder if this is some Zen-like, unitive, null state that he has achieved, the altogether everywhere, or if it's emotional collapse and cognitive resignation. Either way it resembles senility. He keeps the lights off and the blinds shut in his office. He pats the pocket of his fleece vest, takes out a memo pad, flips to a blank page, clicks the push button on his ballpoint pen with his thumb, and writes himself a note. I squint to make it out. The office is so hot and dry it hurts to swallow. He closes the memo pad, clicks the pen. I feel like my intercellular substance is drying up, the walls of my cells are puckering, my body's shutting down. I'm losing my will. Crust is building up on my nasal septum. The thing is I want to like this man who's retying his thin and scraggly gray hair into a ponytail with a maroon scrunchy. He adores Blake, after all. ("Energy is eternal delight.") He has presented a paper on the violation of boundaries in *The Marriage of Heaven and Hell*. He likes Blake and Wordsworth and Yeats. To what then do I attribute his languor? Maybe there's trouble at home. He finds it difficult to concentrate. Maybe his wolfhound, Albion, is having seizures due to an astrocytoma on his frontal lobe. Surgery's out of the question, I'm afraid. And what with his arthritis, the sweet old dog can barely walk.

But perhaps it's not domestic distress at all. Perhaps the English chair is feeling sorry for me and embarrassed for himself because he is privy to what I will soon find out, and he knows he should never have agreed to dragging me 2,340 miles across the country for this dog-and-pony show. There are—I'm told by another candidate, just so I know what's going on—five candidates for the job. Three are in-house. One is the sister of the director of the creative writing program. (And another dated a girl from Requiem when he was in prep school in Connecticut.)

IN THE corridor, the candidate who spilled the beans, lifted a corner of the veil, unmasked the harlequins, introduces me to Hokey Mokey, the Ginsu poet. (He's a knife that needs no sharpening.) I shake his hand. Hokey Mokey, I think. Where have I heard that name before? Hokey Mokey's handshake is limp and thumbless, his fingers folding like a contessa's. He ogles my unruly hair when he says he is so looking forward to the faculty interview at five. I tell him I have to hurry to meet Realtor Sharri for the real estate tour. Where do you live? I ask him. Manhattan. When you're in town, I mean.

The man on his way to the La-Z-Boy Gallery orders sausage pinwheels with his poached eggs. I ask the waitress for the time. Nine-ish. Hillary says Hokey Mokey must be new. Sharri drives down Stephens, and I see that the comic-book store is having a Halloween Day Price Massacre. And the French bistro on Higgins, For Crepes Sakes, will be hosting a Miss Ooh La La Contest. The whole idea of the real estate tour seems cynical and fraudulent. I tell Sharri I'm not likely to get the job, but I would like to see the town if she wouldn't mind. She scolds me. Not with that attitude, you won't get the job. I tell her they'll likely hire a local, and she'll be out a commission. Sharri says she can't live her life thinking negatively.

She wants to get an idea of where to look and asks what size house I own now. I tell her I rent a house. I've never owned one. I have failure written all over me; I can feel it. She explains to me how I am being fiscally foolish, but the car is so hot that I'm falling asleep. We drive up the Rattlesnake, down Pattee Canyon, through Linda Vista. I want to confess all of my incompetence. I don't know what to do in case of emergency, Sharri. I can't solve

for x. I have no savings account, no 401(k), no investments, no
IRA. I can't hit a curve, and I can't operate the DVD player.
When I point out a house I like, a Craftsman bungalow not far
from the university, Sharri is forthright enough to suggest that
this particular school district may not be what I'm looking for. I
have no kids, Sharri. The Hmong, she says. The Belarus. What
about them? I say. Refugees.

WE ASK the man eating his sausage pinwheels for the time. He
wipes yolk from his chin with his fingers, holds his wrist toward
us. Nine twenty-five. Hillary says we should pay the bill and leave
for school. She asks me how the faculty interview went, and I tell
her how the couple of dozen professors—all, with a single Asian
exception, white—sat at the seminar tables arranged along the
walls of the classroom, somberly attired in that starched and
creased but casual manner, all inexplicably well coiffed, thanks to
some secret cowboy mousse, while I slumped in my chair with
my crappy flyaway hair and my itchy, bloodshot eyes and my
cracked and bleeding lips, breathing through my mouth, and my
new interview shirt (on sale at Marshalls) made me look bloated
and pale, dangerous and dyspeptic, and a bearded critical theorist
said, So tell us why you want this job, and I told him, I'm not sure
I do. (And this was where an adverb could have come in handy.
"I'm not sure I do, *actually*," would have made all the difference.)
I'm here to find out, I said. Well, that set off a flurry of scribbles.
Fair enough, he said.

I had meant to be honest, but I know I sounded arrogant and
flip. Still, the English professors smiled collegially and main-
tained their polite demeanor except for Mr. Hokey Mokey, who
squirmed in his seat and folded his hands each time he spoke. He
repeated everything I said and then asked me if I really meant it:
You contend that a plot is necessary in a short story. Did you

really mean that? *Why else would I have said it?* Did you really
mean to imply that fiction is at least as well written as poetry? *Not
that it is, but that it ought to be. And I didn't imply it, I said it.* And
you honestly mean it? *That's why I said it.* That's ludicrous. *With
all due respect, Professor Hokey Mokey, fiction has to do everything
poetry does, plus tell a story.* Hokey Mokey brushed a lash from his
eye, yawned, and smiled. I watched to see if he put the lash on
the back of his hand.

I HAVE three shots of vodka at the Ox with the candidate who
let the cat out of the bag before I go to dinner at Shadows Keep
(nouvelle American—no *kab yob* [pronounced kai-yaw], no
draniki) with the Director Whose Sister, etc., and with Hokey
Mokey and his betrothed, and with a Deconstructionist and his
wife. Before I even get to taste my first pan-fried oyster (in Montana! what was I thinking?), Hokey Mokey drops his pococurante
pose, points his knife at me, and demands to know why he was
not hired two years ago for the poetry position at my university.

Oh, you're *that* Hokey Mokey, I say. Always nice to put a face
to a name. Hokey Mokey's intended cradles her teacup in both
hands and stares into her white Darjeeling. Sometimes she
wishes her honeybunch would temper his badgerly ways. But
isn't that why she loves him, after all? The Deconstructionist rests
his fork, prongs down, on the edge of his plate. His wife sips her
blush. The Director Whose Sister, etc., pats her mouth with her
napkin, and suddenly I hear John Denver singing "Country
Roads," and I think maybe we're experiencing a divine interven-
tion here, or it's a short circuit in my tinnitus, but then I realize
it's the unobtrusive Shadows Keep sound system.

All eyes are on me, and I wish there were no *here* here, wish I
were on the watery planet Urizen in the pinwheel galaxy Los,
where poems are written in foam and the people have a word for

feeling like you've been strapped to the knife-thrower's wheel of death.
I really want to know, the impalement artist says. Did you find
someone who wrote crime poetry? Well, Hokey Mokey, we
didn't like your lugubrious and self-regarding poems of po-mo
disconnection and ponderous desolation, didn't like your ironic
skepticism and fashionable obscurantism, but still we were willing to overlook all that, so we gave you the telephone interview
and asked you what you thought of Kentucky, and you laughed
and called your students hicks, and the interview was over. Two
of my colleagues walked out of the room, one (the one from
Kentucky) holding his fingers over his nose. We found you
pompous and, frankly, more than a little creepy. *Dickhead* was, I
believe, the popular assignation.

That's what I wanted to say. What I did say: The truth is,
Hokey Mokey, that we were under some unstated, but quite
apparent, administrative pressure to diversify the faculty, if you
catch my drift, and we had an in-house candidate who seemed to
fit the bill, and we didn't think it fair to ask you, a white man, to
fly to Miami to jump through hoops and then send you home
with false hopes. And with that I ordered another Ketel One martini. I smiled collegially, raised my glass. Here's to Grizzlyville! I
said. Here's to the sunless city!

THAT NIGHT at the Edgewater I dreamed that I lost my real job
in Florida, where Diane DiPietro used to teach, because I'd
applied for this bogus job in Montana, Montana, the Glory of the
West!, and so I started the Famous Writers School, Inc. in Winnipeg, Manitoba, where my intense, brilliant, and acerbic friend
James grew up and which is 477 miles southeast of Flin Flon.

"If you can write this sentence—'It is universally acknowl-
edged, that a single man in possession of a good fortune, must be
in want of a wife'—then you might have what it takes to become

a famous, respected, and handsomely remunerated writer. Act now! Send for the Famous Writers Aptitude Test. If you test well, or show other evidence of writing proficiency, you may enroll. Write in your spare time in the comfort of your home! Writing today offers a life of financial reward, personal recognition, and the freedom to live as you please!" Among those who took the aptitude test was one Mr. H. Mokey, and I wrote back to him explaining the difference between articulation and accomplishment and suggesting that the only way he'd ever be famous would be to slaughter a colony of Montana Hutterites. And that's when I woke up.

The Hmong believe that we are born with three souls. When we die, one goes to the land of the ancestors, one is reincarnated, and one stays in the grave. The one that goes to the land of the ancestors collects its placenta, climbs the heavenly stairs in thirteen days, and crosses a salty river and a bitter spring. The journey home is a lonely one. Forty thousand Hmong died fighting for the United States in the Vietnam conflict. When the U.S. lost the war, the Hmong lost their homeland. One hundred and thirty thousand of them fled to the United States, three hundred or so to western Montana. Their journey to America across the great salty river to the Bitterroot was a lonely one.

Hillary's brother fought in Vietnam with Charlie Company, Eleventh Brigade, Americal Division. He was killed on the Ides of March, 1968, and his death may have precipitated the slaughter of 350 unarmed civilians—the size of five Hutterite colonies—at My Lai the next day. Praying children were shot in the backs of their heads by American fighting men. Women were gang-raped before they were executed. Elderly peasants were hacked to death with bayonets. (My Lai is 8,389 miles west-southwest or east-southeast of Requiem, Mass., where M16s were manufactured at Harrington & Richardson Arms Company.) I fell back to sleep and to dreams where I was once again the dean of the Famous Writers School, and we were off on our Semester at Sea, aboard the good ship *Jane Austen* somewhere off the coast of Winnipeg, and in my welcoming address to those students who doubt that stories need plots I quoted the Hutterites (who conscientiously object to war): You are either on the ark or off the ark.

IF PLANCK length is the smallest measurement that has any meaning, then we have to say that the universe came into existence when it was already 10^{-43} seconds old, and we can never know what happened before (in this sense a meaningless adverb) that moment or understand in what sense the universe came to be 10^{-43} seconds old. How could that have happened outside of time? The universe is the effect; there is no knowable cause. Is there then a purpose to existence? We'll never know. Are space and time independent of their contents? In what matrix do space and time exist? Why precisely three spatial dimensions? Why did the Big Bang happen? What is the fate of the universe? When does the present become the past? How many stars in the sky? Why do we wonder? Why do we sing? Why do we laugh? Why do we need to die?

WHY DO we feel the need for sausage pinwheels? Why do we eat them? The opposite of Planck length would seem to be the time it takes for the phlegmatic Grizzlyville University English Department to tell me I didn't get the job. I didn't get the job, of course. You knew that already. I'd give the job to my sister, too. But I didn't hear the news from them. Not a grunt. Not a peep. Not an official letter of regret on the insouciant dean's own linen stationery. Not an e-mail from the complaisant English chair. Chalk it up to that legendary Old West reticence from the last

good place, I suppose. Less is more, they figured, so then nothing is everything. The opposite of Planck length is never. And I
never got the handbook that explains it all.

IN CLASS at the Methodist university, the students sweetly, shyly
confess that they don't quite get my story. It doesn't seem to have
a plot, they say. They suggest an honest-to-God knife for starters,
instead of a chimera. They specifically suggest a twelve-inch
coffin-handled Bowie knife with a clip blade. They suggest gush-
ing blood and oozing gray matter and a woman who will not die.
They suggest a puddle of lungs on the kitchen floor. When they
want to know about irony, I tell them about my friend Shane Fer-
rie who got drafted during the Vietnam War and made up his
mind to flee to Canada rather than kill another human being,
rather than go to jail. But his fiancée, Margaret Mary Foley, told
him that she could not marry a coward, and so Shane found himself in the Army in Phu Loi, a bit north of Saigon. While he was
in-country, Margaret Mary took up with an antiwar activist
named Bliss, became involved with the movement, and eventually married Mr. Bliss.

WHAT HAPPENED to Shane? These days he works on a surveying crew when he *does* work, and keeps a journal of every beer
he drinks, every calorie he ingests, every woman he romances. In
this way, he tells me, he maintains control of his life. Margaret
Mary and her activist are now Republicans. He's the governor's
press secretary. What if, back then, Shane and Margaret Mary
had moved to Manitoba? To Tolstoi, Manitoba, let's say. Tolstoi
for the beauty of the tall-grass prairie. Tolstoi because they were
treated so kindly by the couple at the Chinese restaurant where
they had stopped for lunch. Tolstoi because it was so much more
affordable than Winnipeg. If Shane had moved to Manitoba back

then, I'd be visiting him today instead of avoiding him. We'd bundle up and take a walk after supper out to the Ukrainian cemetery, and there among the Antonychuks, the Biallys, and the Dutkas, he'd confess to me that now that his kids had moved away, he understood the shame of the older generation in town, the shame of being unable to build a community that your children would not leave. A way of life is dying here, he'd tell me, but this is my home, he'd say, and I feel blessed.

LATER THAT evening, at my reading, I spot an old pal from Requiem in the audience. Fred's a poet, living now in the heart of the heart, and a Catholic who has been to church today. His ashes seem to have been applied with a trowel. He's hard to miss. I nod to him, smile. Dust to dust, my friend. Ashes to ashes. Later at the reception, Fred and I, for some reason, talk about Pope John Paul II, his Parkinson's and his poetry. Fred asks me if I know whatever became of Benjamin Zawicki, this lavishly paranoid poet from Providence who taught writing classes in Requiem. My ex-wife was his student. Benjamin was so terrified, so certain that someone would steal his poems that he deconstructed them with scissors, then coded the words, images, metaphors, and lines by color, letter, and number, and squirreled away the fragments in various drawers throughout his house. Benjamin seems to have vanished, Fred says. Maybe he fell apart, I say. Lost his voice.

I'm thinking how I'm someone's ex-husband, a man defined by what he was, how he failed, a dim figure on the periphery of a family's awareness, someone vaguely menacing, but inconsequential, when Hillary introduces me to her student, a young woman from Burkina Faso. The Burkinabé capital of Ouagadougou is 6,829 miles southeast of Walla Walla, the Land of Many Waters. Burkina Faso is plagued by drought and is undergoing staggering desertification. The student tells me a story about her childhood. She went for a family holiday to Lake Bama on the White Volta. She and her little sister played with the bones they had found on the shore. They played House and Army and School. The bones turned out to be the remains of a family friend's wife and children, murdered by the government. Life expectancy in Burkina Faso is forty-four years. The literacy rate is twenty-seven percent. Burkina Faso is a forty-seven-year-old republic with a nine-hundred-year-old monarchy. Every Friday morning in the windswept capital, the Mogho Naba, the king, emerges from his mud palace wearing scarlet robes, clutching a long sword, and approaches his waiting stallion. Every Friday the king prepares for war against the Arabs, against the Berbers, against the French, against the enemies of his Mossi people. And every Friday his attendants plead with him to stay. And he stays—a leader needs to serve his people. He tells his followers the story of Mogho Naba Rawa, the great eleventh century Mossi conqueror. We cannot live with the memories of others, he says. We must have our own memories.

THE BLOND bartender opens the glass door of the popcorn cart and empties the kettle into a green trash bag. She knots the bag, carries it and the kettle back to the kitchen. I'm the only customer in the Quality Inn lounge. I'm sipping cognac. The cable is disconnected from the large-screen TV. The sound is mute, the broadcast picture blurry. A Hoosier basketball game is on. And then the bartender's back with a bottle of Windex and a roll of quilted paper towels. An agitated young man walks into the lounge and tells the bartender that his cell phone got smashed. He needs change to make fifteen calls on the pay phone. He's taken out a restraining order on his girlfriend. I've got a pen. I reach for a cocktail napkin. I write, *His striped tie is unknotted; his blue dress shirt is unbuttoned at the collar.* The bartender makes change.

The young man tells her that he worked here at the Quality Inn South ten years ago when he was like sixteen, and he was the only one of the sixty or so employees who got a date with Judy Isley, who was flat-out movie-star gorgeous and who later died two days before he married Daphne Degnan. Big mistake, that. You sound like you've been a busy man, the bartender says. The young man orders a kamikaze. The bartender tells him that her husband landed his sorry ass in jail last night. Cost her a thousand bucks to bail him out. Her "Cruise to Nowhere" money. The young man takes his drink to the pay phone, lights up a cigarette, punches in a number. The bartender walks back to the kitchen. The young man leans his head against the wall, shuts his eyes, and listens. *His right hand is bleeding at the knuckles.*

The phone behind the bar rings and rings. I figure it's the bartender's husband calling. He wants her to pick him up a pack of smokes on her way home. At least that's what he'll tell her. A pack of smokes and a couple of cans of Alpo for Thor. He really just wants to hear her voice, and he can't figure out why she's not picking up. What's he supposed to think? He's sitting on the sofa, pounding the armrest with his fist. Doesn't she understand it drives him crazy not knowing where she is?

There's an Edward Hopper print on the wall above the popcorn cart. *Gas.* He's not a mechanic, this slight man in vest and tie, bald as a Binghamton poet. Proprietor, more likely, checking the sales figures on these tall red pumps. Triangles of adamant light spill from the neat clapboard filling station onto the driving lanes. Across the narrow blacktop road a sandy ditch and a wave of palomino-colored grass lapping at the trunks of mute and glorious fir trees. The lighted sign above the station advertises Mobilgas. Pegasus seems about to leap the trees. Pegasus, the

winged horse sprung from the blood of the slain Medusa. Pegasus, who opened the fountains of Hippocrene with a kick of his
mighty hoof. *Le cheval volant*, Pegasus, *chez les narines des feu!*
Pegasus, steed of the Muses, always at the service of poets, poets
like Hokey Mokey, love's self-appointed watchman, and like us
kids on O'Connell Street in Requiem, Mass., when we would
walk by Jolicoeur's Mobil Station and scream at the top of our
unpuddled lungs, *Up your ass with Mobilgas!*

   In a moment, the proprietor will take in those cans of motor
oil, stack them by the windshield-wiper display, will cut the lights
on the sign and in the station, will lock the door. He'll drive
home. He lives alone. His house is cozy, neat, but unadorned.
He'll fry eggs and bologna, listen to the radio as he eats, listen for
the news from Europe where the Germans have claimed the
Sudetenland. He'll save the milk he has not finished. He'll wash
the dish, the fry pan, the glass, the fork, and the knife. He'll read
a book in the living room. Zane Grey. The bartender announces
last call, tells me she has to be at her day job at seven. She's an
LPN at a convalescent home. I walk back to Room 128.

I DON'T sleep well in motels. I know the alarm will not buzz, the
wake-up call will not come. I'll miss my flight. All night I strad-
dle the border between consciousness and dreams. I surface, I
check the time, I fall back to a fitful sleep. It's one-fifteen. In my
dream, Hokey Mokey is played by James Woods. We're a couple
of ramblin' boys off to the sunless city to find a plot that I've lost
somehow. When we come to a fork in the Old Planck Road,
Hokey flicks his tongue to sniff the air. This way, he says, and he
points his little arm to the right. One thirty-five. I don't know dot
about Belarus. I do know that Max Planck's first wife Marie died
in 1909. He then married her niece Marga. His son Karl was
killed in action in World War I. His daughter Margarete died in

childbirth in 1917. Her twin Emma died in childbirth in 1919. Planck's son Erwin was executed by the Gestapo in 1945 for his involvement in a plot to kill Hitler. But that's not the plot I'm looking for. Two-ten. Hokey Mokey can move his eyes in different directions at the same time. He can look behind himself. Two-forty. It goes on like that all night. We never reach the sunless city. It is always just a little farther on. You can know where it is but not how to get there, or you can know how to get there but not where it is. Three-eleven. There is the world where I do not get the job in Grizzlyville. There is another world in which I do.

I COULD tell you that the alarm went off at six and that the radio snapped on playing John Denver's "Hey There, Mr. Lonely Heart," but I'd be lying. At four-fifteen, I just got up, switched on the light, found a newspaper to read, saw that in Newark, England, one Dennis Weddington, depressed and out of work, killed himself by hammering two nails into his head, and I surmised that he was not a carpenter, but even so, was the second nail necessary? When John Denver died, I was reading my stories at New England College in Henniker, New Hampshire. Many years ago now—but it seems like only yesterday. I went to the only bar in town with my friend John Candia to have a drink and to catch up on life and literature, and we stumbled into a John Denver memorial gathering. Folks from all over New England had assembled here of all places, and spontaneously it seemed, to honor the fallen singer/songwriter and to grieve for him. They read reverent poems to one another in the dining nook, shared stories about how John Denver had changed their dismal lives. They applauded, nodded, wept, embraced. They lit candles and called for a moment of silence. John and I sat at the end of the bar, drank Guinness, and whispered discreetly to each other about Kerouac and Joyce till we were hushed. John Denver? And hushed again. Daniels Restaurant and Pub had become a church for the night. The mourners, the celebrants, joined hands and sang, "Almost heaven . . ."

WE ARE all blessed with the gift of perhaps. We all feel more than we can imagine. We all imagine more than we can remember. We all remember more than we can know. And we all know more than we can say. I shower and dress and inspect the room one more time for what I may have forgotten. I check out at the front desk and wait for Hillary in the porte cochere. She's driving me to the airport. I've woken with a sinus headache. Feels like someone has plunged an ice pick into that notch above my left eye. I remember that Pietro DiPietro, Diane's dad, was the president of Ascension, a French-Canadian college in Requiem, Mass., and I wonder if that faint memory was the virus that brought on yesterday's Whitman College dream. I see Hillary at the red light in front of the Bob Evans. Hillary, who has lost her brother.

Any meaning is better than none. Ask any Catholic or Methodist or Hutterite or Hmong. You believe in a God who, in his exquisite loneliness, created the universe and little you. Or you believe that we, in our terrifying loneliness, created God. Doesn't matter which. Ask any Vietnamese child kneeling in the mud, praying, choking on her tears, feeling the hot muzzle of an M16 at the nape of her neck, hearing the screams of her grandparents, inhaling the sting of smoke and cordite, knowing that this soldier here behind you, dear, is about to make his own meaning by firing a burst of bullets through your head. At that moment there is no arrow of time for you, there is no there, no then. There is only this singularity, this Planck instant, this big bang. At that moment you are borrowing energy against time and shaping your brief life into a quantum of meaning.

Limbo

D AD TOLD ME once—I was eating split-pea soup; he was looking for his keys and cursing under his breath—that memory's most important job was to forget. And I said, "Well, it's doing a fine job right now." He found the keys under a sofa cushion. "Always the last place you look," he said. He sat back down at the table and dipped his Wonder bread into the soup. He said, "What were we talking about?"

"Memory."

"Right. Not the memory of where things are. That's not what I meant. The memory of who you are, where you've been. Your past. Memory's job is to erase it. Most of it anyway. That way you won't be haunted by what you've done. So you can get on with your life." He slurped his soup. "Two kinds of problems in the world, Johnny. Those you can do something about; those you can't. And you can't change the past."

"You can change the way you think about it."

"Eat your soup."

I had this idea then that my brain was a camera and had

recorded every second of my life, like a TV show, so all I had to do was find the right channel to call up the episode. I had every confidence in God to make a flawless memory for each of us. All we needed to do was to want to use it and then to use it.

The discussion had begun when I told Dad that I was distressed that I couldn't remember anything that happened before I was a year and a half old, and he told me he couldn't remember anything that happened before he was six.

"Maybe you don't want to remember."

"Supposedly I had a dog named Milou."

"You don't remember your dog!"

The first eighteen months of my life had vanished. Audrey, on the other hand, remembered being in the womb. She told me she could hear music, the same song over and over—she thought it must have been Conway Twitty because every time she heard "It's Only Make Believe" now she felt this warm buzz at the back of her neck, and her eyes drooped, and she wanted to suck her thumb and go to sleep. She hoped they wouldn't play it at her prom. Mostly, she said, she felt cramped and ignored inside. "It's like sleeping in the trunk of a moving car."

Memory's what you use to find your story. Dad's story begins when he's six. Mine begins with Dad in our apartment over D'Errico's Italian Market. He's in my bedroom, which might also have been their bedroom, only I don't see a bed. Just the crib that I'm in. Dad's across the room in front of the closet, taking off his gabardine topcoat and hat, a gray felt porkpie with a red feather in the hatband. I grab the bar of the crib in my fat little fists and pump my knees up and down doing my happy dance. Dad laughs and walks over and puts the hat on my head, which I, of course, have to touch immediately. The hat falls over my eyes, and I panic until Dad pushes it back on my head. It's so good to see him again. I laugh till I drool. I couldn't talk then, and if Dad said anything to me, I don't remember it. And then Mom's standing in the doorway, leaning against the jamb, with her arms folded. She's smiling.

WHAT I remember about that afternoon that Dad drove home:
My mother thought she was being followed.
My mother thought she was being poisoned by degrees.
My mother thought she was dying.
My mother thought she was pregnant.
My mother thought she was maybe being held against her will in a replica apartment in Vermont.
My mother thought she was Elizabeth Taylor.
My mother thought Elizabeth Taylor was a nun.
My mother wore a black lace mantilla, white cloth gloves, and clutched a *Daily Missal* in her hands. She stood before various objects on the kitchen walls and muttered to herself. The clock; the calendar from Candela's Market with a print of a horse and wagon crossing a wooden bridge on a snowy day; the JFK commemorative plate; the crucifix with palm frond; the decorative copper gelatin mold; the print of Jesus on Gethsemane, weeping over Jerusalem; the red plastic teakettle switch plate. What I thought she thought she was doing was making the Stations of the Cross, meditating on how the clock and company had suffered for our sins. But I couldn't confirm this because she wasn't responding to any of us. Maybe she was trying to memorize the room. Maybe she was trying to ignore us into nonexistence. I've done that sort of thing myself.

Audrey told Mom there were no justified resentments. That got her attention. Mom said, "If you were my kid, I'd slap your face."

"Go ahead."

I looked at Dad sitting there at the table and asked him what he was going to do about this. He told us to leave.

Mom said, "For Christ's sakes, I was only kidding. Jeez!"

Then she said, "No, I wasn't."

She raised an eyebrow, smiled, nodded.

She shook her head.

A quick nod.

A vigorous shake.

A barely discernible nod.

She waved her hand, no.

Dad said, "I'll take care of this. You two get lost."

We went to Veronica's.

DAD PREFERRED to think that our domestic tranquillity began heading south when Mom first got sick in the head, as he put it. My recollection is that neither of them was ever very parental. They liked the nightlife. And everyone loved Rainy; Rainy loved everyone. They stayed out till three in the morning most nights before Dad got the trucking job. I was babysitting Audrey when I was seven. What could I have done if anything had gone wrong? I had the phone number of the Cat Dragged Inn. If they left the Cat, Dad would call with the number of their next stop. But I'd be sleepy and wouldn't write it down. And then I'd try to stay asleep so that I'd miss the bickering, the name-calling, and the sounds of slobbery make-up sex when they got home. But I seldom could. I'd hear the dreadful footfalls on the back stairs, and I'd break out in a sweat. I'd start to pray that tonight they'd be in love, be happy and quiet. Their fighting was, I figured, due punishment for my original sin. Original sin is the sin we did not commit, like we commit actual sin, personal sin. We come into the world depraved and without grace, inheritors of Adam's punishment. And once I thought of my black soul and hellfire and eternity, well, I was up for the night. I'd sit at my window and look out over O'Connell Street. Sometimes Deluxe would sit on the sill and bathe himself, rest his paw on my arm.

If you died with original sin on your soul, if you weren't baptized, in other words, you could never go to heaven. You went to hell or you went to limbo if you were lucky enough to be a baby. Limbo I pictured as an empty bright white room that everyone has forgotten about and in which nothing ever happens. This meant that none of us would ever see little Arthur, who had done nothing to deserve his fate. That's who I thought about those sleepless nights.

I asked Sister Casilda about limbo once, and it was like she'd never heard of it. She had been talking about abortion in class. How what humanists and scientists call a fetus is a breathing, thinking human being, and that abortion is murder. And so those poor victims can't go to heaven unbaptized, I said. The classroom went quiet. "They go to limbo, right, Sister?" She told us all to do a report on limbo, and we'd talk about it the next morning. She told us in the morning that she considered the victims of abortion of having been baptized in blood—they were martyrs. "What about my brother Arthur and the other stillborns?" I said. She said that limbo for them was a state of eternal natural joy. Limbo's somewhere between heaven and hell. To get to heaven, you need a passport. Baptism's that passport. Limbo's not a punishment; it's a pleasant enough destination.

I FIRST met Veronica in the schoolyard when we were six. I was sitting on the basketball court, leaning back against the pole holding up the backboard, arranging my hundred or so baseball cards alphabetically by team. I looked up and saw this sandy-haired girl smiling at me. She had an unopened pack of cards in her hand. She said, "Wanna flip?"

"Who you got?"

We opened the pack. We split the gum. She had a Roger Maris, an Ernie Banks, and a Jim Lemon. We flipped. Veronica wiped me out. I couldn't speak. She offered to give me the cards back. Offered to give me hers, too. I couldn't accept. She could see that I was distraught. This is what comes of gambling, I could hear Sister Maximo saying. Veronica and I sat down. She told me that she thought we were playing for funsies, and so she couldn't keep the cards, really. She put the pack on the ground between us. I was choking back tears. I'd lost my Yaz, my Steady Eddie Bressoud. I ran home.

After that I might be drinking a lime rickey at Charlie's or maybe reading a *Life* magazine at Iandoli's, and suddenly Veronica would be standing beside me smiling a Christmas-morning smile, like she could not imagine wanting to be anywhere else. Or maybe she would bump me, but stare straight ahead like I wasn't there, only I was and she could see me out the corner of her eye. She wouldn't say a word until I did. I found this all so endearing every time she did it. She always seemed so delighted to see me and to be seen by me.

And then her life got sad. Her parents separated, reunited, fought like Rottweilers, separated, and divorced. Veronica didn't blame herself for the divorce like some kids do, but she thought her mother may have. Her grandmother died from sugar diabetes. Her cousin Carl molested her. Her uncle Reno beat Carl with a tire iron, leaving him a brain-damaged drooler. Veronica had to stop her tap lessons at Honey Fellicetti's Dance Studio because her mom couldn't afford them anymore. Then her mom pulled her out of St. Simeon's and put her in public school at Rabbit Maranville Elementary, where Veronica found herself way behind in math and science. When she told her new teacher, Mr. Vanderhoof, that she could diagram compound-complex sentences, he said, Why would you want to do that? Her brother came home from the war in a sealed coffin.

Audrey played in the parlor with a suitcase full of Veronica's old Barbies. The dolls, Audrey let us know, were saving up the money they made waitressing at Ken's Diner to buy Gene Autry's Melody Ranch. They liked to ride and they liked to sing. Veronica and I made lunch. Boiled rice with margarine and ketchup. Raspberry ZaRex to drink. Veronica told us her mom was dating a Puerto Rican guy named Mike who was in the Coast Guard.

"They're out on the lake now with his cabin cruiser. They could have asked me to come."

I said, "I hate boats."

Audrey said, "Boats are a measure of success."

I said, "How many boats does Dr. Bondurant have?"

"A speedboat and a yacht." Which she rhymed with *hatchet*.

After lunch Veronica let her hamster Ringo out of his cage, and we watched him try to burrow through the linoleum on the pantry floor and then chew his way through one of Veronica's orthopedic shoes. Meanwhile, at home things hadn't gone so well.

WE HEARD Deluxe before we saw him. He meowed. We stopped at the front steps, called his name, and waited. Audrey peeked under the porch. He meowed again, and we looked up. He was twenty feet up, nestled in the crook of an oak limb, and he couldn't or wouldn't come down. He whined for our attention or assistance, but he couldn't be coaxed from his roost. I clucked for him to come. Audrey stamped her foot and commanded him to get down here on the double. He blinked, wailed a little.

When we got upstairs, Audrey went out on the piazza to reason with Deluxe. I went inside. Caeli was sweeping up pieces of what had been my grandmother's bone china off the kitchen floor. She stopped when she saw me. She put her arm around my shoulder and squeezed. Nunzie was on the telephone, pacing in front of the fridge. When he saw me, he turned to the wall, wagged his finger at the ceiling, and said, "Pardon my French, Your Eminence, but you tell that Kraut bastard that he plays ball here, or I'll have the Hub pay him a little visit. Trust me, he does not want to speak with the Hub. Capisce?" Dad sat at the kitchen table, holding an ice pack to his forehead. I saw that the window by the table was shattered and the storm window beyond it cracked. I said, "Where's Mom?" like I didn't know, like I wanted to find out.

Caeli said that Mom had pitched a bit of a fit. "She's sick. She put her face through the window there. She wasn't trying to jump out or anything. The ambulance came for her. They gave her something to calm her down."

Dad said that Mom thought he was someone else. He didn't look to me like a man who'd lost something dear to him, but like a man who'd grown accustomed to loss. Resigned and resolved. "I'm so sorry you had to live with her like this."

Caeli said, "She'll get the help she needs now."

Nunzie hung up the phone. He said, "I don't know why you have to live like a fucking gypsy, Rainy."

Caeli put her hands over my ears and smiled.

Nunzie said, "You got a family here."

"A family I have to support."

I said, "You're leaving again?"

Caeli said, "What did the bishop say?"

Dad said, "It's just temporary. I'm working on a solution to this whole mess, the kerfuffle. Goddamned can of worms."

"I want to know where you are every minute, Rainy," Nunzie said.

"I'll call."

"I can have you driving a cement mixer for Caputo Construction tomorrow."

"When I get back, maybe."

"You got three weeks."

Nunzie had prevailed upon the bishop to call off his Catholic Charities social worker and to find Audrey a room at St. Anne's. "It's not an orphanage," he told me. "It's a children's home." This until Dad returned in three weeks, he promised. I'd be staying with the Morrisseys. Audrey couldn't because of her age and because she had special needs, Nunzie said.

I said, "What are you talking about?"

He said, "She's a little touched in the head like your mother."

"Is not."

Nunzie looked at Caeli and shrugged. Caeli said, "You'll see her every day after school."

Audrey came in and said we had to call the fire department. I called the O'Connell Street fire barn and explained Deluxe's problem. The fireman told me they didn't do that sort of thing. "That only happens in the movies, kid. We've got better things to do."

I said, "What are you doing now?"

He said, "Don't be a wise guy."

I asked him what I was supposed to do, then. He said, "Have you ever seen a cat skeleton in a tree?"

Boysville

I was thinking about what I would do if Spot died. Would I buy another dog? Another setter puppy? Call him Pavlov? Would I do things differently this time? Obedience school. Dry food. Walkies. Heel. Spot stopped gnawing his pig ear and stared at me.

I said, "What?"

He woofed.

"You can't read my mind, Spot, so don't even pretend to."

"Ouah, ouah!"

Spot had been listening to conversational French language tapes with me and had been affecting a laughable French accent lately. I told him I was thinking about his aunt Audrey.

A dismissive woof this time.

"You don't have to believe it. That's your business."

Spot and I were on the deck after supper, he with his delectable chewy pig ear and me with my healthy pomegranate martini, chock-full of antioxidants. Annick was working late at the theater building the sets for the Dania Beach Playhouse production of *Grease*. What had me thinking about a Spotless life was what had happened to the Hargitais' apricot pug Hedy earlier in the week. Attila and Linka Hargitai live five houses down where the tidal estuary and canal empty into the lake. The indomitable Hedy had been out in her backyard yipping furiously at an unflappable six-foot iguana, who placidly munched on pink hibiscus blossoms. Whenever Hedy barked, she turned in tight little excited circles, always spinning to her left (the Shaquille O'Neal of pugs). Maybe her circles got her dizzy, but for whatever reason, Hedy drifted too close to the iguana, who flicked his tail and swept Hedy over the retaining wall and into the water. Poor girl couldn't climb back up the three-foot wall, though she struggled mightily to find purchase.

A couple of kids fishing for snapper on the footbridge saw what had happened, dropped their Shakespeare Ugly Stiks, and ran to the rescue. They tried to scoop Hedy up in their landing net, but that only frightened and confused her. She turned and swam for the middle of the lake. There she was bobbing toward the island, and then she wasn't. And then the water roiled and reddened. And then the crocodile surfaced.

When the grieving Attila tried to take revenge on the crocodile that evening by firing several rounds from his .38-caliber Colt Commander at the monster, he was arrested. You can't kill an endangered species. You can't fire a pistol in the city limits. Attila hasn't given up, however. He injected a Butterball turkey with strychnine and tossed it in the lake. But if the croc ate Attila's turkey, he or she felt no ill effects. Mrs. Maradona told me she ran into Attila at the marine flea market over in the jai-alai parking lot. He was carrying a harpoon. He seemed gleeful, she said. A little distracted, but gleeful.

That afternoon I'd gotten an e-mail from my friend Gaspar in Requiem letting me know that our old (as in "long ago") English professor, Walker Roberts, had died unexpectedly. He was seventy-two miles into a hundred-and-fifty-mile charity bicycle race across the state when his heart gave out. He was dead, they figured, before his head met the pavement. Turns out his arteries were ninety percent blocked, that he'd had a heart attack a year earlier, which he was apparently unaware of. And now I couldn't stop thinking about him and how he was not much older than I was. What would Spot do if I died?

I took Dr. Roberts for Literature and Social Change when I was a sophomore. I was all about social change in those days. I was earnest, literal-minded, and a complete stranger to irony. I remember our spirited exchanges about Doris Lessing. I thought *The Four-Gated City* was profound and prophetic, and he thought it was polemical and pompous. Dr. Roberts liked to stand with his hands in his jeans pockets when he lectured. When he made an amusing remark, he smiled and looked at the ceiling. His blue eyes were not quite aligned with each other. If you asked him a question, he would smooth his mustache before he answered.

I met my pre-Alice girlfriend Ray in that literature course. She let me borrow *Under the Volcano*, which I still have and still have not read. The class met in a room on the first floor of the Mark Saunders Science Building. There was an upright piano in front of the room, its fall board closed and secured with a padlock. I was quite taken with Ray's charm, wit, intelligence, and Slavic beauty. Smitten in spades, you could say. She folded her hands on her lap when she spoke, and she spoke so eloquently and articulated so precisely. She could spin a pencil around her thumb, fold a paper rose, touch her nose with the tip of her tongue. I changed my seat to the one beside hers. Soon we were taking the bus together, stopping for coffee at the Jersey Bar. And now Walker Roberts is dead; Ray lives in Requiem and does I-don't-know-what, and I am far far away.

Not long after I had left Requiem for good I heard from Gaspar that Walker Roberts had been stabbed by a disgruntled or obsessed student. The guy just barged into Walker's office with a serrated kitchen knife and lunged at him over the desk. The obsessed ones are the dangerous ones. And the dangerous ones are an occupational hazard, I've come to find out. If you're breathing and you have a line of credit, you can get into a public university after all. No background checks, no psychological workups. So one day you're in a room with one of your best and brightest—you want to ask her to apply for your graduate program—and she suddenly accuses you of stalking her through the back alleys of Coconut Grove and dressing as a priest while you do it. You notice the classroom door is closed. You back away slowly. Or you get a hundred threatening daily e-mails from a screwball who can't write a coherent sentence but does manage to savagely murder someone with your name in all of his short stories. Or the woman who sends you and your girlfriend anonymous letters discussing the details of her torrid and longstanding affair with you. Sooner or later, after a judicial hearing or a restraining order or two, and if you're lucky, they usually drift back to their sad little lives, but there are days when dealing with sociopaths makes you want to quit the business and maybe do something less worthwhile and less stressful. Like drive a cab. Or do some landscaping. But then you remember your allergies.

Annick came out to the deck with a glass of red wine and kissed me on the head. Spot ran to her, wagging his mighty tail, his whole backside, in fact. Annick took his face in her hands and kissed his nose. He whined to her.

She said, "You two bickering again?" She sat in the chair beside me.

I said, "He started it."

Spot gave her the poor-puppy eyes.

She told me I was older and should know better.

"You always take his side."

It was the first day of hurricane season, the day you look at your house and your possessions and wonder if they'll all be here in six months. You wonder is it too late to call about the shutters. Annick told me they caught the kids that did it.

"Did what?"

"The thing with the monkey."

A couple of tourists kayaking the Dania Cutoff Canal had come upon the crucified skeleton of a monkey nailed to an Australian pine. Looked like it was a warning to the other monkeys. Maybe some kind of voodoo Santeria ritual or something. This sort of thing doesn't happen in Iowa, they told a reporter for the *Sun-Sentinel*.

I said, "How did they catch them?"

The kids bragged about it on MySpace. Posted photos of the monkey, nailed and alive.

BLACKIE SLEPT in our apartment with me (but only after I'd removed the milk from the fridge) so that we could keep Deluxe company, but Deluxe was depressed, confused, and aloof. He curled himself into a furry mound on Audrey's pillow, tucked his tail under his chin, and slept. He ran to the door whenever he heard the latch bolt click, but then collapsed in a heap when he saw it was me or Blackie, or maybe it was Caeli peeking in to see if we needed anything at Iandoli's. He wouldn't chase his marbles, could only manage to give his plaid catnip mousie a cursory swat now and again. Blackie sat at the kitchen table and worked on the storyboard for *The Drone*. *The Devious Dr. Diabolus* was on hold while Blackie looked for backers. *The Drone* was an adaptation of my own creation, actually. A serial story I told myself every night of my childhood from when I was six or so until I was eleven, when

I suddenly found myself more interested in the mysteries of girls and the afterlife than in the now-pallid thrills of adventure. The Drone of my fantasies was named Frankie Raines. He was me, of course, with a sexier name and a better haircut. He began life as an orphan and cowboy, the charismatic leader of the bunkhouse gang at the Circle T Ranch in Catville and defender of the downtrodden in rural Requiem County, but by the time I was eight, Frankie had become a secretive, some would even say furtive, boy of singular crime-solving skills, unassuming, unrelenting, and uncompromising, a stealthy superhero without superpowers, but with a finely calibrated moral radar and a refined ability to read a face. He was a human lie detector and an extraordinary liar himself.

Blackie changed Frankie's name to Conbert H. Benneck. Not unsexy, Blackie argued, retro-sexy. We decided for the sake of Blackie's serial movie that Conbert grew up in an orphanage called Boysville in Central City, USA. He was a shy kid and preferred solitude to organized violence. He was assigned to keep the bees in the Boysville apple orchard. Conbert's birth is shrouded in mystery. His father might be the president, for all we know, his mother the queen of Slovenia. Blackie drew pictures of young Conbert in his white oversized overalls, mesh helmet, and leather gloves. The other boys began to call him Honey.

AFTER SCHOOL that Friday, I met Audrey at St. Anne's, and we walked over to Farrell Field. The sun was already going down over the tops of the triple-deckers on O'Connell Street. We played on the swing set. Audrey hung by her knees from the sidebar and talked to me upside down. She wiped her runny nose with her mittens. My ears were so cold they burned. Audrey said she really didn't mind the orphanage so much. I could smell burning leaves. I told her not to keep wetting her lips; they'd chap.

"Then I'll look like I'm wearing lipstick."

"It'll hurt like heck."

"You have to suffer for beauty, Mom always says." She dropped to the ground, pulled up her wool hat, and showed me the nasty-looking stitches on her forehead. She told me Cosmo Haddad hit her with a turtle. "Pretty neat, huh?"

"He what?"

"A red-eared slider."

"Why?"

She shrugged. "Because he's a spaz? He eats Vaseline sandwiches."

"Does not."

"On Wonder bread." Audrey sat on a swing and twisted in circles until the chains were braided as tightly as possible. "And then Cosmo Haddad killed Shelly, stomped on her shell. He told Sister it was an accident."

"I still don't understand why he hit you in the first place."

"He wet his pants. He caught me sniffing the air. He lost it. I was handy. Plus his father is dead, and I called him Cosmo Had-a-dad."

"Not cool."

She lifted her legs, and the swing uncoiled, spinning her like mad. She stood, tried to walk, lost her balance, and fell. "I love being dizzy, don't you?"

She told me that the kids at the orphanage were not really orphans except for this very tall boy named Ryan O'Brian or Brian O'Ryan, she wasn't sure, who said he was going to join the Army as soon as he could. Mostly the parents were all poor and couldn't afford to feed the kids. Or they were in jail. Billy Maloney's dad shot a bank teller during a robbery in Fall River. Audrey told me that mostly the kids all did what they were told to do and then whined or pouted about it afterward. They were starting to grate on her nerves.

I asked her if the nuns had said anything about her boots. She told me she'd worked that out. Then she said she wanted to visit Mom in the hospital.

I said, "They won't let us in."

When I went to see Audrey on Saturday morning—I was going to surprise her with a trip to the movies, *2001: A Space Odyssey*—a nun with her sleeves rolled up, wearing rubber gloves and an apron over her habit, holding a damp rag in one hand and a can of Bab-o in the other, told me that Audrey was with her brother. I thanked her, said, no, I was her cousin Carmine from Lowell.

"You look familiar," she said.

"I've got one of those faces, Sister."

I expected to find Audrey at home under her bed or in her closet reading. She had been home—her hat was on the kitchen table—but she was gone, and so was Deluxe. The Morrisseys hadn't seen her. I walked to the field, to the schoolyard, to Iandoli's, to Charlie's, back to the orphanage. I went home and stared out the window. I walked to the church. Audrey hadn't taken the stroller for Deluxe. I thought about calling the cops, but I knew that could only end badly. Where would she have gone? There were no Sandilands, after all.

It turned out she had been riding the bus for hours. She had Deluxe in her schoolbag, and as long as she stroked his head, he was content and quiet. I saw her get off the bus in front of Charlie's, and I ran downstairs, told her I was worried sick. She told me not to get all up in her face like that. "Take a pill, Johnny Boy." Violet made us lunch. Audrey said she used her bus tickets to get around. She said she was trying to find the hospital to visit Mom.

I told her she could get in big trouble like that, wandering around the city by herself, could get kidnapped or something.

She told me that some old guy in a blue parka and brown leather gloves followed her off the bus, up Front Street, into Woolworth's, and out the back to Exchange Street. She lost him in W. T. Grant's.

BLACKIE TOOK us to the sixth-floor solarium at Four Crowned Martyrs and told us to sit and wait. Twenty minutes later he wheeled Mom in and parked her beside us. Her face was bruised blue and contused. Her bottom lip was split in the middle and swollen. She had a Band-Aid over her nose. Mom looked at Audrey and me and said, "Haven't you tortured me enough?"

I said, "Hi, Mom."

Blackie said, "It's Johnny, Frances. In the flesh."

Audrey said, "I learned a new song, Mom."

Mom leaned toward me, pointed to Blackie with her chin, and said, "I'm supposed to listen to your minion, am I?" She took a pack of Pall Malls out of her robe pocket.

Audrey stood, very formally, clasped her hands at her waist, and cleared her throat. Mom lit a cigarette, waved the match in the air, and dropped it to the floor. Audrey sang "Moon River" until Mom asked her to please, please, just stop it, please!

I said, "There are no substitutes, Mom. You've watched too many science-fiction movies."

"I have, have I?"

Audrey slumped on the couch beside Blackie. He put his arm around her shoulder.

I said, "You're Frances; she's Audrey. I'm your son. I'm Johnny."

"Well, of course you think you're Johnny. That's how you've been—what do they call it?—programmed. You can't help it. Your ignorance is your strength."

"So you think I'm lying?"

"You're not listening. You would have to have a will in order to lie. You're a machine, bub. No heart, no soul."

"So where are we from, and who sent us?"

"She's the liar," Audrey said. "She just doesn't want us anymore."

I said, "So you think you're important enough for some superior race . . ."

"Did I ever say anything about a superior race?"

". . . to worry about?"

"Gave yourself away there, my friend." She smiled.

"What threat would you pose to them or to the government or to whoever you think is doing this?"

"I know things."

"Like what?"

"Wouldn't you like to know?" She laughed and the laugh became a coughing fit.

"You're killing yourself with the smokes, Frances," Blackie said.

"I'll give you credit," she told me. "You've learned how to seem."

WHAT AUDREY had said about Mom's not wanting us seemed improbable, but I did need to consider the possibility. But I figured if Mom really didn't want to be with us, she could have packed her suitcase and left. That's a lot easier than all this pretense and hysteria. She could have dumped us both at the orphanage, for that matter. She could have had the Welfare people warehouse us in some squalid foster-care facility. She was telling imposters to leave her alone, not telling us. At least that's what I preferred to believe.

I walked Audrey to St. Anne's. When we got to the gate, she stopped and kissed my cheek, thanked me, and said so long.

"I'll walk you to the door."

"I'll be fine. Really."

I opened the gate and we walked up the path to the steps. Audrey thanked me again, shook my hand.

"I'll wait till you get inside."

I opened the door. She peeked inside, looked left and right, and took off running down the hallway, her boots clomping on the hardwood floor. She waved without turning back. "Adios, Johnny Boy!" She cracked me up.

I called Mom while Blackie was downstairs taking a shower. She said she was so happy to hear from me and told me about the recent visit from the aliens, the clones, the robots, whatever they were. Said she was disappointed in Blackie's falling for their ruse. "When I get out of here, we'll go to Whalom Park."

"It's December."

"We'll go sledding on Asylum Hill."

"How do you feel?"

"This little guy just doesn't want to be born."

"You're not pregnant."

"Why else would I be here?"

"You had a breakdown."

"Jeez. They've got me on so many meds I can't think straight."

"You'll get better."

"Have I been under a lot of stress lately?"

"I think you get confused when you see things, Mom. Maybe you should close your eyes when you're home. Wear an eye mask." I was happy to be talking to the old, confused, but not delusional Frances again. I felt sad that she had to try so hard to find herself when all I had to do was wake up, and there I was. "Can't wait till you get home and we're one big family again."

"Don't let's get carried away."

"It'll be like it was."

"'Like it was' made it like it is." She hung up on me, and that was the last time I spoke with her for several months. The doctors decided that Mom would be better off, that she would recover more readily and more fully, by not seeing us or seeing Dad. And by the time we spoke again, I had another mother.

Your Beamish Boy

IT OCCURS TO me now that my real struggle was not *in* the past, but is *with* the past. I mean the effort *now* to have *then* make sense. Of course, there's nothing I can do to change what has happened, and, in truth, I wouldn't change a moment of it; otherwise, I wouldn't be parked here at the desk, your beamish boy, doing what I'm so busily and contentedly (for the moment anyway) doing. Writing. I'd be some*where* else, doing some*thing* else. Or I'd be dead. I subscribe, as you can see, to a chaos theory of time, in spooky action at a chronological distance, you could say. I believe that had I not flapped my wings in alarm and fluttered away from a budding romance with Chrissy Nolan—even now I get a chill at the sound of the name—when I was seventeen, I'd be tending bar in Spooner, Wisconsin, or some place like it, wondering if I'd have to bail one of the kids out of jail again this weekend and if the Ski-Doo would start up and how long could I sit here in the dark alone, drinking shots of Canadian Mist after closing.

There are so many things best left unremembered. I won't

even get into l'affaire Nolan except to say that four years later Chrissy sicced her overbearing and woeful husband on me by telling him that she and I had been having a fling for quite some time and that the baby wasn't his. So Mr. Farley James called me up and told me he'd be over to my house in fifteen minutes with a gun. I told him if I didn't come out to start the shooting without me. I stayed in the house—and away from the windows—until he stopped his screaming and went away.

DAD SHOWED up out of the blue one afternoon a week before Christmas and took Audrey out of St. Anne's. I didn't know what was up, and Dad wasn't talking. I didn't ask, maybe because I didn't want to know. I thought, I'll just relax like this is just another day in our lives. Dad called Dr. Reininger. I eavesdropped from the living room. Mostly he said, "Uh-huh, uh-huh." Then he called the hospital, and I heard him say, "Not until when?" We ordered a large mushroom and pepperoni from Pizza π. Audrey scraped off the mushrooms and gave them to Deluxe, who licked the sauce and ate the bits of cheese. School's good, we said. That's good, he said. Veronica? She's good, I said. Good. Yeah, it sure is cold, I said. Freezing, Audrey said. Your mother's going to be fine, he said. Got a little something they call Cotard something or other. She just needs some rest. Good as new, I said. Fit as a fiddle, he said. Audrey said, What's going on?

Dad said, "I want you kids to get packed. We're going on a Christmas vacation."

I said, "Where to?"

Audrey said, "We can't leave Mom." She cried.

"Mom's not up to it, sweetheart," Dad said. "But she wants us to enjoy the holidays. Trust me."

"We'll send her a card," I said.

Audrey said, "Will we have a tree?"

"Of course," Dad said.

"And presents?"

"Wouldn't be Christmas without presents."

Audrey bent down and told Deluxe we were all going on vacation. Dad said Deluxe'd be better off with Caeli. Audrey looked at me, her little chin trembling. I told Dad I didn't think Deluxe's coming was up for debate.

We packed our suitcases and the litter box up in the bunk of the cab. Plenty of room for the three of us to nap or lounge back there. The sun was just coming up. Violet ran out from the house with a cooler full of sandwiches. Dad hammered the tires, hopped in, blasted the air horn, and we were off, bobtailing it to points unknown to us. By evening we were pulling into a truck stop as bright as any city there in the mountains of Virginia.

Dad parked the rig beside a mobile chapel at the edge of the parking lot. He said the walk would do us good. Audrey said, Carry me. Dad bent over and Audrey leaped on for a piggyback ride. The chapel was a semi trailer resting on its support legs with a door in its sidewall above the auxiliary tank and a flight of fold-out stairs to the asphalt. JAMMERS FOR JESUS was painted on the side. A small sign by the door read, CHAPLAIN BUCK ALEXANDER, AVAILABLE 24/7/365. We could hear tinny organ music from inside like it was being played on an eight-track machine. We headed for the restaurant that Dad called the Chew and Spew. It was like a carnival in there, noisy, flashy, garish. Lots of shouting and laughing and smoke. We sat in a booth. We were the only kids in there, and the only women were the waitresses. Audrey ordered a bologna burger and a Coke float. Dad got the Montreal smoked meat sandwich, and I got a grilled cheese. A guy in a cowboy hat at the booth across the aisle was telling his buddy how he blew his turbo and figured to spend the night here, so he was fixing to find himself a lot lizard to kill the time. Audrey kept trying to get Dad to tell us where we were going. Disneyland? she said. The Emerald City? Dad said he'd never tell. She said that wasn't fair. But he did say we'd get there by tomorrow night. Our plan was to fill the tank, drive to a motel about an hour down the road, get some rest, let Deluxe stretch his legs and do his business, wake up early, and drive.

A clean-shaven guy with enormous earlobes, wearing bib overalls and a white dress shirt buttoned at the neck, stopped at our booth and smiled. The cuffs of his shirt stopped above his wrists. He had a Bible in his left hand. He held his right hand above his head, looked at Dad, and said, "Brother, can I ask you, do you have any kind of spiritual belief?"

"Pardon me?"

"Have you accepted Jesus Christ as your personal lord and savior?"

"I'm trying to sit here with my family and enjoy my smoked meat."

"Do you believe there's a heaven and a hell?"

"I'm asking you nicely to leave us alone."

Audrey slid her float to the edge of the table.

The man who might be Chaplain Buck Alexander said, "Let us bow our heads and pray."

"Let's not and say we did," Audrey said.

The man said, "Brother, if you fell over and died right now, right here, if your face hit the Formica, I mean, if your heart stopped beating, where would you go?"

"Heaven," Dad said.

"But would God let you in?"

Dad put his sandwich down and said, "All right, that's enough, now. If you—"

"If what you believe is not true, would you want to know?"

Audrey said, "Oops," and poured her float down the gentleman's pants legs.

DAD GOT pulled over for speeding on Highway 11 outside of
Cleveland, Tennessee. Audrey and Deluxe were conked out in
the sleeper cab. I was studying the road atlas, trying to determine
from our previous course and from our present direction where
the hell we were headed, constructing what I would now call a
fourteen-hour cone of probability that stretched from Biloxi to
almost the Texas border to Shreveport. I would have a better idea
when I saw what highway we took out of Birmingham if, in fact,
we were going to Birmingham. The truck continued to idle, so I
could hear Dad and the cop outside, but not what they were saying. Their voices both sounded calm as pudding. Dad hopped
back up into his seat and wished the trooper a merry Christmas.
The trooper tipped his Stetson and said, "You be good, now, Mr.
Donais. Safe home." Dad ground the gears into first, put on his
blinker, and eased out onto the highway. He said, "I need to paint
a biblical verse up there on the cab. They like that down here.
'Except a man be born again, he cannot see the kingdom of
God.' Something like that."
    "Where's the ticket?"
    "We settled out of court."
    "What did he call you?"
    "Donais, as in Raymond Donais. My alias, my nom de guerre.
Got to spread those moving violations around somehow."
    Dad told me to reach under my seat and take out the attaché
case. I did. It was scuffed brown leather with a sticker of Yellow-
stone National Park on the top. The clasps were rusted, and one
side of the handle had been repaired with twine. He told me the
combination and told me to open it. A bottle of aspirin, an
Argosy magazine, and a little black address directory. He told me

how to release the false bottom. In the secret compartment I found a dozen sets of fake identifications, a couple even had photos of Dad.

"You're breaking the law."

"Yes, I am."

"Do you ever forget who you are?"

"I get to live a dozen lives."

"When do you get to be my father?"

"Don't be melodramatic. I'm always your father."

"Or you're always pretending to be."

"I can tell the difference between who I am and who I made up. Ray Donais, he's from Newark, New Jersey. Rusty Driggs is from Round Rock, Texas, and he talks like this here—" Dad was hardly moving his lips when he spoke. "And he wears this big old rodeo belt buckle."

"And Roscoe what's-his-face?"

"He's me, too."

Now, having written that unmasking scene, and in the interest of full disclosure (and because I might be grilled about this someday on *Larry King Live*), I have a confession to make. My father and I never had that dramatically convenient conversation. All of Dad's revelations leaked out over the following few days, but what would have been the point of dragging it out over multiple scenes? My way you get the accumulated facts, the streamlined truth. I'm sorry if you're offended, but sometimes a writer needs to bend the truth to fit a more efficient and attractive shape. And sometimes the writer finds that he has to flat-out make things up because that's the way he wants or believes his life to have been. So he changes the truth to change the facts because he's trying to make sense of his life, and the life he knows he lived is not always the life his fallible memory recalls. Let me give you a case in point.

Last night Annick and I went to eat with Ricky and Nikki Vladimir at their house in Coconut Grove. Built in 1915. Dade County pine, coral fireplace. Gorgeous. They're married and are both writers. Ricky also had a long career in public relations and knows all the celebrities you've ever heard of. Spot stayed out on the patio with Pumpkin the aging wiener dog and tried to get her to play take-away or pounce. The Vladimirs' stories led from something like JFK to Ike to Richard Nixon to David Frost to Diahann Carroll. Diahann, it turns out, lived in Ricky and Nikki's apartment building in Manhattan with her little daughter. She was trying to make it in show biz in those days. One afternoon she asked Ricky for his advice. Should she give up show biz and become a hairdresser? Under no circumstances, Ricky told her, and we were thinking, What might not have been!

That's when Nikki raised her arms and protested. She said, These are good people, Ricky (meaning Annick and me), and they need to hear the truth. So she told us what really happened, a story that involved her mother's black chauffeur, Lincoln, who would occasionally run Diahann up to 125th Street in Harlem to get her hair styled at Rose Meta's salon. Rose Meta was Joe Louis's wife and the best stylist in the city. And Diahann would never have said anything like what Ricky had accused her of saying. Not in a million years. Ricky said, Are you sure? Never! Ricky pointed to the hassock (in the role of a living room chair) to his right—I can see her sitting right there and asking me point-blank. Never happened, Nikki said.

I kind of liked Ricky's story better, though I did appreciate the supporting cast that Nikki wove into hers, especially that chauffeur. But should we trust Nikki's memory just because she more assertively told the story? Here's the thing. When I got home last night, I went online and Googled "Rose Meta"—no such gal. Not exactly. Joe Louis did marry one Rose Meta Morgan (annulled two years later) and Rose Morgan did co-own a beauty shop in Harlem called the Rose Meta House of Beauty. I know that if Ricky thinks harder about it, he'll remember the blouse Diahann was wearing when she had her moment of doubt. And he'll remember Diahann's daughter's name—Suzanne! Yes, and Suzanne was across the room watching cartoons with her feet up on the coffee table.

AUDREY WAS asleep beside me with her thumb in her mouth. The truck's engine was off, but my body kept vibrating. The silence and the stillness were what woke me. Dad was gone. To the bathroom, I figured. Deluxe put a paw over his eyes. I had been dreaming I was in a dark and cramped theater watching a young woman dance on a bare stage. She wore black. She had no arms, no neck, and no stomach. Just air where all that business should be. She tapped and brushed, scuffled and riffed, and kept up what I knew to be delightful patter even though I couldn't make out a word she was saying. I thought about her parents, how proud and how sad they must feel. The door opened and Dad shook my leg and said, "Wake up, lazy bones."

Audrey stretched and moaned.

I said, "Where are we?"

"We're there."

"Where?"

"Monroe, Louisiana."

"Why?"

"We're spending Christmas here."

"What's that smell?"

"The paper mill."

I sat up on my elbow and looked out the window at the silhouette of a house. The drapes were opened in a large picture window in the living room, and margarine-colored light spilled to the lawn. The window looked like a drive-in movie screen hung up out there in the dark. I crawled into the passenger seat. Now the window looked like an illuminated painting in a dark gallery. And the subject of the painting was this wash of stark light. In a corner of the living room stood a flashy aluminum Christmas tree with lavender ornaments. There was a starburst clock on the wall above a blond console television. A turquoise couch. Over the couch and facing the window was a huge mirror in which I could see our truck and my own groggy face. I waved to myself to be sure. The Christmas tree seemed to be revolving. There did not seem to be a shadow in the room.

Dad said, "Let's go in and say hello."

Dad opened the back door, and we stepped into the house like we owned it. The kitchen smelled like tuna fish. He shut the door and dropped his keys into a soup bowl on the counter. He put his hands on our shoulders and called out, "We're here!" A woman and a little boy about four walked in. She couldn't have weighed ninety pounds. She had light brown hair cut unfashionably short, shorter than Dad's, and bright blue eyes. She was all smiles. She clapped her hands and said, "You two are so precious."

Dad said, "Kids, this here is Stevie."

The little boy scrambled across the floor on all fours. Stevie said, "He don't bite."

Dad said, "Drake likes to play doggie." Drake rolled over on his back.

Stevie said, "He wants you to pet him."

Dad picked Drake up and held him on his hip. Drake panted and licked Dad's face. Stevie said, "Let me take a picture of this." We all stood rather stiffly, and Stevie raised her hands to her face like she was holding a camera. She said "Smile," shut one eye, and pumped her finger. She said, "Click!"

Audrey remembered that Deluxe was still in the truck. Dad put Drake on the floor and said he'd fetch Deluxe. Audrey asked Stevie if Drake minded cats. Not at all. Drake sniffed my shoes. I patted his head, asked him how he was. Stevie said, "You two must be starving. I've got you some sweet tea and spaghetti-tuna casserole. Sit. Come on." I asked her whose baby photo was on the fridge.

"That's Elvis's baby girl, Lisa Marie."

"You know Elvis?"

"I met him once when I was in high school. He was with the Hayride over to Shreveport, and he stopped in on his way back to Memphis for pie and coffee at the Dinner Bell where I was waitressing. He wasn't much of anything then except a very handsome and polite boy. Of course, I'd heard him on KWKH. He signed a napkin for me."

Deluxe leaped from Dad's arms to the counter and from the counter to the top of the fridge. He swatted a glue stick to the floor and yeowled. Stevie said, "I've been looking for that. Thank you, kitty." Audrey asked Stevie if Drake liked dog biscuits.

I said, "Drake doesn't say much."

Stevie said, "He doesn't talk at all."

Audrey said, "Does he know any tricks?"

I said, "Do you know why?"

Dad grabbed a Jax beer from the fridge, wrapped a paper-towel jacket around the bottle, and joined us at the table.

Stevie said, "Had the doctors take a look. They don't know. His hearing's just fine. Might be something serious, they say. Might could be he has nothing to say. He's just not ready yet. Time will tell."

Audrey said, "Be nice if he could tell us what he likes so much about being a dog."

Dad coaxed Deluxe down with a saucer of tuna from the casserole.

Stevie said, "He understands us well enough, don't you, sweetie?" She smoothed Drake's hair. He smiled.

Dad said, "So what do you think?"

Audrey said, "I'm sure glad we're not in that truck anymore."

I said, "I don't know what to think."

Dad said, "You're wondering what the setup is."

"I think I know what the setup is."

Audrey said, "What are you talking about?"

Dad said, "We'll talk in the morning. I think we could all use some sleep. Look at the time."

That was fine by me. I was hoping this would all go away, that what I was thinking was so obvious was in reality a misperception easily explained away.

Stevie showed us to our rooms. Drake and I had a room with bunk beds, and Audrey had a room to herself. She cried and said she missed her mom. She said she didn't want to sleep alone. She was scared. She looked at me, cried some more. Dad said, "Okay, you can sleep with Johnny." She said she wanted to sleep with Stevie, and she hugged Stevie and put her head on Stevie's stomach.

Stevie said, "Of course you can, honey." She kissed shrewd little Audrey's head. So Dad and I ended up on the bunks. Audrey and Stevie slept in her double bed with Drake and Deluxe curled at their feet.

I stared at the ceiling and said, "I don't want another mom. I want Mom."

Dad said, "That might not be possible."

"But it might."

He said, "We'll talk tomorrow, all of us. A family meeting." And then he was snoring away.

I said, "Goodnight, Roscoe." What does he think he's doing? I figured I'd never sleep, but I was so tired I thought I heard a voice tell me that at night the sunflower dreams of the sun. And then I was deep in dreamland, and Blackie and I and a crew of eager orphan boys, whom I couldn't see but knew were with us, were on our way to Central City to film the final episode of *The Drone* (*The Death of the Drone?*), and to pass the time because it seemed like we'd never get there—"They keep moving the city farther away," Blackie told me—I told him about the dream I'd had while we were driving through Louisiana, how I was abducted by my own father and taken to live with my "real family," and I had a brother who thought he was a puppy but was actually a spider monkey, and he would wrap his tail around my shoulder while we sat on the couch and watched TV and ate peanuts. He liked me to scratch him under the chin. Blackie said that would make a great movie, and I said I was just happy that I woke up, and he said, "Go wake up your brother," and I said, "Haven't you heard a word I said?" I shook my head and looked out the window, but it was night, and all I could see was my reflection, and I waved at it, and I became aware that I could no longer hear the hum of the diesel, and that's what jolted me half awake, and I realized I couldn't hear any traffic at all on O'Connell Street and how odd that was, and I opened my eyes and saw the ceiling a foot in front of my face and understood that I wasn't in Requiem anymore, and then I felt a tug at my leg and heard, Arf! Arf!

Five Years Next Week

I FOUND DAD out on the carport, sitting at a picnic table, drinking coffee, smoking a cigarette, and shaking his head at whatever he was reading in the newspaper. He said, "You're up!" It was cold enough to see your breath and for Dad to be wearing a bulky cardigan sweater, but it felt like spring to me after the deep-freeze of Requiem. The backyard grass was green, and a mockingbird sang in what I would soon learn was a pecan tree. I sat in one of the aluminum lawn chairs and tucked my bare feet under me. A half dozen clear plastic bags of water hung from the roof of the carport. "What's that about?"

"Keeps the flies away. Flies got these, what do you call it, these multifaceted eyes, so when they look at the water they see like a thousand other flies looking back at them. Scares the shit out of them or something. Anyway, they go crazy and scoot, and we never have any problem with flies when we're eating out here."

I wondered how come we didn't know about that in Massachusetts, and what else didn't we know about? Besides the picnic table and chairs, there were a barbecue grill made from an oil barrel cut in half, a bag of charcoal briquettes leaning against the house, a green plastic sandbox in the shape of a turtle. The shell was the cover, but the cover was off, upside down, and filled with a few inches of water and leafy debris. Next to the sandbox was a banged-up red and white tricycle with rusted wheel spokes and ragged red, white, and blue streamers on the handlebars.

I said, "Does Mom know about this?"

"I don't think she should. Do you?"

"What you're doing isn't right."

"Stevie and I aren't married."

"So what's your plan?"

"I'll play it by ear."

"It's not a piano."

Dad put the cigarette out and folded his hands under his chin. "Johnny, believe me, I didn't plan for something like this to happen."

"What about Mom?"

"You don't know what it's like to be lonely."

"How can you say that?"

"Sorry."

"What does Stevie know?"

"Everything."

"Even your real name?"

"Yes."

"And she's okay with that?"

"You'd have to ask her."

I FOUND Stevie in the bathroom, sitting on the ledge of the pink bathtub. At first I thought she was polishing her fingernails, but she was painting the tile grout with Wite-Out, and her fingernails were, in fact, clear and filed to the quick. I sat on the toilet and tried to figure out what I should say after "Hello." I said,

"Audrey's in Drake's room trying to teach him to speak. To talk, I mean."

Stevie inhaled from the jar of Wite-Out and then screwed the cap shut. She said, "What's your favorite smell?"

I said, "Ditto copies. The ones with the blue ink."

"Mine's the fresh-ground coffee in the machine at the A&P," she said. "I didn't steal your daddy away from your momma. I want you to know that. He came to me. And I sent him away. And he came back. More than once. And I said no. And he said yes. Yes, yes, yes."

"So how long have you two—"

"Five years next week."

I stared at the jam jar on the shelf above the sink, at the three toothbrushes in the jar.

"My husband had died, and I was vunerable." Vulnerable.

"How did he die?"

"Cal drowned in a rice paddy over to Vietnam. Would have survived the gunshot wound in his side, they said, if he could have turned his head."

"Yikes."

"Most people didn't even know we were at war in 1963. Not like today when it's on the news every night."

I tried to guess whose toothbrush was red, whose blue, whose yellow.

"I love Rainy. But I have no claim on him."

I figured Dad's was red 'cause he had red at home. Drake's would be blue.

"I've got no skills," Stevie said. "No training, no checking account, no money to speak of. I live in this rent house behind the Piggly Wiggly. When it rains the yard floods, the roof in the living room leaks. All I've got are the days given me, and I'm happy for each one."

I shrugged my shoulders and clenched my jaw. "I don't know what to do."

Stevie knelt by the toilet and hugged me, and I let her. I may even have cried though that was not something I did (or do) very often. Whenever I felt the crush of sadness choking my breath, I would simply and involuntarily shut down, go numb. And I would think how I should be sad, any normal person would be sad, but I'm not, so why aren't I, and why can't I stop with this distracting blather and let myself feel something other than this fragile, icy calm? But there was nothing I could do about it. I had learned—somewhere—that crying solved nothing. Perhaps the meliorating tears would relieve my ache, but my feelings, I knew, were not the point.

Stevie patted my back, told me everything would be okay. "Let it go," she said.

I said, "You know he lies."

She smiled. "Like a mirror."

"Maybe he has another family in Nebraska."

"Rainy doesn't mean any harm with his stories."

"He never told us about you and Drake. That was a lie, not a story. The story was he's driving a truck out West. He's stuck in a blizzard. He needs a valve job."

Stevie said, "We've got us a muddle and a half here, and we need to sort it all out after a while, and we will. Your daddy's got some deep thinking to do. We all have. But just now your momma's in a bad way. She needs to be alone with the doctors, so she can recover herself. There's not a thing that you or I can do about that. Am I right?"

She was right.

"You and Audrey are on your Christmas vacation, so let's all try to have some fun and be sweet to one another."

Which sounded fine to me. We shook on it. And then we

heard Audrey shout, "He did it!" We hurried to Drake's bedroom. Drake said it again, his first three words. "I'm a dog!" And then he smiled and said his fourth. "Momma," or more accurately "Mo-mo-ma," but close enough. Stevie gave Drake a big hug and told Audrey she was a genius.

Audrey said, "Drake did it."

"You're brilliant."

"Tomorrow we'll work on 'love.'"

We went to the kitchen and ate what Stevie called biblical measures of peach cobbler for breakfast and toasted Drake with our bottles of Big Red soda.

Stevie said, "He's a big boy now!"

Drake even ate some of the cobbler with his fingers before he shoved his face into the bowl.

Audrey said, "Where's Dad?"

"Might could be he's out Christmas shopping," Stevie said. "I'll bet that's it."

Audrey said, "You have Santa Claus down here?"

"Do we ever!" Stevie dropped some peanuts into her Big Red, and Audrey made a face. Stevie slid the bottle to Audrey. "Go on, taste of it. You'll see."

TURNS OUT that Monroe's Santa Claus wore a camouflage suit, combat boots, and a green beret, and he parachuted into the parking lot of Howard Brothers Department Store on Louisville. You could see that he was aiming for the bed of a Ford pickup, but a gust of wind carried him into the Nativity scene, where he knocked over and decapitated a Wise Man. The crowd cheered wildly when he told us that he was supporting our boys in Vietnam and that the little Communist children don't have a Christmas or a Christ. "Ho Ho Ho Chi Minh," he yelled, "Ho Chi Minh will never win!"

Audrey spoke for herself and Drake when they finally got their minute on Santa's lap. She wanted a brown suede fringed jacket like the Range Rider's or a pink diary with a lock and key. And a ballpoint pen. Drake, she told Santa, wanted those Rock 'Em Sock 'Em Robots. And bring something for Johnny Boy, she said. Something bookish. She stood and remembered. "You know we're not in Requiem, right? We're in Monroe. On Concordia." Santa said he knew. They all smiled for the camera.

Dad came out of the store with a color wheel for the Christmas tree. So now the revolving silver tree changed colors from red to yellow to blue to green unless you flipped a switch and kept the wheel from turning and then you could have your choice of a tree in one of four colors. I preferred blue. It just seemed calm to me. Like Delaware is calm. And France. Like the clear sky.

Dad gave Audrey and me $15 each to do our Christmas shopping, and it took us several trips to Howard Brothers and to Spat's Pharmacy to spend it all. I bought Dad some Soap on a Rope, Audrey a pair of fancy cowgirl gloves with fringed cuffs, Drake a Matchbox truck and trailer, not unlike Dad's. I bought Mom a mauve monogrammed handkerchief set and Stevie white pelican salt-and-pepper shakers.

On Saturday, Stevie took me fishing at Bayou DeSiard while Dad took the kids to see *Chitty Chitty Bang Bang* at the Paramount. We fished with twelve-foot cane poles and used Spam for bait. Stevie sprayed her Spam balls with WD-40, and this recipe seemed to work. I caught several bream, which we tossed back. Stevie caught a thirteen-inch gaspergou, usually a spring fish, and a thirty-inch buffalo, the largest fish I'd ever seen. Stevie cleaned the fish right there on shore and put the fillets in the freezer at home. On Sunday, we all skipped church. I was the only one even vaguely interested in going, and though Stevie was sure there must be a Catholic church in town, she wasn't sure where it could be. Dad took Audrey and Drake bowling. Stevie and I went fishing in the slough by the Ouachita River. We caught a bucketful of blue cats using this awful-smelling blood bait. Stevie panfried the fish for supper with hush puppies, coleslaw, and fried okra. Here's something else we didn't know about in Requiem, food this delicious. Dad sprinkled pepper sauce on his okra. He told Stevie how he used to take me fishing all the time. I reminded him that while he may have had good intentions, we actually only made it past the Cat Dragged Inn and to the lake once. And that one time he fell asleep in the boat. "And it was so hot that all of our shiners died in the bucket. We didn't catch a thing. Not so much as a nibble. We drifted into a bed of water lilies."

Dad said, "You've made your point."

Stevie said, "Is that when you were sick?"

I said, "Sick?"

"His cancer," Stevie said.

"You never had cancer, Dad."

"It's not something I wanted to worry you kids with."

"You've never even been to a doctor."

"That's enough!"

Stevie said, "Let's play Clue after supper."

Drake's next words were, "Lead pipe."

WHILE WE busied and entertained ourselves, Deluxe befriended the lovely Orbison, an elegant and vainglorious red and blue Siamese fighting fish who lived on the coffee table in a heated ten-gallon tank with a porcelain sponge diver. Deluxe was fascinated with this exquisite creature who seemed to defy gravity. And Orbison seemed quite taken with Deluxe and his attention. Whenever Deluxe hopped up onto the coffee table, Orbison swam in enthusiastic circles, rippled his long and flowing fins, and then nosed up to the glass and primped himself for Deluxe. He might blow a bubble, execute a graceful turn, or fan his pectorals. Deluxe spoke to Orbison in muted, sweet meows and chirrs. When Deluxe left the table, Orbison retreated behind the frond of plastic kelp. He seemed to deflate. He'd sink to the bottom of the tank and lie there listlessly by the treasure chest. There were times I saw him slam his head against the glass. If Deluxe was gone too long, Orbison punished him by swimming to the opposite side of the tank and keeping as far from the circling and apologetic cat as he could until he felt that Deluxe had been punished enough.

I HAD always harbored decidedly mixed feelings about Christmas, equal parts breathless anticipation and suffocating dread. School was closed, and that, of course, was liberating. But everything else was closed as well, and that disruption in the social routine I found depressing. Now we were all prisoners in our homes. What if I needed double-A batteries for my new transistor radio? Alka-Seltzer for the imminent indigestion? I could go for a walk and listen to the crunch and squeak of my boots on the packed snow and imagine I was the only survivor of a nuclear holocaust, but I'd look up and see all the flickering blue TV lights in the apartment windows and realize I was not welcomed in any of their lives, was not privy to any of their secrets.

You got toys and games for Christmas, and you distracted yourself for hours by playing with them until even you grew bored. You spoiled your dinner with ribbon candy that looked like spun glass, didn't so much taste as tickle, and stained your fingers red and green. And then the delicious meal itself with the turkey and the mashed potatoes and the cranberry sauce and the pies, the pies! But then you'd look outside and see that it was getting

dark already, shit!, and you'd realize that this day of extravagant
indulgence was ending and wouldn't return for another year, and
when it did, it wouldn't produce quite the thrill it once did, and
you'd get that awful it's-Sunday-night-and-Ed-Sullivan's-on-and-I-
haven't-done-my-homework-and-it's-too-late-to-start-now-so-
let's-face-it-my-ass-is-grass-at-school-in-the-morning feeling.

After my grandmother Grace died, Christmas in Requiem
didn't amount to much. Audrey and I would be up at the crack of
dawn. Rainy and Frances, hung over, would sleep until the afternoon, by which time Audrey and I would have opened every gift,
played with and broken all the new toys, and would have
watched *Suzy Snowflake* for the umpteenth time and fallen asleep
in front of the TV. We'd wander outside to play, maybe go sledding down the hill by the schoolyard, eat a late dinner of left-
overs, and go to bed.

That Christmas in Monroe, Dad bought me a Daisy Lever-
Matic BB gun, made to look like a Model 94 Winchester, the rifle
that won the West. It came with a box of BBs, a tube of gun oil,
and a paper target that had a baseball game on it. Hit the bull's-
eye—home run. Audrey liked it. She offered her diary in trade. I
asked Dad why he bought it for me.

"I thought it would make a good starter rifle."

"Why a rifle, I mean?"

"It's what boys do."

The only boy I knew back in Requiem who had a rifle was
Philip Cooke, and Philip was a nasty fool, a juvenile delinquent
who used his rifle to shoot birds off wires and squirrels out of
trees. Every once in a while he'd point the rifle at your face and
threaten to shoot your eyes out.

"I don't really want to kill anything."

"That's what the target's all about. You shoot bottles, cans.
Like that." He handed me the instruction booklet and told me I

could read it on the way to Stevie's mom's house, which was where we were having Christmas dinner. This was north of town, up in Sterlington.

"Rule number one," he said. "No shooting the gun in the house."

Stevie's mom, Dorsey Ann, lived in a tiny old house about a half mile up a gravel road off 165. Stevie leaned out the window of the car and hollered, "Hello, the house!" In a deuce, Dorsey Ann was outside waiting for us where the road became yard, and she gave us each a hug as we climbed out of Stevie's Buick. Dorsey Ann smelled like vanilla. She introduced us to her friend Eldrid Gomillion, her sweetheart, I figured. And I was right. Eldrid's hair was cut short on the sides, longer up top, and a wave of his dark hair fell over his forehead. He had on a black knit tie and a starched blue work shirt. Eldrid nodded and smiled at each of us.

Four rough-hewn columns held up the extended roof over the front porch. The white paint on the house itself had faded and chipped, came off like dust on your fingers. There were a rocking chair, an extra refrigerator, and a glider on the porch. There was also a framed photo by the door of a man in a dark suit and a fedora standing at a microphone. Gave the porch a living room kind of feel. Dorsey Ann told me the man was Uncle Earl. Governor Earl Long. Drake and Audrey made for the johnboat at the side of the house and climbed in. They played pirates until dinner was ready. Drake's new words were *grog* and *arrgh*. Me, I walked through the house while the adults parked themselves at the kitchen table and opened a bottle of what they were calling Christmas cheer. You walked in the front door to a hall with a hat rack, a telephone on a table, and a fabric wall hanging featuring an American flag that said I'M HAPPY TO BE AN EXTENSION HOME-MAKER. The kitchen was to the left, the parlor to the right, and the bedroom to the back.

I sat on a loungey, overstuffed fabric chair with pleated, pillowy arms and put my feet up on the matching ottoman. There was a wall of autographed celebrity photographs: Ferlin Husky, Perry Como, George Jones, Edd "Kookie" Burns, Allen Funt ("Smile, Dorsey Ann, you're on *Candid Camera!*"), Paul Anka, and Don Rickles. There was a baby food jar on the chair-side table with thirteen of Stevie's baby teeth, like so many flakes of vermiculite. Next to the jar, Stevie's bronzed baby shoes, bowed laces and all. Next to the shoes, Stevie's first-place Ouachita Parish Spelling Bee trophy. I had never been in a spelling bee. The trophy was a golden bowl, and folded inside the bowl was Stevie's parish fair blue ribbon for her Flemish Giant rabbit. I imagined what my life would have been like if I had grown up here in Louisiana. I'd know boys with rifles, apparently. And girls who won blue ribbons. My backyard would go on forever. I'd be alone more often. If you were crazy and you lived out in the country in Louisiana, would anyone even notice?

We had baked ham for dinner with sweet potatoes and spicy cheese grits. Banana cream pie and vanilla ice cream for dessert. After dinner, Dad loosened his belt, drifted to the parlor, and fell asleep on the couch. Audrey and Drake headed outside to play. Eldrid excused himself and walked to the shed. He got a bucket of white paint and a brush and painted the tree trunks. I watched him through the window. I looked at Stevie. I said, What's Eldrid up to? Dorsey Ann said, Southeast trunk disease. Stevie said that the early winter sun can warm the bark so it cracks, and the delicate tissue beneath gets injured, and the tree dies. Trees need a new coat about every winter. Yes, I said, sure, I'd like coffee. I tasted it. With cream. Tasted again. And sugar. More sugar. Thanks.

Dorsey Ann pursed her lips and shook her head. Then she told Stevie and me how she went to visit her baby sister, Stevie's aunt

Ginger Rae, last Thursday. For my sake Dorsey Ann prefaced her story with some family history. "Ginger Rae married the youngest, plumpest, and laziest of the six no-account Futch brothers and moved with him to Farmerville. Boy's name is Talmadge Sims Futch, but it should be Fatso Futch. When he's not sacking groceries at the Piggly Wiggly, he's parked on his pooched-out bohunkus on that reinforced BarcaLounger in that sorry-ass double-wide they call a home. Pardon my French."

Stevie said, "Momma, he's not lazy; he's got that illness."

Dorsey Ann said, "He's a four-hundred-pound narcoleptic grocery clerk who hasn't satisfied his poor wife in a coon's age, hasn't seen his own little mister in who knows how long."

"He has his good points."

"He don't beat his wife no more."

Dorsey Ann poured herself more coffee. Freshened Stevie's cup. "That wasn't very Christian of me speaking ill of a person like that, no matter how regrettable he is. I apologize." She put her face in her hands. "The man can't even lie down, you know that? Doctor said Talmadge's own fat would crush his cold little overworked heart." And then she mumbled something, sounded like "We can only hope," but Stevie cut a look at me, smiled, and we let it pass.

All this talk about lardaceous Talmadge had me thinking about my friend Jumbo McPhee, who at eleven, when we joined the Boys' Club together, weighed three hundred and some pounds, and he was shorter than I was. And I weighed 115. The rule at the Ionic Avenue Boys' Club was you swam naked in the pool. (We what? It's for sanitary reasons. How's that work? Get in the pool, pussies!) The other kids were unmerciful in their mocking and derision of Jumbo. These were the same kids who held your head underwater for sport, who cheated at Snaps, and extorted your snack money. Jumbo seemed able to ignore it. He was hippopotamusly obese, but miraculously graceful. He could dive from the board and enter the water without a splash. Jumbo (née Alistair) wanted to be a doctor and went off to McGill University in Montreal. And that was the last I heard from or about him.

Dorsey Ann said, "So Ginger Rae's at the kitchen table writing this letter. I get myself an iced tea and break off a piece of praline. I sit down. Ginger Rae says, 'Sister, tell me what you think,' and she reads the letter.

"She goes, 'Dear Theda—' I says to her, 'Who's Theda?' She says, 'Bob-next-door's wife.' Then she clears her throat and continues reading. 'I know I have been a burden on you and our children. I have failed at being a loving daddy and a dutiful husband.' And then she crosses out *dutiful*, and says, '*Worthwhile* husband.' She nods her head, puts the pencil back on her ear. 'Please don't blame yourself for my untimely passing.'

"'What's going on here, Ginger Rae?'

"'I'm doing Bob a favor.'

"'Writing his suicide note?'

"'Bob doesn't even own a pencil. He can barely spell his own name. Bob Cobb. I'm being neighborly is all. This letter is too important to let him screw it up.'

"I tell her you can't help a person kill hisself, though I'm thinking to my own self I might could try in Talmadge's case. Then she explains to me how it was all a ruse: the letter, the vacuum cleaner hose, the closed garage door, the idling Ford station wagon. What she was writing was a fiction story, not a real suicide note.

"Bob is trying to win back the love and devotion of his wife Theda. The zing has gone out of their marriage. She takes him for granted, he thinks, and Ginger Rae figures he's right, and she should know because she gabs all morning, every morning, with Theda right there in Theda's kitchen.

"Ginger Rae and Bob had come up with a plan because his suicide attempt has to appear real and not just some melodramatic
stunt, which would only make Theda pity Bob, and pity, as we
know, is just a baby step away from contempt. Ginger Rae tells
Bob that Theda gets home every afternoon at four-ten after dropping the kids off at choir practice. She gets the supper into the
oven, picks the kids up, and is home again by five-twenty when
Bob gets back from his job with LP&L.

"They decide that at three fifty-five, Bob will attach the hose
to the exhaust and run the hose through the back window. Then
he'll shut the garage door. At four he'll start the engine—they
want the smell of exhaust to be overpowering when Theda
opens that door."

Stevie said, "This isn't going to end well, is it?"

Dorsey Ann said, "Bob took a comic book for mature readers
into the car with him. *Blood of the Innocent*. He sat there reading.
This was on Friday. He must have heard Theda's car pull up to the
house, checked his watch, and smiled. She was home at four-ten on
the dot. He couldn't wipe the smile off his face. But Theda wasn't
alone. She stumbled into the kitchen in the arms of Warren Hart-
line, who is Talmadge's boss at the Piggly Wiggly." Dorsey Ann
shook her head. "Sometimes the world is so damn small you just
want to spit nickels. The next time Bob checks his watch he probably can't make out the time, but it must feel like he's been there
for hours or days or weeks or he hasn't been there at all. Meanwhile, Warren and Theda do their rutting right there on the
kitchen floor, and when they come to, Theda thinks she hears a
distant humming, and then Warren hears it, too, and he thinks it
might could be a flying saucer landing—he's heard that hum
before—and they run out to investigate, and when the trees aren't
all lit up golden and the sky is empty of aircraft and the grass is not
burned in a perfect circle, they follow the noise to the garage.

"The car door was opened like maybe Bob had realized that something had gone wrong, but he realized it a smidge too late. His body was slumped. His ass was in the seat, and his head was on the garage floor. I imagine he thought, Why am I sitting like this? And Theda knows it's Ginger Rae wrote the note. Matches the handwriting on the Christmas card. Ginger Rae figures they'll work though the uncomfortableness at the funeral. Meanwhile, Ginger Rae's babysitting the twins while Warren, when he isn't working or dealing with his own wife and kids, helps Theda work through her grief or her loss or whatever."

Dorsey Ann and Eldrid were leaving at six to drive over to Jackson to see her sister Kizzie. Kizzie was blind, I found out, and so was her seeing-eye dog, Jake. Jake was seventeen and probably didn't hear very well, either. And he had those arthritic hips, but Kizzie wouldn't put him down and get herself a new seeing-eye dog. She told Dorsey Ann that you don't toss out a person when they can't work. He's a dog, Kizzie. So Kizzie and Jake rode cabs around Jackson. She took him to the vet's about every other day.

Before we all left, Dorsey Ann called us into the parlor and gave us our presents. We were her adopted grandkids, she said. Drake got a Slinky, Audrey an *I Love Lucy* paper doll book. She gave Dorsey Ann and Eldrid big hugs. Eldrid blushed. I got a Kentucky Derby racing game, which I still have, although Whirlaway is now lame. It was dusk now and when you looked out at the painted trees it seemed like they were all unattached, all hovering three feet over the land. A few darker minutes later, the trees had vanished and been replaced by glowing three-foot fountains of limestone. Stalagmites in the bayou.

On the drive back to Monroe, Drake and Audrey slept beside me in the backseat, Drake's head on Audrey's arm, Audrey's head against the door's armrest, both their little mouths open. I sat behind Stevie, my head against the cold, vibrating window.

Stevie and Dad spoke quietly to each other, their subdued conversation a slow dance to the radio music. Marvin Gaye bet you
wondered how he knew. Dad smiled, lifted his eyebrows. I
couldn't see it, but I suspected he and Stevie were holding hands
up there. I looked out the window at the chaos of stars and
understood that this was the happiest Christmas I'd ever had. No
one had screamed in anger; no one had fumed in a corner; no
one had behaved spitefully, and no one had lost his patience.
Nobody had gotten sick from overeating; nobody had kicked a
toy across a room, and nobody had stormed off leaving a trail of
threats and epithets. Nobody had gotten drunk and passed out.
I sat in the backseat smiling to myself without even trying. I
liked it here, liked the possums and the roadrunners, the stubby
cotton fields, the swirling river, the still, black bayous, the Spanish moss dripping from the live oaks. I liked the music and
cadence of the speech. I liked not being frozen. I refused to
admit then that this was not my bona fide life, that this was not
my home, these not my people, the road ahead not my future.
The present, I convinced myself, was the only important time
because the present is what you will remember, and where you
feel emotion. And now, writing, remembering that drive that
night, the hum of the tires on tarmac, the sweet wheeze of
Drake's breathing, the massage of soft music and whispered
voices, I feel tranquil and fortunate more than I feel sad. When
I think of that drive I see the black Buick as from above, the two
beams of yellow light leading us on, the car sliding into the
future through the dark. And I see my head on the window as I
drift to sleep, not thinking about her.

The Bathtub

WHILE WE WERE enjoying our cozy and affable Christmas down South, Mom left the hospital and made her way home. There was then, and there remains, some confusion as to exactly how she executed her escape. My best guess is that she simply woke up, got dressed, shoved her valuables into her purse, took the elevator down to the lobby, and walked out the front door while the hospital's skeleton staff was busy entertaining the patients with carols and cookies in the rec room, and the duty nurses were sipping eggnog at their stations, and the receptionist was trying to explain yet again to an addled mother-in-law how to follow the yellow lines to the maternity ward. Mom walked home, or she rode a bus, or she hailed a cab. She took the extra key off its hook in the shed and let herself in. She would have turned up the heat a bit, checked the fridge, maybe called out our names. She might have noticed that the pilot light was off on the stove and figured she'd call Blackie later to light it.

She went down cellar and hauled a five-gallon jerry can upstairs and poured the gasoline into the bathtub. And then she took the second can and did the same. No one would be using the lawn mower till April anyway. She undressed, put on her shower cap, and settled into the tub. She closed her eyes against the fumes, tried taking shallow breaths through her nose. Already she could feel the gasoline washing away the stink of her rotting flesh and suffocating the maggots that were eating away at her skin and her muscles. Before she could relax, though, she needed a cigarette. She remembered the opened pack of Pall Malls she kept for emergencies in the cookie jar on top of the fridge. She stepped out of the tub, wiped her feet on the bath mat, tiptoed to the kitchen, got the pack, tapped out a smoke, and popped it in her mouth. She rummaged through the junk drawer for matches. No matches, but an ashtray. She looked under the sofa cushions, under the sofa. She looked behind the TV. She swept the magazines off the coffee table. She moved the ottoman. She scoured through her closet and found a book of matches with a bluebird on the cover in the pocket of a ski jacket.

Upstairs, Nunzie clipped on his Knights of Columbus cufflinks and straightened his tie in the mirror. He slapped on some Canoe, lifted his chin, and checked his profile. He wet the tips of his middle fingers and smoothed back his eyebrows. He asked Caeli if she smelled gasoline. She did, now that he mentioned it. She pulled the blankets up to her neck. Nunzie, who was supposed to be dropping off a fifth of Johnnie Walker Red to the monsignor at the rectory, bent over and kissed Caeli on her forehead. She held his wrist. He told her he had to get home before the kids got too antsy, and before his brother-in-law, Paulie Mook, and family showed up for cocktails and lasagna. He said goodbye and left by the front door.

Downstairs, Violet had one of those headaches that starts behind the eye and shoots straight back to the base of her skull. Through all that gray matter like an arrow. She closed her novel,

The Minister's Confession, and shut her eyes. She put her head back. Red popped open a can of Narragansett and put his feet up on the coffee table. He stared at the football game on the tube. Blackie couldn't figure out where the smell of gasoline was coming from. Now it sounded like someone was moving furniture upstairs. He followed his nose to the back porch and up the stairs. The door was opened. He called out to Rainy. "You home?"

Frances said, "I'm in the tub."

"You smell gasoline?"

"Well, yeah . . ."

Staging

O F COURSE, we didn't know about Mom's disturbing adventure as we drove through the dark toward Monroe. Dad would hear the news in a phone call long after we kids were all tucked away in bed and dead to the world. But before we return to the morning after the drive and after the gasoline bath, I want to jump ahead to last night and to the conversation I had with a real estate client, a gentleman from Columbus, Ohio, named Martin Abbott.

The housing market here in South Florida is in the doldrums, so Annick tells me. There are any number of million-dollar-plus homes for sale on the Hollywood Lakes, and they are simply not moving. This situation has local Realtors in a panic, which turns out to be good news for Annick, who, as I mentioned, augments her theater income by staging houses, expensive houses. What Annick does is she makes the houses irresistible to the prospective buyers, helps them, in other words, see themselves living there, relaxing, entertaining, loving, growing old gracefully in this luxurious and thoroughly charming new home.

Most houses are sold in the first ten minutes, Annick says, so
first impressions are crucial. Appearance is everything, she says.
I say, That's pretty shallow, isn't it? She says, It's love at first sight
or it's a no-sale. And this makes me think about the first time I
saw Spot. There he was in his kennel out in Belle Glade with his
mother and his brothers and sisters. Spot was the setter puppy
with one ear flapped over his head and his tongue lolling out. He
was the one puppy not at Mom's teats. He saw me, yipped,
jumped up, and fell over backward. I whistled to him, and he ran
to me, kind of sideways, and slammed into a pole. Then he sat in
a dish of water and yipped at me some more. I said, That's the
dog for me. The first time I saw Annick in a bookstore, I thought
she was adorable, but she thought I was a stalker until I convinced her to have a coffee with me and turned on my not-
inconsiderable charms. When even that didn't work, I begged for
her phone number. The first time we kissed, we were on Hollywood Beach, and as my lips met her lips, a gust of wind blew the
Panama hat off my head.

   House shoppers, like editors, are looking for a reason to say no.
So you don't give them a reason to say no. You transform that
property into a home, a home owned and loved by a close-knit,
prosperous family with impeccable taste just like the potential
buyers'. You get rid of all the clutter, all the detritus of the former
owners (a clown painting, what were they thinking?), and you call
the Maid Brigade to make the place shine. You have the landscap-
ers mow the lawn, trim the hibiscus, plant the bougainvillea,
sweep the terrace, and prune the goddamn oleander. You see that
the rooms are well lighted. You put some Mozart on the sound
system. Maybe you see that the rectangular ebony extension dining room table, which you bought at Restoration Hardware and
move from house to house, is set for two. The beeswax candles in
their pewter holders are lit, as are the wall sconces.

When even all that magic didn't work on the house at 500 Adams, Annick had a brainstorm. She'd hire actors from the theater company to play the Andersons. The Andersons own the home and truly regret having to move, but Bob's being transferred to the Tokyo office. The faux-Andersons will model loving family behavior and show the prospect all the amenities of the house until that excitable prospect and his cautious wife finally agree that the house is a bargain at any price. But last night the actors couldn't make the showing because of a rehearsal for *The Fantasticks*, and the potential buyer was in town for just the one night, so I was recruited. I was Bob Anderson. Annick made me get a haircut, and not at Supercuts as usual, but with Rudy at the Elite Group. I looked sharp, she said, distinguished. I said, You're lying through your teeth. All right, you look better, she said. Frazzled. You got this Keith Richards kind of thing going. He'll think you're rattled and motivated to sell. This'll work. So the lie was that my family, Marianne, Bob Junior, and Roberta, are already on their way to Tokyo, the wife settling the kids into the American school and getting the house in shape. I'm here tying up loose ends. I answer the door, say hello to Sissy Stroczek, the real estate agent. I shake the gentleman's hand. "Happy to make your acquaintance, Mr. . . . ?"

"Abbott," he says. "You can call me Martin."

While Sissy walks Martin through the house, I sit, as per my instructions, in the leather chaise in the den, reading cartoons in an old *New Yorker*. I've got a snifter of Hennessey V.S.O.P. on the maple side table. Go easy on the cognac, Annick told me. Remember, you're Bob Anderson, and Bob Anderson is a man of taste and moderation. Like I'm not, I said. I can hear Sissy pointing out the unique architectural details of the house: the Dade County pine floors, the pilastered doorframes, the egg-and-dart molding, the recessed lighting, the louvered interior shutters. All

I hear from Martin, though, is the occasional Uh-hum. I wonder what's wrong. Why is he here when it seems obvious he doesn't want to be? Why is he leaving Ohio? Early retirement, maybe. In one of the cartoons, Charles Dickens is sitting across the desk from his editor, and his editor, looking at the manuscript, says, So why can't you make up your mind? Was it the best of times or the worst of times? I know that the real Bob Anderson is moving into new digs up in Boca. He's bought a mansion across the street from Yanni. He's divorced and childless.

And then Sissy realizes she's left the paperwork for the house back at the office. She slaps her forehead. She'll just scoot on over and get it—be back in ten. This is all part of our script. The ten will become twenty. I'll chat with Martin so that he feels comfortable here. I'll fashion some kind of compelling narrative about the Andersons and their beloved house, so he'll be ready to sign on the dotted line when Sissy returns. Martin says, sure, he'll join me for a drink, and we move out onto the deck. I take the bottle. I say, Martin, can you see yourself in this house? He nods, but not convincingly. I change the subject. I say, You're going to love it here in winter. Trust me.

He says, "My son died."

"I'm sorry." I'm hoping I heard wrong. "How? What happened?"

"Dallas was twenty-seven. It was so odd, so unnecessary, so unfair." Martin sips his drink. "He was crossing a playing field on his way home from work. He'd been living with us again ever since his divorce. Moved back into his old room. Anyway, there were kids out playing soccer in the field. The ball rolled toward Dallas, and he figured he'd give it a boot, bend it like Beckham, you know, but he sclaffed the kick, hit the hard dirt a few inches behind the ball, and broke his great toe."

"Ouch."

"And then he made it worse, no doubt, by walking home."

This isn't in the script, of course, and I'm feeling like a shit, pretending to be someone I'm not while this man is pouring out his soul. I don't say, I'm not really an investment banker, Martin. I'm a writer, and I'm going to steal your story. I just listen.

"There's nothing they can do for a broken toe. No cast, nothing. It stays broke."

I ask Martin if he has a photo of his son, and he takes out his wallet, slips the picture from its plastic sleeve, and hands it to me. Dallas is wearing a party hat and has a noisemaker in his mouth. He's smiling and his arm is around someone's shoulder. Someone you can't see. Like an ex-wife, maybe. New Year's Eve, I figure. His eyes are red dots. I say, "Good-looking boy," and give Martin back the photo.

"He kept his toe elevated as much as he could." Martin sips the cognac and looks up at the full moon above the coconut palm. "Elevated the foot, iced the toe. But, of course, he had to work."

"What did he do?"

"Reference librarian. Columbus Metropolitan Library. Main branch downtown. He bought himself a cane at a medical supply store to take the stress off the toe. Then his back started hurting. Evidently the spine was all out of whack, what with trying to compensate for the toe and all. Saw a chiropractor for a while. He wore a slipper on the right foot now. Shoes hurt too much. So he was running an errand for his mother, picking up a jar of paprika at Meijer's, when a car pulls out in front of him. Dallas slammed on the brakes, must have crushed his toe, and the pain shot through him, and he shut his eyes or lost control or something. Smashed into a big-ass maple tree. Jaws of Life. DOA."

"Jesus, Martin, I'm so sorry."

"His mother. She can't live in that house anymore."

I want to tell him the price is negotiable.

"Dallas was our one and only."

We can work out a deal that's good for both of us.

"That kick, that was the beginning of our end. The end of the Abbotts."

I'm thinking Martin and his wife will carry Dallas with them wherever they go.

"You're a lucky man, Bob."

"I know."

"Don't let anything happen to those kids."

"I won't." I tell him, no, I don't have any pictures of the kids, and I'm wondering if he thinks I'm a no-account dad. I see a picture of the two of them in my head. If he asks, I can describe them, right down to Roberta's braces and Bob Junior's mole.

"Coming here tonight was my way of telling myself not to surrender to the darkness, you know."

"You've got your wife."

"You've been kind to listen to me."

"Your days will grow lighter, you'll see."

"It's the nights I can't handle."

We hear Sissy at the front door. I tell Martin I'll get rid of her, and I walk inside. Sissy says she can't just leave me here. I say you just did. I'll lock up. I'll call. I think I can seal this deal. She says she'll give me a half hour. Thanks, Sissy. You're welcome, Bob.

When I go back to the deck, Martin is gone. At first I figure he's in the bushes taking a leak. Or he's just checking out the grounds. I call his name. I sit and wait. He hasn't left a note or a business card or anything. I check out front and see that his car is gone. I figure I'll finish both our drinks. I think about the loss of a child, how devastating that is. Maybe that's how my mother felt. Maybe that's what drove her nuts. She was crazy with grief for her abducted children. And we two imposters in the house even made it worse. Never mind that she hadn't lost us—it was enough that she believed she had. How does a mother survive the disappearance of her children?

A Door, A Jar

WHEN MOM TOLD Blackie that she was luxuriating in a tub of therapeutic gasoline but not to worry, she knew what she was doing, she'd even cracked the window, Blackie asked her if she was decent, but then he thought, What the hell difference does that make? He knocked at the bathroom door. I'm coming in, Frances. And a good thing he did. Mom had the unlit cigarette in her mouth and the matches in her hand. Blackie snatched the matches away.

"What a gentleman," Mom said.

"I'm not lighting it for you, Frances. Jesus H. Christ Almighty, you could have blown us all to smithereens."

She said, "Define *decent*."

He said, "Not now, Frances."

She said, "Oh, Blackie, if you had only waited another minute, all my problems would have been over."

"What the hell do you think you're doing?"

She told him how she was rotting away from the inside out, how she was basically just a shell and all her organs were so much decomposing mush, and how the gasoline would cleanse her flesh, or the fire would finish her off, and she didn't much care which way it went.

"You're not dying, Frances, but you almost did." Blackie helped her out of the tub and into her robe. He drained the tub of gasoline. "We'd all be dead now. Charred slabs of smoking meat. What were you thinking?"

"I wasn't going to drop the match in the gasoline. Not at first."

"It's the fumes that burn, Frances, not the liquid."

Blackie led her downstairs, where Violet got her into the shower with a can of Boraxo and a sponge. Red nearly had a seizure. He was hyperventilating and dribbling his beer. Blackie called for an ambulance and let the hospital know the situation. He called Caeli with the news. Red called the fire department just in case. Send the inspector, he told them. When the ambulance arrived, Mom was sipping tea at the kitchen table, her hair turbaned in a towel. She said the gasoline had done the trick. "Just what the doctor ordered. Fit as butcher's dog." She looked at the paramedics, held out her hand. "To the ball, gentlemen." On her way out the door, she said, "Don't wait up for me."

Red looked at Blackie. "There's something wrong with her."

"Yes, there is."

"She's mental."

"She's getting help."

"We can't have her living upstairs."

"I know that."

Blackie then opened all the windows on all three floors, but not for long, for a half hour, maybe. It was twenty degrees and blustery outside. Caeli stopped by to say she was on her way to the Holiday Inn. Would anyone care to join her? Red said, Thanks, but no thanks. He was crying. They heard her cab honking its horn. Red wouldn't say what he was crying over, and he was angry at Blackie for calling attention to the tears with his concern. Violet asked Blackie to help her in the kitchen. She told him quietly that Red had slept every single night of his life in this house! "He was born in the bed we sleep in. In that same room. And he has this crazy idea that if he doesn't sleep here, he'll croak. End of story."

They each had this uncomfortableness in their temples, not a headache exactly, more like a swelling, a tightness. Blackie noticed that he couldn't smell the gasoline anymore. Neither could Violet or Red. But it was there. That's what the fire inspector said as he waved his hand in front of his face. How can you stand it? Blackie figured you smell something long enough and something about that smell or within that smell makes you not smell it. Every smell has an anti-smell. Or maybe the smell carries paralyzer cells that go to work on our nasal neurons or something. Blackie told me all of this on the phone.

I'd called Blackie the day after Christmas, after Dad gave me a report of his middle-of-the-night conversation with Blackie. Blackie said they stayed awake all night in the kitchen with the windows opened a bit and two oscillating fans circulating the air. They ate the rest of the Christmas goose and played Parcheesi. "Johnny, your mother can't be living here."

"Not till she's better."

"You two and your old man, fine. You understand?"

"Yes."

I wanted to leave for Requiem right away and said so. Dad said there was nothing we could do till Mom was back being peculiar and inexplicable again and not morbid and suicidal. Then we'll see. He called Four Crowned Martyrs while I sat there beside him. He held the phone away from his ear so I could listen in. The nurse, or whoever it was, told Dad that Mom had scrubbed her body raw with steel wool trying to scrape away the rotting skin. That's what she told us, the nurse said. And now she's demanding to be buried. She's convinced herself that she's dead and doesn't understand why we can't smell the decay. The nurse told Dad that they had Mom on a new medication, and they were hopeful it would work. Dad thanked her and hung up. I said maybe if she had her family . . . But even I didn't believe what I was going to say.

Audrey wanted to stay. No one in Monroe made a stink about her boots or about her taste in music—it was their taste as well. You could hear Patsy Cline over the speakers at the A&P. And Audrey had her pal, the increasingly loquacious Drake. And she was certain that I would never leave her.

Dad said, I want the best for you kids, and Stevie is the best. I couldn't argue. She treated us better than Mom ever did, sane or loony. Stevie was sweet, loving, happy, interesting, and interested. I said, Stevie's great, Dad, but she's not Mom. You don't get to pick your mother. I said maybe if we went home, we could coax the old Frances from the new and unimproved Frances. Dad told me I was living in fantasyland. I reminded him that I had school starting Monday.

"There are schools in Monroe."

"I'm in my last term at St. Simeon's. I graduate in June."

"Audrey's happy here. You're happy. I'm happy."

"What's happiness got to do with it?"

Monday came, and I didn't go to school. Audrey did, and she came home all excited. She told me that the best part was there were no nuns. The teachers are normal people. They dress normal; they watch TV, go to the store, and tell jokes. They're the people in your neighborhood. I was out in the yard with my faux-Winchester, shooting at the target and even hitting it once in a while. Audrey said, You can't mope your life away, Johnny Boy. She put her hand on my shoulder. Number Eighteen: Be open to everything and attached to nothing. Then she told me she had homework to do. The New Math. Words and numbers together. Fabulous!

When he got home, Dad came out to the yard. He said, "Squeeze the trigger; don't pull it." He tried to reason with me about school, about settling in Monroe, but I kept shooting the rifle like he wasn't there. He said, "Johnny, put the rifle down and let's talk man to man."

I told him I was pretending the target was him.

"You want to shoot me?"

"No, I want to pretend to shoot you."

He walked in front of the target. "Shoot me."

"Dad, I don't want—"

"Shoot me!"

So I did. I didn't aim. I just squeezed. Hit him in the left leg.

"You shot me!"

"You told me to."

"Jesus Christ!" He sat on the grass and grabbed at his leg.

I put down the rifle. "Sorry." I could see a little rip in his chinos over the knee. And a little blood.

Stevie and the kids came running out, wanting to know what the ruckus was all about.

I said, "This is what happens when you have guns around the house."

Stevie checked Dad's leg. "You'll live. Nothing, really."

"It hurts," Dad said.

She took Dad inside, fixed him up with iodine and Band-Aids. I apologized. Dad told me to get in the car. We're going for a ride. Drake wanted to go, too. Audrey wondered where the bullet went. BB, I said. I went out front and waited. Dad limped out. I asked him where we were going. He didn't answer. We went to the Mohawk Tavern on Louisville. We sat at a booth, let our eyes adjust to the dim light. Dad ordered a Jax and a Dr Pepper. I told him I wasn't hungry. He ordered a bowl of gumbo and a slice of red velvet cake. Two forks, two spoons. All the customers were white, and all the staff were black. Thin, elderly gentlemen in black slacks and white jackets. Dad rubbed his knee, stretched his leg, sipped his beer. He told me he'd gone through Korea without getting shot. I apologized again.

And then he apologized to me for my crummy childhood. He said, I didn't plan on your mother losing her grip. Whenever Dad took me to a bar in order to ream my ass, he ended up talking about his own childhood. And the beer helped fuel the memories. The only time Dad didn't lie (I think) was when he was drinking. Then he got sad and pensive. It was almost worth getting into trouble to get this time alone with him. All I'd need to do was mention a name of a childhood friend, and he'd chuckle and launch into a story. All of his childhood memories were sweet ones. He was a man in love with his youth and with the people who lived there. Tubba Henry, I'd say. Oh, Christ, he'd say, and he'd tell the story about the day he and Tubba and the Tomaiolo twins got caught stealing apples from Mr. Aiello's apple orchard and chased by the old man himself. They battered him with his own apples until he went inside and called the cops. By the time the cops arrived, they were long gone. Maybe he thought I was the only person interested in his past. And I was because it was my past, too.

He asked me his favorite question, what did I want to be when I grew up, and while I thought about the possibilities, he told me that when he was twelve, he wanted to be a pilot.

"But you're afraid of heights."

"That's why I'm not a pilot."

On Harp Hill, in my experience, no one really chose to become this or that. Son followed father into whatever job of work the father did. A plumber's son became a plumber, a cop's son a cop, the bookie's son the bookie, and like that. You'd have the occasional priest, of course, and a used-car dealer or two among the disaffected, but that was it. Women married and settled into homemaking or else they didn't marry and worked in an office downtown, nursed, or entered the convent, God forbid. Doctors, lawyers, and other professionals came from other neighborhoods. I knew I didn't want to drive a truck, but assumed I would. One day Dad would hand me the keys and a bill of lading and say he'd see me when he saw me. He'd park his ass on the La-Z-Boy, pop open a brewski. Be safe out there, Johnny. It's like an H, remember. And someday I'd have a wife and children whether I wanted them or not. This was the natural order of things.

I said, "I think I'd like to do a lot of things. I'd like to be a scientist, have my own lab out in the desert. Then maybe work on a ship or something."

"What are you best at in school?"

"Reading and writing."

"And you're proud of that?"

"And I'd like to be a fireman and a scuba diver."

"You're going to have to pick one."

"Why?"

"One's what they pay you for." He wiped his napkin, signaled the waiter for another Jax.

STEVIE SOLVED my problem. I don't know what she said to Dad or what she promised him, but at breakfast the next morning, Dad told us to pack our stuff. We're taking a road trip.

Audrey said, "Where we going?"

Dad said, "Stevie wants to see snow."

I said, "Home?"

Audrey said, "What about school?"

Stevie said, "We're not going to let school get in the way of your education."

Drake said, "Snap, crackle, and pop."

I said, "What about Orbison?"

Stevie had already taken care of that. Her hairstylist Rochelle at Ivy's Chez Beauté would be moving in for as long as Stevie needed her. Rochelle's manicurist roommates Tracy Goode and Darlene Killeen were driving her out of her mind with their constant bickering, filing, and spritzing, so she was looking forward to peace and quiet. We packed our bags and put everything into the truck. Deluxe rode with Dad in the rig. I rode up front with Stevie in her Falcon and kept an eye on the kids in back. I was like the social director. We aired up the tires, gassed up the tanks, and drove on out of Monroe at noon. Dad and I kept in touch on the CB radio. "Come in, Johnnycake; this is Rainy Day. What's your twenty?" We played a dozen games of Botticelli, played License Plate Geography, Twenty Questions, Name That Cow, Inky-Stinky, and I See Something Red. We played Let's See Who Can Stay Quiet the Longest. We called Rainy Day on the radio and asked to speak with Deluxe. We told scary stories about guys with hooks and halitosis. We must have sung "Eddie Koochie-kacha-kamma-toesinarra-toesinocha-samma-kamma-waukee Brown" thirty times. In three days we pulled into Requiem.

You've Got the World on a String

Y OU'RE SITTING ON a rainbow. And from your perch, at long last, you can see how your book is going to end and in only five or six easy chapters, and you picture yourself at the Dania Beach post office dropping the weighty manuscript into the mailbox and driving over to Discount Liquors for a celebratory bottle of the good stuff. You feel like you've just taken twenty milligrams of Endural, and you're indestructible. It's like you're twelve again, and you just walked out of confession, knowing that nothing bad can happen to you now, and even if it does, so what, you're going to heaven. And not only that, your cholesterolemia is responding to the new meds, hallelujah!, and the problem with the lawn sprinkler turned out to be a seventy-nine-cent washer, and you passed your kidney stone without too much squirming and screaming. It's a wonderful life, mister. You've got that string on your finger. It's there to remind you of something. You forget what. Maybe that all of this untrammeled prosperity is about to end.

Last night I met my friend David for supper at the Universe

Café. I parked where I always park, in the empty Bank of America lot on Tyler Street. We order drinks and the walnut, honey, and Parmesan appetizer. We like sitting under the mimosas, watching the folks walk by on the boulevard, and talking about books. Last tourist season, all of the waitresses at the Universe were from Montevideo. This year they're all from St. Petersburg, where David and I have, coincidentally, spent many a white night, drinking Russian Standard at cafés along Nevsky Prospect, watching the folks stagger by, and talking about books. Lena brings the martinis and reads us the specials. We tell her about our writing classes at the Summer Literary Seminars. She wants to know if we're from the "University of I-over." We decide to split the chicken satay and the calamari.

David tells me he got a call last night from an old flame, the exquisite stepdaughter of a famous British author of spy novels. Daddy had more money than God when he died, and left all of it to a niece and a nephew. He left the breathtaking stepdaughter a gold typewriter and a signed first edition of his second novel. I've brought along a book I picked up at Hittel's used book store, and I read the author's greeting aloud: "'These pieces of moral prose have been written, dear Reader, by a large Carnivorous Mammal, belonging to the suborder of the Animal Kingdom, which includes also the Orang-outang, the tusked gorilla, the Baboon with his bright blue and scarlet bottom, and the gentle Chimpanzee.'" David says, Oh, yes, Logan Pearsall Smith. Born in Philadelphia, but settled in England. His sister married Bertrand Russell. And then he tells me which character Smith is in Anthony Powell's *A Dance to the Music of Time*.

After the meal, David and I wave so long to Lena, who's trying to make sense of the French-Canadians at the next table. Poutine? she says. Vladimir Putin? *Nyet? What this poutine is? Spasiba, Lena! Da svidaniya!* We get to the parking lot, and my car is gone. The lot is empty. What the . . . ? David says, No, that can't be. I stand in the parking space and turn in a circle. Nothing. I do that thing that incredulous cartoon characters often do. I squeeze my eyes shut and rattle my head. When I do, I hear cowbells. But when I open my eyes, the car is still not there. I borrow David's cell phone (got to get me one of those) and call the number on the heretofore ignored DON'T EVEN THINK ABOUT PARKING HERE 'CAUSE WE'LL TOW YOUR SORRY ASS IN A HOLLYWOOD MINUTE sign and tell the woman who answers that I think she may have my car.

She says, "Does it look like a lunch box?"

"That's it."

"A hundred bucks."

So I take a hundred out of the Bank of America ATM, and they take their $2.50 fee, the unneighborly scoundrels. I grab the cash and the receipt, and David drives me down Gasoline Alley to Pembroke Road, a neighborhood of convenience stores, broken glass, used car dealerships with razor wire atop their chain-link fences, and our grail, the impoundment lot. We go in, and I put my mouth up to the hole in the security window and say I just called about the lunch box.

"The maroon one?"

"Salsa, actually."

Her name is Chantal. I ask her if she has to work through the night. She does. And when the Chinese takeout next door closes, it can get pretty eerie, let me tell you. She's got a canister of pepper spray and a handgun, a 9mm Smith & Wesson police trade-in, in her desk drawer. She's used the pepper spray. Most nights she gets to nap a bit. Or she'll turn on the TV. She's dating a BSO deputy, and he'll swing by when he's on duty, which I figure he is doing tonight because Chantal is wearing a pleated black sleeve-less V-neck dress with strands of silver and turquoise, and I know she's not trying to impress scofflaws like me. Bobby is the deputy's name, and he's sweet as Bajan rum, she says, but he's married. Chantal counts out my twenties and checks my driver's license. I ask her if she sees herself working here in ten years. She puts a hand on her hip, cocks her head, raises an eyebrow, and stares at me. My bad. David tells her she looks like a young Diahann Carroll. She says, Who's this, now?

And then this morning Spot wakes me up with a paw to my face and lets me know that we're out of Snausages. All right, I say, we'll go to Publix. He runs and gets his leash and when he gets back, he's a little irritated that I'm still in bed. He barks and drops the leash. He picks it up and woofs out the side of his muzzle. Okay, I'm up, but you got to let me pee first. He follows me to the bathroom and sits. I ask him nicely not to watch, and he pretends to look at the ceiling. I kiss Annick goodbye, and she tells me to pick up some Advil Liqui-Gels. Will do. Anything else? Kashi GoLean, the crunch not the cereal.

I'm in the Express Lane with my Ten Items or Fewer behind a sunburned woman with a buggy full of groceries and a handful of coupons. I look at the woman. I look at the sign. I look at the cashier, Dulcie. I silently count the woman's items. (Does anyone need five bottles of green ketchup?) I roll my eyes. The woman wants to pay with a traveler's check, and it's clear that Dulcie has never seen one before. The manager is summoned; the confusion is sorted out, and the woman waddles (that's not nice!) away. I'm about to tell Dulcie my idea for an Express Lane checkout that would stop automatically at the eleventh item when I realize I don't have my credit card. I apologize and go through the wallet one more time. Dulcie mumbles something about this not being her day. Spot, who's waiting for me outside Ice Cream Cohen's, is not at all happy. He won't move. I explain how I left the card in my other pants—we'll scoot home, get it, and hustle back. He woofs. What don't you understand, Spot? No money, no Snausages. I tug the leash. He goes limp.

But the credit card is not in my pants pocket. You guessed that already. It's in the ATM, of course. Or was. I ask Annick what to do. We're screwed, I say, but she reminds me about the PIN number. Right! Annick says all her muscles ache; she couldn't sleep, and she feels like shit. I need to call someone about this, I tell her. Annick says call the number on the back of the card, and for a few seconds that even makes sense. I imagine the woman who has my card now and wonder if she's a medium or something and can divine the PIN number just by feeling the card. That would be just my luck. Maybe she can sense my interest in the History Plays. But even if she can, would she know the date of the Battle of Agincourt? I'm not making any sense, of course. Anyway, I get the card canceled. I grab $20 from Annick's purse and head back to Publix. I see that the garbage has been picked up, but our garbage bin is not in the driveway. I check behind the oleander, check with the neighbors. Someone stole our garbage bin. Jesus! What kind of people . . . And ours is cracked, banged up, and lopsided. Theft-proof, you would think. But it is also the only bin in the neighborhood without the address spray-painted on it because that's too white-trashy for Annick, which is also why I can't leave bread on top of the fridge or dish soap on the rim of the sink. Cream needs to be in a creamer, butter in a dish. And there'll be no Pop-Tarts in this house. Annick says my characters can eat and drink whatever they want, Go-Tarts!, Kool-Aid Jammers, Blinks, Tang, Lunchables, or Uncrustables, but *we're* not going to.

I go back in the house and tell Annick about the bin, and I'm a little loopy at this point. I'm slamming things down and raving about common human decency, and I call Waste Management, and Javier says they'll get me a new one for $50 and I'll have it in ten days, the same day my new credit card arrives. Annick tries to get up, but she can't walk. I tell her I'll call Dr. Khani and make an appointment. She doesn't need one, she says. You know this could be the flu, I tell her. Annick gets her medical advice and her homeopathic remedies from her friend Ellie who's a chiropractor. And then she takes my prescription meds when she needs them to sleep or decongest or whatever. She lies on the couch and turns on the TV. She calls Ellie, leaves a message. Spot curls up at her feet. Bob the Builder is teaching children about divergent thinking.

This afternoon I decide to pressure-clean the deck. I want to surprise Annick. But the pressure cleaner, which I've used like five times, doesn't work, or I've forgotten how it works. Annick's the mechanic in this house. So I get on the phone, and I call the 800 customer-service number, and I'm put on hold several times, and I get a beep on the call-waiting service, and I answer it, and it's Audrey. I ask her what she knows about pressure cleaners.

She says, "I need money."

"I'm fine. How are you?"

"Did you hear me, Johnny Boy?"

"Daxson out of work again?"

"He does the Lord's work."

"How much?"

"I'm sorry. I am. You're the only one."

I tell her I want her to come visit, knowing that she will not. She's calling from a pay phone. I'm to send the money to a PO box in Minot as usual. She's careful that I can't find her. North Dakota is all I know.

WE JUST got back from Publix. Mr. Inconspicuous and his dog Casual, just out for a stroll past the Dumpster in back of the supermarket. First we have a plastic bag of garbage, and then we don't. Annick's asleep thanks to my Ambien, and I'm at the desk, writing what you've just read because if I don't write, I'll be up all night fantasizing about catching and punishing the bin thief. Is a bin thief even capable of feeling shame and humiliation? I've written myself back to where we were, it seems. Ready to move back and move on. We're in Requiem. It's freezing. Dad has forgotten his keys. Audrey has a spare in her boot.

Red and Violet come upstairs in their pajamas and robes when they hear the footfalls on their ceiling. Dad jacks up the heat. The radiators clang and hiss. Stevie leaves her jacket on. Red hands me a shopping bag full of mail and says how happy he is to see us, but I can tell he's a little flustered by Stevie's presence. Violet hugs Audrey and shakes hands with Drake. She has tears in her eyes and a miner's lamp on her head. It's a Christmas gift from Red. So she can read in bed without disturbing him. Red pulls Dad aside and tells him he doesn't know if this domestic arrangement with Stevie is kosher. The gal's name's not on the rental agreement or anything.

Dad says, "There is no rental agreement, Red. And this is our family now."

"And what about Frances?"

"We'll wait and see."

"What are you, Mormon now?"

"Stevie and I aren't married."

"And that's supposed to make me feel better?"

Violet takes Red's arm and says they'll let us settle in. They head downstairs. Deluxe sniffs around the parlor and finds an old friend, a blue cloth mousie missing its cotton eyes, behind the sofa. He bites onto the mousie and hops up on the TV, where he settles into his Easter basket. I stand in the bathroom and stare at the bathtub. I guess I expect to understand something, but I don't. Smells like bleach. Stevie checks the fridge and decides we need groceries right away. She and Dad head off to Iandoli's. I want to call Veronica, but the phone is dead. I go through the mail and put the utility bills in one pile, the medical bills in another. I toss out the catalogues and the *Reader's Digest* after I read the article on Joe Valachi and the Cosa Nostra, which Nunzie once told me did not even exist. We had been talking about drug trafficking. Nunzie was helping me with a paper I was writing for civics class. He said if the Mafia existed, it would not dirty its hands with drugs. Trust me. It's your Puerto Ricans behind it.

I said, "How do you know?"

"I'm a lawyer, aren't I?"

"But Joe Valachi says—"

"Joe Valachi is a *blatta*. Capisce? A cockroach." And then he put the sole of his shoe down on an imaginary bug and crushed it into the floor.

I give Audrey and Drake all the holiday cards, and they cut out the pictures and arrange what we'd now call a graphic novel on the kitchen floor. Then they cut out speech balloons and write the dialogue. The story's called "What Will Santa Do?" and it's about how it's Christmas Eve, and Santa's favorite elf, Danny, is very sick, and Santa has to decide between delivering gifts to all the girls and boys of the world or getting Danny to a hospital in Hartford, Coconut, which is the only place they treat Danny's condition, which is called crimson fever, and which is almost always fatal in elves. Already his tiny heart is pumping so fiercely that he's bleeding from the eyes. It turns out that Audrey and Drake's Santa is a compassionate boss, a loyal friend, and many children are left in tears on Christmas morning, and many parents are left to wonder just what their evidently devious and undeserving children have been up to behind their backs.

I open the annual holiday letter from Uncle Gunner and Aunt Tree and read it. There's a photo of their dog Blaster wearing fabric antlers, sitting by a fireplace. *Tree and I are halfway through our marriage counseling sessions, and Dr. Burl is amazed at our progress. And so are we, quite frankly. I'll admit it took me several weeks to recover from the disturbing revelation of Tree's affair with Herb Gallant—I mean who could figure she'd cat around with a fat and balding fish and game officer—but my subsequent dalliance with Lucille Potvin helped both to ease my pain and to level the therapeutic playing field.* And so on. I find out that their older boy, my cousin Errol, is now an import-exporter in Tucson, and his teeth have started to fall out. The other son, Blaine, is in a band with an obscene name that came in second in the Hampton Beach Battle of the Bands on Labor Day weekend. And he's in AA now, and he's at step nine, *and this letter will serve as his amends to all parties offended and/or harmed.*

Stevie and Dad come in laughing and hauling the groceries. Stevie can't believe they didn't have grits at Iandoli's. This is barbaric!

Dad says, "They don't sell grits anywhere in Requiem."

Audrey puts on the country music station and dances with Drake to "It's Only Make Believe." Stevie thinks we'll have raviolis. How does that sound? It sounds great. With a nice pesto sauce. Dad unpacks the groceries, and I put them away, since I'm the only one there who understands Mom's storage system. She keeps her olive oil in the creamer, her cream in the sugar bowl, sugar in the coffee can, coffee in a fruit bowl, fruit in the bread box, and bread in the oven. Canned goods go under the pantry counter; boxed goods over the counter in the cabinet by the window; herbs, spices, bottled and jarred food in the cabinet next to that. Tomatoes go on the windowsill.

After supper I perk a pot of coffee and set out the Fig Newtons on the kitchen table while Dad and Stevie do the dishes. Audrey and Drake started a club at supper they were calling the Junior Thunder Riders. You have to be a cowpoke and devotee of Dr.

Valentine Bondurant to join. They're out in the back hall now building some kind of clubhouse. The first thing they made was a sign that said NO ADULTS ALLOWED PLEASE. The storm windows rattle in the wind. The three of us sit at the table, quiet and smiling. What have we wrought? I wonder. I'm going back to school in the morning after more than a week's absence and will probably get yelled at, maybe slapped or exiled to the cloakroom until I learn my lesson, but I don't care. I kind of miss Sister Casilda. I only hope no one has messed with my desk.

I say, "Dad, you'll have to write me a note."

"What should I tell them?"

"That I've had a wicked case of crimson fever."

Audrey, of course, is finished with the nuns, so Dad has agreed to enroll her and Drake down the street at Robert Benchley Elementary, the rhyming school, as Audrey calls it. I ask Dad when we'll get to see Mom.

"When they let us."

"And then what?"

Dad looks at Stevie and then at his coffee. Why did I just stir up the future when I'm so comfortable sitting here and talking without Mom around? When I think how sweet this is and that Mom can't be part of it, I feel guilty. Traitorous. That's why.

After our baths, we crawl into bed. Dad set up a cot for Drake in Audrey's room, not in the Junior Thunder Riders' bunkhouse. Stevie tucks them in and reads them *Pecos Bill* start to finish. She comes to my room to say goodnight. I ask her how she likes it here so far.

"Like it fine."

"It's cold, though."

"You miss your mom, don't you?"

"Thanks for getting us home."

"You're welcome."

"How did you get him to go for that?"

"Was his idea. I think he wants to do the right thing by everyone. Come clean. Where do we go from here?"

"It's not just for him to decide."

"And we'll remind him of that."

When I mention school in the morning, Stevie tells me about her very first day of school, how she got lost walking home. First she was in a line of students, and then she was alone and didn't recognize the neighborhood. She stood by a wisteria and waited for her mom. Then she tried to retrace her steps to school but came to a shabby yellow house. She pretended her doll Cindy was with her and they assured each other that rescue was on the way. Let's not cry. A lady came out of the yellow house and yelled, You don't belong here, girl; this ain't your house. And now she did cry. A grizzled old yardman, a stranger, rode up on his bicycle, a lawn mower balanced in the basket and a machete slung across his back. He asked little Stevie where she lived, but she had forgotten her address. There it is, on your lunch box, he said. See, right there. Eleven-oh-one Filhiol Street. Does that sound right? It did. She climbed up on his crossbar and he rode her home.

I say, "Did you ever see him again?"

"For a long time I did, but I don't think he remembered me. And then he was gone."

I fall asleep and dream about Mom with antlers. She's munching on cucumber plants in Red's garden. And then we realize that I'm holding a rifle. She backs away. I say it's just an air rifle. She asks me if I'm going to shoot her.

"Do you need shooting?"

She's a Mental Case

I DIDN'T GET to see Mom again until April when she was
released from Requiem State Hospital. When Dad was not
on the road, he visited Mom on Sundays, visitors' day. He'd take
Mom a carton of Pall Malls and a case of Beemans gum. He
wouldn't take me along. He said, The nuthouse is not a place for
kids. Some Sundays he'd come home so shaken that he could
hardly breathe. He'd sit at the table, pour himself a belt of
whiskey, and say, You wouldn't believe what goes on in there. All
the phones are off the hook. You know what I'm saying? People
stumbling around in circles mumbling to themselves. They all
think they're invisible. And your mother's afraid. She thinks
everyone is watching her. And, you know, she's right. The nurses,
the aides, the doctors, the other patients—they're all staring,
waiting for the first unseemly gesture or unsuitable word. We
need to get her the hell out of there, Johnny. She sends her love.

Our timing was fortunate. Apparently around 1967 or '8 or so
there was a paradigm shift in the Massachusetts mental health-
care industry. Someone had figured out that warehousing fragile,

skittish, and volatile people, locking them in rooms with barred windows, was not, in fact, caring for them, was not curing them, but was instead shattering their lives. Maybe that someone had looked up *mental* and *health* in a dictionary and learned that together they meant something like "to return the mind to soundness and wholeness." *Return* is the operative word, of course. If you've never been whole, if you've always been cracked, well, just unpack your bags. Life in the asylum was harrowing and hopeless, the industry admitted, and so a move was begun to reintroduce those able patients, those not utterly helpless and profoundly disabled, to the community.

Mom moved into a halfway house on Main Street across from the city's methadone clinic and two blocks from Elizabeth Bishop Park, where the junkies liked to assemble and to sleep in the warmer months. And that's where I visited her, in her new and temporary—her halfway—home. The house itself was a three-story Neocolonial that must have been grand in its day. There were two windowed dormers facing the street on the top floor like a pair of glassy eyes, and a long flight of flagstone stairs leading to a columned porch. The original clapboards had been not very artfully covered with white aluminum siding which was dented in places and fading to gray. A hand-painted sign was planted by the forsythia bushes. NO TRESSPASSING! OR LORTERING! KEEP OFF OF PROPERITY!! The building, I found out later, was owned by my dentist and his lawyer brother, notorious slumlords. Dr. Grenier liked to work without Novocain to save time. He filled eighteen of my teeth and pulled three. All eighteen cavities fell out within five years. But let's not get started on my teeth.

I pressed the buzzard, Audrey's word for buzzer. Nothing. I knocked and waited. A man in a satiny blue and yellow Paramount Drum and Bugle Corps jacket answered the door. He was

eating out of a can of Chef Boy-ar-dee Lasagna and Egg Noodles. He had a marinara mustache. He said, Welcome to the
House of Redundants. He licked his spoon, turned it over, and
licked it again. I told him I was here to see my mother and said
her name. He said, My wife didn't leave me, my friend. I left me.
And then he turned, farted, and shuffled away down the hall.

Mom's room was in the back of the house on the first floor. I
knocked. The hall smelled like cat piss and cigarettes. I yelled out
my name. Mom said, It's open. Come in if you're beautiful. She
was sitting at a table in front of a bright window, so I could only
see her in silhouette. She held out her arms. She could have been
looking at me or away from me. We hugged. She said, It's really
you, Johnny. She smiled and wiped her eyes. Out the window, a
row of galvanized garbage cans and the backside of Atamian
Auto Body. Mom was doing a crossword puzzle. She asked me
what my poison was. She had ZaRex, instant coffee, and tap
water. I said I wasn't thirsty.

She said, "Six-letter word for *the future*."

"*Utopia*."

"Starts with an *o*."

"*Offing*."

"That's not a word."

"It is."

"The opposite of *awning*?"

"*The foreseeable future*."

She had a framed color print of the Virgin Mary over her
dresser. Mary's heart was exposed and a tongue of flame licked
the air above it. A garland of white roses encircled the heart
although you couldn't really know that because you couldn't see
the back of the heart. You just assumed it. At first glance, Mary
seemed to be about fifteen and completely befuddled by this
extracorporeal event, but then you look again, and she seems to

be thirty, jaded, and bored, like she might be thinking, And now for my next trick.

Mom took my hand in hers and kissed my fingers. "So great to see you again, Johnny."

"Me and not my replacement?"

"Yeah, what the hell was that all about, huh?" She shook her head. "Jeez, Louise!"

"You scared us."

"I'm sorry."

"It's okay."

She wiped her eyes with a balled-up tissue. "Look at me; I'm supposed to be getting better."

"When are you coming home?"

"It would be a little crowded, don't you think?"

"Dad told you about Stevie."

She nodded. "I'm just trying to be here now." She tapped her fist on the table at each word. "Be here now." She closed her eyes.

"Are you okay?"

"Thinking too far ahead freaks me out."

"Do you have a radio on?"

"I don't own a radio."

"I hear music."

"It's from upstairs. It travels through the hot water pipes. What are they singing?"

"'Volare.'"

Mom explained that she was doing crossword puzzles these days as a way to stay sharp, alert, focused, and aware. She had read an article in the paper about it. Crossword puzzles and walking ward off dementia. If my grandmother had done puzzles, maybe she wouldn't have wound up running naked down Fairmont Avenue at three in the afternoon. It was part of a bigger self-improvement kick she was on. "I'm going to get well," she said.

"I know you are."

"I've been to hell, and I've come back. That's how I feel." She spooned coffee crystals into her mug, walked to the sink, and filled the mug with hot water. "You know what hell is like, Johnny?"

"Fires."

"Not the hell the priests made up to keep us in line. The real hell. The hell on earth." She sat, sprinkled Cremora into her coffee, and stirred.

"No," I said, "I don't know what it's like."

She looked out the window. "Hell is being lonely, bored, poor, unnecessary, and inconsolable." She shut her eyes and folded her hands. "And when you're there, you feel all brittle, like you could snap apart at any second, like you could sit down wrong and just break your hip, fall to pieces. Or you could take a step, and your leg would crack and splinter. So you don't move. And you can't hold a thought. A thought sparkles and fades. And then another lights up, and then a galaxy of them, and then they're gone. If you can't hold a thought, you can't help yourself. The best you can do is be still and keep your balance because you know if you fall you won't get up." She held the table with both hands and looked at me. "You have no control of your life in hell. Everyone else wants to be the boss of you. Everyone knows what's good for you. Even though not a one knows what you're thinking or feeling. And if you tell them what you're really thinking or feeling, they don't like it or they don't believe it. The voices aren't real, they say. Well, if they weren't real, I wouldn't hear them, would I?"

"But now you're in control, right?"

"I'm learning how to act appropriately in the milieu."

"What?"

"I tell Dr. Reininger that he's helping me even when he isn't. I ignore the side effects of the Nirvanax and smile."

"Are you just pretending to be better?"

"I'm healthy enough to know how to act. I may not be the sanest person in this house, but I'm the strongest. I'll be the first one to leave. Me and Charlie." She shook her head. "I worry about Audrey. She's so much like me."

"Who's Charlie?"

We walked to the hospitality room so I could meet Charlie. A guy about four hundred pounds sat lounging on and occupying most of the couch. He was wrapped in a soiled bedsheet and nothing else. His hair was long, greasy, and gray. The skin on his feet was purple. His ankles were swollen. He asked me what I thought of his marvelous tits. Mom told him to zip it. She said, "You seen Charlie?"

"Nope."

"What time is it?"

"I don't have a watch." And to prove it, he held up both of his enormous arms.

She told me, "He'll be here soon." She looked at the man on the couch. "What was going on with Pat and Azad last night? All the screaming."

He picked up a can of Reddi-wip off the coffee table and squirted some in his mouth. "Azad was Satan again, and he wanted to have his way with St. Patricia."

"If you see Charlie, we're waiting for him in the room."

A guy passed us in the hall. He wore a T-shirt that said I'M NOT A GYNECOLOGIST, BUT I'LL TAKE A LOOK. He held a lit cigarette about six inches in front of his face and leaned his head toward it as he walked. Like a carrot on a stick.

When we got in the room I asked Mom about the fat man, what was up with him. Exhibitionist or something?

"That's Fausto Rossi. He's with the DMH. He's our social worker."

"He's in charge?"

"In a manner of speaking. People here dress like rodeo clowns."

As if to prove her point, a man Mom called The Fox stuck his head in the room. He whistled and waved. Mom introduced us. He had Cole Porter lyrics written on his khaki pants. "Miss Otis Regrets," the whole song. He also had written his address, phone number, and the total miles he had walked in 1968: 11,874. He'd torn the sleeves off his gray sweatshirt so that the world could see his tattoos. A crucified Jesus on one arm, a blood-dripping dagger on the other.

Charlie's surname was indeed *Brown* like the comic character. Mom showed me a photo of Charlie. Beatle haircut, beads, yellow-tinted specs at the end of his nose, bongos between his knees. He's in a cemetery. Mom smiled at the picture and told me how sweet Charlie was. "We're engaged."

"You're married."

"I'm a new person now, Johnny. White Owl married Rainy."

"You don't even know this guy."

"I knew him in another life."

"Now you're scaring me."

"You don't think this is the only life we live, do you? That would be pointless, wouldn't it? You need to read the *Diamond Sutra*."

The aroma of patchouli arrived before Charlie did. He came in all smiles and gave a hug to Mom. He bowed to me, shook my hand. His hair was now down to his waist. He was wearing a green plaid kilt with knee socks and a tank-top T-shirt. He took a tube of ChapStick from the little purse around his waist and applied it to his lips.

Mom told me that Charlie had been a psychology professor at Lewis University down the street. We sat at the table.

"I had a little disagreement with the chairman. Long story short—they're living in the Dark Ages over there."

"And then his wife walked out on him."

"And I had a little breakdown. My way of healing."

"And Charlie is already out on his own. He's just here waiting for me. Isn't that romantic?"

I said, "Why are you dressed in the Scottish costume?"

"Well, laddie, I was a crofter in Aberdeen my last trip through."

And then somehow we got talking about the NASA moon mission scheduled for the summer. Charlie explained how the moon was our ancestral home but had been destroyed by a nuclear war. And all the time he was talking about this, he was looking at me out of the corner of his eye. You'd have thought we'd learned our lesson, he said. We had to start all over from square one on earth. And if we keep going insane like we are, the earth will end up a barren, pockmarked planet like the moon. And I said that if that happens then the dead will have no place to come back to for the next life.

He said, "I know you. We've met before, Angus, in another life."

I looked at Mom. She smiled.

He said, "Angus Twigg. We were mates. Worked for the same laird."

"No, we didn't."

"Donal Muir. That's me. Ring a bell?"

"How could it?"

"Do you remember the afternoon with the laird's daughters down at the Spey?"

"No."

"I wouldn't admit it, either. You're serious, though, you don't remember?"

Mom said, "You should come to our regression group."

He said, "A little hypnosis will bring it all back. You'll see." And then he stepped back and looked me over. "It's so great to see you again."

Charlie said he needed to leave for a dental appointment. We walked out onto the porch. I saw a man with an eye patch and spurs on his boots slapping a woman. Charlie told me to ignore it.

"He's hitting her."

"You a cop? A doctor? No, you're not. This is not your affair." He kissed Mom and said so long. The woman on the sidewalk told the man with the eye patch she was sorry. He said, "All right, then," and they embraced.

I said, "Will we be invited to your wedding?"

"There's my funeral first."

"What are you talking about?"

"Remember when I thought I was rotting away? Turns out I really was. Metaphorically. Anyway, this'll be a symbolic burial. You're invited, of course."

THE FUNERAL took place on Easter morning. Mom's invitation said, *Dear Sane People: When you're crazy, you can't die, even if you want to, even if you try to. No relief; you suffer instead. Well, I'm no longer crazy, so I'll be buried at 10 A.M. by the lilacs in Elizabeth Bishop Park.* Stevie thought this whole production was macabre and melodramatic, not to say disrespectful and even blasphemous. Dad shook his head. I went to Mass alone—I had enough on my mind without the stress of eternal damnation weighing on me because I had committed a mortal sin—and then to my mother's mock funeral. When I arrived, the residents of the halfway house were gathered by the grave. Charlie had built a plywood coffin, and The Fox had dug a shallow grave. He leaned on his shovel. Mom was already in the coffin, hands folded, eyes closed. I said,

Hi, Mom! Charlie put his hand on my shoulder and said, She's in a better place now. Fausto, still dressed in his sheet, but wearing sandals, cleared his throat. I guessed that the woman with the startled eyes, bravura makeup, and rosary beads was Pat, and the unshaven gentleman at her side, Azad. He had hooded, darkly circled eyes and the nub of a lit cigarette in his mouth. His gratuitous galoshes were unbuckled and his brown slacks were tucked into them. He wore a herringbone topcoat and a lamb's-wool hat. Charlie slid the lid onto the coffin. I was happy to see no hammer in his hand. Fausto said, "Friends, we are here this glorious morning to acknowledge the passing of our dear friend. We are bereft, bothered, and bewildered. Every death is a birth; every birth a death. Frances is dead! Long live Frances! Her death and rebirth are delightful, delicious, de-lovely." Or something like that.

We were asked to throw a clump of earth onto the coffin. I wondered what the long-term effect of this service might have on me. I knew it was all make-believe, a *Marat/Sade* fantasy, but I wondered why these adults weren't taking life seriously. And then I remembered they weren't all that normal, were they? But then who was? My teachers? Intelligent women dressed in medieval peasant costumes, living together in a big house, humbling themselves before the fussy parish priests, and venting their frustrations on captive children? A father with two families?

Charlie and The Fox lifted the coffin lid, and Mom sat up and looked around like she was stunned. Charlie gave her his hand and she stepped out of the coffin. The Fox leaned the lid and then the coffin against a lilac bush. Mom sniffed her arm, narrowed her eyes, and sniffed again. The maggots were gone, she said; the putrefaction had ended. Everyone applauded. Such was the milieu.

Fausto looked into the empty grave and said, "We could roast a pig in there."

"Or a dog," Azad said.

Pat said, "I could eat a horse."

"I have," Charlie said.

"I ate a monkey," The Fox said.

"That's not right," Pat said.

"We cooked it."

"We?" Fausto said.

"Me and another zookeeper."

Mom told me goodbye, and they all headed off to this Catholic Worker place on Congress Alley called the House on the Rock for an Easter dinner.

On my walk back, I cut over to Ionic Ave. and past the Boys' Club, which I normally would have avoided because of the knucklewalkers who hung out on the front steps. But even if they had pummeled me, I wouldn't have felt it. I was already so distressed by my mother's blasphemous dumb show that my bones were humming. My whole body trembled, from cells to skin. I thought this was what a clapped bell must feel like. I'd been hammered by Mom's indifference . . . no, by her sterling contempt. How could she have chosen those abject fools over Audrey and me? I thought I'd either break apart or leave the ground. I started running down Beacon to Madison, past Esper's Ice House, and down Washington to the railroad bridge with the Oilzum Man painted on it. Just his head with an orange driving cap and a pair of goggles. An upper lip like a bird in flight. He looked like a man of mystery. And I always kind of thought or hoped he was looking out for me. I caught my breath. He told me that Mom's pistons were knocking right now. I'd need patience, and she'd need an oil change. That's a metaphor, he said. Love, he said, is the cream of Pennsylvania crude. No more chatter, no more ping, no more stalling out. All right, then.

I came out to Ash Street, where there were, improbably, two gas streetlamps, and they were burning still at noon on this empty block. Sometimes I thought I was the only one who knew about them. Dad used to sing a song about an old lamplighter who "made the night a little brighter." He told me the songwriter was from Requiem, and I wondered if these relics were here as a sort of tribute to the man. They just hadn't gotten around to putting up a plaque on the brick wall of the abandoned tenement building there. The lamplighter, as I remembered, had a lonely heart. The brick wall was a canvas of pentimenti. At the top of the building over the blank windows, ROOMS was written in white block letters. Beneath that an ad for Tom Moore cigars, America's favorite. Behind the MOORE and still faintly visible, COCA-COLA 5¢. And to the side of those ads, REAGAN BROTHERS SALOON, WINES AND LIQUORS.

Water Street was what remained of the city's old Jewish neighborhood and the only place there would likely be activity on a Sunday morning. I stopped at Epstein's Feed and Grain to look at the bunnies and chicks like I always did. I ended up buying two peeping yellow chicks for a dollar. One for Audrey, one for Drake. Sheppie Epstein put the chicks in a lunch bag, and I tore a couple of small holes so the chicks could breathe. Audrey called hers Durango, Drake called his Drake Junior. We let the chicks loose on the kitchen floor. Deluxe came blasting into the room and slid into the fridge. He started clicking and then chirruping and yowling, shaking his butt and twitching his tail. He pulled his ears back and crouched. I caught him in mid-assault and put him in Audrey's room, where he threw himself against the door and howled. We put the chicks in a shoe box and put the box out on the back porch. Dad said he'd build a catproof cage in the morning, but in the morning the chicks were dead. The cold, Stevie figured. We tried to bury the dead before the kids woke up, but we heard their feet on the kitchen floor. At first they suspected Deluxe, but we assured them Deluxe couldn't have opened the door. When they stopped crying, they made Popsicle-stick crosses for the graves. We buried Durango and Junior in the backyard and went to Charlie's for doughnuts and chocolate milks.

In Their Summer Dresses

ALL FIFTY-FOUR graduating Stormy Petrels from the eighth-grade class of '69 and their families, some of the dads and uncles already drunk or stoned, assembled outside St. Simeon Stylites church at nine A.M. on the first day of summer. We students lined up as we had rehearsed, in alphabetical order by height, as Sister Philomena, our drill instructor, had it, and by gender. We followed a procession of seventeen nuns (including the reclusive, one-eyed Sister Fidelis, the convent's cook) and four priests up the aisle to our pews, boys on the right, girls to the left, as Mr. Gallipeau played "Pomp and Circumstance" on the pipe organ. The girls wore their cheery summer dresses and the boys, maroon blazers and black ties. I also wore white cotton gloves and cordovan scuffs. I was suffering through an excruciating case of poison ivory, as Audrey called it, from my toes to my neck. Beneath my white oxford shirt and black chinos, my skin was blotted with calamine lotion and smeared with Rhus-lo cream. And still the shiny blisters oozed their toxic resin, and the bright rash burned me till I wanted to scream. And I knew if I started scratching the demonic itch, I would never stop. I prayed for relief instead. Earlier, Blackie had offered me a Benadryl and brandy cocktail, to dull the senses, he said, but I foolishly passed. I sat in the front pew between Eddie Dumphy and Richie McMahon. They each gave me plenty of space. Eddie had splashed himself with Jade East, and the smell set me to sneezing. Richie was writing HATE on his knuckles with a ball-point pen.

Requiem's auxiliary bishop Martin Scanlon, a hefty, officious fellow, gave the graduation address. He rocked on his heels as he spoke and closed his eyes at the end of sentences. He told us that this sacred and solemn ceremony marked the end of our innocence. He had a large gold and onyx ring on his left pinky. Today, he said, we would step out into the disagreeable world as young Catholic men and women, as soldiers of Christ, and we would immediately come under siege by the Satanic forces of Secular Humanism and Popular Culture. He pulled a handkerchief from the sleeve of his cassock and wiped his brow. We would need vigilance and fortitude to survive. We would need to take the offensive against the heathens who would strip us of our Faith. I looked around. Did this make sense to anyone? Some of us, he said—and here he paused and made eye contact with various students—some of us would lose our Faith, especially those of us whose shortsighted parents had seen fit to enroll us in public schools along with Protestants, Jews, Jehovah's Witnesses, pagans, and atheists. Some of you girls will become godless whores in no time at all.

Someone behind me stifled a laugh. Richie McMahon said, "Ramona Espy," in a stage whisper. The blood rose to Bishop Scanlon's enormous head; his eyes widened; he lifted up on his toes, fumed, and erupted. He said, The fall from grace has already begun, I see. Richie whispered, "From Grace Canio," and jerked off the air with his tattooed hand. Bishop Scanlon said, Our future drug-smoking reprobates, our sons of Belial, think that indecency is funny, think moral turpitude is funny, think eternal damnation is funny, think blasphemy is funny, think depravity is funny. You impenitent savages, you barbarous deviates, you would thrust daggers into your dear mothers' hearts. ("Breasts," Richie whispered.) And then the bishop gave us our diplomas.

After the uncomfortable, interminable, but liberating ceremony, we gathered on the school steps for our class photo. Big smiles. I saw Bishop Scanlon, chewing on a cigar, get into a black Lincoln and drive away. I couldn't know it, but this would be the last time I would ever see some of my classmates. Donald Mulrey was struck by lightning two days later while playing golf at Green Hill with his father. That winter Claire Walsh fell through the ice at Coes Pond and drowned. Other disappearances were less dramatic, but no less surprising. You're with the same people every day for eight years, and then, presto!, they're gone. Many of us stayed at St. Simeon's for high school. Others went on to public schools. I went off to Holy Martyrs Prep, for what reasons, I don't know. I suppose because it was out of the neighborhood and I was looking for adventure. It was an all-male school and had an esteemed academic reputation, which I would soon learn was undeserved. And no nuns. The teaching brothers (Xaverians) were rumored to be severe disciplinarians, and discipline, I was told, built character. So I spent four miserable years (don't ask me why I stayed) being punched, poked, slapped, shoved, and verbally humiliated while being told how special I was, how fortunate, how cared for, how respected and loved. So why couldn't I be good? I left high school a battered wife. But that's another story.

Smooch Penney also went to Martyrs. He didn't take well to being sucker-punched. He showed up at school one morning with brass knuckles and went looking for the assistant headmaster. Mrs. Spillaine, the secretary, told Smooch to get to his class. Brother is busy, she said, too busy for the likes of you. Smooch sat in a chair in the front office and lit up a cigarette. That got her attention. When Brother Delmore, a six-foot seven-inch cross-eyed thug, came lumbering out of his office, Smooch slipped on the knuckles and coldcocked him. Broke his cheekbone. Laid him out flat on the Astrakhan rug. Mrs. Spillaine called the cops. Smooch picked up his book bag and walked out the door. He finished his last two years at Al Banx High, graduated as class valedictorian. Then he spent a year at Georgetown, a year at Boston College, and a year at a Carmelite seminary in Georgia, where he slept on a marble slab, took a vow of silence, and gobbled up mass quantities of LSD, which I shipped to him in weekly care packages. He did a tour of duty in Vietnam, came home, and opened a real estate business. I said, "Why real estate, Smooch?"

"Barry," he corrected me. "I stopped asking the big questions."

"Why?"

"I want answers. I decided to make my future, not wait for it to happen. Now, what kind of home are you looking for, Johnny?"

"I'm not, Barry."

"Everyone is."

WE WENT to the house for a backyard party. Stevie had made a devil's food cake with a marzipan diploma and my name in brown icing on the diploma. The aunts, uncles, and cousins from Lowell and Holyoke were already there being entertained by Caeli and Violet. I hadn't seen my cousin Louie since I was five and he was the age I was now. He was still as sullen as I remembered him. I said, Hi, Louie. He said, Who the fuck are you, Bugs

Bunny? He meant the white gloves. I said, Poison ivy. Step away, freak, he said. Louie was not in school and was not in the Army, either, because he had tried to rob a liquor store in Lowell, and the clerk clocked him with a quart bottle of 'Gansett. He served thirteen months in Concord.

My cousin Dev shoved one of the little Ludys and snatched a comic book from her hands. The little Ludy, Brenda, I think it was, ran crying to her mom, my aunt Maggie. Dev was a year younger than I was and completely out of control. Always had been. There was something organically wrong with him, I was sure, but I never found out what. He had a sloping forehead, icy blue eyes, a wide face, a large lower lip, and a brutal temper. I had seen him head-butt his dad because his dad, Uncle Roland, who was blind, by the way, had told him he could not have a fourth honey dip doughnut. Over the years Dev had clubbed me with a Tonka backhoe, a transistor radio, and a glass bank. He never smiled, and his gaze never seemed to advance beyond his reach. His was a shrunken and frightening world. (And now I'm going to dream about him tonight.)

There were ten towheaded Ludy children, all younger than I, from six months to eleven and a half years, seven boys, three girls, no twins, all of whom would grow up to be handsome and strapping mechanics and heavy-equipment operators. Audrey and Drake busied themselves playing fawning waiter and wait-ress until they grew bored and organized the littler Ludys into a rousing game of Statue Man.

BLACKIE WAS filming the day's festivities, making a documen-tary he was calling *Graduation*. His artistic life had taken a recent and dramatic turn when the two of us saw a movie together at Req Tech's *Film at Eleven* Sunday morning cinema series. The movie was the Maysles Brothers' *Salesman*, the story of four real-life door-to-door Bible salesmen. The movie starts in Requiem County in the snow and the sleet and ends up in the sunshine and warmth of Miami Beach. You might think the radiant geographic shift would suggest a happy ending. And here's an eerie coincidence: Before the movie was made, Violet had bought a Catholic Bible bound in antique gold Fabrikoid from the skinny salesman in the movie. Mr. Baker. The guy with the bow tie and the three fingers on each hand. Blackie remembered Mr. Baker sitting at the kitchen table with the Bible opened to a page of color illustrations of the Vatican and talking about the Swiss Guards who were taller than most of your Italians. Blackie said, You don't forget hands like those.

After seeing *Salesman*, Blackie talked all the way home about going back to St. Anthony and shooting more of Nora McCabe and Baby, more of the aides and the nurses, and the other old-timers in the rec room. He called the nursing home the next morning and found out that Nora had died about three weeks after we had visited her. Blackie was stirred by our good fortune in talking to her when we did, by his prescience, as it were. But he was also distraught at his myopia. I didn't recognize what we had there, Johnny. That won't happen again. Seeing, he said, really seeing, is a moral imperative in this crazy world. Looking hard has to become a way of life.

Blackie had been seized by the idea that you could make a documentary movie as emotionally compelling as a feature film, but with the extra and extraordinary power of its being absolutely real. Absolutely true, Johnny, true! He didn't say it then, but I'm thinking it now—this was the difference between fiction and memoir. Blackie hadn't completely abandoned feature films. In fact, when he made them, he figured to use their profits to bankroll his docs. His important work was now to capture objective truth, to witness lives, not to judge them. It was like he'd had a religious conversion, only his religion was reality, and he was a zealot.

So now Blackie had a two-and-a-half-foot-long portable camera with a zoom lens balanced on his shoulder like a bazooka. Miss Teaspoon walked beside him with a reel-to-reel audio recorder slung on her shoulder and a microphone shielded with Acoustifoam in her hand. *Graduation* was going to be Blackie's calling card for producers. He'd show them what he could do, and they'd hand him money for his full-length project, *Convent*. The bishop and I are talking, he told me. Sister Casilda is on board.

I said, But what if nothing out of the ordinary happens today? He said, You trust that life is interesting and that something poignant or exhilarating or spectacular will happen, and it will. If you look at life beautifully, it will reveal its beauty to you. And if you bring a family together, with all the history there, then something wonderful or catastrophic is bound to happen.

Mom arrived carrying a tray of Vienna rolls stuffed with bologna salad, a favorite of mine. She kissed my head and handed Stevie the tray. She regarded my gloved hands and told Stevie that when I was a kid, my hands were covered in warts, dozens of warts. It was heartbreaking, she said. All the other kids were afraid of him. Children can be so cruel. Stevie said how her mom thought warts came from handling frogs. Mom said she tried everything to get rid of the warts. Witch hazel, castor oil, apple cider vinegar, vitamin this, that, and the other. She prayed. She tried to burn them off. And then one morning he woke up, she said, and they were gone. A miracle, Stevie said. He stopped lying, Mom said.

She put her hands on my shoulders and held me at arm's length the way she did when I was little and she'd say, Look into my eyes and listen to my words. She smiled. "Look at you, Mr.

Graduate!" She touched my cheek with her hand and nodded. "It wasn't easy for me to come here today."

"I'm glad you did."

"What I mean is I didn't get you anything."

"That's okay."

"I'm not apologizing."

"Okay."

"An apology is a step back." She held my hands like we were maybe going to dance. She gazed into my eyes, cocked her head. "You know why all this has happened, don't you? You're an Aquarian. I'm Libra."

"Astrology?"

"You've become a little too reliant on me."

"But you're my mother."

"I've had to give you your space. Believe me, it wasn't easy."

I started to protest, but she placed a finger on my lips. She said, "And I think it's working out. You're turning out to be a fine young man. A little too conventional for my taste, perhaps, but you'll grow out of that. Maybe." She looked to the buffet table. "You guys have a cozy little thing going on here."

Dad had his hand on Stevie's lower back. She had her head on his shoulder.

Mom said, "You've eased me right out of the picture."

"It wasn't my idea."

"She's a malleable sort. The kind your father can appreciate."

"You don't know her."

"You, on the other hand, are drawn to independent women like me. It's in your stars, Johnny. But you'll always feel threatened by us."

I wanted to tell her I felt threatened by almost everyone, but she told me she should mingle and joined her friends. I could tell that she saw today as her coming-out party, new boyfriend, new wardrobe, new mind. She had on a silky black dress with gold signs of the zodiac on it. She was shoeless but wore ankle bells. She wore small diamond-shaped sunglasses and violets braided in her hair. Charlie Brown carried a six-pack of Piel's Real Draft beer in each hand. His hair was in pigtails. He looked at me and said, "I've got one word for you, Johnny—*information*." He and The Fox wore identical plaid shirts. Must have gone shopping together at the Salvation Army. The Fox's date was a fifteen-year-old named Crystal, who apparently did not talk. The four of them sat in a circle on the grass, held hands, and closed their eyes. Blackie filmed Crystal as they all returned to earth and opened their eyes. Mom wanted to know who was making a pharmacy run. Crystal worried a loose front tooth with her tongue. The Fox said, I'll need some cash.

Even though we were just supposed to be ourselves, whatever that might mean, and not perform for the camera, that can be a difficult challenge for some people, especially if performing *is* their life. Aunt Priss and Uncle Eudore's adorable five-year-old twins Kiki and Tsipi sang "Side by Side" for Blackie. Miss Teaspoon smiled, tapped her foot, and mouthed the lyrics. "What if the sky should fall?" And then Uncle Kayo arrived in a sleeveless butterscotch maxidress with a scoop neckline, an empire waist, and a slit up the right leg. He had on a wide-brimmed straw hat, overlarge sunglasses, and a pair of mango pumps with low heels and buckles that I would later hear him refer to as "kicky." He put down the Pyrex casserole dish with his cottage cheese lasagna, smiled into the camera, and gave me a big hug. "We're so proud of you, Johnny."

"You're wearing a dress."

"Like it?" He did a turn.

"I'll get used to it."

Uncle Kayo had gone to Holy Martyrs, where he'd been an all-

city tailback on their western Massachusetts championship football team. He loved his alma mater, he said. Never punched, not
once. He took off his hat. His wig was a black bob sort of thing
with bangs. He sang the school fight song for Blackie. "Boola
boola, boola boola, that's the war cry of Holy Martyrs Prep . . ."
After prep school Uncle Kayo turned down a football scholarship
to UMass because he didn't want to leave his older, simpler
brother Pete alone. The two of them joined the Ringling Brothers Circus and traveled the country, running a funnel cake concession for four years until Uncle Kayo met Aunt Lottie in
Wisconsin and/so (not sure which) Uncle Pete leaped to his
death from the Ferris wheel.

Mom leaned back against her arms, and looked up at the sky.
Her eyes may have been closed. Audrey sat between Mom's legs,
the better to study Crystal. Crystal flipped her hair over her ears,
and so did Audrey. Crystal rubbed her nose with the heel of her
hand. So did Audrey. Crystal sniffled. Audrey said, "When your
tooth falls out, could I have it?"

"I might need it." Crystal could talk.

Audrey nodded. "Nice tattoo."

"Thanks."

Crystal had a homemade tattoo on her left forearm. BORN TO
BE WILED. Audrey asked her if it hurt. "Not now but when you
got it."

"Like a motherfucker."

"Who did it?"

"Richard Cary, my ex-ex-boyfriend, the faggot."

"He misspelled *wild*."

Crystal checked her arm. "Nuh-uh!" She shook her head. "No
one ever said it was, so I guess it's not."

"It *is* a word."

"There you go."

"Spelling's overrated anyway."

"I hate spelling with a passion."

"What's your favorite subject?"

"History's cool."

"Does your mom know where you are?"

"She doesn't even know where she is."

I heard Louie howl and tell someone to let go of his arm before he broke it. I saw Red frog-march Louie across the lawn to Aunt Jan and Uncle Joey. Red said, Go ahead and tell your parents what you were up to. Dad put his hands on Red's shoulders. Red released Louie. He said, We're waiting, punk. Louie flexed his arm and winced. What had happened was that Red caught Louie in Garnet's room rifling through her dresser drawers. Louie was not especially repentant nor particularly clever in his explanation—"I was looking for a book of matches"—but he did apologize for being where he was not supposed to be, and Red looked at me (and I looked at the ground) and reluctantly agreed to let him stay.

Uncle Joey said, "Louie, if you need some money or whatever, just ask. Always ask. Asking is easy and legal."

Louie said, "I don't *need* anything."

Despite that assertion, Louie *would* always need something. First it was heroin. And then after a second stretch in prison, he needed Jesus. And we all thought, Louie is saved; he has turned his life around; he was blind and now he sees. But then Jesus apparently reneged on his promise of prosperity, so then Louie found what he needed in motorcycles and crank. And then he was dead. Louie had been president of the Lowell chapter of the Outlaws Motorcycle Club. He was buried with his Softail Deluxe and his sawed-off shotgun. Eulogies were delivered by bikers who then poured beer over the casket. One freezer-sized guy with a bald head and a white goatee recited a treacly poem he'd written called "Ode to an Outlaw" in which he rhymed "V-rod" with "Gee, God" and in which Louie ended up on a road trip through Paradise with Heaven's Angels.

Cousin Dev, by the way, was a tad more fortunate than Louie, lived a far more conventional life, but eventually he did succumb to his vast Typhoean rage. After his second wife left him, Dev bought a bungalow in Newton. His neighbors had an ancient beech tree in their yard that had spread its limbs over Dev's yard. Dev asked Mr. Mann if he'd call a tree service and have them prune the tree. Mr. Mann wouldn't hear of it. The tree is magnificent, he told Dev. It's a treasure. Dev tried the city commission, but they were unable or unwilling to help. After an October storm, Dev woke to find his yard ankle-deep in copper leaves. He was furious and determined to take care of business. He got out his ladder and his chain saw. He put on his goggles and leather-palmed work gloves, climbed the ladder, fired up the saw, and attacked a limb. Well, he must have hit a burl in the limb, and the saw bounced back into his face.

Veronica arrived finally, but only to tell me she was leaving—not the party, but the city, the state. What? I opened her gift, a copy of *Franny and Zooey*. "I loved it," she said. She took the chair beside mine, sat on her hands, and swung her feet. Her mom and her mom's boyfriend Mike, the guy in the Coast Guard, were moving to Mobile, Alabama, and Veronica was going with them unless she could convince her dad and his girlfriend to take her in, but she wasn't even sure she wanted to do that. In fact, she was sure she didn't want to. Life with Lord and Lady Budweiser would be too distressing. Wheelock or Mobile, what's the difference?

I said, "Want some cake or anything?"

She shook her head. "I got to go pack."

"When are you leaving?"

"Thursday."

"Will you write to me?"

She nodded. (She never did.)

So what do we do now? I wondered. I said, "Maybe you'll move back like we did."

"I have to go." She stood waiting for me to say something, do something. I knew I couldn't very well kiss her in front of all these people. Didn't want her to catch poison ivy, either. And I couldn't cry, even, though my erstwhile girlfriend was leaving me before we even dated. I shook her hand with my gloved hand. She said, "Congratulations," forced a smile, turned, and ran home.

Stevie took Veronica's seat and put her arm over my shoulder. I told her what Veronica had said. She pulled me toward her. "I wish I could make it better," she said. "I'm feeling a little lost myself."

"Why?"

"I'm not sure I want to know the answer right now."

"You miss Monroe?"

"You'll find another girlfriend."

Drake and the little Ludys were playing Red Light Man, the aunts and uncles, Whist. Dad, Red, and the older Ludys were jacking up the shed. Blackie was filming Crystal, who was doing Audrey's makeup. Coral lips, jade mascara.

"Penny for your thoughts," Stevie said.

"Just wondering what's going to happen to all of us."

"The future's the door we're always opening, the room we're always walking into. And we never know who or what's going to be in there waiting for us."

"Dad says people don't change."

"Does he?"

"You are who you are."

"I've seen people change whether they wanted to or not. I've changed."

I noticed that Charlie Brown and The Fox were missing in action. Dev was busy peeling the bark off the white birch. Louie blew smoke rings at Blackie's camera. I thought maybe it's best this way. A clean slate. We got what we needed finally, a stable family for Audrey and a cute little brother thrown in. You can have anything, but you can't have everything. I watched Stevie watching Dad watching Mom. Mom seemed to be asleep on the grass. Or else she was passed out. I told Stevie I'd better check on her. Stevie said she'd start cleaning up a bit.

I shook Mom's arm.

"Johnny?"

"Where's Charlie Brown?"

"We had words." She sat up.

"How do you feel?"

"Like I was having a nightmare, and now I'm just dreaming."

"Hope you wake up soon."

"How's she treating you?"

"Stevie? She's nice."

"I'm glad."

"You're not upset?"

"He's her problem now."

Crystal told Audrey she had to go. She got up with Louie's help and put her arm around his waist. He whispered in her ear. She took a fifth of schnapps out of her purse and said, "I've got my fuckin' this." And off they went. Side by side.

Later that evening, Blackie brought the tape recorder upstairs, and we sat at the table and listened while I opened my gifts and made out thank-you cards. I had a small pile of checks and crisp new bills in front of me. Blackie asked me if I wanted to be executive producer on *Convent*. I said if he really needed the money . . . He said he was joking. On the tape The Fox said, "I wish I didn't have two wives already." Uncle Eudore, a landlord, said, "Well, when he dangles those juicy properties in front of me like that, I just get hard."

Blackie said, "You can't write lines that good. People are going to put writers out of work."

While Blackie advanced the tape, I opened a card from the Sandilands. Ten bucks and this note: *Congratulations! I understand you won't be needing to babysit any longer. Lucy and Desi will miss you. We're moving to Nantucket. The Captain* (his mark).

Blackie said, "Don't look at me." He stopped the tape and pressed *play*. "Listen."

Aunt Lottie says, "I can't find a decent pair of size-twelve capri pants, but Kayo can find a lovely pair of size-eighteen shoes. It's not fair." In the background you can hear Uncle Kayo telling someone how he's disappointed with his manicure. He tells whoever it is that the nail color is called I'm Not Your Waitress.

Aunt Lottie says, "It's what Kayo wants. Who's he hurting? No one, that's who. It's a phase he's going through, like golf. Two years ago he was all Titleist this and Wilson that, and match play and bunkers and g-d water hazards. And I'll tell you what else. He's not drinking. Knock wood. Watching the figure. And he's got more zip, zoom, zing, and zest, if you catch my drift. Where it counts."

Audrey snuck up behind Blackie and put her hands over his eyes. "Guess who?" she said.

"I know it's you."

"Gesundheit!"

Blackie rewound the tape. "Julie Sullivan."

"What?"

"That's Sister Casilda's real name."

"She told you?"

"She's from Springfield."

"What else?"

"Red hair."

Dead Reckoning

THREE YEARS LATER, Stevie left Dad, but not us, immediately after she'd learned that he had left her. She threw him out, actually. I was sixteen, and we were safe. Dad, as you may have suspected, did indeed have yet another family out West, and Stevie found that out the day the newer woman called our home in a panic. Their baby, meaning Rainy's and her baby, was critically ill and in the ICU at a Boise hospital. Stevie said, How old is this baby? She's two? She sent me down to the Cat Dragged Inn to fetch Dad.

When Dad left that night—I drove him to the airport for his Requiem-to-New York-to-Denver-to-Boise flight—Stevie told him not to bother coming back. He said, We'll talk this over when I get home. No, we won't, she said. He told me the baby's name was Nevada and what she had was meningitis. I said, How can you do this, Dad? Not now, he said. I said I hoped the baby was okay. I dropped him at the terminal. He hopped out, leaned in the door, and said, I'll call you with the news. I doubt it, I said.

Stevie had the locks changed. She stuffed all of Dad's personal

belongings into the truck. Audrey and Drake helped her. He had
less than you might expect. Dad didn't bother trying to get back
into Stevie's good graces. He rented a studio apartment at the
Elmwood Arms so we could visit when he was in town, which he
seldom was. He had this little kitchenette, two-burner stove, single sink, an under-the-counter fridge, a TV, a Castro convertible,
and a Formica table with two chrome chairs. Baby Nevada survived her crisis.

DAD, DRAKE, and I had come back to his apartment from our
Boys' Night Out. We'd gone candlepin bowling at Colonial Lanes
and then over to Coney Island for hot dogs and chocolate milks.
Drake fell asleep on the pull-out. I sat at the table while Dad
washed his work clothes with Woolite in the sink. His apartment
key was attached to a length of black and green gimp, braided in
a reverse knot stitch. And that got me remembering the gimp
lady, who was this college girl who'd come to Lake Park about
once a week in summers (or maybe it was just one summer) and
do crafts projects with gimp and key rings and scraps of leather.
Irene, I think. Or Eileen. She wore red plaid shorts and a white
sleeveless blouse, had black hair, blue eyes, and the whitest teeth.
Gimp trumped swings and bocce as far as I was concerned. I
thought, Finally after six years of school I'm learning something
useful.

One day I made a small, thin, heart-shaped coin purse for
Mom, sewn together with red gimp. She loved it. She told me
she'd keep an emergency dime in it so that if she was ever lost
or in trouble, she could make a phone call. What she actually
kept in the purse was a double-edged Gillette Blue Blade. One
morning I saw the purse on the bathroom counter, and after
admiring the handiwork, I decided that I needed a dime for a
Creamsicle or something, and I poked my finger in the purse.

I bled until I thought I'd faint. Audrey heard me howl, turned white when she saw me bleeding into the sink, and ran to get Violet.

Dad soaked the clothes in the rinse water. I asked him how he met his newish girlfriend Heidi. He told me they met at a church service at a Transport for Christ mobile chapel at a truck stop in Laramie. When I reminded him that he didn't go to church, that he was not even remotely tolerant of religious zealots, he said that after you've survived a jackknife on I-70 in a white-out blizzard, you haul your blessed ass to the nearest church, and you get on your knees and thank the good Lord for saving your life. I said, It sounds like he was trying to kill you. And there was Heidi, he said, her head bowed in prayer. When she looked up, and our eyes met, well, that was that. Some years later I'd learn from Heidi that they had actually met at a casino in Jackpot, Nevada, where she worked as a blackjack dealer.

I said, "So you see this woman, and she's cute, and you forget about your girlfriend, your wife, whoever, your kids; it's all out the window."

He said, "A lot of guys, they'll have affairs. Slam, bam, thank you, ma'am. Love-'em-and-leave-'em types. You're tempted, you know. You're on the road, you're lonely, and so on. Don't roll your eyes—you'll be there. Well, I was not made that way. When I love a woman, I need to take care of her."

His wallet was on the table. I asked him if I could look through the pictures. He squeezed the excess water from his shirt and pants. He said, Knock yourself out. He draped the clothes over the clotheshorse by the radiator. There was a seventh-grade photo of me, my blond hair looking dark like it did every year. How could Carlton Laporte Studios be so consistently wrong, and who were they paying off to get the school contract? There was a second-grade photo of Audrey with her eyes deliberately

crossed. I said, "You ought to update these, Dad." Drake as a toddler, Little Nevada on her mom's lap.

"She's your half-sister."

"Does she point at my picture and say, Who's that, Daddy?"

"She calls me Papa."

Dad heated a cube of salt pork in a skillet. He took a jar of
horseradish and a plate of cold string beans from the fridge and
set them on the table. I said I'd pass. "You want a beer?" he said.
"You're old enough for a beer."

"How old am I?"

"Old enough."

"I told Stevie we'd be home."

He slid the salt pork off the skillet and onto a paper plate. He
sat and spread the horseradish on the meat. He licked the knife.

"When I married your mother, I figured, you know, that was
it. One wife, two kids, maybe three, a steady job, a union pension, an apartment and then a bungalow, maybe a summer camp
on Cool Sandy Beach. Die in my sleep, fat and happy."

I realized I hated the way he ate, never really closing his
mouth, chewing far too much, way too vigorously, running
his tongue over his gums, sucking at his teeth, the clicking jaw,
the audible swallow. Every mouthful of food was like a skir-
mish. What else I didn't like was how he inspected his handkerchief after he blew his nose. In fact, I had a list of
irritations—the way he'd drink milk right from the carton,
wash his hair with a damp face cloth, smell his shirts before he
put them on.

I heard a key snick in the front door lock. Dad looked up, the
fork an inch from his mouth. Mom walked in. She said, "I didn't
expect to find you here, Johnny."

I looked at Dad. "She has a key?"

She said, "Sometimes I need to get away from Mr. Brown."

"She's still my wife. What's mine is hers. The least I can do. Like I said, I don't abandon people."

Mom said, "I could use a martini, Rainy."

SO DAD and Heidi live in Idaho these days, and if Dad has another family, I don't know about it. The two of them spend a good deal of their time on the road. Dad still drives, and Heidi's his able copilot. They could retire, of course, but they're having the time of their lives, trucking around the country with their GPS and their forty-channel CB radio, and Heidi's twenty-thousand-song iPod. ("And every one of them songs is country, hon.") Heidi cooks on a hot plate in the cab. They've got a dog-house sleeper, but prefer motels. They've got a Web page where they post *Today's Photo* (Heidi by a sign advertising "THE THING!" ONLY 135 MILES!); *Thoughts* ("I don't live to drive, I drive to live"); *Jokes* (Q: What's the difference between a Jehovah's Witness and a Peterbilt? A: You can close the door on a Jehovah's Witness). And there's a map where you can follow their route and progress. This morning they left Taos for Santa Fe. According to *Heidi's Journal* they spent last night at the Sagebrush Inn, ate chile rellenos at the Adobe Bar, and stayed up past their bedtime dancing the two-step in the cantina.

Nevada, the half-sister I've never met or spoken to, lives in a small coastal town in Alaska. Dad says she's a reader like me, cut from the same cloth, two peas in a pod; the two of us would get along like gangbusters. Heidi also has two sons from an earlier boyfriend. The older son, Curt, is a banjo maker in Arkansas. He has a gray beard to his waist and looks about a hundred, but he's in his late fifties. Morris is a sportsman, a hunting and fishing guide with his own outdoors show on a cable network. I saw him on the show one time standing in a wheat field in an orange vest and cap, rifle sloped on his shoulder, whispering to his dog. Suddenly a bouquet of pheasants rose and scattered not ten yards ahead of him. I changed the channel.

FOR A couple of years now my dreams have presented themselves on many nights as a computer file. *Documents and Settings\HP_Administrator\My Documents\My Files\Dreams*. I open the menu, click on *New* if I'm feeling adventurous, or click on the title of a recurring dream, and download. I get full-screen, DVD-quality visuals and stereo sound. I can link to other dreams, freeze the image, jump ahead, replay, mute the sound, zoom in or out, enhance the color, save with changes. I'm sure I'm not the only person this happens to. Of course, my dreams are a Windows application, so they're prone to gotchas and crashes. Annick says my dreams at night would be more user-friendly and reliable if I switched to a Mac during the day, but she's talking to a guy who typed his first novel on an Atari without a hard drive and would still be using it if they had not stopped making the parts. Thirty-six single-sided disks.

Anyway, one of my recent dreams is *Reunion*. It's just below *ReqMem* on the menu, and in it the lot of us are back in the old O'Connell Street backyard for a gathering and cookout. Red and Miss Teaspoon are there even though they're dead (ALS/peritonitis). Red's sitting by Violet in her wheelchair. He's sipping a 'Gansett and stroking her hair. Miss Teaspoon is quiet, and she's shimmering, and sometimes she vanishes for a few moments. Annick is there in the role of Stevie, watching over everyone, making sure they have enough to eat and drink. Blackie's filming it all with his old camera. There are seventeen nuns in matching floral print housedresses and pale white hose sitting on bleachers where the shed used to be. They're all eating cake and humming Gregorian chants. "That's going to make a nice soundtrack," Blackie says. Nunzie's there with Caeli. Another

Nunzie is across the yard with his wife, who is veiled in black lace. The Sandilands made it. The Captain and Ivy wear matching blue yacht-club blazers, white duck pants, and admirals' hats. Ivy says, "You remember the twins, don't you, Johnny?" Will and Grace have flown in from North Dakota to see me. Some nights they're Regis and Kelly and they've driven up from Greenwich.

Mom's wrestling with her new boyfriend on the grass. Dad's truck is idling out front on O'Connell Street, and he has a map unfolded on his lap, but he and Heidi seem to be enjoying the party. Heidi's boys are scarfing down the hot dogs like they're in training to go up against Takeru Kobayashi in a competitive eating competition. Deluxe is sprawled on a branch of the birch we buried him under. He died the way that Dad wanted to. Veronica tells me she married a man who owns a flow-control valve company in Birmingham and she plays golf four days a week at the country club, and I don't tell her how disappointed I am in her orthodoxy, and Annick reads my thoughts and tells me I have no right to be so arrogant.

Alice is not invited, but some nights she shows up anyway, looking beautiful and twenty-nine. I feel the pressure to keep everyone entertained. Some nights there's a pétanque match. Dad introduces me to Nevada. We shake with one hand and embrace with the other. She's brought me a salmon. "Copper River," she says. It turns out that she reads mysteries, thrillers, suspense and crime, whodunits, cozies. Our conversations go something like this.

"You like Grisham?"

"Haven't read him."

"King?"

"Haven't read him."

"You'd like him. Clancy?"

"Nope."

"Kuntz?"

"Nope."

"Mosley?"

"Nope."

"You've read Crichton."

"I haven't."

"Sue Grafton."

"Nuh-uh."

"Who do you read?"

"William Trevor."

"Who?"

Every time I see Garnet she's across the yard from me. I wave, but she doesn't look up. I wade through the waves of guests, and when I arrive at where she was, she isn't. I want to tell her how I've written about her, how she is not forgotten. I want to say how sorry I am. I want to thank her for all she did. And then she's standing beside me, squinting at the house. I tell her about the dedication in the memoir. She tells me it means nothing to her. She's beyond meaning. She's dead. Meaning doesn't cross that barrier.

We're all, we suddenly realize, waiting for Audrey to arrive. We wonder what she'll look like, what she'll have to say for herself. We wonder what's keeping her. Caeli checks her watch. Someone says he saw Audrey earlier at Speedy's waving goodbye. People have run out of things to say. The nuns have stopped humming. They're licking frosting from their fingers. At this point scenes from the dream begin to repeat themselves. Dad rubs the scar on his leg again. Curt braids his beard. Folks begin to drift away. The sun is going down. There's a chill in the air. The ashes in the Weber are cold. Spot's under the bleachers with a birdhouse in his mouth. Once again, the party has been ruined by great expectations. I decide that I don't like the dream any-more, and I wake myself up.

CHARLIE BROWN became Charles Brown when he became the administrative director of the city's methadone clinic. In his new role he became a local countercultural celebrity and hero as a forceful and vociferous advocate of the poor, the homeless, the addicted, and the disenfranchised. He surprised me, I'll admit. Folks urged him to run for the City Council, but he wanted noth-ing to do with the "establishment," as we called it then. He gath-ered a—*devoted* would not be too strong a word—a devoted group of acolytes and assistants, who admired his passion, com-mitment, and eloquence. He shaved his head. He looked more like Elmer Fudd than a Buddhist monk, I thought, but the new fashion aesthetic proved alluring to his followers, one of whom owned a large farm in King Phillipston and donated it to Charles. About a dozen folks, including Mom and The Fox, moved into the commune they called Laing House. Charles ran the place like a hippie boot camp. Mom found herself only one of several "wives." Power may have gone to Charles's head. There were rumors of a financial scandal and sexual improprieties. He van-ished and turned up nine months later in San Francisco, the guru to one of the Grateful Dead. And from there it was just a small step to artist management, concert promotion, and a mansion in Marin, where, as far as I know, he still lives.

Mom never wanted for suitors, marginal characters most of them, rode hard and put up wet, but attentive and affectionate enough, so that even before Charles Brown made his splash in *Newsweek* when his wedding to a flower child in Golden Gate Park was featured in a special issue on the Haight, Mom was liv-ing with a soft-spoken fellow named Dennis LaPlante, who had cerebral palsy. Dennis quit his job at H&R Block, and the two of them opened a vintage clothing store in what had been a used book shop downtown. They called the place the Glass of Fashion, but Mom always referred to it as Rags to Bitches. She started to dress like a femme fatale in a forties noir movie. Dressed to kill, Dennis said. She looked radiant and dangerous. I bought all my Rooster ties and Cowichan sweaters at the store. Business was booming, but Dennis was also selling cocaine out of the men's dressing room, and one day he sold half a gram to an undercover cop (Lenny Cox, Kenny's brother) and got busted. So Dennis went to jail, and the store closed. Mom told me she was going to visit a friend in Santa Fe, and I never heard from her again, not in person. The occasional postcard, the annual phone conversation. Dad stayed in touch with her. She had no friend in Santa Fe, of course. She waitressed at the Plaza Café for six months and then moved to Tucson and then to Flagstaff. Dad said she was looking for a place where she fit. She worked a season at the El Tovar in the Grand Canyon. She moved to Los Angeles. Dad sent her money for a flight back to Requiem.

After Audrey enrolled at Requiem State, Stevie and Drake moved back to Louisiana. A couple of years later Stevie married Skeet Dryden, a wealthy gentleman of leisure from a prominent Monroe family. As a young man Skeet had gone off to Yale and then settled in Manhattan. He published a critically acclaimed novel, *Bobby Reynolds, In Person*, when he was twenty-two. He wrote teleplays for *Studio One* and *Playhouse 90*. And then he stopped writing because, he claimed, he had nothing else to say. He knew Truman Capote and Nelle Lee—three Southerners in the big city. After his father died, Skeet moved back to Monroe to care for his mother. He and Nelle are still in touch.

Stevie could remember the scandal in Monroe that accompanied the publication of Skeet's novel. Decent citizens were outraged when they read in *Time* magazine that Skeet was writing about homosexuals and insanity and miscegenation in little "Madison, Louisiana." The nerve! When the public library refused to purchase the book, it was effectively banned from Monroe, there being no other place to get yourself a book in those days unless you wanted to drive over to Jackson. Fortunately, everyone's over that now. Skeet's about as close to a celebrity as you have in Monroe. People find it endearing that he clips grocery coupons and recycles string and tinfoil. He and Stevie take a trip or two every year to Europe or to Latin America. Drake owns a car dealership in Monroe. In his TV commercials he rides onto his car lot on a golden palomino, lassos his sales staff, and makes them promise to sell their new and pre-owned automobiles at the lowest possible prices. He sold me my salsa lunch box. We talk about once a month. Usually about Audrey.

Remember Keefe Smith? The balding reporter I found in our kitchen the morning after one of Mom's parties? Ben-Gay on the scalp; black, tasseled loafers, and op-art necktie—that Keefe Smith. Well, these days Mom and Keefe are married or they're attached, I'm not sure which. They live together and have for ten years, at least. Mom hasn't spoken to me—not even when spoken to—in a dozen years. She won't answer the phone or acknowledge birthday or holiday cards. Keefe sends me a note every few months letting me know how Mom's doing. Good days, bad days. Laughing, crying. Chatty, withdrawn. Docile, belligerent. He sees that she keeps her medical appointments and takes her drugs. He loves her. He keeps the wolves from the door. Mom doesn't know about Keefe's correspondence with me, or she would tell him to stop, and he would. She's angry at and frightened by her past. Keefe doesn't know why exactly and says he doesn't need to. He has a hunch.

All this writing about Mom, all the looking at photographs

and home movies, has had me missing her. At least I think it's fondness I'm feeling. And curiosity, I suppose, though that sounds cold to me. I want to know how she's doing, but she has made it hard to care very much. I want affirmation, too. Recognition. And that's perhaps hostile of me. I'm your goddamned son, Frances. I wonder if I have the right to impose myself on a woman who is so obviously unwell. Anyway, I decided to pay her a visit to see if the two of us might reach some sort of closure or commencement. Maybe if she saw me, I figured, saw herself in me—I have her hazel eyes, long nose, and high cheekbones— she'd exhale all that fear. So last week I flew to Providence, rented a car, and drove to Requiem.

Mom and Keefe live in the Fafords' old house on Barry Street. I was in that house dozens of times as a kid. I remember Donald and I playing marathon games of Risk at the kitchen table while his mom baked bread and listened to her Édith Piaf records. Their linoleum floor was made to look like bricks. They always seemed to have the same shopping list on the fridge: milk, eggs, yeast, King Arthur flour, Fluff. If I happened to be there after supper on a summer evening, we'd go out to the backyard and watch Mr. Faford's homing pigeons circle the neighborhood until he shook his coffee can of pigeon pellets and called them back to the loft. I wondered how the pigeons could hear the rattle from that high up and without any discernible ears.

I arrived unannounced, figuring if I told Mom I was coming, she'd have sold the house and left town. I parked out front. As I opened the fence gate, all the lights in the house went out. Someone peeked out from behind a window curtain. The doorbell didn't work. I opened the screen door. Taped to the little window on the inside door was a sign, NO PEDDLERS AND NO SOLICITORS. I knocked. I waited. I said, "I know you're in there, Mom." I knocked again. "I can wait all night." Next time I knocked a friendly shave-and-a-haircut. "Please, Mom." Keefe opened the door, handed me a bottle of whiskey and two high-ball glasses. He stepped out onto the porch and closed the doors behind him. We sat on the glider. He said, "She doesn't want to see you." He poured whiskey into the glasses. We toasted to better days.

He told me that 119 billion people have lived on earth. "And how many do we remember?" We toasted the first man to eat an oyster. He said, "One of every seven people on earth is a Chinese peasant." We toasted peasants.

"Does she talk about me?"

"No."

"Never?"

"Never ever."

I told him about being in this house as a kid. He told me he bought the house from Mr. Faford. "He moved into one of those assisted living places."

"I'm surprised he'd leave his pigeons."

"The pigeons were long gone. This crazy old coot named Buffone—lives in the house behind us—he killed the pigeons."

"What?"

"Stood on his porch with a shotgun and blasted them out of the sky. Said he couldn't stand the cooing anymore."

"Did Faford call the cops?"

"He was losing it by then. After Donald died, he—"

"Donald died?"

"Some kind of cancer. Knocked the old man off his rocker."

"Fuck!"

"Amen."

I held out my glass. Keefe filled it. He said half the languages in the world will disappear in this century. "That's half the worlds." Keefe told me he had to stop being a reporter when he got sick. He was in a wheelchair for a year. Mixed some booze and Tylenol and woke up paralyzed. He's given up Tylenol. "They didn't think I'd walk again."

"Are you sure it was the Tylenol and booze?"

"You think it's a coincidence?"

He spent some time in therapy and gained his strength back. But they had to replace his knees. He's fine now, but has to walk downstairs backward. "After that everything is easy," he said. "Piece of cake." He fixes burnt-out washing machines now and sells them. Buys them at the Salvation Army or picks them up on the street on bulk pickup days. Got a Toyota pickup, a beater, and a ramp he bought from U-Haul. He's got a little shop in the garage. It's mostly WD-40 and paint. I told him about the memoir. He said, "Call it *Mother's Little Helper* or *The End of My Rope*." He wanted to know who was going to play him in the movie. He thought Sean Connery was a good choice. He said, "Call it *Try Being Honest*."

"I like that," I said. "Got any others?"

"*Lying in Bed*."

Keefe told me his dad owned I See the Light in You Press and fancied himself a Wiccan-Buddhist-Jew. He's still going strong. Lives in Vermont. He publishes books on topics like UFOs, crystals, yoga, astral projection, homeopathy, and angels. "He's always been very keen on the idea of the Divine. Once when I was a kid, he took me to Boston to meet God. I got all dressed up. God turned out to be some schmo who bent spoons."

Keefe said that as a boy he wrote and illustrated comic books. He had dozens of them. He was obsessed. He'd created a super-hero named Sloth who walked upside down, was always on his way to a crime scene, and slept for three years at a time. I told him about *The Drone*. He told me his dad thought comic books were for cretins. Keefe's personal favorite creation was Peninsula

Man, who was green and surrounded by water on three sides and who drowned many of the fiends he encountered and lamentably a few of his allies.

I heard a door slam somewhere in the house. I looked at Keefe. He said, "I came home from school one afternoon and found my father burning all my comic books in the rubbish barrel. He did it, he said, because I had disparaged God. What I'd done was tell my brother that if God was so intelligent why did he make teeth that decayed. My brother squealed on me."

"One and done," I said and held out my glass. Keefe poured. "To fathers," I said.

"To fathers."

I said, "Do you know why she won't speak to me?"

"She says you know why."

"I don't."

"She thinks you did something to Audrey."

"Something?"

"Unsavory."

"Why would she think that?"

"Audrey told her so."

I told Keefe I didn't understand why Audrey would lie about me, or why Mom would believe her, or even why Mom would speak to Audrey but not to me.

"You're hurt."

"I'm perplexed."

"Frances tells me you're quite the liar."

"I *had* to lie to her when I was a kid."

"And now you lie for a living."

"Writing stories, you mean?"

"You make them up."

"Not to deceive anyone."

Keefe shrugged.

Sheet lightning brightened the sky over the Pingetons' house. I remembered Tommy Pingeton lifting his T-shirt to show me the scar he'd gotten when he impaled himself to the liver on a picket fence. Last I heard he'd moved to Alabama.

Keefe said, "You mother was blind, but now she sees."

"She found Jesus?"

"She lost her sight."

"When?"

"For a year. She keeps her Cadillacs in a jar on the mantel."

"Her what?"

"It's what she calls them. 'Cause they cost so much. Her cataracts."

"She saved them?"

"She's a sentimental woman."

"I want to see her."

"That's not up to me."

"Once more before she dies. Or I do."

"You'd only upset her."

"Your mother worked at the Corner Lunch, didn't she?"

"Every time I remember her she's wearing a hairnet and a white uniform. She's riding a bus, smoking a cigarette. Cooked there for fifty-one years. Died in their kitchen."

"I'm sorry."

"When she was at work, and I was home alone, I'd sit in her closet and smell her on her clothes." He finished his drink and set the glass on the deck. He stood, held the two doors open for me, and ushered me into the darkened living room. The screen door slapped shut. He switched on a floor lamp by the fireplace and waved me over. The house smelled faintly of apples and bleach. He handed me the thin glass jar of cataracts, little white crystals floating in what looked like Karo syrup. I saw a corked glass test tube on its side. I picked it up. A couple of safety pins. I said, "What are these?"

"From your first diaper, she tells me." Keefe excused himself and walked down the hall to convince Mom to come out of hiding, I figured. I shook the tube.

"Sounds like a little rattlesnake, doesn't it?"

I looked across the room to the corner by the draped window and saw Mom almost disappearing into her plushy chair. I said, "You scared me half to death."

"So Caesar has crossed the Rubicon."

"I didn't come to fight. I came to make nice."

"You came, you saw, you concord."

"So what have you been doing with yourself?"

"Well, I certainly haven't been sitting around drinking Manhattans for ten years, if that's what you mean."

I smiled. I thought she was joking, but I couldn't see her face. I sat on the sofa and leaned forward. "You know I didn't do anything to hurt Audrey. I wouldn't."

"You came to tell me that?"

"I came because I missed you."

"Do you have any kids, Johnny?"

"A dog."

"You're lucky. The experts, they've proven that people with children are not as happy as people without."

"This is Mem's rug, isn't it?"

"I had it cleaned."

Dad's mother made the rug for us when I was six or seven. She'd gathered up decades of family woolens from her attic and our cellar, blankets, suits, slacks, dresses, and whatnot, all the clothes that kept us warm, cut them into strips, braided them, and wove them into an oval rug. My baseball pajamas are in there and Audrey's security rag, Mr. Binky, my grandfather's blue gabardine trousers, my grandmother's wheat-colored bathrobe, and a great-uncle's doughboy uniform. Generations of the family all together on my mother's floor.

Mom said, "All of a sudden one day I was beside myself. Until that moment I'd been fine. This happened not long after I lost Arthur. And I've never really been able to recover."

"You seem better."

"I maintain, but that takes all my strength. All my energy. I've got nothing left for you. I'm sorry. But you don't want me to be the way I was. And I don't want that. You understand?"

"Trying to."

"I know how it's supposed to be. For every body there's one person, and the body and the person stay together over time and space. We don't become someone else when we move or when we age. I know this sounds crazy, but ever since that day I've felt another Frances inside trying to shove me out. I'm barely holding on."

WHICH BRINGS US to Audrey.

When Stevie and Drake moved, I expected that Audrey and I would continue to live in the apartment we'd grown up in. And I hoped Drake would spend his summers with us. Audrey knew I'd pay the rent until she could afford to chip in. I had a decent job at the neighborhood community center, Friendly House, working with kids after school, distributing surplus food, and driving seniors to markets and appointments. Audrey laughed at the idea of living with me. She said with Alice moving in, it was getting mighty crowded. We were in Howard Johnson's on Route 9 having coffee and pie after a movie. She wore a long white frilly sleeveless dress over her jeans. The jeans were rolled to her calves to show off her two new Japanese ankle tattoos. One was a winged, fire-breathing dragon, the other in Japanese characters, a quote from Sei Shonagon, "All small things are adorable." Her hair was cut unfashionably short so that the tops of her ears peeked out. She had on red espadrilles. She said, "Johnny Boy, I'm getting married."

"Very funny."

"I'm serious."

I didn't even know she had a boyfriend or had ever had a boyfriend. I said, "What the hell are you talking about?"

The boyfriend was a guy named Walston Hull who owned Hull Home Improvement and was thirty years older than Audrey. Older than Dad, I pointed out. "Where'd you meet this geezer?"

"We're getting married Saturday."

"You weren't going to tell me?"

"It was a spur-of-the-moment thing."

"I'm not invited?"

"Some judge is going to marry us in his living room. In and out. No big deal. We've got our witnesses."

"Who?"

"Walston's ex and her husband."

So Audrey married Walston Hull and moved to his farm in Cold Spring Brook. He bought her two horses. I said, "Audrey, that's carrying the cowgirl thing too far." She named the horses Tess and Jude. I was not encouraged to visit. Audrey said, "Walston doesn't care for you."

"What's wrong with me?"

"He thinks you think you own me."

"If I did, you wouldn't be with him."

"He thinks you're frivolous and unambitious."

Audrey stopped by about once a week with her laundry. She told me she and Walston didn't sleep together. He snored something awful. She slept in the barn with Tess and Jude and a radio. They didn't eat together because Walston only ate peanut butter and chicken, though not at the same time, and he wouldn't touch vegetables. He drank only water and Lipton tea. They didn't have sex. Walston had two kids from the first marriage who spent every other weekend with him, high school kids only two and three years younger than Audrey.

I said, "That's not a marriage, Audrey."

"All marriages are alike?"

"I don't know what it is."

"It's my life."

"Get it annulled."

"Goodbye."

"Come home."

I was beside myself. Caeli told me to butt out. It was Audrey's life, not mine. "The thing with Walston will run its course, you'll see. Audrey will be fine."

But I wasn't finished with her. The next time she brought the laundry, I took her to the El Morocco for kibbe sandwiches. When we got there, she told me she didn't eat meat anymore. She ordered a salad and gave me the feta cheese.

I said, "What do you want to do with your life, Audrey?"

"I'd like to live in an immense house deep in the forest and bake breads, gather wildflowers, and read in front of a cozy fire."

"You want to live in a Grace Livingston Hill novel?"

"That would be splendid."

"Be serious for a minute."

She put down her fork and picked up her napkin. She leaned across the table and wiped my chin. "I want to be curious enough and brave enough to live the life that comes my way."

"That's asking for trouble."

"Nothing I can't handle."

"You should want to take control."

"*Should!*"

"You're drifting."

"What do you want to be?"

"A writer, you know that."

"Bullshit."

"What?"

"If you wanted to be a writer, you'd be writing, not talking about it. I'm sick of your talking about it."

Audrey had another admirer, one of my old teachers, in fact, the sixty-something British history professor William W. Williams. Dr. Williams owned a three-legged border collie named Tippy who followed him everywhere. He was a member of the Society for Creative Anachronism and spent his summers in Europe as a Hundred Years' War reenactor. He liked to lecture in costume—a very popular routine with the local press and the college's PR department. He might be Sir Walter Raleigh, in a starched ruff, smoking a pipe and regaling us on his journeys of discovery. As Henry VIII, Dr. Williams tore at a turkey leg, his lips glistening with fowl fat, and told us about meeting his betrothed Anne of Cleves. He pulled back her veil and screamed, "A horse, a horse! They've sent me a horse!"

Dr. Williams deferred his retirement so that he could keep Audrey in his life. I didn't say it, but you may have guessed it: Dr. Williams was married and the father of four grown children, all medical doctors. Audrey was working as an assistant to the secretary in the History Department. She and Dr. Williams had lunch—something brought in from the Falcon Pub—every day in his office with Tippy curled on her doggie bed beneath the desk and Thomas Tallis playing on the tape deck. All very romantic, according to Audrey. After lunch he'd brush her hair. She found his flirtation exciting, but was not above complaining about it to me. Too many gifts, too many phone calls. He's very needy, she said. She got rattled when he actually touched her hand.

As a junior, Audrey took an abnormal psych course and caught the eye of the professor. This time the professor was a woman, Dr. Claire Young. Audrey wound up telling Dr. Young about Dr.

Williams and Mr. Hull. Dr. Young asked Audrey if she was happy. No, she was not. They agreed that possessive men seemed to be a problem in her life. She was in need of emancipation, was she not? It was time, Claire told Audrey (they were, by then, on a first-name basis), it was time to become the subject and not an object. Claire and Audrey went horseback riding on Saturdays.

And this all led to Dr. Williams's abrupt retirement, to Audrey's divorce from Walston Hull, and to my last face-to-face conversation with Audrey as we folded laundry in my kitchen. Claire had accepted a tenure-track associate professor position at SUNY Cortland, and Audrey was going along as Claire's amanuensis.

"Are you two lovers?"

"Claire said you'd say that."

"I'll come visit."

"I can't heal myself with you in my life. Maybe in a year, two, five. I've got a load of damage to undo."

"Audrey, you're all I've got."

"Ask yourself why."

"I'll miss you."

"You can be a real pest, Johnny Boy."

You already know from a previous phone call that Audrey's now living with a man named Daxson—Daxson DeNeil—and that they're settled somewhere near Minot, North Dakota. Daxson's a fundamentalist Christian fanatic, which suggests to me that he's heavily armed, unemployed, self-righteous, and paranoid. Maybe I'm wrong about Daxson, of course, but since Audrey is unwilling to share much information about her spouse, I have to imagine the son of a bitch. Every time I picture him, and I don't know why, he's wearing smoky white robes and a white turban, and I'm guessing that's inaccurate realistically, even if correct metaphorically. The name *Daxson* is medium blue, and *DeNeil* is a light orange with maybe a bit of pink. Coral, call it. So that's probably why I see him with blue eyes and coral skin.

Audrey told me that Daxson is a millennialist who thinks the end times are upon us, the rapture is imminent, and there's nothing much else to do but hunker down, pray, and keep the invading infidels off your property, even if you're renting. In other words, he's a pathetic fucking lunatic. Pardon my Anglo-Saxon. You see these poor, deluded true believers, and you want to hold them and tell them it's all right, you'll take care of them. They're like baby hyenas—all frisky, big-eared, wide-eyed, eager, and clumsy, but if you keep them around, you know that very soon, when they get the chance, they'll rip your throat out and eat your heart. Some days I want to scream. But I don't. Instead, every few months I abet Daxson and Audrey's insanity by sending a check. Audrey has to eat, I figure. And I keep hoping that one day she'll take the check and buy a bus ticket that'll get her out of the New Jerusalem and back into our world.

I sent Audrey a cell phone last year—this was just after I read the letter she sent Stevie and which I'll tell you about in a minute. One of those pay-as-you-talk deals. And for a while they used it. But every time I called, Daxson answered. Audrey's out, he'd tell me. Out where? Out in the field. Out to the market. Out at work. Out in church. *Out* out. But he wouldn't tell me where she worked. She didn't, he said, want me to know.

"Are you right with the Lord, John?"

"I'm an adult, Daxson. I'm not afraid of the dark."

"You should be."

"I don't believe in God or Santa or the Tooth Fairy."

"I'll pray for you."

(Don't you hate that?) "Is Audrey okay?"

"She's saved."

How Audrey got to where she is now. Long story short: Claire shed Audrey after two months in Cortland. Audrey found a flat and a job as a groomer at a pet store at the Market Place Mall. One night she took home an adorable Persian cat. When Audrey didn't come to work in the morning, mall security and the cat's owner knocked on her door. Little Miss Wyandotte was reunited with her master, who offered to buy Audrey her own cat, but Audrey was too ashamed to accept, and too ashamed, apparently, to remain in New York. I sent money. She stole Claire's Subaru and moved to Loretta, Wisconsin, where no one has moved to in like a hundred years. She liked the name and the seclusion. She'd decided she was not a people person. She'd decided to simplify her life. She rented an old fishing camp for next to nothing and lived on ramen noodles and bottled water. She was found wandering and confused on a logging road near the Thornapple River and taken to a hospital in Hayward. I would have gone to her, of course, but I didn't know about any of this until much later. At the hospital she met Daxson, a nurse's aide. He healed her, she said. They fell in love. Daxson realized he was a prophet. They married. The Lord told Daxson to move to North Dakota and wait for instructions. Claire's car is, I like to imagine, rusting away by a fish camp.

Finally I got to speak with Audrey. She called to tell me that she was donating the phone to a battered women's shelter.

"How will I reach you, then? What if something happens to Mom? Or to you? How will I know?"

"You've been trying to run my life since I was five."

"That's Daxson talking."

"I do what he needs me to do."

"A decent husband doesn't keep his wife from her family."

"God has a plan for us."

"Christ, Audrey, have you lost your mind?"

"I've never been happier."

"Is he hurting you?"

"I'm going to say goodbye now."

"Look, I'm sorry—"

"Goodbye."

"How can you deny your blood, Audrey? How can you forget everything we've been through together? Audrey? Answer me."

There's a part of me that wants to say, Okay, I surrender. It's over; Audrey, you win. You don't want me around, I'll leave. But no me, no money. This is the self-pitying part of me. I'll let her know that I'll be there when she needs me and back off, respect her wishes. Or maybe it's the humble part of me. I don't know. Another part of me doesn't want to release Audrey into the clutches of the delusional Daxson and whatever apocalyptic fantasy has seized her. This is the melodramatic part of me, the arrogant part of me. I don't know what to do. I do know that she is not as happy as she has wanted me to believe. I read the letter she sent to Stevie.

Stevie, I don't know what's wrong with me. Why I'm never satisfied. I have a roof over my head and a husband who loves me and would never leave me. I've got the job in K. at the market. Daxson drops me off and picks me up. He comes along with me to the library. It's like he doesn't trust me. If he sees me talking to someone he'll say who you trying to impress. Or if it's a guy, he'll say the guy's only interested in me for the one thing. You know, like I don't have a brain. I know that's his fear talking, so I try not to make a big deal about it, but it makes me feel bad. If I say we're fighting a lot, he's says we're not, and that starts a fight. If I say let's talk to someone, a minister or someone, he'll say we don't need counsel, we need more prayer. I don't say this to Daxson, but prayer doesn't work for me. God doesn't seem to be listening. Last night I had this dream. I was filled with air and fixed to a spot on the kitchen floor. I was me, but I had no feet, just this rounded . . . bowl, I guess you could say, or saucer or something, so that when Daxson shoved me over, I popped right back up again. And every time I popped up, I had this big smile on my face, and that made him furious. I'll wipe that silly grin off your face, he'd say, and he'd punch me. Which he never would really. His bark is worse than his bite. I woke up sore all over. I'm not stupid. I know the dream was about my fears of physical abuse. If he ever hit me, though, I would leave. Trust me. I've seen the women at the shelter. But anyway, he wouldn't. He's just so sensitive on the one side and such a perfection-ist on the other—the way men with a calling often are. I know if I open up to him, he'll open up to me. I could write him a letter, I suppose. He could write me back. That would be less threatening for both of us. He can be so sweet, and not just when he's after something. He'll bring me flowers out of the blue. He'll say something nice about my hair. Lit-tle things. I hope you don't think I'm being disloyal to Dax-son, talking out of school like this. Just writing to you I feel better already. I really do. Who knew? And I discovered the solution—write to Daxson. Tell Drake I'm thinking of him. Hi to Skeet. So long. Not to worry. I should have done this a long time ago. Audrey (her mark).

AUDREY'S BECOME a person I don't know at all. I could not have imagined this happening. Not with Audrey. It's like my little water baby has turned to steam, and I can feel her but not touch her, and soon enough she'll evaporate. Did she get lost looking for a father? Was Nunzie right and she's a bit touched like Mom?

There seems to be no evidence of the delightful child in this
sullen woman. On the other hand, maybe she doesn't need my
money at all, and her supplication is just her furtive and peculiar
way of staying in touch.

The Charm of Distance

How do we see the future? With the eyes of the past.

—EDWIN HEDMAN

I'D LIKE TO tell you that what happens next happens next week or next month, but it happens three years from today: It's just before noon. I'm sitting here writing. Spot's giving himself an unnecessarily noisy bath over on the futon. Outside the window, a squirrel is asleep on the bird feeder. I'm working on a story about a woman who's writing her husband's suicide note. She's reading it over for the tenth time and wondering if she's made him sound too sympathetic. She scratches out *self-loathing*. That's not a word Jack would ever use. She changes *rid of me* to *without me*. She calls her boyfriend to see what he thinks. His wife answers. They gab about what they'll wear to the Art Basel vernissage. I make a note to buy a copy of *Elle*. My cell phone—I finally got one, and Annick tells me I can watch the Marlins on it; I remind her about the TV—anyway, the cell phone vibrates and starts walking across my desk. The phone has this feature that lets you listen to the caller's message as it's being left. I let the phone dance against my coffee mug. The wife says, Do you think Dan's been acting funny lately? Annick's voice greets the caller. Spot looks around, perks his ears, and arfs when he doesn't see Annick. He does that every time. Audrey says, "Johnny Boy, pick up."

I push *talk*. Nothing. I push it again. "Audrey!" Goddammit! Again. "Audrey?"

"You have to come get me."

"Where are you?"

"I'm at work."

"I mean *where* where?"

She's in Livia, North Dakota. She tells me Daxson is in Williston for a couple of days, and she wants to get out before he gets back. There's no one she can stay with. She doesn't want anyone else involved in her mess. "Just hurry, please."

"I'm glad you called, Audrey." I'm glad I sent her the number.

She gives me the address, and I remember to write down the number she called from. For me that's incredibly efficient. I call Annick with the news. She heads home. I book a ticket for the morning on Expedia. I tell Spot I'm going to fetch Aunt Audrey. He runs and gets his leash.

It takes forever to get to Bismarck via Charlotte and Denver. On the flight from Denver I sit next to a man from Zap, about ninety miles northwest of Bismarck. Works out at the Garrison Dam. Grew up in Minneapolis. He says he moved out west because he thought the great distances would force people together, thought the absence of neighbors would drive the lonesomeness away. Was he ever wrong! But he's been here now too long to leave. He tells me he's fifty and has been married thirty years, and he and his wife are considered youngsters in Zap. When we die, the town dies. You can't have economic development if you have no young people to work. Lost half our population in ten years. He asks me how Audrey wound up in Livia of all places. I say she came by mistake. He says no one comes to Livia by mistake.

We land in Bismarck in midafternoon. I rent one of those new Quark Charms, the hybrid they're all writing about, drive it to the Kirkwood Mall, and buy a pair of gloves and a blue knit hat that says UNIVERSITY OF MARY MARAUDERS on it. I buy a hat for Audrey. It's bitterly cold and windy. I drive north through Washburn and see the signs for Fort Mandan. I roll down the window and try to imagine the Corps of Discovery braving the elements that first winter. I roll up the window. There's a Lewis & Clark Interpretive Center nearby, and I wonder if Audrey might want to stop in on our way back. We've got so much catching up to do. I keep rehearsing our reunion, what I'll say, how she'll react. I see tears and smiles, a hurried embrace, and a sprint to the Quark. I keep seeing her driveway as gravel, and I see the spray of stones onto the brown lawn as I peel out. I remember the old Nez Percé woman who kept her tribe from murdering the explorers. Watkuese. She'd been kidnapped in her youth and later cared for by whites. Eventually she made her way back home. Watkuese means "Lost and Was Found." Like Audrey.

It's dark when I reach Livia. There aren't that many streets in town, so Audrey's is easy enough to find. Wherever you are, you can see the Livia water tower and the grain elevators. I park out front of Audrey's house. There's no driveway. There are no lights on in the house. There's no mail in the mailbox. I knock at the front door and then at the side door. I check the address stenciled at the curb. I walk around the house and try to peek in the curtained windows. I sit in the car and then decide that Audrey must be out picking up last-minute items for the trip. Little shampoos and breath mints, things like that. She couldn't know when I'd arrive. I drive around town looking for her. On Main Street Peterson's Department Store is closed for the night and so is Dell's Diner. Everything else looks closed for good. I see a dog walking along the railroad tracks leaving town.

This time I park down the block. I don't know why, really. If Daxson is around, he won't see me? I decide to call the number Audrey called me from. No signal. Just great. At nine I figure I'd better find a place to sleep. I wind up in Kenmare at the San Way Ve Motel. I ask the clerk about the motel name. He says, What about it? It's odd. It is? Room 12 has dark plywood paneling and dim lighting. There's a black vinyl chair facing the bed. Beside the chair is a low table, and on the table a white compact fridge, and on the fridge a white towel, and on the towel a small white microwave. The blue carpet worries me, and so does the floral bedspread. I can see my breath. I crank up the heat. The TV's on the dresser. There's no remote. My nose bleeds, and my hair hurts when I take off the knit cap. I turn on the shower, let it steam up, humidify and warm the room. I get a phone signal and try the number. No answer. I call Annick and fill her in. I have a bad feeling, I say.

In the morning I drive to Livia. I go by Audrey's to check for signs of life. There's a beige pickup on the front lawn and smoke curling from the chimney. I knock, and Daxson opens the door a few inches. He's thin, balding, and sallow. His glasses are too large for his face. He says, "We don't want any."

"Good, I don't have any." I know I'm not tough, but I figure I could pin this insect to a mounting board if I have to. "I'd like to speak to Audrey. Tell her it's her brother."

"Audrey's not here."

"We both know she is." I shoulder my way into the living room and close the door behind me. Daxson says he'd be within his rights to shoot me as an intruder.

I say, "If you had the balls, you could," and I don't know where that came from. Do I really say that? "Audrey!"

Audrey walks into the room, and when she says, "Johnny Boy, what are you doing here?" I know that her call to me is a secret from Daxson. So how then did I find the place? I decide that I've hired a detective.

"I was in the neighborhood."

Daxson says, "Audrey, what in the Lord's name is going on here?"

I say, "Don't you have a hug for your brother?" She does, but it's a limp one, a so-sweet-of-you-to-drop-by-with-the-fruit-basket-for-Mama kind of hug. I tell her to get her coat and we'll take a little walk. We can catch up; she can show me the sight. (My singular little joke about Podunk.) She's gaunt and lusterless, but still beautiful. Lost some weight and some muscle tone. North Dakota will do that to you.

"She's not going anywhere," Daxson says. "How did you find us?"

"I was in the area researching a book on Lewis and Clark, and—"

Daxson says, "Bill Peterson."

"What?"

"Told you where we lived."

"I can't reveal my sources."

"It was Peterson. Can't keep his mouth shut."

I look at Audrey, cock my head, raise my brows, widen my eyes, lift my shoulders like, *What's going on here, Audrey?* She stares at her feet. I give her the hat I bought her. "Let's go. We've got some family issues we need to discuss."

Daxson says, "I'm family."

Audrey says, "Johnny Boy, I think you should leave."

Daxson puts his arm over Audrey's shoulder. She slips hers around his waist, leans her head on his bony shoulder. She says, "We're just fine here, Johnny Boy. Nothing for you to worry about." She looks at Daxson and smiles.

Someone in the kitchen, it sounds like, says, "How's that for abuse?" Daxson turns. Audrey smiles, says it must have been someone walking by.

I say, "How about a cup of coffee for the road?"

Daxson says, "We don't drink coffee."

"Try Dell's," Audrey says.

I stand there looking for some kind of signal from Audrey. Daxson watches her too. Audrey twirls the hat in her hand. Daxson gets the door.

The coffee at Dell's is washy, the creamer is powder. I'm disappointed, but not surprised. Everyone in the place is smoking cigarettes, including Marie behind the counter. Marie tells me that Dell died in 1976. My guess is that all these guys in caps and coveralls are farmers whiling away a winter morning. I'm thinking they should go to Florida for the season if they've got nothing better to do. Why suffer this gloom and cold? I have a weak signal, so I call Audrey's number again. Turns out to be the number of Bob's Super Valu in Kenmare. I ask for Audrey, and they tell me she didn't come to work today. Some kind of flu. Says she'll be out all week. I wonder if I should call the motel and reserve the room for another night. I'm not leaving without Audrey.

I take a walk and stop at Peterson's Department Store. I figure that's Bill Peterson reading the newspaper he's got spread out on the counter. He doesn't look up when the little bell over the door tinkles. I browse around. The wooden floor creaks. I love this place. The goods are displayed on long tables and are separated by glass partitions. Hairnets, pacifiers, Lepage's mucilage, glassware, costume jewelry, scarves, marbles, silk coin purses, sunglasses, aprons, cake mixes, jack-o'-lanterns, spark plugs, lunch boxes, cigarette lighters, handkerchiefs. There's a pile of dusty boxes of model airplane kits—something to pass the time at the San Way Ve. I buy a metal grabber, which is this long arm with a two-fingered hand at the end that helps you reach items on the top shelves of your cabinets. Annick will love it. She'll say it's silly, but she'll love it. I buy a wooden honey dripper and a ceramic salt pig. And I find a treasure, a Big Indian Chief writing tablet made in, believe it or not, Requiem, Mass., by the Arrow Wholesale Company on Water Street, which was the same street where I bought the chicks for Drake and Audrey. Sounds like a sign to me. I didn't know such a tablet existed. There's a Plains Indian in full feathered headdress on the red cover and a line to write your name below his photo.

At the counter, the man I'm thinking of as Bill Peterson asks me where I'm from and what I'm doing in town. When I say Florida, he looks up. Florida has just made Spanish an official language, and I know this has upset some folks in the heartland. But he doesn't mention it. I tell him I'm here to see my sister Audrey. He squeezes the grabber to make sure it's working properly. I say, "Do you know her?"

"Know of her."

I pay up and compliment him on his store. I say so long. The bell above the door tinkles.

He waves and goes back to his newspaper. He says, "Don't be a stranger."

I put my loot in the Quark. Except for the tablet. I carry it with me. Maybe I'll get a chance to see what the wife is up to in my story. How's she going to pull off a murder that looks like a suicide? And then what happens to the boyfriend's wife? (At least now I know the boyfriend looks a lot like Daxson.) It takes me two hours to walk down every street in Livia. Guys drive by in pickups and lift their index fingers hello. I watch the train rattle through town. One hundred and seventeen cars. I write that down. The Livia High School building is for sale. The pickup is still in Audrey's front yard. I write down the tag number. Back at Dell's I have the place to myself. Marie's reading a romance novel called *The Lord of Lambeth Manor*, and she tells me to help myself. I pour my coffee, more sludge now than wash, and carry it to a table by the window. I say, "How's the book?"

"It gets me out of Livia. That's all I ask. All Claire Devereaux's books are the same, but that's what I like—dependability." Marie tells me that Claire Devereaux is also Carole Sheehy and Della Jordan and Janelle Moore. "She's like a writing machine."

A woman and a boy who looks about twelve walk in and stamp their cold feet. They say hi to Marie. Marie says, "Two cocoas and two doughnuts coming right up." She puts down her book, crushes out her cigarette.

The woman helps the boy out of his hood, his cap, and his jacket. He has a long, narrow face and enormous ears. The woman smiles at me. She's got dimples and blue eyes. When she takes off her hat, her thin blond hair lifts from her head with static electricity. The tip of her nose is red. She keeps her scarf wound around her neck. The boy looks at me. I smile. He has a wandering eye. Marie brings their order, and the woman thanks her. The boy thanks her. Marie says, "Cold one today." The boy says, "Cold one today." The woman tells him, "Stop that, now." He says "Stop that, now." The woman holds the boy by his shoulders and turns him toward her. She says, "Stop repeating." He flaps his hand and then bites it. She gives him his powdered doughnut. She sees me watching and smiles. Then she says, "Excuse me, but do I know you?"

"No."

"You look familiar."

"I've got one of those faces."

"Minot?"

The boy says, "Why not Minot?"

I tell her I've only driven through there once. Yesterday.

She looks at me sideways and smiles. "What brings you to Livia?"

"The climate."

"It's a frozen wasteland."

"I was misinformed."

And she says, "I think this is the beginning of a beautiful friendship," and we laugh.

I tell her about Audrey. She knows Audrey. "That's her table." She points to a table in the back of the diner. She knows Daxson better. "He keeps a tight leash."

I refill my coffee and join her at the table. I introduce myself. We shake hands.

"Chloe Melville," she says. "That's my boy Bix." She points out the window at a blue house with white shutters. "Our home."

"So what brought you to Livia?"

"A husband."

"He's gone?"

"How did you know?"

"Just a guess."

She sips her cocoa. "He was a good man, but fragile."

"Do you ever think about leaving yourself?"

"You writing a book?"

"Sorry. I didn't mean to—"

"I'm kidding. Yes, I have. Often. But people here are all so good to Bix. Livia's like his family. I can't take him away from that."

"And they take care of you."

"They do their best."

I tell her about Audrey's phone call and about the confounding visit to her house this morning.

"Sounds like you need a few minutes alone with your sister. That should be easy to arrange."

"He won't let her out of his sight. He's a monster."

"No one in Livia would say that."

"She lives in fear."

"Sometimes men behave one way at home and another way in public. This way with this woman, that way with that woman."

"So I've heard."

She raises an eyebrow and smiles. "Daxson helps people out. Does plumbing, repairs, yard work—all free. You have to listen to a little God talk, but that's not so bad. Some folks even like it."

"So what do we do and when do we do it?"

She checks her watch. "Does *now* work for you?"

"Perfect."

"I'll hike over to his house and let him know my pipes *are* frozen. You wait till you see us go in my house. And then go talk to Audrey."

"That sounds too easy."

"Should we have something go wrong?"

"No."

"Make a better story that way."

She asks Marie to keep an eye on Bix. Marie puts her face on Bix's arm. "I've got my eye on him." Bix laughs like crazy.

Chloe puts on her coat and hat. I thank her. She tells me she likes an adventure in her day.

I say, "What happens when he finds out you betrayed him?"

"You trying to talk me out of this?"

"No."

"My pipes *are* frozen. I could fix them myself with a hair dryer and some blankets, of course. I just think a man should be able to see his sister."

Ten minutes later Chloe's back, and she's out of breath. "They're gone, and they left in a hurry, it looks like." She says the side door was wide open and a kettle of water was boiling away on the stove. "The kettle was full, so they can't be far."

Bix stops staring at the fluorescent light and says he wants to go home now. Marie says would he like some pancakes. He sure would. Chloe says you can only leave Livia going east or west, toward Kenmare or toward the wildlife refuge. Marie says in Kenmare they could pick up Audrey's paycheck at Bob's Super Valu. Bix drapes himself over the counter and sings the word *pancakes* over and over. I wonder what the future holds for him. I see him in a green apron and glasses. He's rubbing his hands together. He's in a restaurant, it looks like. I realize I won't probably see him again in the flesh. I say so long to him and he covers his eyes with his hands so that I can't see him.

We haven't driven a mile on 2A when we see the beige pickup off the road and Audrey behind the wheel. I run to the truck. Audrey gets out and we hug. She's got an angry bruise on her cheekbone and blood soaked through her Marauders hat.

I say, "Were you in an accident?"

"Daxson was."

"Where is he?"

"Under the truck."

"Is he alive?"

"I don't know."

Chloe gets on her hands and knees and looks under the truck. "He's moving." She gets on her stomach. "Daxson, you lie still, now. We'll have an ambulance here in no time."

I say, "Should we pull him out?"

"Might be something broke."

"Move the truck?"

"His jacket's caught up on the manifold." She turns to Daxson. "Where does it hurt?"

"Where's Audrey?" Daxson says.

"Who?"

"My wife."

"You must have hit your head pretty hard. You don't have a

wife." She looks up at us and smiles, tells Daxson to stop mumbling; she's the answer to his prayers. "God sent me to save you."

I ask Audrey how she got the bruise. She tells me she resisted being kidnapped, so Daxson hit her with a cross.

"No, he didn't."

"Yes, he did."

"No one would believe it."

"He had it in his hand—the only thing in the house that he cared about."

I lift her hat. Her hair is matted with blood, but the cut is not very deep. We'll get a butterfly bandage in Kenmare.

Chloe stands up and says, "What happened here, Audrey?"

"The piece-of-shit truck stalled out. Daxson got out to wiggle the wires like he always does. I slid over and backed her up a few feet, put it in first, and ran him down."

I say, "You hit him?"

"And then I backed over him."

Chloe tells us to hit the road. She'll take care of everything.

I say, "How?"

She says, "Don't you think I can come up with a convincing story? I was out for my walk, and I saw everything, saw my neighbor, Mr. DeNeil, get out of his truck and walk around to the front. I don't know why. Forgot to set the hand brake, I figure. The truck rolled over him. These things happen." She tells us there's a Cenex station about three miles down 2A. "Stop there and call 911."

"I could try my cell right now." No signal. I say, "What happens to you when Daxson starts babbling about how his wife ran him over?"

"I'll shake my head, look knowingly at the deputy, and tap my head with my index finger. And I'll look sad and concerned."

"But eventually they'll find out he has a wife."

"And you'll be long gone. And anyway, before he decides to make a federal case out of it, I'll explain to him about assault and battery, about how the heathen sheriff's department would like nothing better than to see him suffer, about how his landlord, my good friend Bill Peterson, might be forced to evict him. I'll think of something."

We all hug goodbye. I tell Chloe that for some reason I see her living in Saskatchewan in a few years.

She says, "Have we had this conversation before?"

"How is that possible?"

"It's just weird. I feel like I'm remembering the future."

"That *is* weird."

"You'd better get going."

At the Cenex station I make the 911 call while Audrey cleans up in the restroom. The attendant, a kid about sixteen, sits at a metal desk and plays solitaire and watches the last black-and-white TV on earth. The picture keeps rolling and fluttering. He whacks the oil-stained TV cabinet. He adjusts the rabbit ears. He moves a piece of aluminum foil up one of the antennas. He's wearing fingerless knit gloves and a hooded sweatshirt with a picture of Uncle Sam on front. Uncle Sam is saying, ZIP IT, HIPPIE! I ask the kid what he's watching. He puts a black jack on a red queen.

"*Guiding Light.*"

"How are things in Springfield?"

"Tammy's dead."

"Accident?"

"So they say."

"You don't sound like you believe them."

"Alan had the motive and the opportunity. What's the third thing you need?"

"Wherewithal?"

"Huh?"

"The means."

"That's it. He had all three."

I hear a siren and look up to see a sheriff's cruiser heading west on 2A.

The kid looks out the window and sees my car. "Never seen one of those before."

"It's a Quark."

He peeks at the next card in his deck. "You mean quark like a duck?"

"You don't notice them, but they're everywhere."

Audrey comes back and hands the kid the little key on the significant ring. She asks him if they sell coffee.

"No, ma'am, we're a gas station."

On the road to Kenmare, I say, "You'll stay with us, Audrey. No arguments. End of story."

"Till you're sick of me."

"I got you back at last."

She stares out the window at the fallow wheat fields and the lowering sky.

I say, "What made you call me finally?"

"I couldn't see ahead of me. I couldn't imagine anything but what dreary little I already had. I got scared." She touches my shoulder. "The charm of distance was wearing thin."

I think of how three years ago while I was writing about this very rescue and escape, I had imagined the two of us driving the Quark all the way to Chief Yellowhorse's Trading Post and exchanging our blue hats for a goldfish, but when I looked out back behind the trading post, I saw this dusty and dispirited bison tethered to a post, tramping along a circular rut bringing him back to where he'd been, so I reimagined us heading southeast, a beeline to Monroe and then Mobile and then home. Sweet home! We've got the radio blasting, and we're singing along to Bob Wills for all we're worth. Every mile it gets warmer and brighter. And then we see Dad thundering toward us in his big rig, and we wave out the window and throw him kisses, and he blasts his air horn hello! When I think of that drive, I see the chromium Quark as if from above, see it picking up speed as I shift the engine into quiescent mode, and we drive on deep, deep into our shiny futures.

We drive into Kenmare. Audrey says, "Don't stop, Johnny Boy. Let's put the miles behind us."

At the edge of town we turn south on 52. She says, "The meaning of life is that it stops."

"Bondurant?"

"Kafka." Then she says, "Can we just drive all the way?"

"That can be arranged."

"So, I hear you write books."

"I do."

She leans her head against the window and closes her eyes. "So tell me a story."